He Is Just Away

A Novel

LESLIE WARDWELL

Weston Heights Press.

westonheightspress@gmail.com

Library of Congress Cataloging-in-Publication Data:

ISBN: 979-8-9927644-0-6 (ebook)

ISBN: 979-8-9927644-1-3 (paperback)

ISBN: 979-8-9927644-2-0 (hardcover)

"Do not follow where the path may lead. Go instead where there is no path and leave a trail."

— Ralph Waldo Emerson.

"Not till we are completely lost or turned around … do we begin to find ourselves."

— Henry David Thoreau.

I

Mary Jane Nutting felt her baby's foot sweep across the inside of her abdomen below her ribs, while butterfly wings flitted beneath her diaphragm with each labored breath in the damp, biting early January waterfront air. Standing on the blackened creosote wood planks of Noble Wharf, free of frost and snow, the acrid smell of mothballs riled her nerves and stomach as she stood among a milling, anxious crowd, all waiting to board the S.S. Halifax bound for Boston.

Dressed in layers of heavy charcoal-colored linen for warmth, she wore one of her mother's lace bonnets to protect her ears from the blustery wind with little effect. With no extra money for a warmer jacket, she kept her gloveless hands tucked under her arms. Leaning slightly over her swollen midriff, she peered at her flat-heeled, scuffed loafers, worrying about how long the worn leather would last before a hole formed in the sole. At their age, she thought one might first split along the outside edge. She had not considered the weather on the streets of Boston and hoped her thick wool socks would keep her warm and dry, but she conceded the worst could happen, being a twenty-four-year-old unwed mother forced to leave her home.

The wharf was abuzz with hundreds of souls, a diverse gathering of classes from commoners to the wealthy. The less fortunate wore wool, the middle class donned linens, and the affluent flaunted furs, high-laced boots, and wide-brimmed decorative wool hats. Every respectable woman wore an outer jacket with epaulets over a silk skirt and cotton petticoat. The wealthier the departing tourist, the more luggage piled and displayed at their sides.

Mary believed the less fortunate had saved and scrimped for the seven-dollar one-way ticket to begin their journey toward the American Dream, while the wealthier class booked round trips into the city or chose a more adventurous all-points west railway excursion across the vast, open frontier.

A woman dressed for a brisk mid-winter ocean breeze in a dark emerald bustle skirt, a boned bodice, and an outer jacket bumped her valise into Mary's side, nearly knocking her off balance. Only the slight tackiness of the wooden planks beneath her shoes kept her from toppling.

"Oh, dear," the woman said, swiveling her beaver bonnet to glance over her shoulder. She stopped when she noticed Mary, clad only in a full-length, long-sleeve maternity gown, moving a hand to her protruding stomach and the other to her hip. The woman's travel companion also shuddered his step, and together, they exchanged uneasy glances, their eyes darting side to side as if searching for someone lost. It was only Mary and her unborn child who stood resolute.

"I'm sorry, we really should have been more careful," the woman apologized, turning to Mary with an exaggerated roundabout survey of the dock's charged crowd. "Have you lost your husband?"

Mary's expression remained indifferent, as this was not the first time she had answered this question today. "No. He's just off to the washroom, and I'm awaiting his prompt return." Although she did not smile, she hoped her stoic demeanor would convince the couple to take her at her word and that no one would be forced to look around uncomfortably for signage and catch her in a lie.

The emerald woman adjusted her hair stick and linked her husband's arm. "Rest assured, then. Have a delightful trip to Boston and safe travels," she said, flicking her gaze toward Mary's midriff. "And do take care of yourselves," she said as they walked away without so much as a second glance.

Mary took a deep breath to steady herself and exhaled, trying to hold back tears. She had come this far, and there was no turning back. Her mother had said it was a divine sign that a new steamship had begun daily round trips between Noble Wharf and Boston's Lewis Wharf in the Italian North End. The fare was steep for her, but the twelve-dollar round-trip ticket, thick and sturdy in her hand, felt comforting as she rubbed it like a worry stone between her thumb and index finger.

She carried her belongings in a stout canvas satchel with a sturdy handle and shoulder strap, and since her mother could not afford to have it monogrammed, Mary helped her affix a small silver brooch pin to identify it in case it got lost on board. Despite her mother's insistence, Mary knew that if she were to fall asleep, however unlikely that might be, she would keep the shoulder strap across her bosom and her wrist through the handle, knowing sleep on the overnight voyage would be arduous and likely improbable.

The S.S. Halifax was docked, her boilers lit, and a crew was preparing to keep her on schedule. Mary knew she had more time before the morning departure, so finding a washroom became her priority before boarding. At eight months pregnant, her bladder felt as tiny as a butternut.

Before searching for a ladies' washroom, she stole a discreet glimpse at her late father's Waltham pocket watch to check the time, ensuring she still had about an hour before the boarding whistle would signal departure. She scanned for anyone nearby with fixed stares, careful not to attract attention to herself. Once she confirmed the time, she closed the watch and slipped it back inside a hidden pocket her mother had sewn into the hem of her maternity gown. Alone and without her mother's help, who remained behind with her younger siblings, Mary found herself a pregnant, unwed, and frightened young woman.

After a quick relief, she sat alone on a bench, awaiting her departure, her mind racing with unanswered questions as she gazed across the harbor, beyond Lower Water Street, and up the hill where she envisioned her mother pacing in their modest south-end apartment. How could she have let this happen? It was her fault that her family had to uproot from their farm in Stewiacke, but her mother, younger teenage brother, and sister did not hate her. They had been distant at first, but as the scandal surrounding them intensified, they did their best to protect her even more diligently.

Months ago, isolation from neighbors and the threats of retaliation from her baby's father's family reached a breaking point, forcing her mother to leave their small farm and move the family to a two-room apartment on the hill above Water Street. Here, away from prying eyes and gossip, they could try to sort things out while her mother made ends meet by cleaning houses near Saint Mary's University. Traveling alone on an overnight steamship to Boston had not seemed feasible two months earlier. Although whispers and misdeeds may not have followed them from Stewiacke to Halifax, that did not quell their paranoia and fear.

If she chose to stay and give birth as a single mother, the rumormongering about her having a child out of wedlock would resurface. Therefore, her mother, Rachel, had convinced her that traveling to Boston to deliver the baby, leaving it at an orphanage, and returning home was the most sensible path forward for the family.

As Mary sat there, the baby's foot—or perhaps an elbow or knee—pressed against her abdomen, seeking more space and a comfortable position. She gently pushed her fingers into her middle, feeling the soft bump and wondering whether it was a boy or a girl. As she ran her fingers over her midsection, she felt the appendage moving again, closed her eyes, and tried to envision it as a heel or elbow, pushing harder to see if she could distinguish any tiny toes. A serene smile spread across her cheeks as a tear rolled down her nose, catching at the corner of her lips.

Her lower back and nut-sized bladder both began to ache, leaving her uncertain if she could continue as she held her swollen midsection and nervously tried to rub her worries away on her ticket. When the lone steam stack's boarding whistle blew, it did not bring relief, but she knew she had to decide her future somewhere between another trip to the washroom and climbing the gangway steps.

The ship appeared awkward and top-heavy, with a raised deck above a row of porthole windows. Mary imagined it tipping and floundering somewhere between the outer harbor and the New England coastline, and if that were to occur, she would not be forced to decide anyone's future path.

2

The accommodations aboard the S.S. Halifax were cramped, and Mary opted not to spend the extra dollar for a shared stateroom, much less a dollar and a half for a private room, where she assumed the woman in the emerald green dress was sharing with her husband while hanging up her furs.

The flat bench seating might have been more comfortable if she weren't pregnant. Unfortunately, she couldn't reach the footrest in front of her and didn't want to stand and linger near the privy either. Sleeping overnight was not an option.

Leaving the harbor, she sat lost in thought, gazing out a portside window as the landscape of Halifax and Georges Island gradually faded from view. Acadia was the only home she had ever known, with the small rural communities around Colchester filled with local farmers and those whose ancestors had left Nantucket—either pushed out by the expansion of the tiny island's whaling industry or seeking to establish their own Quaker settlements. Some stayed, some returned after the whaling boom ended, and the rest moved on.

Mary's memory was haunted by the loss of her father, George, who had passed away when she was only thirteen. Her younger brother, George, was ten at the time, and her sister, Agnes, was just six. There had been no accident on their small farm, but her father was nearly thirty years older than her mother, and his heart had grown hardened. The long hours spent swinging a scythe during the brief Nova Scotia summers and harvesting hay for the winter took a toll on a man of sixty-five.

Rachel had wanted to bury her husband in the field where he had fallen, believing that's where he would have preferred to end his days. However, they ultimately buried him up the road in the Eastville cemetery, where Rachel hoped it would be easier for the children to move on at their young age. Out of sight, out of mind, isn't that how it goes?

Mary felt someone sit beside her, but they stood up again before she could welcome the warmth of the stranger's body. She turned, expecting another high-class traveler, perhaps the woman in emerald green, but instead noticed a couple dressed much like her. What she had felt was the man sitting without noticing her condition before standing, tipping his hat, and switching places with his companion. Mary desperately wished it had been her mother who rushed to board with a last-minute change of heart to be with her.

The woman sat next to Mary, wearing an empathetic expression, tucked her valise between her feet, and glanced at Mary's satchel. "You might be a bit more comfortable if you put that heavy bag on the floor," she said, gesturing with her linen-gloved hand toward Mary's shoes. "It's okay… I won't let you lose it."

Mary gazed into the woman's kind eyes and noticed her petite button nose. She thought her eyelashes were the prettiest she had ever seen and felt herself melt at her warm, upturned smile. She couldn't believe it; a few hours earlier, she had walked away from her mother, choking back tears, afraid that everything was beyond her control. She wanted to trust her mother's plan, but feeling and seeing her baby move changed everything. Confusion and dread filled her, leaving her unable to understand why her body and thoughts seemed to act on their own. If not for this strange woman's kind face studying her now, she would have been inclined to start crying, seek out someone in a steward uniform, and plead to be let off the ship.

The woman gently rested her hand on Mary's thigh and whispered, "Will you come back home?" She then took Mary's hand in her own, soothing it softly with a gentle, rhythmic rub of her thumb. "Both of you?"

Mary could see the woman searching for an answer in her eyes, probing her thoughts. "I…" she stammered, noticing the woman's hand and feeling the warmth radiating on her leg. She struggled to maintain eye contact with this woman, knowing she had no answer. Finally, she relented. "I want to, yes," she choked out.

The woman gave Mary's hand a gentle squeeze before switching to a gentle pat. "Everything will work out… not to worry. What's your name, dear?"

"Mary Jane. My mother calls me Mary Jane, but my brother and sister call me MJ." Feeling relieved, a faint smile appeared as she glanced at the silver brooch pinned to her satchel and remembered her mother's fingers rubbing it before securing it to the heavy canvas.

"Well, I shall call you MJ, and my name is Annie, Annie Hatt, and this is my husband, Richard." She turned slightly, hooking her thumb sideways at the man who had sat next to Mary for a moment before realizing it wasn't an appropriate place to be. He tipped his hat, checked his pocket watch, and pulled the brim low over his eyes.

Mary fixated on Richard's watch chain, hanging from the front of his wool vest. Her father had let his gold watch chain dangle extra low from his pants pocket, and it bothered her, knowing it could easily snag on something while he worked in the fields on their farm. Sometimes, her father noticed her staring and swung it around like a Vaudeville burlesque dancer, and she would always shout, "Daddy! Stop that!" Her father had a knack for knowing how to embarrass her on a whim, and sometimes, he'd do both: swing the drooping chain, waggle his hat over his head, and sashay, leaving swirls on the dusty, hay-chaffed ground with his footsteps. That was always too much, and she'd run back into the house every time, mortified with embarrassment.

Annie asked, "Do you have a jacket?"

"No, but I have two layers of linens under this dress."

"May I see your shoes?" Annie tilted her head down for a better look as she waited for Mary to pull up her maternity gown. "How about we find you a sturdy pair of boots when we get to Boston and out of this steel trap?" she suggested, raising her eyebrows and gesturing at their surroundings.

"I'm not…" Mary's voice faltered. "I don't have much extra money to spare. I was hoping I wouldn't have to walk too far to find a…" She pursed her lips, unsure exactly how to respond but more frightened to hear her own answer.

"Nonsense. A fine young woman deserves a fine pair of ladies' boots. They won't always stay hidden under that maternity gown." Annie glanced at Mary's midsection and whispered, "How far along are you? Do you know?"

"I don't know," Mary answered honestly. "I'm not sure, maybe… eight months?" She shook her head and moved Annie's hand from her thigh to her bump. "Believe it or not, I saw the baby move under my skin!"

"Did you, now?" said Annie, raising her eyebrows and appearing surprised. "Is this—your first?"

"God, yes!" Mary quickly turned to the porthole to watch the passing North Atlantic whitecaps, feeling embarrassed, knowing Annie was pretending to be surprised. A small wave of shame fluttered through her mind, but it vanished when Annie held her hand again.

"It's a wonderful feeling—isn't it? The little buggers move around a lot, especially in the last month. No more room, eh?"

"I know!"

"You get used to it."

Mary pushed through her mental fog. "You must already have children."

Annie held up six fingers. "Six. Four boys and two girls." She held her tongue as Mary silently opened and closed her mouth three times. "Richard needed sons to help build fishing boats in Owls Head—where we live—and then I needed daughters to help care for them all. Wouldn't that have been a pickle if we kept having boys?" She paused, watching Mary's blank expression. "Our second son, Robert, is probably about your age. He's twenty-four, no?"

Mary nodded, finding it all unimaginable to comprehend.

"Reuben, Robert, Ada, Omeda, Henry, and Clifford were our last little ones. Clifford's five, and I think that's all I can manage!" Annie said, wiping her brow with an exaggerated, playful gesture. "We're headed to Boston to fetch supplies. We need to restock our boat-building business." She nudged Mary, leaned in closer, and whispered, "It's our only time to ourselves."

Mary thought of her mother back on land, watching over her teenage sister, Agnes, and hoped her brother, George, would help with chores. The last thing her mother wanted to do when she came home from house cleaning was to clean her own. George hadn't been able to contribute to the family coffer much, delivering papers in town, and she felt terrible when he got fired as a mason's apprentice. Laying bricks required them to be stacked in a straight line and plumb, and he hadn't learned those skills on their farm before their father passed away. At least Agnes wasn't a child and could care for herself during the day, but Rachel still didn't want her to venture out and find a part-time job. Worrying about one daughter out of sight was enough.

"Omeda," Mary said. "I've never heard that name before."

"It means good-natured." Annie sounded confident even though she didn't appear entirely sure. She leaned closer to Mary, nudging her in the ribs again, and whispered, "Well, that's what we told her, and she believes us because she has plenty of confidence for fifteen."

"My sister, Agnes, she's seventeen," Mary said, looking away with a heavy sigh. "My brother is old enough to care for himself. At least we all keep hoping so. He's twenty-one and delivers papers."

"Where do you all live?"

"South end, in the city, near Saint Mary's on Kirby's Lane, off Tower Road. It's a cozy spot. Two small bedrooms, a small bathroom, a small kitchen." She glanced at Annie, shrugging her shoulders. "See the pattern?"

"And your mother?"

"She cleans houses for others near the university. It's all through word of mouth, and she takes whatever work she can find."

"You're alone… and if your mother is with your younger sister, then where is—"

Mary interrupted, having been asked many times before. "He's gone. My father died eleven years ago." Feeling Annie's gentle coaxing, she elaborated, "We worked our farm in Stewiacke, the five of us. A few animals, a couple of cows, our horse, Trigger, four pigs, and a henhouse. Grew our own crops. We always had enough hay for Trigger and sold the rest to some neighbors for extra money. Father sometimes traded hay for corn, and they helped us after he died. George was too young back then, so folks picked up the slack, and we bartered to survive." She paused, looking down at her bulge, as she couldn't help but wonder if it was her fate to meet Annie on this day on this ship to share her life.

"Then this," she said, rubbing her abdomen. "It happened so quickly. It felt like overnight all those folks who helped us now shunned us because they blamed me." She began to cry. Inside, the stress was building, and the baby could feel it, kicking her bladder what felt like every other minute, and she started to stand. "I should go to the privy before it turns into a disaster all over this bench," she said, struggling to get up.

"Here, here, let me help you," Annie offered, reaching for Mary's satchel. "Let me take this for you and move it out of the way. We don't want you to trip and fall."

At first, Mary held on tightly. She possessed only limited funds and a few extra changes of clothes, but she eventually relented. "All right."

"Richard, wake up," Annie poked her husband's shoulder with a stiff finger and a stern, unflattering scowl. "Watch our bags while I help this young lady to the washroom."

He straightened, surveyed the cabin, and adjusted his hat. "Sure. Everything okay?"

"Of course. Now, please move your feet and let us pass."

"Is she... you know?"

"No, of course not," Annie scoffed. "We're just going to use the ladies' facilities, that's all," she said, standing up. "Keep an eye on our bags and save our seats, for God's sake."

Mary struggled to stand and scanned the cabin. Everything was gray yet clean, with plenty of glowing lights illuminating the walkways. Passengers seemed to keep to themselves, gazing out the portholes from their benches or with their chins down, dozing like Annie's husband, Richard. She could see the dark red-painted floor of the boat decking wrapping around what she assumed were the interior staterooms. Looking behind her, she saw the same, but it was much further away—no further than the distance from their old farm's backdoor to the barn. Doors with straight handles on either end likely separated compartments, and she remembered that more people were boarding from two gangways on the wharf than she could see in this area. Up front, to the right of the door, she finally spotted a sign labeled "Washrooms" with an arrow pointing toward the middle of the ship. She couldn't see past the interior wall, and if there was a line, she had no idea. She'd have to walk around the corner and hope for the best.

As she started to step forward and noticed Annie standing there, blocking her path, she said, "It's okay. I can make it. I'm spryer than I look. I'm not a waddling house yet."

"Don't be silly. I'll go with you."

"It's all right. I've talked your ear off long enough. You need a moment to check on your husband." Mary stepped forward again, but Annie stayed put. "I'll be fine. I trust you to keep an eye on my bag, and when it's your turn, I'll watch yours." She pointed to the sign a dozen rows ahead. "It's just up there around the corner. I'll be right back."

"Okay," Annie relented, turned sideways and sat back down. She swung her knees toward Richard so Mary could slip past, and he stood up, giving her the entire aisle space on the bench. "Five minutes, and I'll come looking for you," she said, sounding like a mother bear.

• • •

After Annie watched Mary disappear around the corner, she locked eyes with her husband during an ironic, pregnant pause.

"Is it bad?" Richard asked his wife.

A rolling fog of worry settled over Annie's face. "Yeah," she admitted. "It's bad—for sure." She couldn't imagine being in this situation. She knew she had to stay calm despite the desperate urge to wrap her arms around this young woman and squeeze the story out of her. But at that moment, she could only fathom the burden of being ostracized by neighbors and family.

She was only twenty when her first child, Reuben, was born, and she married Richard less than a year later. To think of what this young woman was experiencing now—fatherless and somehow forced from her home due to something she didn't understand and didn't dare ask about yet—this girl was running scared and felt like she had no options or support here.

Annie turned to Richard and whispered, "She's going to Boston to have her baby, and my gut tells me she's going to give it up for adoption. I can feel it"—she squeezed his elbow—"mother's intuition. I can see it in her eyes, and she's scared, but what she's afraid of, I don't know yet."

"Annie, should we get involved? Why?"

"Because we're good people, Richard, that's what we taught our children." Annie glanced around nervously. "She's running from something or someone, and as a mother with a conscience, I can't let her dock in Boston, a city where she's never been. To do what? Find a hospital and give birth on her own? Put her baby up for adoption? Or even locate an orphanage? It's America, and *we* don't even know those answers, let alone her. She's all alone!"

Richard didn't dispute her, and she wouldn't let his logic play a role in their discussion.

"That baby is Acadian, one of our own," Annie said, fidgeting with her wedding ring under her glove. "I'm not abandoning her, even though her mother has put ideas in her head, but I don't think she wants to or can go through with it." She drilled into Richard's eyes. "You gather what we need, the minimum, and we do a turnaround tomorrow. Can we pull it off and get everything done on time?"

She wouldn't change her mind, no matter how little time they had to finish their business before the afternoon departure. All she could do now was fidget with her wedding ring, wondering if five minutes had passed.

• • •

A man sat on the first bench in the starboard row, dressed in wool from head to toe. His charcoal gray derby hat was slightly lighter than his closely trimmed beard but matched the color of his buttoned vest worn over a long-sleeved, off-white linen shirt. His black and white pinstriped pants were tucked into scuffed black leather square-toed boots.

He observed the young woman as she approached the aft washroom, visibly pregnant and not dressed to afford a stateroom. As two older women directed her to the head of the line, he noticed her shoes as she stepped forward and realized she wasn't wearing a jacket for this time of year. It wasn't cold inside the ship, but it wasn't warm either. While stroking his black mustache and massaging his thoughts, the door opened, and as the young lady reached for the handle with her left hand, he had a clear view and saw that she was not wearing a wedding ring.

A few moments after she emerged and disappeared around the port side corner, he rose and walked toward the stern.

• • •

Once Mary settled in, tucking her satchel between her feet and under her knees, she apologized to Annie, "I'm sorry it took longer than five minutes, and I hope you didn't worry too much." She ruffled her gown and smoothed her lap. "Everything came out okay."

Annie covered her mouth, trying to suppress a chortle, but failed. "I see you have a sense of humor. Good for you. Now"—turning to face Mary—"it's settled, then."

Mary changed the subject. "I'm starving." She realized she didn't remember packing an overnight bread snack. What was she thinking? She hadn't considered it, and that was the problem; not thinking is how all bad situations begin. She couldn't bear to meet Annie's eyes, so she spread her knees, reached down to unbuckle her satchel, and hoped her mother hadn't let her down. Unfortunately, she couldn't reach her bag, and the baby let her know it wasn't pleased with being squeezed. "Ouch," she yelped, sitting up abruptly. Fortunately, she didn't have to find out if her mother had let her down when Annie handed her a small tin of soda crackers. "Thank you," she said, accepting. "So what's settled?"

"Do not do this."

"What shouldn't I do?" Mary feigned as she opened the tin. Upon seeing the crackers, she nearly drooled, and the baby kicked in excitement.

"Don't do what I think your mother persuaded you to do."

Annie watched Mary hesitantly nibble on her first cracker before they both turned to see if Richard was listening or dozing. Although expressionless, he seemed to be paying attention.

Mary took another cracker, but she hesitated as it reached her lips. Tears began to flow, and she leaned against Annie's shoulder.

"I don't know what to do," she said, her tears mingling with cracker crumbs as they dribbled onto Annie's sleeve. "I don't think… I don't want to." She couldn't hold back the dam any longer, burying her face and tears in Annie's neckline.

"Oh," Annie said, stroking the edge of Mary's bonnet before tugging at the chin strings, untying them, and gazing at Mary's thick dark brown hair tied up in a tight bun. She pulled the stick, allowing the wavy locks to cascade over her shoulders, stroked it gently, and whispered, "Everything will come out just fine."

Mary snorted, "Like I have a choice!" Tears streamed down her face as she tried to force a laugh. "Will you stay with me?"

Annie looked at Richard, who seemed confused and uneasy.

"Oh, honey, we're not staying."

Mary sat up straight. "No? Why not?"

"Because you're not staying either. We'll try to get some sleep and dock in the morning, and I'll stay right with you while everyone gets off this boat. Then we'll get right back on after Richard takes care of our business, and we'll all go home together."

"You'll talk to my mother when we return? Help convince her there's a chance I can keep my baby without causing any trouble?"

"Of course. There was no need to overreact like this."

Mary rested her head on Annie's shoulder and balanced the tin on her baby shelf, inhaling deeply. "But you don't understand," she whispered before drifting off.

3

The man had watched the trio disembark from the gangway onto Lewis Wharf in Boston's North End. He was unsure if the pregnant young woman was the daughter of the older couple, but his instincts suggested otherwise. He had kept a close watch on board and hadn't seen any signs of mother-daughter affection. There were no smiles, no kisses, only fear and tension—emotions he recognized all too well.

He was a grifter, never physically suited for a job as a manual laborer, and never able to sit behind a desk all day, either. His mother had told him from her deathbed that he'd never amount to a hill of beans. 'You have no ambition or patience,' she told him. Even from a young age, he always felt like his head and legs buzzed like a beehive, keeping him moving and distracted, unable to concentrate on any task. He spent the overnight trip not sleeping but instead kept a watchful eye on the trio as he paced the stern section, rehearsing scenarios in his head.

He had no idea how long he would have before the trio vanished into any of the granite buildings lining the marketplace along the harborfront. Still, he would find a way to separate the young woman from the couple without causing a public ruckus.

He leaned against a granite-block doorway, watching the two women sit on a knee wall with their backs to the harbor. His ears rang, and his feet itched to move, but he knew he had to suppress the urge. Biding his time, he munched rhythmically on a paper bag of sugared popcorn and peanuts—a delicious blend of sweet and salty that was almost addictive, he mused. It was his first time trying it, and it made it harder to focus on his grift, but he had a plan when he slipped back through the warehouse doorway to buy or steal another bag.

• • •

"Go to the tackle shop and place our supply orders," Annie instructed Richard. "Do you remember everything we need for the new jack boats?"

"Yes, seines, more hand lines, and traps," he replied.

"How much new and spare canvas sailcloth do we need?"

"Best guess? One bolt for each deliverable jack."

"And rope?"

"I don't need any," he replied confidently. "We still have plenty from our last trade on Cape Breton."

"Just make sure everything is scheduled for the same train, and for heaven's sake, have them put it in writing." She gripped Richard's jacket sleeve, tugging at it to make sure she had his full attention. "Don't try to memorize it all," she pleaded. "The last thing we want is for everything to arrive home while we're not there to claim it, and with our luck, it'll be sold out of the back of the station. If we don't leave the harbor, we'll have time for the turnabout."

"I'll handle it, Annie. We've been through this before."

Annie relented, moving on. "MJ and I will find a place on the wharf to stretch our legs and take a break. We have about three hours… I guess."

Annie and Mary watched Richard head off toward Warehouse Row, with Annie wanting to stay as close as possible and find a place to rest near a washroom and food. Lewis Wharf was more expansive than the docking area in Halifax, and with the number of departing and arriving passengers from other ships, she didn't want to make Mary anxious. This was not Stewiacke. Hundreds of Italians filled the wharf, coming and going, shopping, and shouting.

Annie wondered what the bearded man had been eating from the bag. With his pinstriped pants, he was hard to miss standing in the archway next to where Richard had gone inside. Was he looking right at us? she wondered after he slipped into the shadows. She turned to Mary and gently squeezed her hand. "You holding up all right?"

She felt Mary grip her hand and turned further after noticing the young woman craning her neck to see the vast harbor filled with boats. Mary's eyes were as big as Nor'easter snowballs. This city away from home could leave anyone speechless. Although she had known Mary for less than a day, she already felt responsible for the young woman's well-being and the urgency of her unborn baby. Even though she was a stranger, a mother is always a mother. Yet, when she returns Mary to her mother, she must remember her language.

"Bladder check?" Annie asked.

"I'm too nervous to move. I'm shocked I can even talk with all this noise." Mary kept turning her head from side to side, absorbing all the passing faces and voices. "I've never heard anyone speak Italian before. Only a bit of French." She closed her eyes. "I have no idea what everyone is saying, but the sound of their voices is like music."

"Are you sure about the washroom?" Annie asked, double-checking— still no sign of Richard navigating his way through the crowd.

"I can't explain it. I don't have to go." Mary swiveled to watch the people, envying their dashing happiness. "Honestly."

Annie was startled as Richard appeared front and center. "Oh!" she gasped. "Done already? That seemed quick."

"Not really," he said, firmly placing his fists on his hips. "This time, they need your initials on some papers for the financing and shipping."

Annie glanced at Mary, who looked at Richard, who gazed back at Annie—a three-sided dilemma. Annie stood and reached for Mary's hand. "Okay, I guess we get to go sign our names and push some papers," she said, looking perplexed at Mary, who hadn't offered her hand. "Can I help you up?"

Mary glanced at both of them. "Is it all right if I stay here? I won't move an inch… I promise," she said, crossing herself. "I'm warming up in the sun, and it hardly smells like fish or low tide," she said and winked.

Annie looked befuddled, growing uneasy, but finally relented. "Okay, but not one inch! You understand? Don't make me worry!" Turning to

Richard, she said, "Let's be quick. Go on… go." She focused on Mary. "And watch our bags too!"

"Yes, Mother."

"Not yet," Annie quipped, turning to follow Richard as he wove through the crowd toward Warehouse Row.

The man wearing pinstriped pants had retreated into the shadow of a doorway, clutching two brown paper snack bags. After the older couple passed through the next archway and vanished inside the warehouse, he moved forward and stepped out after them.

4

Mary stood and stretched her arms over her head, turning to face the harbor as she gazed over the brick knee wall at the choppy water, mesmerized by the moored sailboats, schooners, and dinghies swaying in the whitecaps. Seagulls perched on every mast and ladder, cackling like an out-of-tune orchestra. She could see the tall granite-white obelisk of the Bunker Hill Monument across the inland waterway and the cyclical flash of brilliance from far-off Boston Light on Little Brewster Island. The scent of the ocean wasn't foreign to her, experiencing both the frigid North Atlantic and the swift-moving high tides of the Bay of Fundy, with its rocky coastlines and the fishy odor of salted cod drying on endless wooden racks in the coastal breezes and warm rising sun of Nova Scotia's eastern shore.

She recalled the few times during the summer when she and her family visited the high cliff beaches and discovered a handful of Mi'kmaq arrowheads when she noticed a man standing beside her, too close to ignore, holding two small paper bags. He turned and smiled at her, showing tiny bits of white food caught in his teeth and on his black mustache.

He offered one of the bags. "Would you like to try a handful of salted popcorn and peanuts?" he asked with a friendly, insecure smile. "They're quite tasty, I must confess."

When Mary first tasted the salted popcorn and peanuts, her stomach rumbled. The salty-sweet mix rolled over her tongue, bringing a wave of euphoria. It beat those bland soda crackers, which were neither sweet nor salty. She raised her eyebrows, smiled, and murmured, "Mmmm," acknowledging the deliciousness.

"Here," he said, presenting the whole bag to her. "Take it. I couldn't possibly eat both bags."

Mary gladly accepted the paper bag, carefully placing a second hand on the bottom to avoid accidentally dropping it and spilling the treasured contents. "Thanks," she said, pulling it closer. "I don't—"

"You're welcome," he said with a stop gesture. "It was only a nickel." He waved dismissively. "Don't worry. Hopefully, your parents won't mind when they return."

Mary noticed his palm was clean and free of calluses, which her father's hands had never been. "Oh, they're not my parents," she said, glancing over her shoulder at the warehouse. "We met yesterday on the ship. They're nice. They have a boat-building business back home and came here to buy supplies," she said cordially.

"Oh, I just assumed you were their daughter…" He paused briefly to look away. "Anyway, I work for the supply company"—he gestured with his thumb over his shoulder—"and they're such valued returning customers that my manager asked me to fetch you"—he darted his eyes down and up without missing a beat—"and your bags to come inside," he said, tipping his derby. "May I?" He reached for the Hatts' valise and her satchel.

Doubt pierced Mary's innocence, but now that she was standing, she had no choice but to find a washroom as the urge was too strong, and inside the warehouse seemed like the best place to start. She squatted, suppressing a groan, and grabbed her bag by the handle, wincing at the pressure on her bladder.

"Just theirs," she said, pointing to the valise. "I'll be fine. You know the Hatts?" She realized she was in a predicament—holding the snack bag in one hand and her satchel handle in the other, unable to get the strap over her shoulder. She struggled to lift the heavy canvas bag, and he quickly reached for it. However, Mary handed him the paper bag instead, forcing him to set the valise back on the ground.

"Yes, of course," he replied, shifting his weight from one foot to the other as he squeezed the snack bags until they crinkled in his strong hands. "They come here for business quite regularly. I just assumed you were their daughter," he said again.

Mary tossed the strap over her shoulder. "No, I'm not, but thank you. I'm MJ, by the way," she said, offering her hand to mollify his nervousness.

He was left holding the bag—two to be exact—so he handed one back to Mary and started to reciprocate before hesitating. "My hand"—he wiped it on his trousers—"it's all sticky from the sugar and all." He picked up the valise and gestured for them to move off the dock toward the archways. "Nice to meet you, MJ. My name is Frank."

As they started walking toward Warehouse Row, he asked her, "So, does MJ stand for Mary Jane by any chance?"

• • •

Inside the maritime supply office, Annie scribbled her initials as quickly as each sheet of paper landed before her on the desk. "How many more are there?" she asked, pausing for a moment and not caring who responded first, whether it was Richard, the salesman at the desk, or the younger apprentice standing behind him.

"That's it for the orders, ma'am," the salesman behind the desk said, scooping up the stack of receipts and exchanging them with another handful held by his helper. "Only a few more to sign off on regarding the shipping options and delivery schedule."

Annie looked at Richard as if the delay were entirely his fault. "I didn't have to deal with any of this the last time we were here."

She was growing more nervous by the minute. This was taking too long, and she didn't want to leave Mary alone outside in public. It was still early in the day, and hundreds of people were milling about, but that was both a good and a bad sign. She had to assume Mary needed to relieve herself, and she had left both their heavy bags as an extra burden. It was foolish to have listened to the young woman and let herself be convinced to leave her alone.

5

A few steps into the warehouse, Mary's eyes began to adjust to the dim light. It was chillier inside these granite walls than outside by the waterfront in the sunshine. The entrance was an arched granite tunnel leading to an open courtyard. She shivered as the draft swept past her linens, but her hands, clasped beneath her bosom, were warm enough. She felt the baby shift over her bladder and quickened her pace.

Before reaching the courtyard, Mary spotted the washroom doors—ladies on the left and gentlemen on the right—and had nearly passed them without noticing the signs mounted flush on the door fronts. "I need to stop here for a minute," she told Frank, framing her girth with her hands, making her pregnancy abundantly clear.

"Right… of course"—he gestured toward the ladies' door—"I'll be"—he scanned the courtyard and pointed—"right over there on that bench."

Mary thought, 'Not another bench! My fanny will be flat forever if I keep sitting on benches!' Her back muscles had started to stiffen, and she was losing patience. "Fine, but could you please check on the Hatts while I'm busy?"

"Yes, absolutely. They're over there." He swiveled his pointed hand across the narrow courtyard, his finger wavering slightly, not focusing on any specific window. "But perhaps"—he glanced up, pointing higher—"they might have been taken to the second-floor offices. That's typically where all the sales offices are. The inventory is only on the bottom floors."

Mary couldn't care less about the building's details; she pushed the washroom door open with her hip and disappeared inside.

• • •

Frank sat on the courtyard bench, waiting for Mary to return from the washroom. While he considered how to take advantage of this young woman's situation, he had no idea whether her travel companions had wrapped up their business.

Although his trip to Halifax to find a job had been short-lived, he might never stop smelling the cod fisheries he'd worked at along the coasts of Newfoundland and Labrador. Seeing more flies than stars in the night sky had turned him against all seafood, making this return to Boston feel like torture.

He wasn't stupid, regardless of what his mother had told him on her deathbed. 'I have patience. I'm ambitious, and I will make something of myself,' he thought, cursing his mother. This young woman was about to give birth and wasn't married (that alone spelled trouble). The couple traveling with her was simply in the right place at the right time to take pity on her, but now it was his turn to relieve them of any moral duties they wished to fulfill.

He watched Mary emerge from the washroom, her satchel slung over her shoulder. She glanced back down the archway toward the warehouse entrance, and for a brief moment, he wondered if she would return outside out of guilt. Instead, she pivoted, seeing him sitting on the courtyard bench and making eye contact with her.

He waved casually, wiggling his fingers, and called to her, "Mary Jane, over here." He was ready for his next ambitious move as she approached. "How are you holding up? Is everything okay?" he asked, attempting to sound empathetic, though the words he felt might have come out stilted.

Mary hesitated, looking perplexed.

Frank studied her expression, unsure whether her predicament would lead her to cry, vomit, or force a strained smile.

Finally, she replied, "I don't think so." Rubbing her forehead, she said, "I just don't know anymore."

Now, it was Frank's turn to hesitate. He needed more information and some extra time to be ambitious. "All right, well, I'm a pretty good listener, and it just so happens we have a bit more time," he fibbed about one thing. "While you were freshening up, I quickly checked on how the supply purchases were going and how much longer they might take and…" he paused, lying again, then said, "turns out the…" he rubbed his fingers together, pretending he'd lost the couple's name on the tip of his tongue.

"The Hatts," she replied, falling into the trap.

"Ah, yes, the Hatts. It's been a busy morning. My apologies. A co-worker informed me that my supply boss and the Hatts were ushered to the train station offices to arrange and schedule the delivery back to Halifax." He paused to gauge her expression and, sensing no immediate pushback, said, "We'll just go meet them there."

Mary's eyes widened, and her aching spine stiffened.

"Oh, no, no, it's okay. It's not too far away, and I'm sure they were told it would be scheduled quickly. Besides, they knew I was sent to look out for your well-being." The smooth lines kept rolling along. "Here"—he patted the bench—"we don't have to rush. There's no need to get there and find ourselves sitting—"

"On another bench, right?" she interrupted, a faint smile appearing. It didn't take long before she released a short, suppressed laugh to ease the tension.

• • •

Annie darted ahead of her husband across the dock, making a beeline for the knee wall and parting the crowd as they moved forward. When she reached the spot where she thought they had left Mary, immediate panic hit her stomach like a brick from the wall beside which she now stood. Looking left and right, she saw no one sitting on the knee wall and noticed no abandoned bags either. She turned around, glancing back the way they had come, then left and right again. Too many people were milling about on the dock, and she was too short to see.

"Can you see her?" she pleaded with Richard.

"No, there are too many bonnets. Too many hats. Everyone looks almost the same!" he stated the obvious truth to her.

"But she's eight months pregnant!" she shouted. "Help me get up onto the wall!"

"What?" He stared at his wife, hesitating to take her hand.

"Either you climb up and get a better look, or I will! I don't want to lose that girl!"

Richard knelt on the wall cap and pushed himself upright, steadying himself without toppling into the filthy algae and seaweed pressing against the dock pilings.

He scanned the crowd. "I can't see her," he said, trying to shield his eyes from the sun reflecting off the granite facades.

"Look for someone pregnant!" she shouted to him.

"I only see fat men," he said, jumping back onto the deck.

Annie realized that asking passersby if they'd seen a pregnant woman anywhere on this dock was likely futile. She glanced back at the warehouse with its numerous doorways and floors, recognizing that this had become a needle-in-a-haystack problem. Turning to her husband, tears filled her eyes, and his face looked hopeless, but she turned to the open ocean and recited a prayer to Saint Anthony, the patron saint of all lost things.

After finishing, she bowed in reverence and noticed a few scattered peanuts and some pieces of what seemed to be popcorn on the ground, knowing the seagulls wouldn't hesitate to swoop down to grab it.

Feeling stunned, she asked, "What do we do now? And we left our overnight bag with her. That's gone, too." She glanced around the dock near her feet, hoping they'd overlooked it in their haste, but no such luck.

Richard took their tickets from his pocket and held them up to catch the early afternoon sun. "Well, we still have these and the clothes on our backs. What are you going to do?" He looked at her for an answer but received none. "I don't see any other choice but to get on the turnaround in"—he pulled out his watch to check the time—"about an hour and fifteen, maybe twenty."

Exasperated, Annie sucked air in and out through clenched teeth. Why would Mary walk away? A ray of hope struck her, and she proposed, "Let's wait here a little longer. She went off in search of a washroom, right?" She looked at the granite doorways. "She must've gone looking for one back inside." She took a step forward, then looked at Richard, flexing her arms up and down, mimicking herself carrying a bag in each hand. "The poor thing lugged the bags. Her back must be…" she broke off, nearly in tears.

Richard placed his hands on his wife's shoulders. "Let's stay here for a moment. If we head back inside, we might run into her as she comes out, but who knows who will be where and when."

Annie wasn't about to give up and turned toward the warehouse. "We've been here before. There's a courtyard inside, behind the sales offices. Am I right?" She didn't wait for his answer. "I'm sure she's in there looking for us." She started to walk away, feeling a twinge of dread.

Richard grabbed her arm and begged, "Wait… just wait. We're not separating. We don't have time to risk losing each other now."

"We have to go. Now!" she pleaded, pointing at the buildings, reminding him, "The train station is fifteen minutes past the courtyard on the other side of the warehouse! What if she panicked? What if she lost our trust and ran off to who knows where?" Maternal instinct surged within her, and she began to panic over someone who wasn't even her daughter. This wasn't how she envisioned the morning turnaround playing out.

"Annie, how could she lose trust in us when she didn't even know us?" Richard placed his hands on his hips. "For all we know, she might have wanted to steal our bag."

Annie wouldn't put up with it. She hiked up her skirt linens and swiftly crossed the wharf planks toward the warehouse with Richard reluctantly close behind her, trying to keep pace.

6

Mary stared at her hands, all ten empty fingers. No matter how often she opened and closed her hands, a ring never magically appeared. She remembered trying for so long to hide her morning sickness from her mother, but four months into the pregnancy, her mother had begun to suspect the worst. Concealing her growing midriff beneath bulky dresses had bought her maybe a month. Her brother George had been unaware of her condition even though he had spent so much time around the farmhouse, barely paying much attention to her and her sister.

It had been a humid night in late August when she, her sister, and her mother were having supper in the kitchen. She remembered slouching in her chair, trying to keep her waist hidden below the tabletop. She made eye contact with her mother and recalled wishing her hair was as rich, deep, and auburn red as her mother's Scottish heritage when something awful about the earthy smell of the vegetable stew churned her stomach. Trying to swallow it down was a mistake to dawdle, and she never made it out the back door. No time to say, 'Excuse me.' It all came up and out all over the kitchen floor, with some splattering on the bottom panel of the back door.

"Mary Jane!" her mother exclaimed as she kneeled beside her daughter. "What…" she began to ask, but Mary had already pushed herself out the door and onto the back porch.

The first thing Mary thought at that moment wasn't the inquisition she knew she was about to face from her mother, but her sister, Agnes, who would be traumatized by the sight and sound of it all. She couldn't recall whether her poor sister or mother had eventually cleaned up the mess.

• • •

Frank watched Mary as she examined her hands. He knew that no wedding ring meant no husband, which suggested an out-of-wedlock child. Her fingers looked dainty and not swollen, and there was no sign of a ring indentation, so he proceeded cautiously. "I won't judge you, MJ, I promise," he whispered, crossing himself and pretending to stick a pin in his eye. He took off his derby and held it over his chest. "I can help you. I have friends who can help with the baby," he offered, studying her face for any reaction. "I only work here in the city, but I live just outside it, to the west." He considered pointing west but realized she wouldn't know which way was which or care at that moment. "There's a nice quiet town where I live, and…" he hesitated, then whispered even lower, "a good orphanage and churches. There's also a well-respected midwife in town."

"Okay… I'll meet your friends and listen to all the options, but I can't stop feeling guilty or being a burden. It's like a gale is roaring inside my head." She took a deep breath and composed herself. "The Hatts are too generous. I'd be *such* an imposition on them." She bounced her feet, darting her eyes around the courtyard while clutching her gown above her knees. "There's a midwife, you say?"

"Yes," he replied honestly.

Before standing up, Mary glanced at the Hatts' bag and asked, "How is this going to work? You're supposed to take me to meet them? We have their valise."

Frank rounded the bend, clearing the last hurdles. 'I'll show you patience, Mother,' he thought before responding carefully, "Wait here. I'll return it to the office and tell them you feel unwell, and I'm taking you to find help. They'll have to return here and retrieve it when their business is done." He made an assumption and kept the lies rolling along. "I'm sure the

Hatts mentioned your condition once they were inside, so I'm sure they'll all understand."

He rose from the bench, grabbed the Hatts' valise, and walked into the tunnel, looking back at Mary, who nodded and waved. When she turned around, he slipped into the men's washroom and shoved the suitcase in the trashcan.

• • •

Annie and Richard hurried down the granite warehouse corridor, making their way toward the courtyard in the back. As they stepped into the open air, Annie felt a surge of hope, seeing significantly fewer shoppers inside than the crowd at Lewis Wharf. She scanned the courtyard, searching for Mary, her eyes moving counterclockwise from each archway to each bench around the square, but the young pregnant woman was nowhere in sight.

"She must have gone out the back toward North Station," she gasped, managing to take two steps before Richard grabbed her elbow. "Please," she pleaded, but Richard held firm.

"Annie, let her go," he said, lowering the tone and cadence of his voice. "She's gone." The look in his eyes conveyed the truth to her. "For whatever reasons, and I'm sure she has them, her mind must be made up." He released her arm and grasped both of her shoulders. "And forget the bag. It was just clothes, and I'm sure she'll thank us in her prayers."

Annie slumped her shoulders and let her chin drop to her chest. When she lifted her face, she spoke softly, "We should be shopping right here *right now* for her new boots." Tears lingered in her eyes before spilling off her lashes and high cheekbones. "She's going to freeze to death, Richard."

• • •

Frank had a general sense of where he was going when he led Mary into North Station and started looking for the Fitchburg Line of the Boston and Maine Railway. He had grown up in Waltham and spent most of his teenage years moving from one Irish gang to another before working the lines at the Boston Manufacturing Company like many other Irish immigrants who had left the city for the suburbs. The choices for wayward kids in his youth were few: either join a gang or end up in an orphanage, with the fortunate ones being given up for adoption into indentured servitude for the wealthy. The latter would be his prize at the end of Mary's journey.

Mary allowed Frank to take her bag before she stepped onto the train, following him down the center aisle of the rail car, where she collapsed into the first empty window seat in his row. She looked exhausted and barely able to speak. "I've never been on a train before." She leaned on the bag that he had placed between them. "It's a much nicer seat than all those benches," she said, shifting her weight on her haunches and gazing out the window at the people on the platform who moved like ants, marching back and forth while staying in their lines. "Do you take this train to and from work in the city every day?" she asked him.

He didn't, but he felt compelled to respond, "Yeah." He could tell from her expression that she was anticipating more, so he obliged. "The maritime supply store provides me with a small stipend at the beginning of each month, and it covers half the cost."

"Oh, that's generous," she remarked, her eyelids fluttering slowly. "Is it far? Where you live."

"Nah. Less than an hour." This time, he was truthful, but to be thorough, he said, "It would only take half that if the train didn't have to make any other stops between here and there." He tried to smile, hoping it looked genuine, and it seemed to work because, as the train lurched out of North Station toward Waltham, he watched her relax, lean her head against the window glass, and close her eyes.

The cozy warmth of the rail car and the soothing click-clack rhythm of the wheels carried Mary into sleep before the train departed the station.

1882

7

Mary Jane was fourteen when she first met the only son of the new neighbors, their youngest child.

The August summer day was sunny and humid, with no breeze. The tall grasses of the Nutting farmstead drooped languidly while the livestock sought refuge in the shade of a stand of red oaks, old enough to hang over the barn's roof: acorns and fallen leaves from years gone by littered the gray, weathered white pine shingles.

Mary enjoyed the breeze, pulling her bare feet skyward on a simple wooden plank rope swing that her father had hung from an enormous red oak off the back porch. The tree, which centered the yard between the house and barn, was likely three hundred years old and had sprouted before the first European settlers encountered the native Mi'kmaq Indians.

Her skirt billowed at the peak of her swing and fell closed as she descended. Easing to a stop, she heard a dog's bark and watched a golden Labrador retriever racing toward her from the hemlock stand that divided her family's property from the neighboring plot. A small, barefoot boy dressed in short brown woolen knickers and a linen shirt that was too loose for his body, tied at the neck with a bandana, dashed toward her. He was chasing what she assumed was his dog.

"Duke!" he shouted, gesturing wildly. "Stop!"

The dog named Duke stopped and sat on its haunches on the dirt patch at Mary's feet. Even before the boy reached them, she noticed the dog was taller than his frame, and she gently inched her hand toward the dog's head until it obliged by stepping forward, allowing her to scratch it behind its ears. Its flaxen fur was shiny, silky smooth, and cool to the touch.

"I guess he likes you," gasped the boy, stopping to catch his breath. "His name's Duke," he said, bending over with his hands on his knees to regain his breath.

Mary thought his shaggy, thick blonde hair perfectly matched Duke's color and was the cutest thing she had ever seen on a boy. When he finally took a breath, he looked at her with arctic blue eyes that shimmered in the sunlight. She hitched her breath and quickly re-engaged, vigorously scratching the dog's head and chin. "So, his name is Duke… and what's yours?" she asked, stroking the dog's spine.

"William," he replied. "My ma and pa just moved us into the place over"—he pointed to where he had hoped he had come from while chasing his dog—"there. Pa said we're going to be farmers."

"Everyone around here is a farmer," Mary told him. "How many older brothers do you have who will help your dad with all the work?"

"I ain't got no brothers, just seven big sisters," he replied proudly.

Mary took a deep breath and stared at him in disbelief, questioning whether he was too young to count. "You have seven older sisters?" she asked, holding up seven fingers.

"A'yup," he replied, mimicking his father's accent while sticking his thumbs into his empty belt loops. If he'd been chewing on a straw, he would have looked like a Homunculus.

Mary let a barely audible sigh escape her lips, lamenting the absence of teenage boys to crush on. "How old are you, young Master William?" she asked, aware that he was at least half her age.

"I'm six," he replied, echoing her flair for showing the correct number of fingers. "You live here? This your place?"

"A'yup," she teased, pushing herself up again with her toes. "Just our mom and us. I have an older brother and a younger sister." She glanced at him, feeling guilty for mocking his accent, but realized he didn't seem to notice. "I don't have a pa anymore," she whispered as she continued to pet Duke.

"Why?" he asked. "He died or something?"

"Yeah, last year,"—pointing to show him the exact spot in the field—"right over there. He was cutting hay and"—she shrugged her shoulders—"fell over." She recalled grabbing his pocket watch from his vest and clutching it before anyone else could see or take it because she needed something to hold onto, afraid she'd forget him if she didn't.

"Sorry for your loss," William said.

Mary turned to him, her eyes wide with wonder, amazed that such a young boy could know to say something like that. Then she realized it was nearly the only thing she'd heard from the neighbors during her father's funeral and burial.

William stared at her. "What? I'm a good listener. My ma taught me always to listen."

"Well, I guess living with seven sisters means you don't get to do much besides listen," she said. Watching him talk with his hands made her laugh. He was quite the cutie pie, and she was sure he'd break some hearts when he got older.

"I should probably get going. My ma and pa are likely wondering where I ran off to"—he glanced to the tree line—"if they even thought to look. Come on, Duke, let's go." He turned and motioned to his loyal dog, who wasn't ready to leave yet.

Mary shooed Duke. "Go on. You can visit anytime you want!" She watched them jog away and disappear into the hemlock stand, unaware they would become the best of friends over the next ten years.

8

Frank let Mary sleep as they neared Waltham's Roberts station on the way to Fitchburg. It was late afternoon, and the sun was setting behind the station's brick clock tower. She had been asleep for less than an hour, so he chose to wait a few more stops, giving him time to think and stay warm.

As the train slowed to a stop, he hoped the final jolt of the brakes or the steam whistle wouldn't wake her, and they didn't, but she twitched momentarily, and he heard her mumble something in her sleep. Maybe she was dreaming about her worn shoes or trying to shoo something away. It didn't matter to him as long as she didn't wake up with a fright.

While she slept, he took the liberty of searching through her bag for anything useful, only finding extra linens, another dress, a couple of skirts, a hairbrush, and a charcoal-smeared toothcloth. He missed uncovering the small amount of Canadian silver coins her mother had sewn into a few hidden bottom pockets, but he did touch the brooch attached to the outside. Feeling it under his thumb, he found it an odd-looking piece of silver jewelry, star-shaped, with its five sides bent in a swirl pattern instead of traditional points. At least he could steal it from her for the value of the silver if nothing else panned out.

Mary woke up as the train started to slow down before reaching the Lincoln train station. "Where are we?"

"This is Lincoln."

"Are we still in Massachusetts?"

"Yes," he reassured her.

"Is this place named after Abraham Lincoln?"

He had no idea, but he told her anyway, "Indeed, it is." He nodded and emphasized, "Honest Abe, the one and only."

Neither knew that the town was named not after Abraham Lincoln but after Lincoln, England.

"An honest man honored by an honest town?" she asked, laughing softly.

Frank's mouth followed the flow, patronizing her, "You betcha." But his mind raced, trying to think of his next move, but first, they should hop off here while he was familiar with the area instead of continuing to Concord or Fitchburg. He took a deep breath, straightened his shoulders, and confidently said, "This is where we get off."

Frank's mother was undoubtedly rolling over in her grave.

Even though it was January, a hint of spring thaw lingered in the air, and Mary didn't shiver as she stepped off the rail car and onto the station platform. She squinted into the dim light of dusk, trying to see beyond the platform and into town.

Six other people had gotten off with them—three couples. Everyone exchanged pleasantries, including the customary tipping of the men's hats, before dispersing into the early evening.

Mary clutched both hands around her satchel's shoulder strap and asked, "Well? What's next?" After a brief moment of hesitation, she answered herself, "We need to find your friends who will let us stay the night and help me figure out what to do next."

Frank let her take charge. "That's right. I know someone here who can help." The truth was, he did know someone he hoped still lived in town—someone who had been close friends with his parents when they tried to pull him away from the Irish gang as a kid. Whether they would remember him was another question entirely. He wasn't even sure if they were both still alive, much less if they would take him and Mary in for the night. If they weren't alive, his grifting scheme would likely end tonight, with him grabbing the silver and leaving poor Mary to fend for herself.

He extended his hand and asked, "May I take that?"

"It helps keep me warm being snug to my hip," she said, adjusting the strap.

Frank pointed to the steps that led off the back of the train platform. "Let's go this way."

Mary's short gait kept her shoes anchored to the gravel streets of Lincoln. He knew it would strain her back if she fell on the rigid, frozen, crushed stone. Between the early evening dusk and her prominent midsection, there was no way she would spot a patch of ice or snow in time to step over or around it. Being a gentleman, he supported her by linking her elbow as they walked.

Soon, buildings emerged from the twilight as they strolled along. "What's this place?" she asked, pointing into the dusky lowlight.

He recalled the next building that came into view from his adolescence, as it stood out with its white Greek style, featuring four prominent ionic-capped columns and a pediment. "Here we have the town hall," he stated concisely.

"How much further do you think?"

"Not much. A bit further as we get closer to Flint's Pond." He pointed through the winter barren trees to a body of water in the far distance where the early-rising moon reflected. "I used to know a lovely couple who were close to my parents. We would come and visit when I was a teenager." What he left unsaid was about his parents trying to break him free from the gang he'd practically taken up residence with back in Waltham. They'd met during one of the local church dinner exchanges, and these people had been heavily involved with the Lincoln Congregational Church. His parents thought keeping him out of reach would be wise.

At the intersection of Station and Sandy Pond roads, he guided Mary up the front steps of a charming Queen Anne cottage and knocked on the front door. After rapping a second time, they heard light footsteps approaching, which caused the floorboards to squeak inside the entranceway.

"Who's there?" asked a timid elderly woman from behind the front door.

"It's me, Mrs. Gates, Frank Hosman." 'Please, God, remember me,' he prayed.

The sound of a latch snicking came as the door opened slightly. "Franklin? Franklin Hosman, is that you?"

"Yes, Mrs. Gates, it's me," he said, removing his derby hat. "I was coming home from the city and must have fallen asleep on the train… I guess. I woke up just in time to get off here and thought maybe it was a sign from God, as you can see—"

The front door opened, and Mrs. Gertrude Gates looked out at her front porch. "Franklin," she gasped. "How on earth did you even remember…" she began to ask, but upon seeing the young woman standing partially hidden behind him, she changed her line of questioning. "And who is this young lady?" she asked, gasping with delight when she noticed the young woman's condition as she stepped out from behind Frank. "Why, you're married now, Franklin!"

Frank and Mary shared glances, with Mary looking far more offended than Frank.

Gertrude waited with vacant eyes.

"We need your help, Mrs. Gates," Frank said.

Gertrude remained passive despite his appeal for help.

"Please," he pleaded, turning to introduce Mary, "This is Mary Jane. We met at work today. Well, I was working, and she had just arrived from Halifax and didn't—"

Gertrude interrupted him. "Halifax? Then how—"

Frank sensed the tension in his mentor's voice and worried she might shut the door when Mary interrupted. "Ma'am? Mrs. Gates," she said, her tears threatening to freeze in the evening air. "I'm in a lot of—"

"Oh, c'mon. Come in now. Get out of the cold," Gertrude pleaded, motioning for them to enter the house.

Once inside the foyer, Frank removed his boots while Mary slipped off her shoes and set her satchel on a boot bench at the bottom of the staircase. She rubbed her arms and shoulders, trying to shake off the night cold, while Frank rolled his linen sleeves above his elbows and exhaled warmly into his clasped hands.

Gertrude led them into the formal front room. "Come in here and warm up by the fire." Gesturing toward a small Rumford fireplace, she noticed Mary's loafers and wool socks peeking out from under her maternity gown. "Your feet must be cold, dear," she said, reaching for the only rocking chair in the room.

Frank moved it closer to the fire for Mary. Even though it was just for show, he wanted Mrs. Gates to know he remembered his manners.

Mary sat in the rocking chair, slipping off her worn shoes, and rested her socked feet beside the hearth, wiggling some warmth back into her toes. After a moment, she asked, "Mrs. Gates, may I—"

The lady of the house interjected, "Gertrude, please. There's no need for formalities right now. What is it you need?"

Mary pushed herself off the rocking chair, tugging at the front of her gown. "Is there, perhaps, somewhere I could change? I wore extra layers today. I mean, from yesterday when I left home—"

Gertrude waved her off. "Say no more now… of course." She motioned for Mary to follow her into the foyer, pointed up the stairs, and then changed direction, motioning down the hallway. "Down the back hall, the second door on your left is my sewing room. If you're not too tired from your journey, you can change in there, and then I'll show you upstairs to a better room where you can sleep."

Mary reached for her bag, lifted it off the boot bench, and nodded graciously. "Thank you. I'm not sure…" She scrunched her face into a knot and started to cry.

"It's all right," Gertrude shushed her. "No need for any heavy explaining tonight. Just go down the hall, change, and find your way back to the front room. I'll make us some tea."

"Thank you, you have no—"

Gertrude shushed her again. "You'll catch me up on everything tomorrow."

Mary nodded and quietly shuffled down the back hallway, her wool socks gliding on the wooden floor as if she were skating on pond ice.

Frank unbuttoned his vest and draped it over the back of a padded chair before sitting beside the fire across from the rocker. He stood and turned the chair to face the couch, careful not to scratch the shellacked hardwood floor. Then, he moved the chair a few inches farther away from the fire and sat down again, not wanting to be rude by turning his back to Mrs. Gates.

He was a teenage boy whom she and her late husband Roy had tried their best to help so long ago. Now, he was taller and heavier, with facial hair, and his deep brown eyes, which she used to hold and plead with to stay on the straight and narrow, looked different and hardened.

The room wasn't overly spacious. A small loveseat for two faced the fireplace, with a suitably sized square sofa table positioned in the center. A square wool rug featuring a paisley pattern covered most of the hardwood floor. A large wood-framed mirror stretched from the mantel to the intricate crown molding at the ceiling, and a matching wood frame to the mirror encased the floor-to-ceiling windows arranged in a full-sized bay window, offering a view of the wraparound porch. The detailed carpentry of the framing and molding was a hand-chiseled labor of love, perfectly aligning with the half-walled bookcases on either side of the bay window. The roasted chestnut hue of the woodwork radiated a welcoming warmth.

Frank stared at the wall paint as Gertrude entered the room, carrying a tray of cookies while balancing a teapot and three cups.

Taking notice, she said, "The color is Independence Blue." She placed the tray on the sofa table and sat on the loveseat. "You can't quite put your finger on it, can you?"

"No, but it suits the warmth of this room… this house," he admitted. "In the flickering light of the fire, you can see a mix of smoky blue, gray, and… plum?"

"I like to think of it as a blending of north and south."

She poured two cups of tea and appeared to wait for him to get up and help himself.

Taking the hint, he picked up his cup. "May I ask how Mr. Gates is doing? Is he here?" he inquired, looking up as if to suggest that Roy was upstairs.

"He's passed, Franklin." She closed her eyes. "Every day, there's a dull ache in my sixty-two-year-old heart, and I feel it in my bones."

"I'm sorry for your loss," he said apologetically, returning to the rocker with his tea.

She sipped her tea. "Franklin?" When he gave her his attention, she asked, "What kind of trouble are you in now?"

He cradled his cup in his hands, shook his head slightly, and widened his eyes a bit as he answered her, "No, not me… I swear." He whispered,

"She's not carrying *my* baby." He crossed himself and quickly wondered whether that had been the right or wrong thing to do. He whispered again, "I met her on the wharf at lunchtime. She had gotten off the boat from Halifax, and I saw her sitting all alone." He hurried through his words, hoping to get everything out before Mary returned. "I gave her some food, we talked, and one thing led to another. She needs help having the baby." He waited for a response but didn't receive one. "I remember when you and Roy helped me. You had connections through the church." He leaned closer and whispered even lower, "She's not married. I think she came to Boston to have the baby, give it up, and leave."

Gertrude's expression was vacant as she closed her shawl at the corners around her neck with one hand and took another sip of tea.

She reiterated what she had previously told Mary: "There's no need for any heavy explaining tonight. We'll start fresh in the morning. You have my word, and I'll help." She paused, cradling her teacup in both hands, and took a deep sip of her remaining tea. "But there are always three sides to a story, isn't that right?"

Mary quietly returned to the room, and Gertrude welcomed her. "Everything all right, dear?" she asked as she poured a cup of tea and handed it to Mary with a slight tremor in her wrist. She watched Mary, two layers of linen lighter, settle back into her spot on the rocker.

"Yes, thank you. And thanks for the tea. It's been a while." Mary took a sip, resting a hand on her stomach. She moved her hand to her side and let out a small simper, blushing in the dim light.

"The baby enjoying the tea, I see?" Gertrude smiled.

"Yes, I believe so," Mary replied, her cheeks flushed.

"You're carrying pretty high," Gertrude noted. "You might be having a girl."

Mary hiccuped, then composed herself and yawned, covering her mouth. "Wouldn't that be nice?"

"Where are my manners?" gasped Gertrude, picking up a couple of cookies and motioning to Franklin, who stood ready to accept them. "These are new. They just started baking them down in Newton. They're a kind of a soft fig cookie, pretty tasty, I must admit." Gertrude took a small bite.

"Reminds me of a good dense hermit cookie that sticks to your ribs. I don't know if they'll catch on, though," she said, chuckling at her guests' delightful sounds.

41

9

Mary slid between the cotton sheets, feeling more comfortable than ever. The heavy weight of an heirloom patchwork quilt and a goose-down comforter enveloped her like a womb while a goose-down pillow cradled her head. Curling into a fetal position felt so good, and she rubbed her feet together, covered in thick new wool socks, feeling the lanolin soothe her heels.

Mrs. Gates's home was small but filled with comfort and warmth. She particularly loved the sight and charm of her working bathroom, which included a full-size tin bathtub and a flush toilet. After serving figs and tea, Mrs. Gates ran a warm bath for her, allowing her to soak away her chills and immediate fears.

Feelings of exhaustion and fear, wrapped in guilt, jumbled her mind. The warmth of this night, something she could never have predicted when stepping onto the gangway alone yesterday morning, combined with the fuzziness, lulled her toward sleep.

Not wanting to give up her exquisite sensations, she resisted the urge to close her eyes and reached for the bedside table, taking a sip of water. The cool liquid sent a refreshing chill through her, and the baby squirmed and kicked. She returned to her side, pulled her knees up, and hugged herself.

She didn't know what would happen, but she set aside the guilt, embracing the warmth beneath the weight of the blankets. When she finally drifted off to sleep, William filled her sunlit dreams.

• • •

William Fletcher took a break from forking hay into the Nuttings' barn loft and accepted the glass of water that Mary had poured from a pitcher she had brought from the house. He stretched his arms above his head, wiping the sweat from his forearms and leaving a trail of chaff and hay dust. He shook his head and, with a sweaty hand, ruffled his wavy blonde hair, sending more chaff into the air. It was a warmer-than-usual May, and rays of sunlight filtered through the floating particles, some of which clung to his hairless chest. He had grown into a sixteen-year-old young man, standing six feet tall with sinewy muscles and a lithe strength built from a life of homestead farming, and after gulping down some water, he splashed the rest over his face, shaking his head like a dog to shed the excess from his hair.

Mary watched the water cascade in rivulets over his chest, washing away the dust and leaving streaks of glimmering sunlight. The fine, delicate blonde hair on his thick forearms and wrists, developed from near continuous scything, stirred her with a guilty pleasure, and her forehead glistened in the unexpectedly warm late afternoon sun.

She noticed William staring into her brown eyes and flushed cheeks, the hue of pink peonies. Handing her the empty glass, he jiggled it and said, "Thanks," smiling through straight teeth and lips she wanted to be the first to kiss. She paused momentarily, blinked, and, feeling embarrassed, poured William another glass of water.

"You're blushing," he remarked, smiling brighter at her.

"No, I'm not," she insisted. With the sun on her face, she knew that a bead of sweat might fall from her hairline at any moment. Feeling less guilty, she said, "It's hot out, and I'm as flushed as you are… Master William." She arched her eyebrows.

Growing up without a father for half her life, Mary had only two male friends: her brother George and William. From an early age, she never learned that it was a father's job to scare off overly curious boys with a stern look, belt, or worse. Likewise, her brother was never taught this either.

She and William became the closest of friends, seeing each other daily for the past ten years. They became confidants, with him as her muse, sharing their observations, secrets, and laughter. He was always talkative, learning to communicate socially as part of a sisterhood surrounded by the women in his family. In contrast, his father preferred the quiet solitude of working the fields and typically stayed out of earshot.

William smiled as he took Mary's fresh glass of water, their fingers brushing lightly during the exchange. This time, he drank the entire glass without the shower.

"Thanks," he said again, handing it to her. He held it by the bottom, giving her ample finger space this time.

Mary knew he was teasing her, something he enjoyed doing often. She had fallen in love with his icy moonstone eyes the first time he'd stumbled into her backyard a decade ago. Like their friendship, his eyes had grown intense over time, and she held his gaze now as William gripped the fork and went back to pitching hay.

Some of his sisters had hazel eyes, like their mother's, while the others inherited their father's dark eyes. Mary had never met anyone else with such a unique color, which seemed to look right through her, always trying to read her mind.

After school, they spent countless afternoons reading together. Even though they were initially distant in age and reading proficiency, they grew closer with each passing year.

Last year, while reading together in the hayloft with the summer sun shining through the barn walls and illuminating the pages of Henry David Thoreau's *Walden*, she had allowed herself to fall under his spell. After reading the line, 'Things do not change; we change,' she dared a glance at William, who lay beside her with his head resting on his palm, elbow propped in the hay near her shoulder. He hadn't followed her words on the page but looked into her eyes, and at that moment, she felt he was trying to read her mind and thoughts. He smiled at her, and for the first time, a hint of a dimple appeared in the corner of his cheek—one she no longer wanted to tease with a poke or pinch but to kiss fully. It took all her fortitude to close the book and disappoint him by letting him know it was probably getting close to supper time, and she didn't want their mothers to worry about the hour.

Was this love? she wondered as she walked back to the house. She struggled to find the willpower within herself, but she loved him, feeling inseparable from his presence and longing to feel his arms around her shoulders and his hands cradling her face.

She couldn't help herself and turned, glancing back over her shoulder at William's rippling back muscles, knowing she loved him more than ever. The spell had been cast, and she was beyond smitten, unable to control her desire.

She was in love with him.

•••

Mary awoke as the morning sun streamed through the bedroom window's muntin bars, casting lines of sunlight that warmed her cheeks like William's hands in a warm embrace. She never wanted to leave this cozy nest of covers, but the faint sound and aroma of sizzling bacon from the skillet called to her hunger pangs.

Sitting in bed, she noticed things she hadn't seen the night before. The bedroom was small and straightforward, with one front window overlooking the road and a flower-painted wash basin next to the door. Her satchel rested on a bedside chest opposite the window, and the maple bed's headboard and footboard were each adorned with decorative scrollwork. Their farmhouse had never featured such beautiful furniture as Mrs. Gates's house.

Reluctantly, Mary slipped out from under the covers, grateful for her new wool socks as her feet touched the polished wood floors. She glided around the foot of the bed to her bag, careful not to slip, and pulled out another linen gown, slipping it over her head for an additional layer. She paused to touch her mother's silver brooch, rubbing it for luck while worrying that her mother and younger sister were back in Halifax, concerned for her well-being.

She headed toward the stairway, hoping to find Mrs. Gates and breakfast waiting for her downstairs. She and the baby were starving.

Treading carefully down the stairs, she needed no directions other than to follow her nose to the kitchen at the back of the house. She peeked her head through the doorway and spotted Mrs. Gates on her right, dressed in what she considered her Sunday best: a cherry-red dress wrapped in an apron, cooking bacon and eggs in a cast-iron skillet on a large black stove. In the center of the kitchen was a long wooden table, large enough to seat six, with two chairs on each side and one at each end where a basket of muffins took center stage. A floor-to-ceiling baker's rack stood against the wall opposite the stove, filled with colorful English porcelain dinnerware. Beneath the double window sat a soapstone sink with hot and cold faucets—something her family hadn't had while growing up in Nova Scotia.

"Well, good morning, sleepyhead," Gertrude said. "I hope you slept well?"

"Oh, my God, yes. I've never slept in a bed quite like it before in my life. Thank you so much. I don't deserve this."

"Oh, nonsense! I hardly ever have company. It's a pleasure. Pull up a chair and make yourself at home." Gertrude returned to the stove and scooped bacon and eggs onto a plate.

Mary sat at the table, lowered her face closer to the freshly baked muffins, and inhaled their nutty aroma and steamy warmth.

Gertrude brought Mary's plate to the table. "Go on, have one... or two"—she winked—"you're eating for two, right?"

Mary leaned back, rubbing her belly, aware that Mrs. Gates was teasing her. "Sometimes I feel like there's a whole litter in there with all the kicking and turning!"

"Oh dear." Gertrude sighed. "Let's not joke about that, shall we?" She pulled out a chair from the table across from Mary. Sitting down, she interlaced her fingers and urged the young woman to eat. "Dig in."

Mary glanced to each side of the table before turning back to Gertrude.

"Oh, dear," Gertrude said apologetically as she stood and returned with a set of silverware from the drawer in the baker's rack. "It's my fault. I've been a little distracted this morning."

"No, my fault," Mary apologized. She picked up the knife and fork, glanced at the delicious-looking breakfast, and then began to cry. "I don't know what I'm doing."

Gertrude set the silverware down on the tabletop and took Mary's hands. "It's all right. You're not the first young Canadian girl I've ever met."

"I'm not?" Mary asked, reaching for a slice of bacon. She maintained her gaze on Mrs. Gates, searching the woman's bright eyes framed by her wire-rimmed Ben Franklin spectacles.

Gertrude gently shook her head from side to side.

Mary took a bite of the bacon.

"We've got all day and nothing to do but talk," Gertrude told her. "Why don't you start at the beginning? I promise I won't judge you."

"All right," Mary conceded.

10

"Good morning, Franklin," Gertrude said, greeting him at the kitchen doorway. She glanced at Mary, who was wiping egg yolk from the corner of her mouth. "There's bacon and eggs on the stove. Help yourself, and grab a muffin… or two… or three."

"Appreciate it, Mrs. Gates," Frank expressed his gratitude to his old mentor.

"When your plate's full, do you mind taking it out onto the porch?" she asked him. "Mary Jane and I were discussing amongst ourselves."

Frank peeked out the back door. "It's cold out, isn't it?" Without waiting for a response, he said, "May I eat in the front room instead?"

Gertrude sighed, glancing at Franklin to gauge her trust level. "At least grab an extra napkin and keep your plate on the sofa table." She gestured to the baker's rack for napkins and then pointed to the coffee pot on the stove. "There's plenty of coffee," she told him. "And use a saucer, and don't you dare spill anything on my rug, or you'll be out on your keister."

"Yes, ma'am."

After he gathered his plate, took two muffins and his coffee, and retreated to the front room, Gertrude redirected her attention to Mary.

"Can I light a fire?" Frank yelled from the front hallway.

"Of course!" Gertrude snorted. "Sorry, where were we?"

"We had to leave our farm. Once all the neighbors found out from William's mother, we were cut off. Shunned. With no help, there was nothing we could do with the livestock. No one would help with the harvest or wanted the hay." Mary averted her gaze, pulling away from Gertrude.

"Having a baby out of wedlock is scandalous enough. I get why you moved to Halifax. It's away from your home, but here? This far? Alone?" Gertrude lowered her chin and peered over her spectacles, looking Mary directly in the eyes, compelling her attention. "You're not the first to try to escape a transgression." She maintained her focus. "I promised you I wouldn't judge you." She gave Mary a moment, then pressed, "How bad is it?"

The color drained from Mary's face. She stared at Gertrude, holding her breath for what felt like an eternity before finally releasing it. "The father is… just a boy."

Gertrude noticed Mary's pallor and concluded the unfortunate young woman had walked to the cliff's edge and jumped off. She lowered her head and offered a quick prayer.

"When his parents found out… I mean, when my mother told them, his father whipped him good." She turned away, looking ashamed. "He snuck over afterward and told me he couldn't see me for a while… if ever again. I noticed the bruise on his face where his father had hit him." She began to sniffle again. "His eye was swollen shut. His beautiful eyes. They held a power over me like nothing else." She wiped her eyes and nose with a napkin. "Now, one was bruised, and the other bloodshot, and all I could think about was that I'd never see them again as they were before." She lowered her face, sobbing once more into her hands.

Gertrude reached across the kitchen table and patted Mary's arms, pulling her hands away from her face by the elbows. "What exactly do you mean, a boy?" she asked, removing her spectacles and biting an earpiece. "Surely you must mean he was only a bit younger than you? A boy of eighteen? Nineteen? Certainly not a boy anymore."

"No," Mary whispered. "He's barely sixteen… William. His name is William, and he was my best friend." She closed her eyes and slumped forward before crossing her arms and resting her head on the table.

"Well then," Gertrude interjected. "I suppose that certainly changes things a bit, now, doesn't it?" She knew it was time to make a plan and right this faltering ship. "That all doesn't matter in the here and now… does it? First things first, we'll bring a midwife to the house," she said, adjusting her spectacles. "This town has one of the best in the area, and she's delivered more babies than you or I have, or will ever, see in our lifetimes."

Gertrude stood from her chair, turned, and lifted the coffee pot. She re-filled her cup and offered some to Mary, who declined. "Her name is Gladys, and she's my dear friend. We've attended the same church in town our whole lives. The first time we met was in the Missionary Sewing Circle," she said, setting the pot back on the stovetop. "We've been active ever since in the Young Ladies Charitable Mission, which I believe will be a blessing for you." Gertrude sat back down at the table. "There's no time like the present. After breakfast, I'll walk over to her place and fetch her back here. We'll want to know how far along you are, young lady, and plan accordingly, but by the looks of you, I'd say you're pretty far along."

Mary lifted her head and bit another piece of bacon. She murmured her satisfaction as she reached for another piece before chewing the first.

"What does Franklin know? What have you told him, and what have you left out?"

Mary glanced at her unfinished breakfast plate. "Only that I'm not married, still undecided, feeling like a flopping fish, and he would help me find a place for my baby."

Gertrude seemed disarming as she asked, "So he knows nothing about the father?"

"No."

"Good." Gertrude poured a splash of cream into her coffee and stirred it with a teaspoon. "Keep it that way," she urged Mary, taking a sip. "I haven't seen, nor heard, from Franklin in what"—she glanced up to the ceiling—"twenty years? He was a teenager back then, and I was his ward. I'm sure he's harmless now, I hope. Maybe his intentions are honorable. Perhaps they're not so much." She adjusted her spectacles and took another sip of coffee. "Either way, I'm keeping an eye on both of you, and that means staying right here."

"I don't know what to say, Mrs. Gates... I don't know how or why I deserve this."

"You don't deserve this."

Mary's eyes widened as she looked taken aback.

"You do deserve kindness, and that's the Christian way. Someday, God will forgive your sins. You, William, and everyone will be just fine," Gertrude told Mary, glancing at the young woman's unfinished plate, who took notice and kept eating.

Behind them, neither had noticed Frank standing at the kitchen threshold. "Would it be all right if I had seconds?" he asked, startling them both.

"Franklin Hosman!" snapped Gertrude, raising her hands to her heart, feeling it leap like an excited young colt. "I haven't written my last will yet!" She rose, cleaning her spectacles on her apron to distract herself and calm her breathing, and pointed to the skillet. "Whatever's left over is yours." She pulled the wire earpieces around her ears. "When you're finally done, please wash the dishes. You can leave them drying in the sink if you want."

Seeing a clean plate, she glanced at Mary. "Mary Jane and I are going to stretch our legs." Turning to Franklin, she said, "I have a favor to ask of you. Could you walk down to Mrs. Putnam's and see if she'll come around? I would do it myself, but Mary Jane and I are enjoying such a lovely chat. Tell her I sent you, and it's a bit urgent, but please don't frighten her."

Frank hesitated before answering, tilting his head slightly to the side. "East of the town hall?"

"Yes, good guess," Gertrude confirmed. "Go straight through town, and it's the first house on the left, after the library."

"Yes, ma'am." Frank appeared puzzled. "Library? I don't remember a town library."

"That's because there wasn't any while you were in school. It was George Tarbell's dying wish to donate all his money to build a public library. He worked on it with some people from Europe and passed away a couple of years ago, but he saw it through and finished it."

"The Tarbells were the wealthiest family in town," Frank recalled.

"They still are," Gertrude reminded him. "It shouldn't take more than a twenty-minute walk if you remember," she assured him, watching as he scraped the rest of the fried egg and bacon bits onto his plate. "I still keep some of Roy's things in the hall closet. You should be able to find one of his coats that fits you, along with a scarf and mittens."

He turned, sheepishly stealing a glance at the remaining muffins in the basket on the table.

"Yes, yes, take another muffin if you must. I see you still have a hollow leg," she joked, referring to the size of his stomach and how he had nearly eaten her out of house and home as a teenager.

Frank brightened his smile and shrugged his shoulders. He had eaten less than Mary since leaving Halifax.

Gertrude waited for Franklin to return to the front room before suggesting, "Mary Jane, I think if we bring out a couple of nice blankets and sit facing the sun, we should get some fresh air."

Mary shivered. "Please, everyone calls me MJ." She placed the silverware on her plate before standing. "Only my mother calls me Mary Jane when she's upset with me." She stood there, looking down at her empty plate. "That's been quite often this year."

Gertrude stared at the young woman before her. "Nonsense," she declared. "Mary Jane is a name that suits a fine young woman like yourself." She wished Mary would see the confidence in her eyes. "MJ is a child's nickname, and you're no longer a child, so… Mary Jane is how I, Franklin, Gladys, and others here will address you. Is that clear?"

"Yes, ma'am," Mary relented, turning toward the kitchen sink with her plate and utensils in hand.

"Let's leave our dishes right here. Franklin will clean up and earn his keep." Gertrude pushed her chair away from the table and stood, sizing up Mary. "I believe we can find you a jacket and mittens, too." Remembering her shoes, she said, "If I can't find an extra pair of boots that fit you, we can always stuff an extra pair of socks into a pair of my late husband Roy's boots. We're only going to sit on the front porch anyhow, and"—she pointed to Mary's midsection—"we'll keep a blanket fluffed up, just in case anyone is out for a walk today." She took a deep breath, sighing heavily. "We should talk to Gladys before anyone notices, but if by chance some passerby does, I'll say you're my niece visiting from Concord to see our midwife. No need to involve Franklin in any part of the story."

"Yes, ma'am."

Gertrude didn't want to be called ma'am, so she let it go this first morning. "All right, let's get dressed for some fresh air, shall we?" She left the kitchen and headed for the stairwell. "We'll figure this all out... what's best for everyone."

•••

After rinsing the breakfast plates and snagging another muffin, Frank lifted Roy's red and black checkered wool hunting coat off the hook in the foyer closet. A dimple still jutted from the fabric of the collar as it had been there since Roy had passed away. The front pockets were deep, and the wool was thick, so he skipped searching for extra mittens. He'd walk east toward town in the morning sun, so he decided against a scarf—no need to risk overheating or getting an itchy neck. He poked his head into the closet and inhaled the scents of musty lanolin mixed with red cedar.

As he stepped off the front porch, his boots crunched on the frosted gravel that had softened under the late morning sun. He stood on Sandy Pond Road, with Flint's Pond to the west—its size several acres larger than a typical pond, yet it was never referred to as a lake. Immigrant farmers surrounding its watershed provided food and dairy for much of Middlesex County.

Frank made his way east toward the town center.

The air was dry, and the haze of his breath fogged his face. It wasn't cold enough for him to regret not wearing a scarf, but perhaps he'd let his beard grow out unless Mrs. Gates complained. At least his mustache kept the wind off his lips. Sometimes, the most minor things were the most annoying, and having chapped lips ranked high on his list.

The sounds of chickadees filled the leafless maple and elm trees as he walked by the Victorian and Queen Anne homes near the center of town. The tempo of their dee-dee-dee-dee shrills echoed through the chilly air and bare trees.

Some of the town's men and women walked the streets, heading to their jobs, bundled from head to toe in wool and beaver. On this brisk morning,

Frank wished he had a fur hat with earflaps instead of his felt derby, but at least his hands were warm in the deep pockets of the hunting coat. The women, dressed in heavy gowns, used beaver fur hand muffs instead of pockets.

At the town center lay a five-way intersection. To Frank's right stretched Station Road, along with the town hall he and Mary had passed last evening at dusk. To his left, Bedford Road ran north past the general store and post office, continuing to the schoolhouse, which he vaguely remembered tolerating during his Gates mentorship. He ventured straight through the roundabout, passing Station and Weston and onto Trapelo, where the library stood on his left.

He paused for a few moments to admire the new building, which featured a Victorian style that complemented the town's architectural theme but was built entirely of red brick. A black-painted iron fence separated it from the gravel road. To the left of the grand entrance stood a facade resembling a giant fireplace chimney. The words "Lincoln Library" were raised on a centrally framed panel adorned with a floral motif, which included a detailed flower garland hanging between the words. Stairs ascended over a fieldstone foundation to a tall arched entrance, nestled beneath a Mansard clock tower with a slate fish-scale tiled spire.

The architectural details of the mason's work left Frank feeling dejected. During his short time in Halifax, he had failed at apprenticeship jobs because he couldn't plumb rows of bricks, let alone reach this level of detailed craftsmanship.

He kept walking along Trapelo Road toward the Putnam house, which he could see in the distance beyond the library's sprawling fenced grounds.

The Putnam and Gates houses were identical in the Queen Anne Victorian style, reflecting the trends of European settlers and affluent Bostonians who moved westward from the city to build larger estates, including the Tarbells.

The front steps felt solid beneath his boots, but as he reached the porch, the dry cold made the wood decking crackle under his weight. When the front door opened without him having to knock, Frank remembered his manners and removed his derby. "Good morning, Mrs. Putnam." He still recognized her and didn't wait for a response. "Mrs. Gates sent me to fetch you because a young woman needs your services."

"Who?" Gladys asked. "I don't have any expectant mothers in my care right now." She glanced to the side, looking lost in thought. Clearly satisfied there were none, she demanded, "I know I don't, so what's this all about?"

Frank heeded Mrs. Gates's explicit instructions—fetch her and don't scare her. "You probably don't remember me. I'm Frank Hosman," he introduced himself, but he didn't offer his hand. "When I was younger, I came to Lincoln and stayed with Mrs. Gates and her husband." He didn't want to delve into his troubled youth. "My parents were close friends of the Gates's through the Congregational church and—"

"Franklin!" she exclaimed.

"Yes, ma'am. Franklin is my birth name." He placed his derby back on his head and tucked his hands into Roy's coat pockets.

"Now, what's this all about, Franklin?" she asked again.

He noted how much Gertrude and Gladys resembled each other. Both were in their early sixties, petite, with pear-shaped figures, wire-rimmed spectacles, and short hair that was a mix of snowy white and gray, resembling crushed granite gravel. Both widows outlived their husbands and inherited modest wealth.

"I met an unmarried young woman working in the city... on my lunch break... yesterday," he stammered, trying not to mince his words but struggling.

"Working? Where?" she demanded.

In a fleeting moment of panic, Frank almost said, 'Halifax,' but remembered all his traveling haste and answered, "In the north end at Lewis Wharf."

"Good for you, Franklin. It's a nice area to work in, with lots of shopping along the harbor. I venture there on the rare days I'm allowed to leave town."

"Oh." He understood what it meant to be the only midwife in the area— at least the only one with decades of experience and a trusted reputation.

"Step inside while I grab my coat and boots."

II

Annie and Richard Hatt returned to Noble Wharf a day after they had left with one less valise. They had traveled alone after finishing the marine business they had started. Annie couldn't shake the dreadful feeling that Mary's life would end up far worse than better. The young woman wasn't her daughter, but still, her maternal instincts tugged at her heart. She regretted allowing herself to be persuaded into leaving Mary alone in the crowd, wondering for the rest of her life if Mary had been led astray, tricked, kidnapped, or if she was even still alive. She forced the horrific thought from her mind, knowing Mary wasn't dressed for or associated with great wealth. It would take a monster to harm a woman in such an apparent state.

Richard fixed his gaze across the harbor at the Dartmouth shoreline. Their son, Reuben, wasn't expecting them until tomorrow to ferry them back up the coast.

"Should we stroll up to Water Street and find somewhere to stay overnight?" he asked his wife.

Annie wanted to go home. Downtown felt musty and rusty, with the smell of horse carriages lingering in the air. "Any chance we might know someone docked on this side?" she asked, glancing past him up Citadel Hill at the star-shaped fort's cannons, which had long been obsolete.

"Doubtful," he replied, turning inland. "We could spend the rest of the afternoon walking the piers, searching for a needle in a haystack, or we could"—he pointed—"walk one street up and find ourselves a decent meal and a warm bed."

He looked at her, and she looked back at him, both too tired to argue.

12

"Mary Jane, this is one of my dearest friends, Gladys Putnam, and she happens to be the world's greatest midwife," Gertrude extolled about her friend. "Gladys, this is Mary Jane." She looked at Gladys, her expression stone serious. "Since you've known me all my life, I can't lie. And besides, you already know I don't have a niece from Concord, but she is"—she winked—"at least as far as anyone else cares to know."

Gladys acknowledged her friend with a slight nod and wrinkled brow. "World's Greatest is probably a bit too much to boast, but it's nice to meet you, Mary Jane," she said, taking a long look at the young woman's covered midsection. Mary stood to greet her and lowered the blanket. "You look like you're pretty far along."

"Yes, ma'am."

Gertrude pulled the front door open, holding it for them. "Why don't we all go inside and get warm again, shall we?" Once all the women crossed the threshold, she raised her hand to stop Franklin, who looked slightly confused.

He raised his hands, palms up. "Niece from Concord?"

"We need to keep this buttoned down for now, understand?"

"Won't there be others who know that's not true?" he asked.

"Franklin, trust me." She lowered her voice to barely a whisper. "We need to keep young Mary Jane's predicament as quiet as possible until a suitable plan is in place."

She wouldn't reveal what had been shared with her in confidence, so she faced him, standing tall with a stiff resolve, though feeling uneasy as he towered over her. They had been the same height when he was a much younger teenager.

"Okay," he said, easing his broad shoulders.

She studied his face, wary of what his ultimate plan might be. A wealthy Lincoln family would pay something for a child, and there was more than one in this town. It *would* be much harder if word got out that Mary was her niece from Concord.

"Why don't you walk back into town for a bit? Maybe check out your old school?" she asked, hoping it sounded less like a question and more like a command. She noticed him glance inside, hugging his crossed arms tighter across his chest. "Gladys is going to want to examine her. You don't want to be around. This is women's business, after all." She shooed him off the porch, giving him a little nudge. "Why don't you stop by the store and see if they have a warmer hat that fits you? Aren't your ears cold?"

"I…" he hesitated, turned, and walked down the steps.

Gertrude wondered about all his talk of working at Lewis Wharf. "Franklin?" she called after him.

He stopped and turned around.

She could see that his ears were almost as red as the checkered patches on the coat. "If you find a hat that fits and you like it… just tell them to put it on my tab. Ask for Blanche and say you know me, and you're my guest, but for God's sake, don't tell her you're my nephew from Concord or Waltham, either."

She waved him off, stepped inside, and shut the front door.

13

Frank hurried back toward the town center with determination, his leather boots crunching the gravel at double time. The dirty road soaked up the midday sun, melting away the morning's frost. His charcoal derby hat felt warm, but his exposed ears tingled as he neared the five-way intersection, and the library came back into view.

Déjà vu.

This time, he kept to the left, heading north on Bedford toward Chapin's General Store and post office. He had no genuine intention of going to his old Center School and revisiting any of those unnecessary teenage memories.

As much as his mother and the Gates family had prayed for him to find his best path forward, he'd only gone through the motions to please them until the day he was allowed to return home to Waltham. He earned his way back into the gangs because his mother was Irish Catholic, but he was never truly part of a brotherhood because his father had been German.

A jingle bell rang above his head as he pushed open the front door, stepping over the raised threshold into the general store. A wave of dry warmth instantly kissed his left cheek as he turned to face a potbelly stove near the front of the store's spacious, open interior. Six spindle-back Windsor chairs were arranged in a semicircle around the warm stove, and a couple of duffers sipping coffee occupied the two in the middle. Their wool coats were draped over the arms of chairs, and they seemed to be engaged in a deep discussion about horse trading, neither bothering to glance Frank's way even as he removed Roy's heavy wool coat.

The register counter stood directly ahead, lined with gallon-sized glass jars of penny candy—the only thing he could afford. The shelves behind the counter reached from floor to ceiling, pigeonholed with small dry goods and medicines, mostly tonics and tinctures. A rolling ladder on rails rested to one side. Nobody was behind the counter.

To Frank's right, the store seemed to stretch endlessly toward the back. He could see bins and stacks of winter harvest goods, including various squashes, nuts, and preserved items, some of which were pickled. He walked to the rear, passing bushels of carrots, potatoes, parsnips, ginger, and grains. One side featured storage larder doors for cheeses and meats. Although he had seconds of bacon for breakfast, his stomach growled, envisioning the dry, hanging cured hams, salami, and sausages.

Three ladies occupied the post office nook: two stood in front of the counter while one worked behind it. The woman behind the counter appeared well-dressed, wearing a collared, ruffled white linen shirt fastened at her throat with an ivory cameo brooch. Her blonde hair, piled high and held securely with several hair sticks, and her green eyes made him wonder if she was of Polish or German descent. The two younger women being attended to looked more Black Irish, with jet-black hair, dark eyes, and matching dusky dresses.

Frank assumed the blonde was Blanche, a Chapin whose family owned the store and lived next door. His old schoolteacher was a Chapin, and the family had been well-established in town for decades.

They exchanged glances as he walked to the back of the store, where he found a wide selection of winter clothing and accessories. He planned to accept Gertrude's offer while trying on a few warm, waterproof beaver and rabbit fur hats, but he thought they looked better with his hunting coat than with his other clothes.

He donned a pair of earmuffs as the blonde woman approached. "Might there be something of interest I can help you with?" she asked. "The earmuffs are more attractive."

"What do you really think?" he asked, instantly turning on the charm as he traced his finger along the edge of his derby.

She squinted and frowned, focusing on his face rather than his headwear. "What I think is… I don't remember seeing you in the store or around town before." She stepped back and scanned him up and down, appearing perplexed as she brought a finger to her pursed lips. "You're obviously not married since no Victorian wife worth her weight in salt would let you be seen in town wearing that outfit."

Frank flushed with the warmth of the stove and his embarrassment. He started to offer his hand but realized it wouldn't be polite or easy until he lightened his load, so he placed the bulky coat on top of a pile of pants and then doffed his hat and earmuffs, adding them to the pile. Unencumbered and feeling cooler, he finally extended his hand. "Frank Hosman, it's a pleasure to meet you, and yes, you're correct…" He almost said her name but thought better of it, feeling it might be awkward if this wasn't the Blanche who knew Mrs. Gates.

She shook his hand. "Nice to meet you as well, Mr. Hosman. I'm Blanche Chapin. My family owns the store."

Frank paused to consider how much and how quickly he should share about his past in Lincoln. He wanted to avoid an awkward moment, yet he sensed it was heading that way as he struggled to align his thoughts with his words. He felt as if he were slipping into a trance. They were about the same height and age, but perhaps she was slightly older, as he couldn't recall any blonde girls his age from his school days here. He openly acknowledged that she was more beautiful than he was handsome. She captivated his attention with a slim waist, shiny, bright blonde hair, jade eyes, and naturally pouty lips, leaving him nearly spellbound. His mouth seemed poised to disconnect from his thoughts.

"I really think I prefer the earmuffs over a fur hat," she said, saving him. "You have a style, but"—she pointed to the hunting coat—"I'm not sure I understand what—"

"Oh, it's not mine," he interjected. "I'm visiting a friend. It was a spur-of-the-moment decision. I hopped on the train in the city and didn't pack a thing," he said, partially telling the truth. "It wasn't as cold in the north end yesterday afternoon."

"I suppose that explains why I haven't seen you around town." Her eyes flicked back and forth between his as her pupils dilated. "That mustache makes you look like a snake oil salesman. You're not trying to sell me something, are you?" she asked, raising a slim eyebrow.

Frank wanted to spend more time with Blanche and hoped Mrs. Gates wouldn't mind if he chose a different jacket that better suited his style. After all, she had insisted he stay silent. Noticing that no one else was near either counter, he looked past Blanche and asked, "Do you have time to help me find a jacket that's more my style?"

14

Gertrude swept coals from the front room fireplace into a copper pan bed warmer, adding a small piece of elm to keep it burning before the women headed upstairs. She didn't want Mary to feel chilly during Gladys's examination.

She led the way into the upstairs guest room, where Mary had slept last night, and slipped the bed warmer under the sheet. She moved it around for a minute before finally settling it near the bottom corner, out of the way.

Gladys looked at Mary. "You'll need to take off that maternity gown and linens," she said, placing a small black leather bag at the foot of the bed. "I'm going to palpate your abdomen to see how far along you are and feel for the baby's position."

Mary hesitated, glancing at the two older women. "I'm embarrassed… and scared," she confessed.

Noticing the young woman's shilly-shallying, Gladys gently placed her hands on Mary's shoulders. Her smile was as warm as the bedpan. "I'll be able to hear your baby's heartbeat," she said calmly.

Gertrude slipped around the foot of the bed, aware that they were burning daylight and she needed to hustle things along before Frank returned. She pulled open a drawer in the bedside chest and took out a folded garment.

Unfurling it in front of the window revealed it to be a summer nightgown, with natural light filtering through the cotton. She turned to Mary, showing it to her. "There's no need to be modest around us old gals, but if it makes you feel more comfortable, let's put this on." She gave the nightgown a little shake by the shoulders.

Mary unbuttoned her dress while Gertrude moved the bed pan around, and Gladys pretended to double-check her bag's contents as they patiently bided their time, waiting for her to disrobe.

When fully uncovered, Mary reached for the nightgown and began to cry, struggling to pull it over her head. The women assisted her, each gently guiding an arm through the armholes. She shivered, standing completely naked in the room, her skin covered in goosebumps and a patchwork of stretch marks.

"I would be mortified if William saw me like this, no matter how much he loves me. I feel like a fat cow with a swollen udder!"

"It's all right. You're doing fine. Go ahead and lie on your back," Gladys instructed her, gesturing toward the bed. "I think we're all set now," she told Gertrude.

"I'll head down to the kitchen."

After Gertrude left the room, Gladys asked, "Are the bed covers warm? I can move the pan closer to your side."

"I'm fine for now," Mary replied.

Gladys warmed her hands on the sheet covering the bed warmer before sliding them under Mary's nightgown, revealing her bottom half and midsection.

Mary inhaled sharply through clenched teeth, taken by surprise. "Maybe… yeah… could you move the bed warmer a little higher, please?" she asked, attempting to buy more time.

"Sure," Gladys agreed.

The midwife resumed palpating the young woman's abdomen, assessing the baby's size and position, confirming it was still in a breech position. She sensed it moving away from her probing fingers. "I'm going to auscultate your baby's heartbeat."

"What?" Mary asked, attempting to sit up.

"Relax," Gladys assured her. "I'm just going to listen," she said as she reached into her bag for her beechwood Pinard stethoscope, gently coaxing Mary onto her back again.

Mary endured the midwife's finger pressure as she searched for her baby's shoulders and back, bringing the wooden cone to her ear. After what seemed like minutes but was only a few seconds, Gladys reassured her that everything sounded fine, including a strong heartbeat, and tugged the nightgown down.

"I believe we can forgo the pelvic exam. You thought you were… how far along? Seven or eight months? I think you're closer to term."

Mary groaned, releasing a guttural sound that made her chin shudder.

"I would say you have anywhere from two days to two weeks."

Mary's eyes were as wide as Gertrude's tea saucers that they had shared earlier in the day, and she asked the midwife, "What's a pelvic exam? Does that tell you I'm nine months for sure?"

Gladys reached into her bag, using experienced hands to feel for the speculum. Having found it, she pulled it out and offered it to Mary.

The whites of Mary's eyes expanded, and her mouth fell open in shock. She stared at the duck-billed metal contraption until the midwife put it back inside her bag.

"Can you dress yourself?" Gladys asked, zipping her bag shut.

"I think so, yes. Just keep that thing away from me," she said, waving her hands and pulling her knees tight to her stomach.

"Alrighty then… I'm excited to see what my friend is cooking up in the kitchen. We'll see you downstairs."

After Gladys left the room, Mary sat on the edge of the bed, covering her face with her hands. Tears streamed down her arms and dripped from her elbows.

When she decided she'd shed enough tears, she got dressed again and descended the steps, hearing the ladies chatting in the kitchen. She wasn't in the mood for conversation and felt a bit tired. The fireplace crackled, radiating warmth throughout the room and making her eyelids feel heavy. The loveseat looked inviting, so she curled up on it and found a pillow for her head. After adjusting her position, she pulled a folded crocheted afghan from the back of the loveseat and draped it over herself before drifting off to sleep. The heat from the fireplace felt like summer sunshine on her cheeks as she dreamed of her muse, her only love, William.

15

William was now old enough to take on the daily responsibilities of Mary's family farm. As he and his father worked through the daily chores, it eased his father's burden of managing his own property, crops, and animals.

While William filled the pig troughs and spread corn for the chickens in the pen below, Mary dangled her bare feet out of the barn's gable window. He looked up and saw her smiling as he mindlessly shook the scoop, not paying attention to spreading the day's meal evenly, and froze when she tugged her dress up, revealing her bare knees. He'd felt the smoothness of her skin before while lying with her up in the hay loft, and it was exquisite. Working double time, he finished dumping the remaining corn and hurried over to Mary's horse, Trigger, with a bucket of oats and a hay pad before ducking into the barn and climbing the ladder to the loft where he knew his best friend waited patiently.

Mary had retreated into the loft, hidden from the window but still bathed in the afternoon sunlight. She rolled her dress above her knees, leaned against the hay, lifted one knee, and crossed her legs.

William knew she was waiting for him. When he reached the top of the ladder, he hauled it up into the loft because Mary's brother, George, had nearly caught them kissing after sneaking up the ladder and looking for them. They had convinced him they were searching for hen's eggs hidden in nests among the hay piles.

He high-stepped across the loft and gently knelt next to Mary in the shadows while she remained in the sunlight streaming through the open gable. He wanted to cool off from sweating in the breeze, but this was Mary's favorite moment as she unbuttoned his shirt and slid her palm over his bare, slick chest. His heart raced, and his breath hitched with her touch.

He was muscular and tall enough that Mary's forehead brushed against his chin. He felt relaxed and loved, sliding his arm under her neck while they kissed. When their tongues first touched, he thought he might faint and wondered if she felt the same—her shudder gave him the answer.

He loved the taste of her lips, like sweet cream. His hands on her face and in her thick, long brown hair felt so good to him, like a wild animal—it was disconcerting because he couldn't always control his hands, which seemed to have a mind of their own. His heart would pound so fast that he sometimes swore it felt like it was skipping ahead in time.

With his fingers on her flesh, Mary buckled and lifted her leg over his waist, rubbing the inside of her thigh over his as he slid his hand up and down her bare leg, tracing his finger around the knob of her ankle. He felt the rigidness of his manhood poking her stomach, and she grasped it through his trousers. He let his hand glide up her exposed thigh and rest on her hip and made circles with his fingertip on her hipbone. Unable to control himself any longer, he reached for her loins with his fingers, sharply inhaling when he felt her warmth and wetness.

Mary tugged at his belt, her eyes wild and wet, as he clumsily extricated himself from his pants, kicking them off and rolling on top of her. The feel of skin-on-skin contact as he pushed forward and she pulled him in, using her legs wrapped around him, was a sensation neither had ever experienced before.

He slid deep into her warmth, feeling her body arch, and then he erupted in a blinding white light as she spasmed beneath him. With heat radiating and surging through their cores, they screamed in unison, gripping and biting each other's shirt collars to muffle their pleasure from the heavens above.

Their lovemaking concluded as quickly as it began, with Mary wrapping her arms around his neck while keeping him inside with her legs, locking her ankles behind him, and leaving him with no means of escape. Her nose was buried in his ear, inhaling his musky scent.

The two of them remained entwined, napping and cooing, until the chill of the setting sun compelled them to get dressed.

• • •

While Mary lay dreaming, Gertrude and Gladys began crafting a birth plan over scones and tea in the kitchen.

As she led her friend through the front room to the door, Gertrude noticed her young guest clutching a pillow between her legs and groaning softly. "Poor thing must be shivering," she commented to Gladys, who moved to readjust the blanket. "Let me add another chunk to the fire before you go."

"So, Mary Jane will stay with you until it's time," Gladys said, watching her friend sift through the wood bin. "We'll be discreet with the Y.L.C.M. and inquire if any of the Nova Scotian builders would be willing to take on a child."

Gertrude found a small, suitable piece and carefully placed it on the fire, trying not to stir any sparks or topple the coals. "I think it's our best chance to use their empathy," she whispered. "Of course, we won't discuss the crux of her plight with anyone."

"I would say not."

"We have a bit more time," Gertrude said, accompanying her friend to the door.

"Isn't that what I ought to be saying?" Gladys remarked, her tone laced with sarcasm.

"Aren't we too old to be involved in these sorts of things now?"

Gladys glanced at her best friend. "Small town, laborers, wealth, and gossip. We wouldn't want it any other way," she said flatly.

Gertrude snickered and opened the front door, ushering Gladys onto the porch. "Be careful going down the steps, and don't slip." She closed the door once she saw Gladys standing firmly on the gravel road.

Mary stirred from her dreams, feeling the chilly breeze and hearing the front door click shut. She stretched and yawned, pulling the plush afghan up to her chin. With a quick shiver, she was fully awake.

"Oh," she startled, noticing Mrs. Gates in the foyer doorway, looking in at her. "How long have I been sleeping?"

Gertrude walked into the front room and sat next to the young woman. "Probably a better part of an hour or two," she said, tucking the blanket under Mary's feet. "Gladys and I were chatting over tea and scones, thinking about you and how we're going to get through this," she said, gently patting Mary's bent knee.

Mary allowed the flickering flames to almost hypnotize her, and she could feel the warm glow on her cheeks shift as the fire danced. "Tea and scones?" she asked. "Warm scones?"

"Well, of course. Is there any other way?"

"I am feeling peckish."

"Naturally!" Gertrude nudged Mary's bump with an arthritic knuckle. "Don't get up. Stay here. I'll be right back in two shakes of a lamb's tail." She stood and rubbed her knees. "I have pumpkin chestnut, courtesy of our big old town common tree, or maple gingerbread? The store is out of fruit this late… you'll have to wait until spring if you're still here."

Mary let the quip slide and excitedly replied, "Pumpkin chestnut! My mother always roasts chestnuts at Christmas. We had trees on our farm." Hearing herself mention the farm made her feel a wave of melancholy and homesickness, knowing she'd probably never see it, the land, or William again, except in her dreams. She could smell the summer-dried hay in her memories. "Butternuts. Those are my favorite, though. They're sweeter than chestnuts," she said, bringing herself back to the moment.

"Butternuts are my favorite too, but they're the first nut crop to sell out since they're everyone's favorite," Gertrude said, heading to the kitchen.

Mary grew more comfortable with each passing hour. While Mrs. Gates was incredibly nurturing, her home felt like a dream, and she couldn't wait to soak in her bathtub again, maybe after dinner.

That reminded her that she needed to pee. She didn't want to crawl out from under the warm blanket, but nature called, and the baby was bouncing on her bladder, so she slipped down the hall to use the flush toilet, cursing her farmhouse for not having one when she was suffering from morning sickness.

She fast-walked back to the front room, fluffed the afghan, and settled in before Mrs. Gates returned with a steaming teapot and a plate of pumpkin scones. As she watched Gertrude set the teapot down on the table, she noticed some books on an open shelf below and immediately recognized a copy of Henry David Thoreau's *Walden*. Unable to reach it by leaning over her midsection, she slid off the loveseat and fell to her knees. The wool rug was soft enough to cushion her controlled flop landing.

"You have Walden," she said, climbing back onto the loveseat and under the blanket, resting the book on her lap pillow. "It's my favorite book." She looked at Gertrude with vacant eyes, lost in memories of when she read it to her love. "I used to read it to William."

Gertrude studied Mary's young face, free of wrinkles and crow's feet. "I met him once."

Mary riffled through the pages, searching for her favorite passages. "Who?"

"Thoreau."

Startled, Mary slapped the book shut and turned her full attention to Mrs. Gates. "No," she protested. "Really?" She looked again at the book's worn binding and traced her fingertip over the raised, gilded lettering on the spine.

"It's true. Here in town. I was about your age." She turned to look at the fire. "He's been gone now what… thirty years?" She focused back on Mary. "Before he made a name for himself, my late husband Roy knew him at Harvard in the late thirties."

"Harvard?"

"The finest learning institution in America."

"I've heard of it, yes," Mary admitted, embarrassed and impressed.

Gertrude tapped the pillow on Mary's lap. "Did you know that book could have been called Flint's instead of Walden?"

Mary, clearly confused by Gertrude's words, opened her mouth to speak but then closed it, choosing to wait for clarification instead.

"Mr. Thoreau planned to build his small nature hut not too far from where you're sitting right now"—she pointed out the front window—"on the shore of Flint's Pond here in Lincoln."

Mary sat speechless.

"But he got into a bit of a kerfuffle with the landowner, who wouldn't let him build a cabin, so he moved back to where he was born in Concord, near Walden Pond… only about four miles away."

Mary couldn't decide whether her racing heart or the kicking baby kept her from processing Gertrude's words, but she remained speechless. Eventually, she said, "I might have you take me to church tomorrow to give thanks."

It was Gertrude's turn to appear confused. "Tomorrow isn't Sunday, dear."

"It doesn't matter. Somehow, I ended up here, in Lincoln, to find you *and* be so close to where the words were written that William and I fell in love with, reading them over and over again every summer." She began to cry, and Gertrude moved closer, stroking her hair and patting her knee. "At least I can pray to see William again someday," she said, resting her forehead on the book, buoyed by the lap pillow.

Gertrude reached for the teapot, warmed their cups, and handed Mary a scone. "Here, try this while I go get something. I'll be right back."

Mary sipped the earthy tea, savoring the toasted pumpkin and chestnuts, her two favorite winter flavors. She finished the scone in three hearty bites.

When Gertrude returned, she was holding a hairbrush and sat next to Mary. "Scoot over so I can brush your hair."

Mary obliged, feeling Mrs. Gates undo her thick braid with nimble fingers despite her age. Soon, she felt the rhythmic, soothing pulls of the brush and drifted in and out of her thoughts.

"Tell me about Roy," she asked Gertrude, who sighed with a heavy heart.

"Unlike your William, my Roy was older… fourteen years he was."

Brushing the young woman's hair seemed as cathartic for Gertrude as it was for Mary, sharing her story between strokes. "We met here long after he'd finished at Harvard and made his fortune in economics in Boston.

"Wealthy enough to build this Queen Anne and retire.

"This house was our Walden Pond.

"He left ten years ago, buried here at Arbor Vitae under a beautiful blue spruce tree." She glanced around the room. "The color of this room."

"He left you?" Mary asked.

"Oh, that's how I say it so an old lady doesn't cry." She almost started but appeared to hold herself back. "I had it carved to read, 'He is just away' on his headstone."

Mary sniffled when she heard Gertrude take a deep, hitching breath. She turned, and they embraced, crying into each other's shoulders.

16

Blanche nodded approvingly at Frank as he tugged at the lapel of his new leather jacket, lined with linen and accented by a touch of rabbit fur around the collar. He had replaced the beaver earmuffs with the matching rabbit ones.

"So, I'm staying in town with an old family friend, and it was her idea to send me here to find a more suitable hat and coat for the inland weather." Frank held up the hunting coat. "This belonged to her late husband." He noticed a slight disapproving pucker of her lips. "Practical, yes, but…"

"But it's the new year, not hunting season, I get it."

"Thank you—exactly." He took a step, hesitated, and said, "Before we walk back up front, remember I mentioned this trip out of the city was spur of the moment?" He waited for her nod and said, "Right, so Mrs. Gates told me before leaving the house to let Blanche know I'm her guest and to charge it to her tab."

Blanche Chapin hesitated for a few seconds.

Frank struggled to breathe in the silence, dreading rejection until she finally relented and asked, "Gertrude?"

He took a breath again. "Yes, Gertrude Gates."

"You're a family friend of the Gateses?" she asked, double-checking.

He took another deep breath, willing to share the entire story with her. "As a teenager, I visited the Gateses here in Lincoln, giving my parents in Waltham a little break. They knew each other through the Congregational church. I even attended the old Center School next door for a bit, and Carrie Chapin was my teacher." He had inhaled enough breath to finish, yet took another.

"Carrie Chapin was your teacher?"

He nodded.

"She's my older sister."

"You don't say."

"Small world."

"Indeed it is, but I don't remember you in school, and Carrie never mentioned any troublemaker ward of the Gateses."

"Are we like two ships passing in the night?" he asked her, trying to charm his way out of trouble.

She ignored his flirtatious question and led the way back to the front counter, with him following two steps behind, mesmerized by the slow, graceful gait of her legs concealed beneath all that fabric. "Is the Hunt Tavern across the common still in business?" he inquired, feeling luckier she would answer this time.

She glanced back at him over her shoulder. "It still is, but its glory days are long gone."

"Well, then, if you could see a chance to wrap up early today, we could stroll over and enjoy a meal and a drink?"

When she reached the front of the store, Blanche pulled out a small black leather ledger from underneath the counter. She clasped her hands over it and glared at him. "Will the tavern tally also be added to Mrs. Gates's tab today?" she asked him before turning her attention to the conversation at the potbelly stove.

Frank waited for her eyes to return to him before answering. "No, but walking in the cold—I just happen to have a warm coat you could borrow," he offered, coyly holding up Roy's coat as an invitation.

He turned to look at the two men by the stove. "Busy place."

Blanche raised her hands, palms up. "Not really. Just two of the morning regulars draining my coffee pot dry. Mac Donaldson on the left is Lincoln's wealthiest builder with a big house and sprawling farm out by Flint's. And the guy on the right is Jimmy Farrar, one of the town constables."

Frank stopped paying attention when he heard that Mac Donaldson was wealthy.

"Mr. Hosman..." she began, drawing his attention back to her as she leaned over the counter. "Were you a fetching snake oil salesman in another life? Or only in this one?" she asked, smiling.

17

It took Frank two extra trips from the kitchen to the bathroom to fill the bath with hot water from the stove. On the second trip, he stumbled, spilling a little over the side of the five-quart pot onto the floor. He claimed he misstepped over the bathroom threshold, but his breathing told a different story before Gertrude shooed him upstairs to bed.

The Gates's Queen Anne had gas for the kitchen stove and a small tank to heat water for the kitchen and bathroom plumbing. However, the tank didn't quite have enough capacity to fill the bathtub, where Mary was now floating. An extra pot might have been needed if it hadn't been for the baby's displacement.

She floated, weightless, the room awash in the dark amber glow from a kerosene lamp mounted behind the closed door. The space was only big enough for a linen cabinet, a plumbed sink with a small mirror hanging above, and a flush toilet tucked beside the door. She wasn't sure which was her favorite Godsend, the indoor toilet or the bathtub. A gravity water tank was mounted high above the toilet, and she had to reach up on the balls of her feet to pull the chain. Why wasn't the chain a few inches longer? She didn't know and wouldn't ask.

When the tub was filled with piping hot water, condensation formed on the mirror, but the water cooled faster than expected, leaving her disappointed.

The baby rolled, creating tiny ripples of water that bounced off the sides of the tin tub, and Mary inhaled.

"Oh my," she exclaimed, rubbing her belly in circles with both hands. "Did you just do a somersault?"

She rose too quickly, feeling a bit dizzy from the warmth after lying down. Gertrude had left a couple of plush cotton towels on the floor beside the tub, and Mary was careful as she stepped over the wooden frame to avoid losing her balance. She paused halfway, straddling the edge of the box, one foot in the tub and the other on the floor, her hands gripping the frame. Catching a glimpse of herself in the mirror above the sink, she faced herself directly and thought she didn't look pretty with all her parts hanging.

"Oh, William," she moaned to herself in the mirror. "Last winter, we didn't have a care in the world, sitting by the wood stove, reading passages from Walden to each other, our bellies full of mother's roasted chicken."

She lifted her leg while still in the tub and bent her knee. Gripping the frame with both hands to maintain her balance, she planted both feet on the floor without slipping. The squared wooden edge of the tub's frame would not be something to bump against in a fall.

"Things do not change. We change."

She felt that she ought to tell Mr. Thoreau that *everything* had changed.

There was no time for her to get philosophical as she started to shiver, standing naked and covered in dripping tepid water. She dried her front first, studying herself in the mirror with her protruding midsection looking slightly different now, lower, not pressing so much against her ribs.

"What did you do?"

Nothing hurt. She wouldn't panic yet.

She patted herself all over, drying the rivulets of evaporating water, and wrapped one towel around her hair and the other around herself, but it wouldn't fit. She dropped it on the floor, stepping on it to dry her feet.

Turning around and glancing over her shoulder at the mirror, she could barely see any side protrusions. She thought her backside looked the same as it had before her pregnancy and gave her bottom a little shake, pretending to tease William, but only managed to embarrass herself.

The linen cabinet held a few more bath towels and hand towels but no gowns.

She tiptoed over to the door and pressed her ear against the wood to see if she could hear any voices, but she heard none. Bending over to pick up the towel from the floor caused another moment of dizziness, but she did her best to wrap it around her front before reaching for the door.

After lifting the latch and cracking open the door, she faced only darkness. The hinges didn't squeak as she poked her nose into the cool, fresh hallway air, which felt refreshing in her nostrils.

Cinching the towel with one hand behind her back, she opened the door a bit more, enough to poke her head out and look both ways. She did not want Frank to see her in this state of undress, even if by accident.

She whispered, "Mrs. Gates?" Confident that no one was behind her in the sewing room, she stepped into the hallway toward the foyer, hearing no response.

Slipping down the hall towards the bottom of the stairs, she whispered again, louder, "Mrs. Gates?" and prepared to retreat back into the bathroom at a moment's notice.

"Mary Jane?"

"Yes," Mary relaxed, hearing Gertrude's voice.

"Oh dear, I must have nodded off for a bit," she said, shuffling out from the front room. She noticed the young woman's eyes darting about, searching. "Not to worry, Franklin's upstairs, and I assure you he's snoring soundly." She looked up the stairwell. "I'm going to have another talk with that man in the morning."

"I don't have any linens or a gown."

Gertrude threw her hands up in exasperation. "Oh my, where's my head? I'd forget it if it weren't screwed on straight." She started for the stairs and waved Mary into the front room. "Go warm yourself by the fire. I'll be right back down." She took one step up, then turned back. "Again, my head. I won't be able to see now, will I? I ought to straighten up the bathroom and grab the kerosene lamp."

Mary spun on her heels, ducked into the front room, and immediately backed up to the fire. She shook her bottom again, feeling the heat through the towel. When she noticed the glow of the kerosene lamp in the foyer start to fade along with Gertrude's footsteps climbing the stairs, she turned to face the fire, letting the towel fall into her hands. She shook the dampness from the towel and twirled a few times, allowing the fire to dry and toast her body.

She felt utterly carefree.

On her third spin, she remembered the front window and gasped. Frantically, she tried to rewrap herself, failing twice before succeeding the third time.

She crept to the window, barely able to see the porch. The road was shrouded in darkness, with no moon, only emptiness. Her pulse hadn't had much time to elevate, but she exhaled slowly nonetheless. Suddenly, a light flashed on the porch, causing her to jump and drop the towel.

"Here we go, dear. Try these on for size," Gertrude said from behind her, holding a few clothes in one hand and the kerosene lamp in the other. "Oh my, I startled you! I'm so sorry," she apologized, handing the garments to Mary, who realized it was merely the reflection of the lamp in the front window, not someone outside.

Mary took the garments from Mrs. Gates after allowing the elder states-woman to see her in all her glory, stretch marks included, and didn't rush to cover up again. Instead, she said, "Um, when I was taking a bath"—she rubbed her belly—"I felt the baby move, but it moved… differently." She turned slight-ly, giving Gertrude a profile view. "I swear it felt like it did a somersault."

Gertrude held up the lamp and examined her lowered girth. "It's all right, Mary. It means the baby has descended," she said, placing the lamp on the floor. "And yes, it somersaulted. It's where I imagine it should be now, head down." She patted the top of Mary's midriff. "Now, let's get you cov-ered up and step away from the window, for God's sake. There aren't many townsfolk around to see, especially at this hour, but let's get this nightgown over your head."

"So, you can tell if the baby's head is down now? Did you feel the som-ersaults and butterflies with your babies?" She couldn't make out the older woman's expression in the shadows.

"Gladys will know, and, yes, I've helped her on occasions over the years, but no, I haven't. Roy and I didn't have children of our own." She assisted

Mary in tugging the gown over her shoulders, letting it fall freely to the floor. "It simply wasn't in God's plan for us."

Mary hugged her, pulling the woman close. They allowed a gentle sway to comfort them both against the soft sizzle of the dying fire, with its flickering flames casting dancing shadows on the walls.

18

Gertrude and her guests sat together in the kitchen, breaking bread. The only sounds missing from the conversation were the crunching of Frank's bacon and the sipping of coffee. The women in the room were quiet as they ate. Mary noshed on a single maple gingerbread scone, pinching bite after bite with her fingers, while Gertrude fancied a piece of buttered wheat toast.

Frank noticed Mary watching him as he devoured several strips of greasy bacon and asked, "You don't want any?" He held out the remaining pieces between his fingers in a mock offer.

"No, I'm not really in the mood for bacon fat today," she said, popping another dry bite of scone into her mouth.

"Franklin," Gertrude said, interrupting. "You were out a bit late yesterday? Taking a stroll down memory lane, were you?" She locked her gaze with his, waiting for a response.

Frank pushed the last crispy morsel into his mouth, then grabbed a cloth napkin to wipe his face and noticed Mary's look of disgust. Assuming he had smeared a thin coating of grease across his forehead, he wiped everything again, including the corners of his lips and teeth.

"I was, indeed," he replied honestly. "The store has expanded!" He reached for a scone, thought better of it, and grabbed a dry piece of toast instead, taking a bite without butter. "They had a lot of winter clothes to choose from," he said after swallowing the bite of toast. "Blanche was work-ing"—he took another dry bite—"and she was very helpful." He swallowed. "Everything worked out fine, and she had no trouble vouching for you."

He avoided mentioning the tavern meal, trying to recall any hints of his behavior after returning home last night.

"I looked in on the Center School, and I even spent some time sitting and praying for MJ"—he gestured across the table—"Mary Jane and her baby at the Congregational." He knew this was a bold lie.

Gertrude appeared skeptical. "Did you, now? So, Blanche was pleasant and helpful?"

Frank could feel the warmth of the stove flushing his face. "Yeah, she's a nice lady." He'd only afforded a pint of ale at Hunt's, but Blanche had bought him a second, and he wasn't fully awake despite the smell of delicious pork wafting through the air.

He wouldn't tell them that once he laid eyes on Blanche Chapin, with her high blonde hair and long, tall legs, he would have stayed in the store all afternoon until she closed shop and kicked him out.

"We even agreed it was better to pay less for earmuffs than a more expen-sive hat," he said, hoping the cost-cutting would win her over. He noticed the late morning sun through the kitchen window, melting the remain-ing frost and ice on the roof. "And look"—he pointed to the slow water drip—"it's a January thaw, so the earmuffs were the right choice after all." He nodded in self-approval.

"You did the right thing, Franklin, thinking of me and bringing Mary Jane here, and I believe we both agree she appreciates your kindness very much," she said, placing her hand on his wrist. "But you need to get back to work before you eat us out of house and home." She pinched his wrist and asked, "As you mentioned, there's a store on Lewis Wharf in the north end?"

"A fishing and boating supply store," Mary said.

He wasn't comfortable with the direction of the conversation and felt warmth flush his face.

"That's where I was with Annie and her husband, Richard… the Hatts… from Owls Head. I met them on the overnight ship… well, they met me," Mary said, spelling it out.

Gertrude turned away from Franklin. "Mary Jane… would you please excuse yourself and get dressed?" She motioned toward the bright window above the kitchen sink, and Mary followed her gaze. "I think Franklin might be right. It looks like a January thaw, so we should head out. We could walk over to see Gladys"—she glanced at the edge of the table directed at Mary's midsection—"she needs to stay updated on your condition." She stood and took her coffee cup to the stove for a refill.

"That sounds like a plan," Mary said, standing and wiping her hands on her napkin. She carried her plate to the sink, which had only a few crumbs, and brushed them into the soapstone. "Please excuse me." She walked out with her head down.

Gertrude returned to the table and sat across from Frank, where Mary had vacated. "Franklin," she said, focusing her gaze. "Have you changed?" She bore into him, and he looked away. "Look at me," she said without raising her voice. "What did you do?"

These past few days had been the best meals he'd enjoyed in a long time, and he needed to find a way to keep the train rolling on the tracks. A little nudge to the left with the truth, then a little nudge to the right with a lie, were necessary to keep the grift from falling flat.

"There's no job in the north end," he admitted, aware he had overstayed his welcome. "I was in Halifax. I *was* trying to find a good masonry job, but I could never get through anyone's apprenticeships."

Gertrude inhaled deeply and exhaled slowly. "That was a good idea, Franklin," she said, reaching across the table and grasping his wrists. "I'm sure you gave it a valiant effort."

"I gave up. I wanted to come home, and I saw Mary on the wharf after docking," he admitted. "I guess we were on the boat. I assumed so. I dunno for sure," he lied. "She was sitting there all alone, and I only wanted to help." He sniffled for effect.

"So there's no job?"

"No."

"So there's no need to rehash this so-called fishing and boating supply job?"

"No," he replied, lowering his voice. The train was leaning on the curve. "Did you see her with the couple she was traveling with?"

"No," he lied, nudging the train slightly to the right. "She was alone when I saw her. I gave her a snack, and we looked for them." A subtle nudge to the left with the truth. "She seemed confused, lost, and alone. I only wanted to help." He gazed directly at Gertrude. "I guess that couple didn't want to help her after all, no matter how much she hoped they would," he said, unflinching.

She turned to face Franklin, tapping her fingers on the table. "There's likely winter work available, helping the ice cutters, an extra watcher at the pump house, or heck, maybe the Chapins could use some help at the store. James has started a home service delivering meat. He's even rigged up a horse-drawn sled for this winter."

Frank noticed his mentor's neutral expression and firm stance, her hands now planted on her hips. He didn't want to go back to the gangs; he intended to live longer while taking fewer risks.

"Maybe Hunt's Tavern needs a barkeep with room and board," he suggested, more to himself than to her, as he discreetly finished the last piece of bacon on his plate.

Gertrude waved her hands in a flourish. "Besides, Franklin, you don't want to hang around here with women, especially when the baby's born, with the crying and fussing at all hours of the night."

She had a valid point, he thought, before she emphasized, "I'm a sixty-two-year-old widow, sitting in my home with a lost young woman from Canada who could give birth within a fortnight, and I'm trying to stay calm."

He finished his coffee and stood. "Well"—he stretched his arms—"it's too early for Hunt's to be open, so I guess I'll head over to Chapin's, enjoy another coffee in front of their big old potbelly, and keep my ear to the street." Hearing nothing from Gertrude, he turned on his heel.

"Franklin," she called after him, and he stopped. "You may keep the new coat as a gift from me to you."

He nodded his thanks and, with nothing to pack, left the house, aware that he was still ahead.

Gertrude walked to the sink, wiped her hands on her apron, and stood stiffly, gazing out the window at the mottled gray of her winter backyard in hibernation. The lilac bushes, with their spring lavender clusters, had been reduced to a brownish off-white and looked dead on the limb. The crocuses would push up in late March, displaying their purple and yellow if the January thaw lingered; otherwise, the first bloom would arrive in April. The rose bushes looked dead since she had trimmed them down before the first frost.

Her friend, Gladys, loved cultivating gladiolas but often said they reminded her too much of funerals and the passing of acquaintances.

19

January thaws are typical in New England, and this year's Old Farmer's Almanac, issue number ninety-nine, predicted one.

Gertrude and Mary strolled through the town common, thoroughly enjoying the fleeting days of false spring while they lasted. Late mornings to midday offered the best outings as the afternoons softened the roadways enough for deep ruts to form in the refrozen mud from horse-drawn carriages. Chapin's delivery service was the worst offender, but the townsfolk needed their bulk supplies delivered.

The ladies avoided the worst of the trampled road in front of the store by cutting closer to the common.

"That's a magnificent chestnut tree. We have them back home in Stewiacke," Mary remarked. "I wonder how old it might be?"

Gertrude laughed. "It was certainly there before I was born," she said, pointing to the top of its barren canopy, which towered over any other tree or building in the town center. "In the summer, there are so many green leaves that it seems to fill the common." She gestured toward the cemetery beyond the town center, past the tavern and what remained of the town's poor house. "There are more chestnut trees over in the cemetery, and I bet this tree is the mother of all of them between Concord and Waltham."

"Is that where Roy's buried?"

"Yes, but a bit further south," Gertrude said, adjusting her gesture to point toward the public library. "You can't see it from here, thanks to the new library, but if you're up for it, we can continue walking the town loop."

Mary looked at her friend. "If I'm up for it?" she asked, playfully teasing her friend. "I can't have you all lamed up, overdoing it on these daily walks. You're the one keeping up with daily chores, cooking, and cleaning a big house."

Gertrude furrowed her brow. "I'd call it a cottage… maybe we should postpone visiting Roy until I can bring flowers," she suggested, softening her tone. "The crocus bulbs and roses in the backyard were his pride and joy. His roses were more like his children if you ask me. He preferred to work in the yard during spring so he could spend the warm days enjoying retirement on the front porch, sipping sun-brewed tea sweetened with a splash of maple syrup."

After hesitating and studying the front of the general store, Gertrude turned to Mary. "Let's walk up Lincoln Hill. I want to show you my church," she said, relieved that she didn't see Blanche or Franklin outside, though Blanche might have been watching them from the front window. There was no telling how much of the truth about Mary's visit Franklin might have shared with his new lady friend.

Mary glanced at the storefront, following Gertrude's gaze.

They walked up the gentle slope of Bedford Road, leaving the general store behind as they continued to the Chapin residence. Soon, they strolled past the Center School, where Gertrude recounted Franklin's teenage years until they found themselves outside a white, boxy clapboard structure with gabled ends. The clock tower of the Congregational church faced south, down the hill toward the town center.

Gertrude admired the double front doors, smiling proudly. "We've been active members since it was built in 1860."—she turned to face Mary—"That's longer than you've been alive, isn't it?"

"Just a bit!"

Gertrude took a deep breath and gazed down the hill toward her home, partially visible through the bare winter trees. The late morning sun pierced through the cloud cover, warming the higher ground. Soon, it would reach the shadows of the town.

She had only known this young woman for a week, yet somehow, she already felt responsible for her. Although she had never been a mother herself, she couldn't help but think about what this girl's mother must be enduring, knowing she had sent her daughter away without any idea of her whereabouts or whether she was alive or dead. The lack of concern Mary showed left her feeling the opposite. Perhaps she was still in shock or denial, needing to sever her former life to cope with this new one.

"We should go inside and pray, don't you think?" Gertrude said, guiding the pregnant girl toward the front steps. "At least we can warm up and rest our feet for a spell."

"Okay, that would be nice." Mary held Gertrude's gaze for a few extra heartbeats before moving to the door. "I have more to confess, and I'm grateful for the opportunity to speak to God today," she told Gertrude before glancing skyward. "I can see the sky is blue, but I'm thankful I haven't yet been struck down on these hallowed steps."

The elder stateswoman took the lead. "Then I suppose you're in the right place, so let's not dawdle then." She tugged the heavy front door of the church open and crossed over the threshold, holding the door for Mary. "Come in, come in," she urged.

This weekday, the church was empty, so they walked down the center aisle to the front and took seats in the second row of pews after Gertrude paused to kneel.

Mary appeared to be struggling but knelt and clapped her hands before her face, resting her elbows on the back of the front bench. "My thoughts are swirling like a nor'easter. Everything good and bad in my life is jumbled in my head."

Gertrude could hear the girl's labored breathing, and she reached over and rubbed Mary's back, comforting her in her struggle against the inner demons trying to draw and quarter her. All she could do was offer, "Take your time."

Mary took a deep breath, filling her lungs as much as possible, and turned to her mentor with a troubled expression. "There's more to the story.

There's more I need to tell you," she said, beginning to well up, her eyes brimming with tears. "I…" she stammered, her breath hitching.

Gertrude pulled a handkerchief from her sleeve and softly dabbed at her young friend's eyes before Mary turned away, looked up, then down at her hands, and confessed, "I think I have to leave my baby here."

20

Rachel Nutting emerged from the tree line separating the two proper-
ties and stomped up the Fletchers' back porch steps. Her thick, wavy,
shoulder-length red hair danced wildly behind her as she pounded on their
door with both fists.

The Fletcher family had gathered around the kitchen table, enjoying a
late afternoon supper of chilled soup and bread, when the fist pounding
began. Robert, the father and husband, was taken aback by the violent
knocking and urged his wife to take all their daughters to their room
for safety. His eyes immediately shifted to the kitchen corner where his
scattergun should have been leaning, but he remembered it was still in
their bedroom. Pushing away from the table, he wiped his mouth with
his napkin, holding it in place as he struggled to keep his panic and soup
deep down in his gut.

He nodded at William, directing his stare toward the backroom, hoping
he'd understand the gesture to fetch the gun, but William stood frozen.

Hearing a woman's voice behind the fists, he exhaled and opened the
door, and Rachel stormed into the kitchen, driven by adrenaline and fury,
striking his chest and yelling, "You bastard! How dare you?"

Robert backtracked, defending himself as best as he could, but a few
of Rachel's swipes grazed his neck with her fingernails, leaving red marks

but no blood. The fiery Scottish redhead seemed to have an endless supply of breath.

William stood hesitantly behind his father before reaching for the knife nearest to him on the kitchen table.

Rachel's strikes began to slow, and her tears flowed more freely. She looked exhausted. "How could you do this?" she pleaded with Robert. "Sarah Ann!" she shouted, trying to draw the adulterer's wife out of hiding. Taking a deep breath, she called out again, "Sarah Ann!"

Robert watched as his wife opened their bedroom door and stepped out in front of Lydia and Abigail, who were peeking from their room. Abigail ran to join her younger sisters in their parents' bedroom, shutting the door behind her.

"Rachel," Sarah Ann said, raising her hands with palms out. "What's going on? What's the matter?" She took two more steps, positioning herself behind the kitchen table next to William, who stood an arm's length away.

Rachel was now huffing, one hand on her knee and the other pointing at the only woman she had called a friend in the past ten years. A mixture of tears and sweat covered her face as she glanced behind Sarah Ann, where Lydia stood, partially hidden by the half-open door.

Taking a deep breath and rising to her feet, Rachel pointed a finger at her friend and exclaimed, "He's ruined our lives!" She turned, gesturing toward the door. "This farm was everything we had and all we'd *ever* have. Where can we go *now*?" she pleaded.

Rachel huffed like a cornered animal, drew a deep breath, and swung at Robert, shouting, "Keep your fucking husband away from my daughter!"

Robert anticipated the exhausted woman's roundhouse slap, moving swiftly and countering with a forceful, open-handed slap that struck Rachel squarely on the cheek, knocking her to the floor. She stayed down, curled up in a fetal position, dazed and sobbing, clutching her stinging face.

Sarah Ann shot daggers at her husband, her mouth agape.

"Robert? What have you..." she stammered, glaring at her husband. "Our daughters! How am I going to..." She stepped around the kitchen table and knelt beside her friend. "Rachel? I had no..." she began, reaching for her friend.

Rachel lifted her head and faced her friend, her face smeared with streaks of dirt, tears, and sweat from the unswept kitchen floor. She looked like she had the devil in her as she pushed herself to her feet and leveled an accusation at Robert's face. "Don't you have enough babies of your own without fucking *my* daughter? She's pregnant, for God's sake!" she screamed at him point-blank, spewing spit in his face.

Robert didn't move to wipe away her spittle from his cheek. He glanced down at his kneeling wife, his gorge rising, and couldn't unsee the hateful eruption in her dilated pupils.

He knew the truth but didn't want to accept it as he turned to look at William, who stood at the end of the table, holding the knife. He rushed toward his son, raising his fist against him and striking before William even had a chance to react, then pushed him into the corner and attacked him again.

"Goddamn you!" Robert shouted at his son. "Is this how you support this family? Messing around and fathering a bastard?" He grabbed William by the throat with one hand while tugging at his belt buckle with the other.

Next, he'd deal with Rachel's slut daughter after finishing his son's lashing, who dropped the knife and attempted to defend himself with his forearms from his father's punches.

"Robert!" Sarah Ann screamed, jumping up from the floor. "You're hurting him! Stop it!" she shouted. When her husband started fumbling with his belt, she tried to grab the leather strap but was unsuccessful. Some of his backswings struck her before connecting with their son's torso, leaving red welts on them both.

Robert's anger swelled from being overworked and underappreciated since George Nutting's death.

Lydia stood frozen, protecting her younger sisters' hiding place in their parents' bedroom while the chaos unfolded like a slow-motion nightmare.

Robert caught a glimpse of her from the corner of his eye as she emerged from the shadows and slipped into the kitchen. He didn't realize she was staring past him through the wide-open back door, looking beyond Rachel at Mary, who stood in the yard just inside the tree line, her face concealed in her hands.

Mary screamed through her clenched fingers as her mother lunged, Rachel's feet jumping off the floor as she used both hands to slam the dropped knife deep into Robert's back between his ribs, piercing a lung. The force of the blow was so strong that the hilt of the knife fractured a bone in her hand.

Robert struggled to breathe throughout the night, propped up in his wailing wife's lap on the kitchen floor. His breaths grew increasingly shallow until he passed away at dawn's first light, and no matter the explanation or blame, the two families would never be the same.

William's two closest older sisters, Abigail and Lydia, cared for his wounds after their father's outburst following the confrontation with Rachel.

Euphemia and Hannah, their older sisters, ventured out on their own four and three years ago, leaving Lydia and Abigail as the eldest to share in William's homeschooling. Together with their younger sisters, Alice, Clessia, and Frances, they remained with their mother, Sarah Ann.

Lydia, twenty-four, had raven hair and eyes nearly as dark as onyx. Her younger sister, Abigail, was twenty with coffee-colored hair and eyes that matched their mother's. They shared a bedroom on their family farm, and in the months following that dreadful August day, their nighttime whispers were filled with sadness, tears, and, above all, resentment.

21

I tried to see William the next day, but his mother and sisters wouldn't let me. All they did was scream at me to leave."

Gertrude sat at the front of the Congregational church atop Lincoln Hill, listening to Mary recount the events of last summer when William's family discovered the truth about the spoils of their affair.

"I watched my mother grab the knife, and Mr. Fletcher fell to the kitchen floor. Everyone was screaming. I wanted to run home, but I couldn't."

Gertrude noticed Mary's cadence quickening and steadied the young woman with a hand on her cheek. "So you're not certain?"

"I don't know what happened. It all happened so fast. When I came out of the woods, I saw Mr. Fletcher hitting William with his belt and punching him. I knew it was because of me." Mary's lips began to quiver, and her eyes overflowed with tears.

Gertrude clasped her face with paper-thin hands and lifted Mary's head high. "What's done is done."

"My mother just turned and ran out of their house. She raced past me, running home. I don't think she even saw me or wanted to see me."

Gertrude began to worry that either Reverend Richardson or someone else from town would soon enter the church. She didn't want anyone to come inside and see Mary with tears on her face and red eyes. She would confess to Reverend Richardson in her own time.

"My knees are getting stiff," she told Mary, hoping to encourage her to get up and walk. "Aren't yours? Let's head home. I feel like it's tea time," she said, standing up and smoothing her dress.

Gertrude tried jostling Mary out of her daze by helping her to her feet. Together, they exited the row of pews. She gestured for Mary to turn and face the altar, then kneeled again, this time more slowly, so Mary could follow along.

The walk home was uneventful, and neither of them tripped as they tried to keep their dresses from dragging through the muddy puddles.

"Walking is good for you, Mary Jane," Gertrude proffered. "Gladys thinks it will be any day now and says you should earn your room and board by scrubbing my kitchen floor."

Mary gasped. "What? Can't I help with that sometime after the baby is born?"

"That's the point, dear. Good old-fashioned manual labor gets things moving along, and the best way to get the job done is for expectant mothers to scrub the kitchen floor," Gertrude said, rotating both of her hands in opposite directions, miming the act of washing a wall or floor.

"Ewww," Mary groaned. "That sounds like torture. Do I really have to?" she whined.

Gertrude aimed to ignore the confession she had just heard, inhaling the crisp, clean country air, scented with wet red oak and wood-burning fires. "It can't hurt."

• • •

"Who is that?" Blanche asked, noticing the pregnant young woman walking down the hill alongside Mrs. Gates.

Frank lowered the copy of the Concord Freeman he was reading and focused his attention on his lady friend behind the counter, who was pointing out the store's front window. He followed her gaze to two women wearing bonnets.

After folding the paper, he tossed it aside and told her, "I believe that's Mrs. Gates."

Blanche didn't appreciate the insult. "I know who Gertrude is, or else"—she pointed to the new jacket draped over his chair—"that would still be in the back, and we wouldn't be sharing a room over the tavern, now would we?"

It had taken Frank less than two weeks to charm her. She was in her prime years, backed by family money, with few options in town aside from farmers and builders, almost all of whom were tied down with their dirty, labor-worn hands. During the day, he helped her around the store, stocking, delivering, and occasionally negotiating lot purchases when he thought she was being taken advantage of. She kept him out of trouble at night while he worked a second job at the tavern, and two or three nights a week after closing, she stayed in his upstairs room.

"The pregnant girl is Mary Jane," he said.

Blanche's eyebrows quickly shifted from curiosity to pointed anger. "I've never seen her out walking before. How do you know her, Franklin?" Her voice demanding.

Frank hesitated before responding, "She was already there, staying with Mrs. Gates before I came to visit," he said defensively.

"And?" she asked, striking a firm pose and revealing more of the whites of her eyes.

"Gertrude introduced her as her niece from Concord who came to stay, seeking the services of her friend Gladys," he said, picking up the newspaper again and opening it to shield his face from her. "The midwife has a stellar reputation."

Blanche remained suspicious, wondering if he was ducking and diving, fully aware of his penchant for snake oil tactics. However, he was fun, charming, and helpful, and being in the right place at the right time during winter was a significant advantage for her, but still, she had to ask, "It's not yours?"

The blood in Frank Hosman's veins froze, and he stiffened, fluttering the corners of the newspaper, which he gradually lowered and focused entirely on her. "I give you my word, Blanche. That is *not* my baby. She was already a house guest before I arrived," he asserted, using both hands to emphasize his point.

Blanche relaxed her furrowed brow, her complexion smoothing. "It's strange. I haven't seen her, so it's odd not knowing how long she's been here." She hesitated, pretending to sweep dust off the countertop with her hand. "I'll trust you for now, but rest assured, I'll be testing you later to ensure you're not lying."

Frank snorted, ignoring her bluff. "She might be on bed rest since she's been staying inside." He turned to look out the window again, but the two were gone. "Well, she must be quite far along based on—"

She interrupted him, "How fat she looks?" Her voice held the weight of jealousy, though she would claim she was merely envious if asked.

"I was going to say... her midriff," he said, winking.

"You're so eloquent for a city boy—keep talking like that, and we'll make our own face tonight." It was her turn to wink at him, her smile still suspicious.

22

Hot green tea and cozy linens couldn't stop Mary from thinking about her mother and what she might be enduring back in Halifax. She wondered if Rachel spent every waking moment in the apartment waiting for her to knock on the door. Would Rachel feel compelled to walk down the hill to Noble Wharf and look for her safe return? Would her mother expect to see her come back empty-handed or with a child?

She missed William, her family, her farm, Trigger, and Stewiacke.

Halifax was crowded, noisy, and reeked of fish and horse manure. It was perpetually damp, and the wind relentlessly swept into the harbor, trapping the odors against the Citadel hillside.

Taking a small sip of the tea Gertrude had poured for them, she inhaled the warm, uplifting aroma to refresh her memory. "I can't believe Henry David Thoreau's cabin was right here, so close," she said from across the kitchen table, sipping again, then twirling her long brown hair into a bun atop her head. "William would love to know—and see it! Is it still there? His cabin?" Her face lit up for the first time today since her confession at church.

"It is. It most certainly is. Maybe you and William will visit again sometime?"

The light faded from Mary's face as she thought about William's well-being. Her last memory was of his punished, defeated manner, all because of their summer brush. "I haven't seen him in months, not since we left so abruptly," she told Gertrude. "I don't know if he's still with his family or if they stayed." She dabbed her eyes with a napkin and realized she couldn't stop crying. "This all feels like such a surreal nightmare, and everything is so muddled together."

Gertrude listened. "As you said, it's been months, so waiting another month or two won't matter when it comes to the rest of your lives." She finished her tea and stood. "Let's take stock of the pantry and supplies, shall we? Having you and Franklin here this month has hastened my provisions schedule."

Mary was starting to feel overworked, like a rented mule. "Didn't we just sit down?"

"There's no time like the present," Gertrude said, motioning for her to stand. "Did you already forget what I told you earlier?" She walked over to the baker's rack, lifted her apron, slipped it over her head, and cinched it behind her back. Her knotting touch was deft, honed by decades of daily practice.

"Manual labor?" Mary asked, knowing the answer.

"Exactly."

"Okay, I can take care of the pantry inventory, but please, I don't think my back or knees can handle washing the floor after our walk."

"Deal," Gertrude agreed. "At least for now." She bent over and opened the lower cabinets of the baker's rack, peering inside but reaching for nothing. "You couldn't have known, but a few families from Nova Scotia live here in Lincoln."

Mary didn't know where this conversation was headed. She sensed that Gertrude didn't mean to make her do hard labor, but it seemed like a better option than letting her sit around sulking and crying about things she couldn't control—people hundreds of miles away.

"I didn't know anyone back home except for my family and neighbors." Thinking logically, she said, "If any of our neighbors lived here, they wouldn't have been our neighbors back there, right?"

She moved to the baker's rack and squatted next to Gertrude, cradling her abdomen with both hands inside her knees. She could feel her already taut skin stretching even more and closed her eyes for a moment, wondering if her body would ever look the same as it had the last time William caressed her.

"I know I said what I said this morning, but my head is still spinning."

"The Donaldsons are a well-established family of builders. They've constructed many of the homes in this town," Gertrude remarked. "They have money and resources. And an extended family, all living in nice homes."

"Do you really think it matters to me where William and my baby are raised just because we were born in Nova Scotia?" Mary's knees throbbed, and she stood up, rubbing her lower back. "If I decide not to bring this baby back to Nova Scotia, the only other person in this world that I trust is… you."

"Between you and me," Gertrude said, standing and rubbing her kidneys. "We don't have a pair of knees or a back strong enough to keep up with a newborn, let alone a terrible two."

Mary slumped under the weight settling on her shoulders.

Gertrude gently rubbed the young woman's bump. "You don't have to decide tonight, Mary. Besides, you're not having this baby and hopping straight on the Fitchburg the next day. You'll stay here for at least a month… maybe until spring."

"You know, the longer I stay, the less likely I can leave without it. You know that!" Mary exclaimed, growing frustrated and raising her voice, causing the baby to kick. "Ow," she winced, clutching her abdomen. It felt like the baby was kicking with both feet and punching with both fists. Dizziness blurred her vision, and a tightness spread across her back. "Oh," she said, backpedaling and feeling for the chair back. "I think I need to sit down."

Gertrude helped her sit. "Well, it looks like you got yourself out of floor-washing duty after all. I'm as unprepared for the birth of this child as you are!"

Mary groaned, clearly not in the mood for humor. "I don't feel so good, Mrs. Gates. Could I have a glass of water?"

Gertrude went to the kitchen faucet and filled a glass with water, hustling back in two shakes of a lamb's tail.

Mary took a small sip and set it on the table. "Is this it? Is it time?"

"I've listened and learned a lot from Gladys over the years, and I can assure you it isn't." She picked up the water glass and handed it to Mary. "Here, you'd better drink a little more, or you'll end up thirsty."

Gertrude scanned the kitchen as if searching for something she needed. "I'd better put my boots back on and walk over to Gladys's," she told Mary. "Just to be safe." She patted Mary's head and said, "But with a first child, labor can take hours or even days."

"Days!" Mary shouted, her eyes wide and as white as a hen's eggs. "I was eight when my mother had Agnes. I don't even remember what happened. I probably wasn't even there!"

"No self-respecting mother would let her eight-year-old daughter witness a birth, and if she had, I promise you, you wouldn't be here today, never allowing that boy to lay his hands on you."

Shortly after Mary sat down, the contractions eased, and she imagined William calling out her name, asking where she was, and asking if she was okay. She wished he were there now, holding her hand. She smiled and said, "I don't know. It did feel *awfully* good when it happened the first time."

Gertrude guffawed, "Enough," she said forcefully. "Don't be silly," she said more calmly. "I'd better get going so I have time to return before dark."

"You better bring a kerosene lamp. You might need the light walking back."

"Not a bad idea, but let's get you upstairs before I go."

Mary felt much better and didn't want to go to bed so early. "I thought maybe I could take a bath while you're gone?"

Gertrude hesitated, looking pensive. "I'd worry about you being in there alone, without me around," she said with dread on her face. "What if you slipped and fell?"

Noticing Gertrude's concern, Mary reassured her, "Okay, okay." A compromise came to mind, and she suggested, "I guess there's still enough light to read upstairs." Thinking perhaps Gertrude was right after all, she said, "Besides, I'm already in my comfy clothes. No need to get my hair wet."

"Great. We're running out of daylight. I'll add a small piece of elm on the fire and cover the hearth with the screen. No need to chance burning down my house with any stray sparks."

"You mean cottage," Mary playfully corrected her.

Gertrude huffed. "Don't you start with me, young lady."

As Mary was about to leave the kitchen for the hallway, Gertrude reminded her to drink the rest of the water and assured her that she'd be back within the hour with Gladys in tow.

23

Mary screamed loud enough for the entire town to hear. Her agonizing labor reverberated through the walls and the dry winter air with no foliage to absorb the sounds. Her water had broken before Gertrude returned with Gladys, and they found her upstairs, struggling to mop it up with what few linens were in the room. She lay face down on the bed, on her knees, trying to find a position that would ease the pain in her lower back.

Gertrude vanished, snatched a wooden spoon from the kitchen, and hurried back as fast as her knees would allow, giving it to Mary. "Bite down on this. At least you can scream into it without rattling the windows."

Mary bit down with another contraction, collapsing onto her side and curling up. "My bag," she gasped. "In my bag."

"What's in your bag, dear?" Gertrude asked, placing a cool cloth on her forehead.

"My mother's brooch. I need it."

Gertrude glanced at Gladys, and their eyes shifted to the canvas pouch on the bedside chest.

"The silver one pinned to the side?" Gertrude asked.

"Yes! I need it," Mary moaned.

Gertrude left the cloth on Mary's head and walked around the bed to fetch the brooch pin. When she came back, she placed it in Mary's fingers, where it disappeared in her clutch.

Mary rubbed the silver surface with her thumb. "I lost my ticket. I needed my worry stone." She grimaced, huffing. "I'm thirsty."

Gertrude held a glass of tepid water for the young woman.

"I didn't know it would hurt this much," she groaned, taking a sip and spilling some down her chin. "It's warm!" She pushed the glass away from her face, and after trying to wipe her lips with her thumb, she asked, "Are you going to use ropes?"

Gladys exchanged a dismayed look with Gertrude that only stoked Mary's fears. "Ropes?" she asked Mary in disbelief.

Mary bit down on the spoon handle during her next contraction, and after catching her breath, she whispered, "Father would tie ropes around a calf's legs… he and my brother would… pull it out of the mother."

Gertrude covered her face with a hand. Her parchment-like skin was taut, and she spread her fingers, stifling a chuckle.

Mary didn't realize she was about to crack either the spoon handle or a tooth when she bit down during her next contraction.

Gladys shifted to the bed and gripped Mary's face between her palms. "You're not a cow, young lady, and there will be no ropes in this house tonight." She juddered Mary's head. "I think by sometime this morning, we'll have ourselves a new baby."

"Morning?" Mary keened. She refocused, pushed herself back onto her knees, and wrapped her arms tightly around her abdomen. The brooch stayed firmly in her grip. "Can't you just kill me now?" she groaned, drawing her breath out until her lungs were empty, then sharply inhaled and screamed, "Throw me down the stairs—please! I can't take it! I want it to be over!"

Gladys glanced at her friend, who was standing and lighting another kerosene lamp. "It's going to be a long night."

Gertrude nodded. "I've got plenty of sheets and towels."

24

Frank and Blanche canoodled beneath layers of sheets and a goose-down comforter in the small room above Hunt's tavern. There was only enough space for a twin bed and a large bedside table to hold a wash basin. Blanche had brought the comforter from the store, a perk of being the owner, when the short-lived January thaw was smashed by February.

She slipped a bare leg out from under the covers, recoiling when her foot touched the cold wooden planks, and whipped her leg back under the covers so quickly that she bumped kneecaps with Frank in the tight confines.

"Ouch!" he yelped, more startled than hurt.

"I'm sorry, but I can't do it," she said firmly, slipping her arm under his neck and draping her leg over his. "It's too cold for me to use the chamber pot." She shivered and pulled Frank closer, nestling her face against his chest. "I'll wait until I get to the store."

Frank pressed his face into her neck and inhaled the scent of roses. He had no idea how this woman smelled of flowers after working all day in the store, sitting at the bar all evening, and then sweating under the sheets all night, wrapped around him like a snake. Her blonde hair was piled high and felt like fine silk. A strand fell over her face, covering one of her eyes, which studied him intently.

"You're so much prettier than me," he teased her, brushing her hair away from her eye and behind her ear.

She let out a short laugh. "Well, I should hope so!" she said, pursing her lips and scrunching her shoulders. "My ears are ticklish, and you nearly made me wet the bed!"

"Your skin is so smooth, and you always smell like flowers," he said, feeling a warmth spreading across her face.

"I'm blessed with fair skin and fine hair," she said, using her free hand to lift the comforter. After revealing all of her supple skin, she said, "That might be the first genuine compliment anyone's ever given me."

She was as smooth and fair as a Da Vinci marble statue, while he viewed himself as hairy as a black bear. "You look much prettier without your clothes on, and I'm a bit more dapper with mine on," he admitted.

"Well, I'll call your bluff, but thanks. And I'm not *this* natural," she said, tugging the sheet higher until his focus shifted downward. "Don't get me wrong. I'm nowhere near as natural as you, my hairy friend, but I do have a little help." She ran her fingers through his chest hair and then lower, cupping him. "The store stocks a tincture we import from London, which makes life a bit easier and smoother, if you know what I mean."

Frank was oblivious and speechless while Blanche's hands squeezed and roamed his nether end.

"I'm going to save the store money. We don't need to buy it in the city. It's pine resin, beeswax, and perfume," she told him, gently tugging his chest hair.

Frank furrowed his brow and twisted his mouth in confusion until Blanche gave his hair an extra tug. He yelped again, acknowledging with wide eyes and a quick "Yup!"

"The things women do," she lamented. "Speaking of which, I need to open the store, and you have to get Little Joe fed and ready for deliveries."

Little Joe was the Chapin store's delivery horse, pulling a wagon in the summer and a sleigh in the winter.

"My sister might stop by the store this morning to help load the delivery supplies or watch the counter while I help you. You must be looking forward to meeting her after all this time?"

Frank had never been married, and his mother was always blunt when criticizing him as a child. However, his primal instincts were finely attuned to danger, and this straightforward yes-or-no question felt like a trap.

"Of course. If I'm around when she stops by, I'll say hello." He second-guessed whether he had said it with too much emphasis, so he asked, "Who wouldn't want to say hello to their old schoolteacher?"

Blanche flared her nostrils and tugged a fistful of his chest hair, pulling it to the brink of separation from his skin.

"*Old?*"

Frank pried her fingers loose and sheepishly said, "That sound you hear getting dressed? That'll be me throwing myself down the stairs."

"You're lucky you're so adorable," she said, squinting and wrinkling her nose.

Frank chose to quit while he was ahead, reluctantly disengaged himself from her limbs, and got out of bed. "I think I hear Little Joe calling, 'Feed me! Feed me!'"

25

Mary spat the still-intact spoon out of her mouth and grabbed two fistfuls of sheets, crushing the cotton between her fingers with all her remaining strength. Gladys had been telling her to push, always saying 'one more,' but she was lying. Mary leaned as far forward as she could, but she couldn't see between her legs. All she felt was a fire burning and a horse stomping on her back to put it out.

"Mary Jane, push!" yelled Gladys. "C'mon, harder! The baby's crowning. One more! You can do it!"

Mary gasped for air and felt herself floating above the bed, looking down at her body, with Gladys between her legs, both hands inside her, and Gertrude holding her hand, crying and looking frightened. Why was Gertrude crying? she wondered.

"It's coming!" shouted Gladys. "Confess your sins! Now is the time to confess your sins!" she shouted again. "Let this child be born into this world free of sin! Confess!"

Gertrude stroked Mary's face and held back her sweat-soaked hair. "Let it out, Mary, let it out."

Mary felt the baby plowing through her pelvis, tearing her apart, and she screamed at the demons that gripped her ankles.

"I can't do it!"

"Confess!"

Mary huffed deeply three times to steady herself before confessing, "William Henry Fletcher is the father!" she shouted. "I loved him… and I killed him!" she cried out with a final surge of cold relief and heard her baby's cries for the first time.

Gladys held the baby up for Mary to see. "It's a boy," she announced, clamping and cutting the umbilical cord. "Gertrude, I need a hot, wet cloth."

Gertrude handed her friend a lukewarm cloth from the covered pot that had been sitting on the bedroom floor for most of the past hour. "I'll reheat the pot," she said, hoisting it and feeling grateful for the first morning light on the stairs.

Mary winced. Her whole body ached as if she had fallen down the stairs or been stomped on by Trigger, and her face felt swollen and puffy. "Why does he look like a ghost?" Mary asked, her voice raspy and tinged with fear.

"Nothing to be worried about," Gladys reassured her. "I'll have that all wiped off momentarily." She wiped the baby clean of sticky vernix, revealing a healthy glow of redness, and placed the swaddled newborn on Mary's breast. "You two can get to know each other while I tidy up down here a bit and wait for the afterbirth."

"Another baby?" Mary gasped.

"No… the afterbirth," Gladys corrected her, gently tugging on the protruding umbilical cord. "You'll feel the urge to push again shortly, and it'll slide right out. Then, I'll stitch you up. You tore a little," she said, dabbing a clean cloth at Mary's injuries. She held up a small round tin. "This is a new dissolving catgut suture. You'll heal much faster and be back on your feet in no time."

Mary didn't see or hear anything Gladys said. She was intensely focused on her son's face, kissing his rosy cheeks and full head of wispy hair. His eyes were swollen shut, his face a puffy, mirrored vision of her, but she knew they would be blue like his father's.

Gertrude returned to the room, carrying a fresh pot of hot water and some cloths. She helped Mary wrap a fresh cloth around the baby's head and exclaimed, "Oh dear, I can't believe we forgot!"

Mary appeared surprised.

"We spent so much time drinking tea, eating scones, and reminiscing about Walden Pond that we forgot to knit a cap. I'll make short work of that this afternoon."

Mary suddenly felt an urge to push. "I feel pressure again," she told Gladys, who instructed her to go ahead and try. A few minutes later, she held up the bloody afterbirth for everyone to see.

"Eating or burying?" Gladys asked no one in particular.

"Ewww!" Mary dry heaved. "I'd throw up if I weren't already empty and starving!"

Gertrude came to Mary's aid. "The rose bushes will be quite happy, thank you very much."

As Gladys stitched Mary up, Gertrude interrupted and asked, "So, Mary, what names have you picked out?"

Mary struggled to shift her focus from her son to her friend and benefactor. "I haven't picked anything out yet," she replied honestly. "I've been taking things one day at a time, worrying about all the trouble I've caused. I never expected this day to come," she admitted, turning back to her son.

"William is a lovely name," Gertrude said.

"It is. But if I name him William, I could never let him go," Mary confessed. A wave of hormones swelled within her, and tears began to zigzag down her contorted face as she forced herself. "Roy," she stated. "I want to name him Roy."

Gertrude smiled at Mary and gently wiped her swollen face with a damp cloth. "Mary, that's sweet, but you really don't have to do that." She offered the tired young woman a drink of water. "You didn't kill William. You still love each other, and no one can say whether or not you can be a family in the future."

"But he's gone," Mary conceded. "I don't know how I know it, but I do." She cradled her son's head, feeling exhausted and unable to grasp any truths except the need for sleep.

Gladys had finished suturing Mary, and the bleeding had stopped. She moved on to her next responsibility—getting Roy to latch onto a breast. "Here, Mary," she said, encouraging the new mother to lean forward. "Let's get these pillows propped up a bit so you can support his head." To

Gertrude, she asked, "Is there another smaller lap pillow we can use to hold the baby higher?"

Gertrude fetched a decorated needlepoint throw pillow from the bottom drawer of the bedside chest and gently nudged it under the baby from one side of the bed while Gladys lifted him from the other. Holding the back of his head with one hand, she pinched Mary's swollen and tender breast with the other and forced the baby's face inward, stimulating the newborn to feed by stroking his cheek with her finger.

"Ow, they're sore," Mary groaned. She felt her son latch onto her nipple, and instinctively, he started to suckle. Another wave of hormones rushed through her, and she knew she was moments away from falling asleep. An hour ago, she had been in unimaginable pain and was now drifting into complete bliss. "Is he breathing? Can he breathe? I don't want his little nose to get squished," she asked, snapping awake.

"He's fine," Gladys reassured her. "Make sure you and the baby are propped up with these pillows, snug around you so you don't tip over. I don't think you'll suffocate him." She rechecked the pillows. "Give him a few minutes, and then we'll switch sides."

Gertrude patted her friend on the shoulder for yet another successful delivery. "So, how many is this?" she asked the midwife.

Gladys chuckled as she watched Mary nod off while nursing. "Oh, I stopped counting after the first baker's dozen or so."

"You have to admire the beauty of newborn life and motherhood," Gertrude said, wrapping an arm around her friend's waist. "We should be envious of our long-lost youthful days."

"Let's give her a few more minutes," Gladys said. "But before we switch him over, help me gather these linens, and I'll help you soak them." As she and Gertrude grabbed armfuls of soiled linens and towels, she said, "I'll note the birth in my journal for the town records once we're downstairs." She paused, peering over her load, her mouth and nose hidden behind the mountain of linens, before asking her friend, "I lost track of the day, I must admit."

Gertrude set the record straight. "Can you believe it's already the second of February? You should check the almanac to see what the weather will be this month."

PART TWO

26

Sarah Ann Fletcher glanced around the table at each of her children: Lydia, Abigail, William, Alice, Clessia, and Frances, who were seated next to her. Despite the loss of her husband, their provisions from the root cellar were running low. In the weeks after Robert's death, she had been so consumed by anger and then depression that she hadn't kept up with her usual canning and pickling. The last of the summer's hearty vegetables would leave the cellar empty before they could bring in the following spring harvest.

"We need to sell the farm and find a place in Halifax," she told them.

"Can we find help?" Abigail asked. At twenty, she was always the most optimistic among the girls, possessing a cheerful personality and boundless energy. She directed this energy towards homeschooling her three younger sisters. The tragedy of the past summer was buried, and her overtly positive attitude served as a mindful defense.

Lydia looked at her sister with determined eyes. Unlike Abigail, Lydia had withdrawn after their father's death, keeping her emotions to herself and becoming increasingly resentful. Perhaps not as vocal as Abigail, she remained empathetic, nurturing all her siblings like a protective lioness.

"Who? How?" their mother demanded, aware that no answer was forthcoming. She glanced across the table at William. "It was all your brother and father could do to keep both our farm and"—she turned to the east, nearly spitting—"theirs." She shifted her focus back to her son. "If you'd done more chores and less—"

"Mom!" Lydia snapped. Once she had her mother's attention, she glanced around at her three youngest sisters across the table.

Sarah Ann closed her eyes and lowered her chin, reciting a serenity prayer to regain her calm. When she finished, she turned her attention to her three oldest children. "William can't handle everything alone. There aren't enough hours in the day."

"I can help," Lydia offered. "I can handle all the gardening."

Sarah Ann glanced at her enigmatic daughter, who had the enchanting looks of a fairytale sleeping beauty. "Lydia," she said, "you shouldn't even be here. You're twenty-four. You, of all people, should have run away by now, like your other sisters, to find your own life. I'm not stopping you."

"I can do it, Mother," William interjected.

Sarah Ann felt her stomach churn. "Well, maybe I don't *want* you to handle it. Did you think of that?" She rapped the heels of her hands against the table. "Do you think I want to stay here?" she asked, her voice rising. "Do you think I *want* to be in this *kitchen* right now?" she crescendoed.

She apologized to her young daughters after she had regained her composure.

Frances began to cry. Even though they did not witness the brutality of what happened to their father, they still didn't, and probably wouldn't ever, understand. Frances only responded to her mother's raised voice, which calmed after Sarah Ann picked her up and sat her on her lap.

"I don't want to pack up and leave," William said. "Why would you want us to move down to Halifax? What if that's where Mrs. Nutting is now?"

"Mrs. Nutting..." Sarah Ann started, then lowered her voice to a whisper. "She murdered your father, and they ran off like cowards into the night. They could be anywhere in the maritime provinces. For all we know, they could have fled to America, and we might never see them again. Justice may never be served." She bounced Frances gently on her knee. "We'll be fine in the city, don't worry. Your grandmother didn't leave us destitute."

William's lips began to tremble after hearing his mother's words. It had been over five months since he last saw Mary. He glanced at his older sisters, who wouldn't meet his eyes. "I'd rather join the army than move away to the city."

Sarah Ann called his bluff. "Perhaps you should… join the army," she told him, knowing that was precisely her intention for him.

27

Mary had no intention of following Gladys's advice to stay in bed and make Gertrude take extra trips up and down the stairs on her aging knees. There was a clear winner in the debate between a flush toilet and a chamber pot, so she was already spending most of her time downstairs, moving between the bathroom and the kitchen. While she recovered, Gertrude cleverly found some spare throw pillows to put on the kitchen chairs for a softer landing.

Gertrude's kitchen had become Mary's new home away from home. She spent her days sitting, nursing, and chatting while Gertrude provided them with an endless supply of tea, baked bread, oatmeal porridge, and a simmering hearty lamb stew with potatoes and carrots.

"You need to build up your strength and keep that little fellow fed every hour," Gertrude told her, topping Mary's tea cup and buttering her another thick slice of fresh buckwheat bread straight from the oven.

Mary cradled her newborn, nursing him with one arm while she snatched the warm bread. She buried her nose deep into the baked dough, inhaling the hearty, earthy grain, and got melted butter on the tip of her nose. She deftly brushed it off with a finger and licked it clean, not wanting to waste a drop of the rich elixir.

"I can smell molasses," she said, inhaling deeply again. "Now I'm really craving flapjacks! I might not be able to wait for breakfast tomorrow!"

Gertrude stirred a pot of stew, covered it, and returned the spoon to the tray. "I heard Franklin is working for the Chapins and doing their home deliveries, so I should double or triple the usual staples," she said, wiping her hands on her apron. The last thing I remember around here is that we were inventorying the pantry?" She chuckled.

Mary switched the baby to the other side, hissing slightly at the pain from her sore nipple as he broke the latch.

"You ought to send your mother a postcard, Mary." Gertrude walked over to the kitchen table and sat down across from her. "I should have insisted earlier, but—"

"But it didn't matter," Mary interrupted. "If she hadn't done what she did, we wouldn't have been forced from our farm, and I wouldn't have had to choose." She looked down at her and William's son, half nursing, half dozing, eyes closed with cherub-pink cheeks. She adjusted his little knit skullcap, moving it away from his eyes.

"Everyone keeps telling me what to do, and I'm not a child." Roy started to fuss, so she moved him over her shoulder and patted his back. "I let myself be convinced that I had to leave, then that I had to come here, and now you're trying to convince me to leave again." She heard the baby burp and wiped a little spittle from his lips before returning him to her breast. "Part of me wants you to keep him and raise him here in a better home than I could ever provide. Part of me wants to bring him home, and part of me wants to stay because it would be years before I could be with William, and by then..." she trailed off, unable to imagine everything she couldn't control.

"Mary... I can't raise a baby here. I'm too old now, let alone in ten or fifteen years. We could barely handle Franklin as a youngster." Her hands trembled. "I can see in your eyes that you know this."

The stew pot lid began to thump, releasing burps of steam. Gertrude walked over to the stove, removed it using a hand towel, and turned down the gas. When she faced Mary again, she said, "Mary, you have two choices, as I see it. You can either leave the baby here and give him up for adoption to a local family like the Donaldsons, or you can both return to Canada."

Mary felt torn between crying and shouting after being told, once again, what to do. Instead, she asked, "What if I stay?"

"Dear, if you stay, it'll be more of the same that brought you here in the first place. You're a young, unmarried mother with a child born out of wedlock, and people here will talk among themselves. It's a small town, and you can't change this or turn back the clock." She wiped her hands on a towel and said, "I've thought about this and dreaded the day I would have to speak about it."

Mary had to grow up quickly, but she was intelligent. As she stood with Roy, she jostled him, trying to get him to burp again. Satisfied that he was asleep, she gently laid him on his back in a nest of cloth in the top drawer of the baker's rack, which she had repurposed as a bassinet.

She went to the kitchen sink, looked out the back window, and thought, not distracted by any spring colors, but instead faced with a blank slate of defoliated winter gray. She needed to buy more time. Without looking away from the window, she asked, "What if I choose both?"

Gertrude tilted her head and adjusted her spectacles.

Not receiving a reply, Mary turned away from the window. "Can I leave him here with you for a little while, just until I get settled back home? Then I'll return for him. He won't remember any of this."

"I would have no idea when you'll return," Gertrude said, emphasizing each word. "Think about all the possible scenarios where this could go wrong. True, I've grown fond of you in only a few weeks, and I have no doubt you'll come to love this child like no other, but the crux of this problem is time… and you probably wouldn't even write to me, just like you refuse to write to your mother now."

Her tone was sharp enough to stir the baby, and Gertrude took the first step toward the baker's rack. "It's my turn. I'll take him," she said, hoisting the bundle from the drawer and lifting it to her shoulder.

Mary dashed across the room, shifting the cloth from her shoulder to Gertrude's before the baby could soil the woman's beautiful house dress.

"For starters, why don't you sit at the table and write your mother a postcard while Roy helps me finish making supper?" Gertrude motioned for Mary to sit, and she sat as instructed. "I have blanks in the sewing room that cost five cents for postage. I'll take it down to the store and place the delivery order when you're done. It'll kill two birds with one stone."

"I can do that," Mary offered. "I need the exercise."

Gertrude stared at her as if she had three heads. "You *just* had a baby!" She was flabbergasted. "Besides, I'm not ready for Blanche to see you or the baby yet. I haven't figured out the best way to put a lid on the gossip." She bounced Roy over to the stove, reaching for the spoon to stir the stew, and realized she no longer had two hands to lift the lid. "Oops-a-daisy," she said, shrugging her shoulders and smiling. "I'm not ready to give up holding the little bugger, so why don't I go and grab a postcard from the sewing room?"

Mary watched her friend shuffle out of the kitchen with her son and volunteered, "And I'll stir the stew."

28

J.L. Chapin's General Store was unusually busy today for a Wednesday. Nevertheless, some farmers were delivering lamb and mutton while Mac Donaldson and two of his sons dropped off a special order of four ringnecked pheasants intended for the Tarbells' estate dinner.

Blanche's father, James, came in to assist with the meat deliveries, while her older sister, Carrie, who had retired from teaching and was now the principal of the Center School, agreed to help with the morning rush before school started.

While Carrie milled about the store, helping customers, Blanche took turns working at the front counter and the post office. She was ringing up a sale at the front when she noticed Mrs. Gates enter and head toward the post office counter.

Blanche finished the transaction by dropping a coin on the counter. "Oh, I'm sorry," she apologized, not bothering with the coin as her attention shifted elsewhere. Please excuse me. Someone is waiting, and we're so short-staffed this morning," she said, walking away without waiting for a response.

She quickly double-checked the alignment of her bun before Gertrude noticed her approach. She had been late to open after briskly walking across the common from the tavern and hadn't had time to apply anything to her face or properly secure her hair.

"Mrs. Gates," she began, forcing a bright smile. "We haven't seen you in some time," she lied. "How can I help you today?"

"Good morning, Blanche. How are you this fine winter morning?" She did not wait for Blanche to answer. "And how's Franklin? Giving you any trouble?"

Blanche smiled across the counter at the diminutive Mrs. Gates, who stood in her Sunday best: a fox fur coat and matching hat, grinning like the Cheshire Cat. Behind her smile was a mix of envy, jealousy, and a hint of snobbishness toward the widow's wealth and stability, thanks to her late husband. It was something she might never attain, but at least she was determined to have fun trying.

"Franklin has been so dear," she replied. "He truly has. He's packing up the weekly home deliveries as we speak." The muscles in her cheeks began to cramp. "Even Little Joe has taken a shine to him."

Gertrude's attention seemed to refocus at the mention of Franklin loading the delivery sleigh. "That reminds me… I need some additions to my delivery order. Is it too late for this week?" she asked, glancing around. "Where exactly is Franklin?"

Blanche believed Frank, but she wanted to hear Gertrude confirm it. "Additions?" she asked coyly. "What kind of additions do you have?"

Gertrude wrinkled her nose and took off her spectacles, pulling a handkerchief from her purse. Wiping them, she retorted, "Not have—need. As I'm sure Franklin has already told you, he was an unexpected house guest who ate me out of house and home for a while, and I need to restock." She paused, letting out a gentle sigh. "Thank you, by the way, for helping him pick out more appropriate… what might you call them… duds," she said, sounding grateful. "And it's good he's earning a decent day's wage working part-time here at the store and over at the tavern."

When Blanche didn't respond, Gertrude pressed on. "I also have another mouth to feed. My niece from Concord, Mary Jane, is staying with me while Gladys takes care of her needs and services."

Blanche relaxed, nodded, and inhaled, believing Franklin to be truthful. "You're very welcome, and tell her congratulations!" She noticed the small letter Gertrude was holding and offered to take it. "Can I mail this for you?"

Gertrude handed Blanche the letter with Mary's postcard for her mother.

Blanche accepted the parcel, disappointed it was stowed in an envelope and hidden from her prying eyes. She glanced at the address, noting the name and location: Kirby's Lane. "Halifax?" she asked, hoping Gertrude might overshare. "International is five cents, and if we can catch Frank, he'll deliver the mailbag to the station after finishing his rounds."

Gertrude took a nickel from her coin purse and placed it on the counter next to the other coin. "Thank you, my dear." As she left the store, she whispered, "Don't let the little chickadees catch you closing down the tavern tonight."

Blanche rang up the postage and dropped the letter into an outgoing box, not recognizing either the name Rachel Nutting or the Nutting family name. Perhaps she was an acquaintance of Gertrude's late husband. Still, she would mention the name to Frank tonight.

29

Frank worked the home deliveries in a counterclockwise direction around town. First, he walked south down Weston, then east along Trapelo, north up Bedford, looping around past the pump house and back along Sandy Pond, before finishing south again on Station Road to drop off the outgoing mail bag at the train clerk's and return the incoming one to the store. He stood outside Gertrude's house in the early evening, making it one of his last stops before heading to the train station.

"Whoa, attaboy, Joe," he urged the horse, gently pulling on the reins to bring the sled to a stop. The roads were frozen, a bit rutted from the spring thaw, and the gravel scraped and crunched beneath the wide metal runners. The ride was rougher than the carriage, but he didn't have to worry about throwing a wheel while navigating the frozen ruts.

Most of his remaining load was due here, and he gave Little Joe a rub on the head and a carrot before unloading. The first parcel was a small leg of lamb wrapped in parchment paper that he could smell, even though it was recently frozen. He carried a block of ice that had been cut yesterday from Flint's Pond to the porch and set the lamb on top before returning for another load. He was thankful that Blanche had given him this job instead of cutting ice blocks every other day because riding around all afternoon with Joe was much easier on his back, and the horse made for better company.

He placed a bag of wool, a jar of molasses, a sack of buckwheat, two dozen eggs, a box of tea, carrots, potatoes, cabbage, milk, another wrap of meat he couldn't identify, probably brisket, and some dried fruit onto the porch. He glanced at the front door and window before sneaking a carrot for Joe into his coat. There was no bacon, which somehow disappointed him.

The front door opened, and Gertrude stepped onto the porch wearing a housecoat. "Good afternoon, or is it a good evening, Franklin?"

"Mrs. Gates," he said, tipping his derby. The rabbit fur muffs were the highlight of the day. "I'd be happy to help you carry everything inside," he offered.

"Hi Frank, how's it going?" Mary asked, appearing behind Gertrude with her head peeking over the older woman's shoulder.

"Couldn't be better," he replied, somewhat truthfully.

"Franklin, why don't we form a line? You can hand me the goods, and I'll pass them along to Mary inside the house. This way, you won't track in dirt with your boots." Gertrude extended her hands, waiting for the first armful.

She hadn't even given him a chance to argue. He felt a bit hungry and was looking for a cup of coffee and a snack, which he now realized he wouldn't get.

Mary placed all the light items in the foyer but hurried the meat packages into the kitchen larder and checked on Roy in the baker's rack drawer before returning.

When the block of ice was all that was left, Frank said, "I'll have to lug this into the icebox. It's too heavy for you ladies." He gripped the chunk with iron ice tongs and began to lift it.

"Hold on a second, Franklin," Gertrude interrupted him.

She turned to face Mary and told her to go to the kitchen, winking at her, then widening her eyes.

Mary pivoted and hurried into the kitchen to retrieve her son from the drawer, which she closed with a shove of her hip. "Okay, all clear," she said toward the foyer, ducking into the sewing room with Roy asleep on her shoulder.

Frank hauled the ice block down the hall and into the kitchen. After placing it into the larder between the baker's rack and the back door, he was surprised to see only Gertrude standing behind him and disappointed that Mary had vanished. He could smell the simmering stew from across the kitchen, making his mouth water. The rich aromas of mushrooms in gravy made his stomach rumble. The sight of bread on the table and imagining how he'd soak up the gravy nearly made him beg to stay for supper.

"Why don't you grab a piece or two of bread for the road, Franklin," Gertrude suggested, noticing him practically drooling as he stared at the basket on the table. "Isn't Little Joe waiting? He's not even hitched, so I bet he's already heading back to the store's stable without you."

That caught his attention. "Oh, right," he said, tipping his derby hat. He looked down at the floor but didn't see much of anything, yet he still managed to remember his manners and apologize. "Sorry if I tracked in any dirt after all… give my regards to Mary Jane."

As Frank left the kitchen, he noticed the crumpled and bunched cloth hanging over the edge of the baker's rack top drawer. Mrs. Gates was not a messy housekeeper, he thought.

With Frank gone and the front door shut, Gertrude and Mary exchanged deep breaths.

"Good thing Roy's as quiet as a church mouse," Gertrude said.

"Yeah," Mary replied, exhaling slowly. "I was scared for a moment that he might have somehow rolled out of the drawer and onto the floor."

30

How long do you think the mail takes by train?" Mary asked.

Gertrude stopped knitting and rested the baby hat she was working on in her lap. "I haven't a clue," she admitted. "This is something fairly new, but I suspect the mail has to go into the city to be sorted, then re-routed onto different trains, working its way north—probably weeks, not days, that's for sure." She returned to her knitting, scolding herself, "I should have made you send a postcard the day you showed up on my front porch. Your poor mother."

Mary sat cross-legged on the loveseat, cradling Roy in her arms. She had been reading Gertrude's copy of *Walden* to him while he nursed, but it now rested on her lap. "I can't remember the last time I could sit like this," she murmured.

Gertrude nodded toward the open book. "How is everything coming along?" she asked, pointing at Mary's lap.

Mary glanced down. "Oh… okay, I guess. Nothing hurts. It's a bit itchy. Gladys did say the stitches would disappear, right?"

"The stitches actually dissolve, not disappear. You'll be fine as long as you keep things clean and spritz with warm water every day."

"I can't believe it's—" Mary shivered, interrupting herself. "I guess it's a godsend that William will never have to touch me again."

Gertrude glared at Mary, clearly dissatisfied and growing impatient with the young woman's self-deprecation.

"What?"

"Mary," Gertrude said, placing her knitting back in her lap. "You'll be right as rain… now look at him. What do you see?"

"I see…" She paused, her lips trembling and her eyes glazed with a shiny sheen. "I see William."

"Of course you do. It's all you ever talk about."

"I do?"

"Do you ever hear yourself when you're nursing him?"

Mary nodded.

Gertrude could see her struggling to keep her lips from quivering. "You didn't kill him. Your mother didn't kill him, but his father very well might have. You have no idea where things stand."

Gertrude picked up her knitting again, determined to finish it by the night's end.

"I think you should go home after the first crocus blooms, whether or not you get a reply from your mother."

"Okay, I will."

Gertrude snapped away from her work, unable to believe it was as easy as she had heard. "You will?"

"I will, but only under one condition." She handed her baby to Gertrude, who was unwilling to set things aside.

"Mary, I really want to finish this," she pleaded.

Mary extended her arms, lifting Roy by his armpits. "Here, take him."

Gertrude leaned forward and placed her knitting and yarn on the sofa table. She removed her wire-rimmed spectacles and gathered the child in her arms, gently stroking his cheek with a knuckle. Whether she was childless or a mother, young or old, her maternal instincts prevailed.

"You said it. We have no idea where things stand. I don't know if my family is still where I left them. I don't know if they're safe, or if I need to travel back to the farm, or how I would even do that. How can I handle any of that with a baby in tow when I might not even be able to care for myself?"

Gertrude bounced Roy, remaining silent and feeling empathetic.

"I will return home after the first crocus blooms, but on one condition… Roy stays here until I figure our shit out."

"Mary Jane! Mind your language!" Gertrude gasped.

"When will the first crocus bloom?"

"A month, but…" Gertrude stammered, her thoughts racing ahead of her words. "I'm too old. I'd have to find a wet nurse. You could be gone for a month or more!"

"Wet nurse?"

"Who will feed the baby while you're away? He can't have solid food until… I don't know… not until late spring? Early summer?"

Mary reached for her son, pulling him back into her arms. "It's okay," she said, taking a slow breath. "Yes, the thought of another woman feeding my baby is"—she shook her head—"I don't know the words, but I have no choice. And I trust you." She collected herself and then said, "We have a month to figure shit out, right?"

Gertrude snorted, unappreciative of the foul language.

Mary pointed to Gertrude's knitting on the table. "Okay, you can finish now. So far, it looks cute." Suddenly, she handed Roy back to Gertrude. "Oh, wait. Tea! I'll make tea."

Mary closed *Walden* and set it carefully on the sofa table before skipping into the kitchen.

"Hey," she called back to the living room. "Do you still have any of those fig cookies?"

Gertrude didn't hear Mary in the kitchen over her cooing. "What are we going to do about you and your mother? You're lucky you're so adorable with those baby blues."

31

Rachel Nutting untied her boots and left them by the front door of her rented unit on Kirby's Lane. She needed to work extra hours cleaning the homes of faculty and borrow from her son George's wages to cover their expenses. As word of mouth about her services spread across campus, she'd begun to depend less on his help, but she didn't know how much longer he would stay with her and Agnes before growing tired of waiting for Mary's return.

After taking off her jacket and a long-sleeved shirt, she hung them over a spindled chair, where they would be waiting for her again at sunrise.

Sitting on the only frail wooden chair in the small front room that shared a kitchenette, she rubbed her sore feet, grateful for the warmth of the coal-fired air. She wondered if she had the energy to fill a pot to soak her callouses. Ultimately, she decided she did not and leaned back against the uncomfortable spindles, rubbing her bare upper arms, exposed by her sleeveless undershirt.

At fifty, her Scottish red hair was so thick that she rarely wore a bonnet, except on brisk winter mornings when the wind blew in from the harbor. She removed the hairpins, letting her hair cascade in waves over her sore neck and shoulders.

Over the past year, her roots had begun to turn white from stress.

Closing her eyes momentarily, she envisioned strong, masculine fingers kneading her neck and shoulder muscles, turning the soreness into a deep warmth.

It was never going to happen.

She sat there, opened her eyes, and gazed through the front window across South Street at Holy Cross Cemetery and the Our Lady of Sorrows Chapel. It was a place she visited and prayed almost daily since moving to the inner city from the farm, and she could still see the outlines of its modest Gothic design in the lengthening sunset shadows. The interior of the Irish Catholic chapel was sparse, built in a single day around the time of her birth.

Almost every day, returning to the bed where she laid her head, refusing to call it home, she would enter the chapel and pray. She would pray first for Mary's well-being and safe return, second for the safety and well-being of her illegitimate grandchild, and lastly for the future welfare of the Fletchers.

But not today because she was too tired—too tired to feel hungry or to notice any smells from whatever Agnes or George might have been preparing for supper.

"George? Agnes?" she called out, not worried about George, who could take care of himself and often stayed out very late a few nights each week.

"Agnes?" she called again, pushing herself up and off the chair.

In the kitchenette, she struck a match to light an oil lamp and carried it into her bedroom, one of the two she shared with Agnes. As soon as Mary returned, she planned to look for a roomier place, or else George or both George and Mary would venture out independently.

The bedroom was vacant, and George's room was also vacant.

She thought it was strange, but it wasn't that late; still, she panicked. Maybe Agnes had found an after-school job.

In the kitchenette, she heated a teapot until it boiled, and once it started steaming, she used a cloth-covered basket to warm and soften some cut pieces of stale baguette.

She had settled into the two-person table, with its chairs barely large enough for teenagers, when she heard a key turn in the front door and the lock snick open.

Agnes pushed open the front door.

She was her mother's daughter, with long, wavy ginger hair, matching freckles, and green eyes, but her two siblings had inherited their late father's darker hair and eyes. Looking at her mother, expressionless, she stepped into the room, leaving the door ajar.

Rachel stood to greet her daughter and was about to ask if she'd been raised in a barn when she noticed someone else standing outside the doorway. There was no mistaking the difference between a woman's hat and a man's.

Sarah Ann Fletcher stepped inside, her face now tilted into view, illuminated by the lamp's amber glow.

"Hello, Rachel," she said, keeping her hat and gloves on as she shut the door behind her.

Agnes moved quickly, not running, to her mother's side and wrapped her arm around Rachel's waist.

There was no need for introductions. Rachel told her sixteen-year-old daughter to go to their room and shut the door behind her.

Studying the face of her former friend and widowed neighbor, aware it was a stupid question, Rachel asked her, "Sarah Ann… what are you doing here? What were you doing with my daughter?"

Sarah Ann removed her black cloth gloves and hat, holding them in front of her matching black waistcoat.

"What do you want here?" Rachel asked.

Sarah Ann scanned the room. "I'm appalled by the modesty and lack of furniture." She shifted her focus back to Rachel. "At least you have heat," she said sarcastically. "Not much in the way of needing to pack quickly, I see." She took a step forward. "Not expecting guests?"

Rachel dismissed the question. "How did you find my daughter?" she asked instead.

"I haven't found her yet."

Rachel squinted, puzzled by Sarah Ann's intentions, as her heartbeat began to quicken. She wasn't going to play any games and stood her ground.

Sarah Ann was the first to relent. "A well-dressed woman who patiently visits one school after another, asking by name, eventually gets lucky, but it takes time." She stood stiffly and unblinking. "And I'm *very* patient."

"What do you want here?" Rachel asked again, feeling increasingly aware and self-conscious of how much she looked like a haggard vagabond next to someone dressed for second-class travel. She glanced at the front window. "Are you here to have me arrested?"

"No… I want Mary Jane. How hard is that to understand?"

"She's not here."

"Obviously."

Sarah Ann cocked an ear, listening intently, and asked, "Where's the baby?"

"She's not here."

Sarah Ann perked up. "She?"

Rachel believed she noticed a trace of disappointment on Sarah Ann's face and let the tension linger before responding, "Mary Jane isn't here. I've mentioned this before."

"Where is she, then? I want to see her *and* my grandchild. I won't take no for an answer." Sarah Ann stepped forward again. "You *owe* me this," she said through gritted teeth.

"She's not here, Sarah Ann, and I don't know where she is or even if she's alive or dead."

The widow Fletcher studied Rachel's face, searching for any signs of a lie. "You sent her to Boston?"

Hearing Sarah Ann's words brought Rachel relief, knowing her daughter was far from home, and she refused to answer.

"You sent her to Boston by herself… pregnant? When?" Sarah Ann shouted.

Rachel swung her arm toward the back bedrooms and pointed frantically. The only sound she made was a sharp intake of breath through clenched teeth, followed by an exaggerated blowing exhale. She refused to say Agnes's name and age.

"Well, that's disappointing," Sarah Ann lamented. "I would have liked to see her—see them," she corrected.

"How is William?" Rachel deflected, unsuccessfully regaining her composure.

Any trace of solemnity on Sarah Ann's face vanished behind a faint smile. "He's gone too. He's on the train to British Columbia. The army has him now."

"But he's just a boy!" Rachel shouted, trying to stifle herself through clenched jaws.

"Sixteen… seventeen… does it really matter? I was bound to lose him eventually."

"And you call yourself a mother!"

"Oh, isn't that the pot calling the kettle black!"

Sarah Ann started the slow process of pulling on her gloves for the show. "I'll have you know that if you hadn't already been… widowed yourself… I'd have returned the favor by now."

She made several adjustments to place her hat on her head before reaching for the doorknob, where she hesitated and turned to face Rachel again. "Despite my hatred and unforgiveness toward you, I would never harm the mother of my grandchild. I want to see her, Rachel, and believe me… I *will* find her." With her final statement delivered, she stepped into the cold, damp evening air.

Rachel collapsed into one of the two kitchenette chairs, uncaring if it would support her weight. The Fletcher widow's unexpected, confrontational visit had her heart racing. When she turned to call Agnes from the bedroom, her daughter was already standing beside her.

"Agnes, dear," she said, embracing her youngest daughter and rubbing her shoulders. "Did Mrs. Fletcher hurt you? What did she say?"

"No, Mother, she didn't. She came up to me after school and asked me to bring her home. Why is she here? Does this have anything to do with us having to leave the farm?"

Rachel wasn't sure how to respond. She never imagined this predicament would ever happen.

Agnes withdrew a small letter from her dress pocket and slipped it to her mother. "This was in the mailbox by the front door," she said.

Rachel examined the fragile parcel with crumpled corners, barely able to read the postmark, and gingerly opened it with her fingernail. Where on earth was Lincoln, Massachusetts?

"Did Mrs. Fletcher see this? Did she see you take it?"

"No, Mother."

They sat together as Rachel flattened the letter on the table. Unable to read the small inked handwriting at first, she moved the lamp closer, and together they read aloud, their temples practically touching:

Dearest Mother,

I am safe and well, living with a wonderful woman who is taking care of me and my baby, a boy born on Feb 2. I named him Roy. He has William's blue eyes! I shall leave Roy in her care and return home next month. Please stay at Kirby's Lane until my return if you get this. There is much to discuss.

Love MJ

Rachel pushed away from the table and paced the kitchenette in tight circles. She tried to calm her thumping heart, pressing her hand to her chest. The relief of knowing her daughter was safe and alive, having survived childbirth, was overshadowed by countless unanswered questions, and she would have to wait weeks to receive those answers, uncertain if she could manage the stress.

"Mother, why didn't she name her baby after William?" Agnes asked. "We know of no Roy."

"I don't know, sweetheart."

Rachel understood that the only way she could survive another month was to pray twice daily to Saint Anthony in the chapel before and after work.

Agnes looked at her mother. "Mrs. Fletcher probably wants to see the baby," she said, hugging her mother, who returned the gesture in kind.

Rachel's breathing slowed as mother and daughter ran their fingers through each other's hair. At least she had thanks to give, knowing Mary was alive, safe, and on her way home soon. Her first prayer tonight would be to ask for the coming month to pass in the blink of an eye.

Her anxiety subsided until it spiked again when she heard the front door latch snick open. She hadn't locked the door after Sarah Ann walked out, so she tightened her hold on Agnes and pushed her daughter behind her hip, using herself as a shield. She knew it was too late to stop whoever was entering, but she filled her lungs and prepared to scream, only to exhale as she watched her son George step into the room.

He looked surprised as she and his sister stared at him, their eyes and mouths agape. He removed his hat and fluffed his dark hair. He looked himself up and down, checking every part of himself, patting his face, and wiping his mouth with his hand. His face had been clean, but now it was smudged with newspaper ink from his daily deliveries.

"What is it?" he asked as he stepped further into the cramped front room, leaving a trail of gravel dust and specks of snow on the bare wooden floor, which was already starting to melt.

He took off his jacket, draped it over the chair atop his mother's, and asked again, "What's the matter?" With his face now smudged and his ink-stained hands, he looked more like someone who delivered coal than newspapers.

Rachel relaxed her grip on Agnes and was about to respond to her son when Agnes spoke up first, "Mrs. Fletcher followed me home from school today. She's found us."

George turned his attention to his mother. "Is this true?"

"Yes," she admitted. "She was here. She was looking for Mary."

"But, you're—"

"Yes!" she interrupted her only son. "I know exactly what happened. It's not as if it's been so long that I, or anyone else, has forgotten." She spotted the dirty floor. "George, your boots," she reminded him, catching the smell of alcohol on his breath.

He retreated to the front and attempted to remove his boots, tugging at each one while balancing on one foot. He nearly tipped over before dropping to one knee to untie them, his balance slightly off.

Rachel noticed his unsteadiness and asked, "You're late because you've been drinking? How many pints at that Keith doggery? Please tell me you didn't spend all your day's wages on beer."

"Of course not," he reassured her. "It's only me, Frankie, and Tommy Monteleone. I told you about them before, doing brickwork. They bought the rounds this time."

She couldn't read his face, which was all smudged black and shadowy. "For heaven's sake, you look like a mudsill. Go wash your face and hands at the sink."

Agnes was the first to tittle-tattle. "She said she'd never hurt MJ. We think she wants to see the baby."

George spun from the sink, droplets of soapy water spraying onto the floor. "Baby?" he asked, darting his eyes back and forth between them. "Well?"

Rachel sighed and turned to the table, reaching for the letter, but Agnes was quicker and snatched it first.

"Careful with that," Rachel implored her.

"We got a letter from MJ today!" Agnes exclaimed, waving the letter like a saber. "She had the baby a couple of weeks ago, a boy, and named him Roy," she rhymed.

"Who's Roy?" George asked. "Where did that name come from?" He looked as confused by this as they were. "Why wouldn't she name him after me and Dad? Or the…"

Rachel had grown tired of always hearing about the father or the baby's father. There was only one father: Jesus Christ. The father of Mary's baby had a name. "William," she reminded them. "His name is William." With her hands on her hips, she said, "And we don't know why. After everything that's happened, she's probably given up hope of ever seeing that boy again."

She couldn't shake the thought that they might all be widows now.

"She's coming home next month," Agnes blurted.

George dried his face and hands on a towel, leaving it less clean. "Well, she doesn't have anything to worry about. I'll protect my sister from Mrs. Fletcher… and William if I have to."

"There'll be no need for that, George," Rachel assured him. "If we're to believe Sarah Ann, she said she convinced or *forced* him to join the army."

She shot George a look that made him wince, wondering if his mother implied he had choices.

"Whether convinced or forced, who knows? But I'll pray for him nonetheless."

"Where is she?" he asked.

Rachel responded before Agnes, "Somewhere in Massachusetts, in a town called Lincoln. I can ask one of my Saint Mary's faculty members tomorrow. I'm sure someone has an atlas at home."

"How did she get there?" he asked.

Rachel withheld the letter, opting to summarize. "No idea. All she said was… much to discuss."

George lifted the cloth cover from the basket and took a piece of baguette. After biting into it, he said, "Crunchy."

Rachel bit her tongue. Once a child, always a child. "I heated them earlier," she informed him. He would've known this if he hadn't been out drinking on a weekday. "Are those Monteleone brothers a bad influence on you, George?"

He grabbed two more baguettes and deadpanned before heading to his bedroom, "No, Mother, Sicilians make the best friends."

32

March comes in like a lion and goes out like a lamb. When daytime temperatures rise above freezing while nighttime temperatures drop below it, it marks the official start of maple sugar season across New England. The native Indians have been collecting maple sap in the region since long before the Pilgrims arrived.

Frank Hosman scanned the adverts pinned to a wallboard at the front of Chapin's General Store. He could count his gold, seeing all the help needed for sugaring.

Malcolm Donaldson's family owned hundreds of acres of trees on the east side of Flint's Pond, requiring numerous auger holes and buckets. For one month each year, the entire Donaldson family struggled to keep up with the overwhelming number of collection buckets that needed emptying every day.

As the weather warmed and the ground thawed, Malcolm and two of his sons had to restart their home-building projects, which kept them from helping with the maple sugar harvest. When there was a good run, sometimes more than once a day, it meant they needed help—a lot of help spreading profit around.

"So I guess this means I'm probably sleeping alone this month?" Blanche asked, her voice carrying across the open floor.

Frank nearly sprained his neck, wrenching it around. He thought he would feel embarrassed by onlookers and eavesdroppers, but the store appeared empty. Regaining his composure, he sauntered over to the counter, leaned over, and kissed his leggy, blonde, green-eyed beauty of a girlfriend.

"This is my chance to make up for all the dough you've spent on me over the past couple of months," he said, daring to kiss her again. If someone were to walk in the front door, they would only see his back.

"It could be weeks if the season is a good run." She pouted. "A girl has needs."

Frank knew from overhearing the guys in the store that the Farmer's Almanac was predicting a banner year. "I know, twenty-four hours a day for a few weeks. Collecting all day and boiling all night."

He winked at her, aware she was trying to manipulate him with her charm and guile.

"You can't possibly work all day and night. There's gotta be work in shifts."

Frank shrugged with his palms up.

"Oh, stop it, you're teasing."

"Okay, all right," he admitted with a laugh. "Who's really teasing?" he asked her. "I promise I'll grab coffee at the store first thing every morning."

Her playful, pouty look vanished in an instant. "You'd better," she demanded, squinting at him as if placing a curse or spell.

"Who will take care of the weekly deliveries?" he asked, stepping back.

It was her turn to shrug, palms up. "Dunno. This is the first year of deliveries. We might have to cancel. My father can't do it, that's for sure."

The bell above the front door jingled.

Mary walked into the store with a bundle on her chest. She was wearing hand-me-downs from Gertrude's closet: a dark wool plaid skirt that was floor-length on Gertrude but hung just below the tops of the only pair of borrowed leather boots stretched enough to fit Mary without binding. It was long enough to remain modest yet short enough to avoid dragging on the town's gravel roads. The late morning weather was chilly, slightly above freezing, requiring her to wear only two long-sleeved linen shirts. A homemade cotton cloth sling, wrapped around her shoulders and holding Roy, also added to her warmth and shielded his tiny face from the elements. Her thick, dark hair was braided down the middle of her back. Her appearance was neither poor nor Victorian elite.

"MJ? Mary?" Frank called, stepping away from the counter and moving closer to her. Greeting a woman holding her baby was something he had never done before, and his awkward, stilted approach was evident. A friendly hug or handshake didn't seem appropriate at that moment, so he halted, deciding that a hands-up, palms-out gesture would be safe. "Hi," he said, smiling, his eyes drifting to the concealed bundle between them.

"How have you been, Frank?" she asked, softly patting Roy's bottom. "I recognized you right away at the register. Your pinstriped pants and derby are hard to miss."

She scanned the store, sniffing.

When she focused on the potbelly stove and the nearby unkempt wood scrap pile, he noticed that she wrinkled her nose and brought a finger to her lips as if stifling a sneeze.

His brain and mouth could not work in parallel. "Good… good… I've been working," he stammered, doffing his derby out of politeness and inadvertently crushing it against his chest. "Sorry about all the dust and chaff in here."

"That's good to hear," she said, fanning the air around her face and in front of Roy's. "Not your fault. I was used to walking in fresh air."

She looked over his shoulder.

Blanche stepped out from behind the store counter and walked toward them.

Following Mary's gaze, Frank turned and saw Blanche joining them as she offered her hand to greet Mary for the first time.

"Hello. I'm Blanche Chapin. My family owns and operates the store," she said, shaking Mary's hand. "You must be Mary Jane. Franklin mentioned you're staying with Mrs. Gates?"

"Yes, that's true," Mary replied.

Blanche's focus shifted to the baby.

"So, Mary, it seems like you…" Frank began. "I didn't notice—"

Blanche interrupted him. "And who is this little precious bundle?" Her cornsilk hair was piled high, with enough left to frame her face, and a few strands tumbled against the baby's cheeks, causing him to wiggle.

Mary shifted her son, moved the cotton folds away from his face, and gently rubbed his cheek with her finger. "This is my son, Roy." When he finally opened his eyes, she whispered into his face, "Can you say hello?"

Blanche gasped, bending down with her hands on her knees. "Oh my, such beautiful eyes!" She patted her bosom several times, taking deep breaths, before glaring at Frank.

"Thanks, he has blue eyes just like his father's."

Frank composed himself, shrugging off Blanche's stare. "So everything's okay?" he asked.

Blanche placed her hand on Frank's elbow and tightened her grip.

"Yes, everything's fine," Mary replied. "Mrs. Putnam was a godsend. She and Mrs. Gates took care of everything." She lifted the baby out of the sling and rested him on her shoulder, turning so they could see him. "It's warm in here," she said, fanning her face.

Frank drifted with the flow and asked, "Are you going home? Both of you?"

Mary seemed pensive. "I'll head back to Canada next month after the first crocus blooms. That's how Gertrude tells time, I think, when which flowers bloom and when." She turned to Frank. "I don't know what would have happened to me if you hadn't found me on the wharf."

Blanche dug her fingernails deep into Frank's elbow and yanked him closer to her.

He realized that Mary had caught him in his little white lie. He planned to smooth things over with Blanche later and skillfully twisted his arm out of her grasp.

"Halifax?" Blanche asked, pausing. "Mrs. Gates…" she paused again, smiling at Mary and then at Frank. "I was here when Gertrude mailed a letter to Halifax."

"Yes," Mary said. "To my mother."

The front door swung open, ringing the bell. The high-pitched sound startled Roy, making him cry.

Rebecca Smith and Maria Pierce, who worked at the town library, walked in and immediately headed straight for the baby. Both started cooing and extended fingers that Roy instinctively gripped.

"Who do we have here?" asked Rebecca, the former president of the library council who was now volunteering. Her husband, Cyrus, led the town's Masonic lodge.

"His name is Roy," Mary replied.

"And who might you be, dear?" asked Maria, the library's secretary and treasurer.

"MJ," she said, coaxing a smile from Roy as she gently bounced him. Each time his chin touched her shoulder, he smiled. "Mary Jane."

Rebecca and Maria remained silent, their scrunched faces revealing they did not recognize her.

Mary broke the stale pause. "Nutting. I'm Mary Jane Nutting. I'm a friend of Mrs. Gates." She hesitated, blinking several times. "I'm staying with her for a while."

"Oh, Gertrude, of course, yes," Maria said.

"Well, you must be one of Gladys's patients," Rebecca said.

"Yes, she took excellent care of us."

"She's the best midwife this side of Boston, right?" Blanche chimed in. "Do you ladies need my help? Or something you need from Frank?" She gestured toward him.

"Well, it was nice meeting you," the two ladies said in unison.

Rebecca, the older of the two, asked, "I'm sure everyone at the Congregational church has been fawning over the little guy. Tell Gertrude she shouldn't keep you all to herself, and please stop by our Unitarian church after mass if you have the time."

Mary took a deep breath and tightened her lips. Then, she readjusted her grip on Roy and pulled him close with both arms.

"Blanche, could you please assist us?" asked Maria.

"Something you need for the next library council meeting? Something Franklin can help you with?"

"No," Maria said, glancing at Rebecca for confirmation. "I need something from behind the counter that requires a woman's assistance."

"Of course, lead the way." Blanche sighed dejectedly.

Frank stood alone with Mary. "Well, I'm glad everything worked out." He whispered, "Will Gertrude help you with the baby? Find an orphanage or family?"

"No, I've changed my mind," she replied, adjusting Roy in his swaddled sling.

"Can I help you with that?"

"No, thank you. I'm fine."

Sensing Mary's departure, he asked, "Did you come into the store for something? Can I help you find anything?"

"Actually, no. I wanted to go for a walk. I hadn't visited the store yet, and I was curious about what was here."

"Okay, very good, very good," he said, nervously glancing around, wondering if Blanche was watching them and how he would end the conversation. "So I guess… let me know when you and Gertrude need anything delivered." He leaned in and whispered, "The weather is getting ready for sugar season. I'll be swamped this month, and I think the Chapins are postponing deliveries without me." He looked around anxiously. "But if you or Gertrude need *anything*, just let me know, and I'll make time."

Mary smiled. "Thank you. We'll figure it out if we need something."

Behind the counter, Blanche watched as Frank held the door open for Mary and the baby.

33

Rachel and Agnes knelt inside the Our Lady of Sorrows Chapel, their hands clasped around the rosary beads given to them by Bishop O'Brien after Rachel requested a confession. He set them on a path toward the Lord's forgiveness after absolving her and Mary of their cardinal sins.

Early this morning, the building was empty, and Rachel suggested stopping to pray before starting work and school. The chapel's interior was small and modest, accommodating no more than seventy patrons. Stained glass windows from the late 1600s adorned the walls, and wood carvings salvaged from a Flemish church that dated back to 1550 were mounted on the altar.

Mother and daughter prayed, their red manes tied in buns over their ears. There was no warmth inside the chapel except for their own.

Rachel worked the fifty-nine beads between her fingers, praying to Saint Anthony and the Holy Mary.

Agnes remained silent with her head bowed.

"Saint Anthony, Mother Mary," Rachel murmured, thumbing a bead. "Please bring our Mary Jane back to us. Please watch over baby Roy and grant him a place in your flock. Please watch over William and ensure his safe passage and return…"

Agnes glanced around, bouncing her knees and rubbing her arms. "Mom?" she finally asked. "Mrs. Fletcher?"

Rachel exhaled, lowering her beads into her lap. "I'm losing faith," she lamented. "I've been praying for months, and yet she finds us and threatens us. I distrust her. And that's a sin."

"Patience," Agnes proclaimed. "God always has a plan, right?"

Rachel looked at her daughter. "Some plan. I did a bad thing. Now I fear Sarah Ann wants to do a bad thing."

"Mom, people aren't bad. They're messy and might do bad things, but they aren't bad."

"How did you get so grown up for a teenager?"

"I listen when we're here at mass."

Rachel filled her lungs as tears of worry pooled in her eyes. "Now I have to fret about you walking to and from school every day. I can't walk with you, and George leaves before sunrise."

"It's okay. I have faith." Agnes stood first, crossed herself, and draped Mary's rosary beads over her head. "Let's go. We're holding up God's plan."

34

Annie Hatt hurried across the yard from the house to the workshop, bringing a pot of coffee to her husband, Richard, and their sons, Reuben and Robert. Their winter months in Owls Head were spent building boats after dinner, and this offseason found them working on their largest order yet: a thirty-foot, two-masted schooner.

The eastern shore of Nova Scotia, stretching from Halifax to Cape Breton, was founded on cod fishing, boat building, and lumbering. Richard Hatt was a third-generation fisherman and boat builder whose ancestors immigrated to Canada from the small sheep-farming Swiss village of Hemmental in 1751.

Richard learned to sail, fish, and build from his father. He passed these skills on to his two oldest sons, and someday, if he were still able, he would start all over again with his two youngest sons, Henry and Clifford.

He was tall and broad-shouldered, with large, callused hands and thick wrists shaped by years of pulling rope and pushing hand planers to smooth hulls and keels.

At the back of the workshop, a wood stove burned scraps of timber, remnants of the mistakes his sons would learn to overlook as they grew wiser, mastering the art of measuring twice and cutting once.

Lobster traps needing repair were stacked in a corner, away from the drying heat of the stove. The entire long wall of the rectangular building, opposite the side door, was windowless and filled from floor to ceiling with rough-cut poplar lumber of various lengths, thicknesses, and dryness. The end wall, facing the bay, was fitted with double doors and featured a short downhill slipway for launching and retrieving boats from the frigid bay.

Reuben was turning twenty-seven this year, an apple that fell close to the tree, having worked alongside his father since he could walk and swim in the cold, black granite waters of the cove without a fuss. At age eleven, he built his first small eight-foot skiff all by himself, and his father loaded it with rocks and pushed it into the bay; together, they watched it sink. "Someday, you'll build a better boat," his father said, "but that one would drown you!"

Robert had recently turned twenty-five and felt more comfortable hauling lobster traps where the work was demanding yet rhythmic. He didn't have the patience or the mathematical skills to design a curved hull or re-member which woodworking tools were best for each job. His mistakes, not Reuben's, mostly fed the wood stove. His arm and back muscles were chiseled like his jawline, making him the most eligible bachelor in town.

"Here you go," Annie said, offering to refill their cups.

Richard accepted the pour, closing his eyes and inhaling deeply. "I'm sure this is fine coffee that we can afford, Annie, but I can't smell or truly appreciate it. Too many summers drying salted cod have dulled my sense of smell."

Annie ignored her husband's whining. "Are you still on schedule, you think?" she asked him, aware that they had received the train shipment of finishing materials from Boston a few weeks ago.

"Yeah, the hull and cabin exterior are done." He nodded toward Reuben and Robert, working on smoothing the two masts with drawknives. "Robert can finish the mast work while Reuben helps me on the cabin interior."

"How about the sail work?" she asked.

"You and Ada?" he proposed.

She thought the job could be too overwhelming for her and their nine-teen-year-old daughter to handle since Ada hadn't been involved in the family business. They had only received enough cloth bolts to meet the year's orders, and this schooner would need an entire bolt of cloth with little margin for error.

Annie shook her head slowly.

Noticing her doubt, Richard suggested, "I can take care of the sail work and ask my brother, Michael, to help Reuben finish the cabin."

"Okay." Annie breathed slowly, allowing her anxiety level to return to normal.

Richard reacted to her vacant stare. "Annie?" he asked, placing a hand on her shoulder. When she didn't respond, he gave her the slightest of shakes. "Everything okay?"

She snapped out of her reverie. "What? Yes, I was just thinking about our last trip." She shook away the cobwebs. "Thinking about how many cloth bolts we ordered, that's all."

"We ordered enough for the year. I'm sure someone will find a reason to cancel, giving us some leeway."

She took a long sip of her coffee, cradling both hands around the hot mug and lifting it almost to her nose, feeling the warm steam on her cheeks. "No, that's not it," she confessed. "We were at the wharf and were going to buy Mary Jane boots when we finished."

Richard wrapped an arm around her neck and leaned into her ear, whispering, "We tried to find her, but she simply vanished. There was nothing more we could have done, whether it was her choice or not."

He moved his arm from her shoulders and ran his fingers through her short salt-and-pepper hair. A year ago, there had been no gray in her dusky chestnut locks. "After all these years, you're still a beautiful, confident woman—the best catch of my career."

"I know," she agreed. "I've been feeling a bit moody lately, which reminds me of losing her. We were two ships passing in the night. How ironic," she sniffled. "Wherever she ended up, I hope she and her baby are all right." She counted the weeks in her head. "She must have had that child by now."

Richard faced her, ran his large, strong hands through her hair, and kissed her forehead. Then, he locked eyes with her and smiled.

"What do you say we call it a night?" he yelled over his shoulder to his sons.

Robert was the first to drop his drawknife on the shed floor and drain his coffee in three long gulps.

Reuben hesitated. "The stove isn't ready to shut down yet," he said. "I'll keep at this mast for a bit longer." He shot his brother a snide look. "Giving up so soon?"

Robert shrugged, left the workshop through the side door, and jogged back to the house.

"All right, as you wish. But please don't burn down the shed," Richard acknowledged to his protégé son. "It's Robert's turn in the barrel to catch tomorrow's dinner."

After leaving the coffee pot with Reuben, Richard and Annie walked back to the house, hand in hand.

35

"Does this mean we can write back?" Agnes asked.

Rachel wished she had a clear answer to give. "It could very well mean tossing away a nickel we can't rightly afford."

"But we have to try," Agnes urged. "We have to warn her!" She pouted and huffed. "I never wanted her to go in the first place!"

"Shush, you'll wake your brother."

Rachel squeezed her daughter's arm as they huddled beneath their shared blankets to stay warm. Once Rachel was sure she couldn't hear George snoring through the thin wooden wall, she let go. Spending a nickel on international postage to the States wouldn't be such a big deal if her son didn't drink what little he earned with the Monteleone brothers.

"You said it's a small town outside Boston, and she's been there for two months already with someone, and she's had the baby. By now, the post office has to know who she is," Agnes whispered.

Rachel couldn't see her daughter's face in the dark, but she knew Agnes was likely correct, so she gently stroked her cheek. She promised herself she would pay closer attention to her youngest daughter, who was maturing quickly and thinking logically. "I'm sure you're right, but you still can't compare this place to Stewiacke. There's no guarantee that Mary will get a letter—or when."

Agnes rustled beneath the blankets, turning onto her stomach and propping herself on her elbows to face her mother. "Can we write it tonight?"

"No begging. We don't even have a pen or paper here. I promise we'll do it tomorrow, and I'll mail it from the university."

"Promise?"

"Yes," Rachel promised, unaware of Agnes's tight smile.

They rolled over, back to back, surviving another day.

36

Halfway through the spring maple sugar season, the sap boilers had shifted from producing fancy grade to medium amber, and Frank was delivering several gallons to Chapin's General Store.

On his first trip to the store, he held two gallons of syrup in each hand and stopped in his tracks.

Blanche's face was as cold as the frost on a winter morning.

"Hey, darling," he smiled. When Blanche didn't respond but stepped out from behind the counter, his eyes scanned the store.

She was as mad as a March hare and silently pointed for him to leave the jugs in front of the dry goods. She watched him make a few trips before realizing she couldn't stay angry despite his lies about meeting Mary. Holding a grudge took too much energy; besides, she was sure Frank wasn't the baby's father. He and Mary had dark brown eyes, while the baby had blue ones.

When she was a petulant little girl, prone to pitching a fit whenever she didn't get her way, she would cross her arms and purse her lips like a hornpout catfish. Her father scolded her in his own way by saying he hoped her face didn't freeze that way, which eventually scared her straight.

She knew Frank wasn't a gentleman the day he strode into the store, yet he had always treated her like one. She enjoyed his company and knew he felt the same. He wasn't lazy and impressed her with his ambition and drive.

She followed him to where he was carefully stacking the syrup jugs in a pyramid and stood quietly behind him, surprising him when he turned.

"Oh," he quipped. "I didn't see you." He straightened up, dusted off his hands, and turned to face her. "I'm sorry I haven't been around much lately, but you knew I'd be awfully busy this month."

Blanche drew a deep breath and exhaled slowly, choosing to remain silent.

"What's wrong?" he asked, fidgeting with his gloves.

"You know," she said, intentionally trying to make him nervous. He was not wise in the ways of women and had no idea her stone face was a facade.

He ceased fidgeting and stood still, closed his eyes, and tilted his head.

She could tell he understood what this was about. "I'm willing to forgive you," she said, knowing he'd apologize for anything.

"You're so beautiful I can't think straight. I miss you like hell, too."

She was caught off guard. When faced with two choices, she always sought a third, and it seemed he did just that. He was thinking of her, which mattered to Blanche. Her eyes instantly regained their luster as she smiled and moved closer, draping a slender arm over his shoulders. She knew no one was at the front of the store since she hadn't heard the doorbell ring, and a glance over his shoulder revealed that the women in the back were preoccupied. She reached for his crotch with her free hand and squeezed, knowing he was dressed to the right.

Frank squelched, and the whites of his eyes grew wide.

"We'll discuss this later," she told him, brushing her button nose against his ear and feeling his rise. "You'll make it up to me," she said, turning and leaving him high and dry like a pirate ship wrecked on the Isles of Shoals.

37

The late afternoons in mid-March were warm enough for Mary and Gertrude to spend them on the front porch, sipping tea and discussing how long Mary might be away. Gertrude felt anxious because this wasn't about watching Roy for one afternoon; his mother wasn't going to Boston to enjoy a weekend getaway.

She held the baby and bonded with him, noticing that he had grown chubbier from his mother's breast milk. She hoped she could soothe him when he cried for the first time after his mother left.

The sky was partly cloudy, yet enough afternoon sunshine warmed the air above freezing. The towering elm trees lining the opposite side of the road in front of her house stood bare, their budding green leaves still a couple of weeks away. Only a few sparse patches of snow dotted the roadsides, and the only sounds came from acrobatic gray squirrels chattering and chasing each other through the barren tree limbs.

"Oh, look!" Mary pointed through the front porch balusters at a solitary, dusty gray bird perched on the lifeless, straw-colored winter grass.

Neither of them had seen the robin land, but there was no mistaking its bright burnt orange breast. They were surprised by its early return.

"Well, what do you know!" Gertrude exclaimed. "The first robin of spring!"

They watched the solitary bird hopping around on the dormant grass, listening for earthworms in the still partially frosted topsoil. After a few pecks here and there, it gave up and moved on.

"Where there's one, more will follow. Do you know what that means?" Gertrude let the question hang between them until enough time had passed that she assumed Mary either hadn't heard or wasn't paying attention. "It probably means we have about another two or three weeks before the crocus bulbs start to sprout… Mary Jane?"

The squawk of a crow diving into the trees to scare off the squirrels getting too close to its nest stirred Mary from her daydream. "Oh, sorry. I was watching the two squirrels running through the trees. The way they chatter and change directions so fast. The chaser becoming the chased…" she paused, smirking and closing her eyes. "Kind of reminds me of me and William, living and playing without a care in the world."

She turned to Gertrude and asked, "Is Roy awake?" After taking a sip of tea, she shivered. "How did the tea cool off so quickly?"

"No, dear, he's still fine." Gertrude turned to face her, making eye contact and holding Mary's attention. "I think we have only about two or three weeks left. That's still your plan, isn't it?"

"It is. I shall return to Canada and discuss with my mother her thoughts on us all moving here. I believe it could happen. There's plenty of work available, it seems."

She walked to the porch railing, holding her chilled teacup, gazing through the trees toward Flint's pond. She turned to Gertrude and said, "And I want us to bring William too. His mother will agree. I'm sure of it. I suppose she'll gladly give him up to forget about all that's happened and go on raising her daughters, whichever ones haven't moved on."

Gertrude was taken aback, momentarily speechless. Thoughts of uprooting a scandal and its makers from far away to come here raced through her mind. The plan she foresaw was to either send them away or separate them and find a loving, stable home for the boy, not exacerbating the situation by transplanting the seeds of scandal here to grow anew.

"It seems you've made up your mind, but don't you think that's asking too much?" Gertrude asked. "That wasn't part of the plan."

"Telling the townsfolk I was your niece from Concord wasn't part of the plan either," Mary said, looking at her shoes. "I'm sorry… I said that out of fear, not anger."

"It's okay. Neither of us has ever been tested."

Mary refocused on the treeline, setting her teacup on the porch railing. "It's out there somewhere in the distance, close by, isn't it? And at one time, it was almost home to Henry David Thoreau's cabin… William would love knowing this."

Mary excused herself, telling Gertrude she wanted to check on the baby to see if he was still sleeping, bring out the rest of the teapot to freshen their cups and take a moment to forget her lapse in grace.

Gertrude took the opportunity to stretch her legs and stroll around her Queen Anne porch, eagerly awaiting the arrival of spring colors. Her lilac bushes were her favorites, showcasing blue and purple shades against the white-painted porch. She kept those trimmed while allowing the whites to grow into tree form along the edges of the property. At the back of the cottage, bordering the woods and far behind her late husband Roy's rose garden, was a row of azalea bushes that she knew would bloom a deep ruby red as summer approached.

She descended the front steps and crossed the road, checking to see if her best-kept secrets had begun to sprout their base leaves, knowing it was still too early. By early summer, the forest floor across the road from her cottage would burst with pink lady slippers. The native orchids thrived in a dense patch a few yards from the road, far enough away that most passersby didn't notice, precisely what Gertrude and Roy wanted. The wildflowers were common yet elusive, and the bulbs would never transplant. Roy had tried several times to dig up just the bulb or an entire rootball to transplant in the back garden or near the azalea bushes, but they never took hold.

Mary returned to the front porch with the teapot. As she surveyed the porch, she called out, "Gertrude?"

"Over here, dear"—Gertrude waved—"other side of the road."

"What are you doing over there? Aren't your shoes getting muddy?"

Gertrude hadn't noticed her shoes and looked down to see them covered in thick clay sticking to the leather but not wet. "Oh dear," she said, trying in vain to shake some off. She crossed back to the edge of the gravel road and stomped most of it off, but she'd still have a cleaning job to do before supper.

"I brought more tea!" Mary announced.

"I'm coming back. No need to yell."

When Gertrude crossed the middle of the road, she caught movement in her peripheral vision and turned to see a horse walking up Sandy Pond Road toward her. The closer it got, and as she saw the man in his derby hat, the more she recognized it was Franklin, who must be riding Little Joe, though Franklin appeared to have four arms. It wasn't until they were almost at the corner of her lot that Gertrude noticed a woman was riding on Little Joe, sitting sidesaddle behind him.

It was Blanche Chapin.

"Good afternoon, Mrs. Gates," Frank said, tipping his hat. "We were just out giving Little Joe some well-deserved exercise since I had to pause deliveries this month."

"Franklin, it's a pleasant surprise to see you."

Blanche leaned around Frank. "Hello, Mrs. Gates," she said, gripping his waist to avoid falling off Little Joe, who stood eighteen hands tall.

"Ms. Chapin," Gertrude acknowledged, noticing that Franklin was still in his usual clothes, anchored by his silver pinstriped pants. It didn't appear Blanche had redressed him.

"Hey, Frank!" Mary called from the porch, holding up the teapot. "Would you like to stop for tea or coffee?" she asked as if it were her own house. "I didn't realize Little Joe had grown so much. I didn't see him the last time in the dark."

"Sure thing." He paused, turning his head toward Blanche.

Gertrude noticed Franklin whispering something to Blanche.

"Mind if we stop, ma'am?" he asked.

"That would be fine, Franklin."

Frank jumped off Little Joe as if he had been riding a horse all his life, then held up his hands to assist Blanche. He lowered her to the ground slowly enough not to catch her skirt in a downdraft.

"I'd certainly go for an afternoon cup of black coffee," he told Mary.

"Blanche, I remember you run the store. Can I get you some tea?" Mary asked. "That's a beautiful dress and boots for horse riding."

Blanche's blonde hair was tucked under a silk bonnet for the outdoor weather. She wore a dark velvet skirt, matching waistcoat, and knee-high black leather lace-up boots.

"Yes, tea, thank you."

Mary ducked back inside the house to brew both pots again.

"Franklin, could you fetch a couple more chairs from the kitchen?" Gertrude asked, and he followed Mary without excusing himself.

"Who's manning the store?" Gertrude asked.

"Carrie is. We waited until school let out."

"Oh, right. I guess that worked out nicely."

Blanche turned toward the front door and asked, "How long does it take to bring back two chairs in one trip?"

"Shall we?" Gertrude beckoned her up the steps to the porch sitting area, hoping they would stay for only a cup.

"Thank you."

Everyone appears to have remembered their manners today, Gertrude thought.

• • •

Mary was setting out pots for tea and coffee in the kitchen when she heard Roy fussing in the baker's rack drawer. As she picked him up, impressed that he had napped this long, Frank walked into the kitchen.

"He's getting so big," he said.

Mary had to admit he was looking more and more like a cherub. "Yes, he is."

Roy's fussing grew more desperate, and Mary placed him over her shoulder. "I should probably feed him soon," she admitted, glancing at the boiling kettles and hearing the whistle's slow start. "I'll bring out the tray when I'm done with him."

"Right… okay… I came in to grab a couple of chairs." Frank stammered, then left the kitchen with one chair in each hand.

• • •

Outside, Gertrude and Blanche engaged in small talk about store business and the syrup bumper crop. Gertrude made a mental note to pick some up for Gladys and wondered why Franklin hadn't thought to bring her any on this trip. It bothered her how easy it was to hold grudges over minor issues yet forgive larger ones.

Frank sidled through the door, careful not to bump the chairs against the door jamb. "Here are the chairs," he announced.

Blanche tilted her head, peering behind him into the doorway, and asked, "Where's Mary?"

"She'll be right out with the tray after feeding the baby."

The shadowy frostiness appeared to melt from Blanche's face. "Do you think she'd mind if I helped? Maybe she'd let me burp him?" she asked Gertrude.

"I'm sure Mary Jane would appreciate that," Gertrude replied, wondering how long it would take Blanche to get her hands on the infant. "Besides, she'll need an extra pair of hands to carry the drink tray."

Blanche lifted her hemline and dashed into the house like a horse out of the gate as if the horse were wearing heels.

"Franklin and I will keep ourselves entertained. Does that horse need water?" she asked him.

"Oh, he's fine. It's not like he broke a sweat hauling us up the road. He'll trim your yard, whether the grass is alive or dead. He doesn't care."

• • •

Mary stood at the stove with her son over her shoulder, gently bouncing him to keep him calm as she lifted the teapot. "Hi there," Blanche called from the kitchen doorway. Her voice was barely loud enough to catch Mary's attention without startling her.

Mary turned, announcing, "Oh, just in time."

Blanche looked around the kitchen. "I've never been in Gertrude's house before. It feels larger inside than it looks from the outside." She glanced between the stove and the soapstone sink, then back to the baker's rack. "This is a showcase cook's kitchen that belongs in an estate farmhouse. It's bigger and better equipped than my parents' kitchen."

"Her late husband went to Harvard and was quite a clever businessman, she tells me." Mary adjusted Roy, lowering him from her shoulder to her arms. "I was about to feed him," she said. "There's a drink tray on the baker's rack, second shelf, the silver one propped up."

Blanche lifted the tray and brought it to the table with a clean mug for Frank's coffee.

Mary noticed Blanche's height compared to the baker's rack and realized she was roughly the same height as Frank. She removed the whistling teapot and percolator from the gas burners and pulled out a chair, hoping she could feed the baby here without leaving the kitchen.

Blanche reacted when Mary reached for the pot to pour Frank's coffee. "Here, why don't you sit down and care for the baby? I'll pour that," she said, motioning toward the chair for Mary to sit in.

Mary sat with Roy cradled in her arms, waiting for Blanche to come around to the other side of the table to the stove. Instead, she took off her bonnet, gloves, and waistcoat.

"Were you going to bring coffee for Frank?" asked Mary, noticing Blanche drape her jacket over a chair and pull one out for herself.

"I asked Mrs. Gates if it was okay for me to help you with the baby." Blanche moved her chair to the end of the kitchen table and sat beside Mary. "She was fine with waiting, and Frank had already finished his second mug before we saddled up Little Joe. He's not in a hurry, but baby Roy seems to be."

Both women turned their attention to Mary's son, who was squirming and gnawing on his fingers, his tiny tongue working over his knuckles. Neither of which gave him the nourishment he craved.

"Okay," Mary conceded. "Hopefully, he only needs one side." She pulled her shirt up from the waistband of her skirt.

Blanche watched as Mary lifted her linen shirt to reveal her breast, dripping with milk, before the baby latched on, and then Mary draped her shirt back over his head.

They sat quietly, Blanche ogling and mesmerized.

"It's pretty unbelievable," Mary finally said. "All it takes is a minute for everything else in the world to disappear." She closed her eyes, feeling the warmth wash over her. "It feels like the warm summer sun wraps around you like a plush blanket. All the voices and worries rattling around in your skull drift away. The fog lifts, and you feel so calm and clear. It's truly relaxing."

Mary noticed Blanche discreetly sniffing the air while she focused on Roy feeding. She could see goosebumps on Blanche's arm as she seemed to clutch her own breast softly.

She lifted him out from under her shirt when she could no longer feel Roy suckling and wiped breastmilk from his lips with the tail of her shirt. She offered him to Blanche, supporting the back of his head and bottom. "Would you like to burp him? I don't think he—"

"Of course!" Blanche squealed, eagerly reaching for the baby. Absolutely! Like this?" she asked, tenderly taking Roy from Mary and carefully placing her hands to support his neck. She cradled him and said, "He's so adorable." She cooed. "Are you going to open those baby blues?"

"Let me get you a burp cloth. There's some in the drawer behind us," Mary said.

Blanche didn't hesitate and hoisted him over her shoulder. "Oh, don't worry about that," she said, nuzzling her nose into Roy's ear and then the swirl of his fine, wispy hair, inhaling deeply. "I might never wash this shirt again. Why do babies smell so wonderful?" She took several more intoxicating breaths. "Their skin is so soft, oily, and fresh." She gently patted his back in rhythm until he burped, startling her, and she laughed. "Oh my, that was quite a loud belch, just like Frank after a pint of ale at the tavern." She turned to look over her shoulder. "I don't feel any warm spit-up or sour smell, so I guess he's okay."

"He's a good belcher," Mary assured her.

"Do you think he wants more?"

"I dunno. He doesn't seem to be fussing too much now."

Blanche lifted him off her shoulder, placing both hands under his arms. She held him at eye level, facing her. "Aren't you the cutest little one?" She wiggled him from side to side until she had coaxed a smile from him.

He didn't only smile; he giggled for the first time.

"Wow, that's a first," Mary chimed. "I think he likes you." She readjusted her undergarment stay and tucked her shirt back into her waistband before cupping herself. "I'm not too keen on bigger breasts, especially ones that leak all the time." She tugged her shirt away from her skin, examining the front closely. "I'm washing my shirts morning and night!"

Blanche didn't respond except for a fleeting downward glance. "Bigger would undoubtedly round out a corset, but I'd sacrifice my looks to nurse a baby."

Mary didn't know how to respond, so she walked over to the stove to get the tea and coffee pots. "I think it's safe for us to head back to the porch. They're probably wondering what's taking us so long."

Blanche settled the baby back on her shoulder and found clean cloths and a blanket in the baker's rack drawer. "Is it okay if I hold him?" she asked. "There's no way I want to give up this little bundle of heaven yet." She shivered again, inhaling his soft, oily skin.

Together, they walked back to the front, with Blanche leading the way and Mary carrying both pots and two mugs, careful not to let anything slip from the tin tray.

• • •

"Look what I found!" Blanche exclaimed, spinning around so Frank and Gertrude could see little Roy's face resting on her shoulder. She asked Frank, "Do you know what they say about babies?"

An awkward smile swam around his face like a bucket of river eels.

"They're contagious," Blanche teased. "Maybe someday you'll make an honest woman of me, Franklin?"

The eels beneath Frank's face slithered from his lips to his eyebrows, displaying sheer panic.

Blanche's quip didn't escape Gertrude's notice. She bit her tongue, holding back an immediate reaction, but allowed the comment to simmer and stew.

The afternoon sun hung low on the western horizon, and the dry air temperature dropped swiftly.

Frank downed his lukewarm coffee in long gulps. "Blanche, whaddya say? Time to get going?"

Blanche picked up the pace of her baby bouncing and pouted. "Do we have to?"

"It feels like another freeze tonight, so sap's gonna be running tomorrow," Gertrude said, giving Franklin a way out.

"Yeah, gonna have to get an early start." He looked at Blanche and shrugged. "It's past Little Joe's supper time, and—."

"Wait!" Mary interrupted. "Blanche's clothes are in the kitchen." She rushed back into the house. When she returned, she told Blanche, "Here, I'll trade."

Gertrude noticed a wet shine in Blanche's eyes and hoped she wouldn't start crying when she had to return the baby to Mary.

Blanche pouted more but eventually relented. "He's so cute! I just want to eat him up." After securing her bonnet, coat, and gloves, she asked Mary, "Please feel free to stop by the store anytime to visit and let me know if you need any help or have a day off. I wouldn't mind."

"Thank you, that's very kind of you."

Gertrude and Mary held their collective breaths, watching Frank lift Blanche onto Little Joe's rump. She was not a petite woman, tall but not heavy, and he lifted her like a ballerina. He tipped his hat once he got back in the saddle without knocking her off.

"You behaving yourself, Franklin?" Gertrude asked.

"Yes, ma'am," he said with a smile, tugging on Little Joe's reins and heading back toward town.

"Is he telling the truth, Blanche?"

Blanche turned and replied, "Yes, ma'am."

They had only taken a few strides down the road when Blanche reached around Frank's waist and grabbed him through his pants. She leaned into his ear and whispered, "I want a baby."

38

On a busy Saturday morning, Carrie Chapin manned the postal counter. At the same time, her sister Blanche was being pulled in two different directions: helping stock the new spring clothes and selling off the last of the dark amber and cooking-grade syrup supply.

Frank had resumed home deliveries, so he was no help to them inside the store. Blanche could have used his help stacking clothes while she folded, a task that most men she had ever known were unable to master.

April showers and spring flowers were around the corner, and the Chapin General Store was bustling with townsfolk shopping in the warmer weather. Without jackets, they were eager to spend money on a new set of clothes for the year.

The madams Donaldson, Pierce, Smith, and Putnam had all gathered at the register, waiting for someone to ring up their jugs of syrup, dried navy beans, and molasses. Each held tightly to her family recipe for Boston baked beans but was quick to taste each other's batches at the church dinner while taking notes.

Blanche approached the counter, clutching her blonde hair buns as her long, quick-stepping gait threatened to jostle them loose.

Satisfied that her hair was secure and wouldn't fall, she noted everyone's items on the counter. "I see everyone is getting ready for tomorrow's after-church dinner," she said, rolling up her sleeves and grabbing a receipt pad.

Mrs. Evelyn Donaldson, Malcolm's wife, made her way forward among the other women she called friends. While she referred to them as friends, she often gossiped behind their backs whenever she and Malcolm were invited to dinner at the Tarbells, the wealthiest family in Lincoln who lived atop Summit Hill. George Tarbell funded the town library building, and the Donaldson family was the busiest home builders in the area.

Evelyn stated, "I'd also like a pound of salted pork."

Blanche, taller than the others, looked down and across the counter like a judge presiding over her courtroom. She replied to Evelyn, "I suppose you had a profitable sugar season."

Evelyn merely smiled. "You know we did because Frank delivered most of the local wholesale lots to the store. We also paid him for the export barrel deliveries to Boston, which accounted for most of our season's revenues."

Blanche was not impressed. "If you don't mind, I'll write up the receipts for the other ladies first, and then I'll fetch your pork from the larder."

"I guess we'll know whose pot is whose," whispered Rebecca Smith, snickering to her friend and coworker at the town library, Maria Pierce.

Carrie Chapin slid behind her younger sister and interrupted. "Do you recognize this name?" she asked Blanche. "It's addressed to Mary Jane Nutting in town, but there's no address."

The faces of the women outside the counter brightened. Their heads turned in unison at the prospect of overhearing the first fresh whispers of spring.

"I do," replied Blanche, wishing her sister had held off before spilling to the town gossipers.

"Who?" Evelyn asked, sounding like a hoot owl.

Gladys leaned over the counter and said, "I can deliver that if you'd like." She made it sound more like a statement than a question.

Blanche realized it was too late to pry, so she confiscated the small letter from her sister and handed it to Gladys after first noting the postmark from Halifax. She now knew the names of Mary's family and her mother. They were Canadian, a separated mother and daughter.

"Thank you, Gladys."

"What a cutie that baby boy is!" Rebecca exclaimed.

"He sure is, and she hasn't brought him to the library for a visit yet," she pouted.

"Why is this the first I'm hearing about these new town members?" asked Evelyn. "And a newborn baby! Where have they been hiding?"

"Who do you think brought the baby into the world?" Gladys asked.

All around, there is nothing but silence and stares.

Gladys defended herself. "Patient privacy should matter."

Evelyn, the last to know, asked, "Well, where is she living?"

"She's been staying with Gertrude Gates," Blanche said, delivering her answer, aware that Frank's tale about a visiting niece from Concord was a little white lie.

"And how do you know this?" asked Evelyn.

"She's been to the store, and we've visited. You should come into town more often, Evelyn."

All the women glanced at Blanche, but Rebecca was the first to inquire, "Have you been to visit?"

Blanche raised her hands, palms out. "It wasn't a big deal." She shot Carrie a look that, among sisters, she hoped would be understood. (Her sister knew about her relationship with Frank, a former student.) "Frank and I were out exercising Joe, and as we walked by, Gertrude and Mary were having tea on the porch. We stopped for a sip, that's all." She was finished justifying herself to these gossipers. "Well, if we're done with the Spanish Inquisition, I'll fetch your salted pork. A pound, you said?"

"Yes."

"Carrie, could you finish up here with these ladies while I fetch Mrs. Donaldson's pork from the larder?"

The general store was a central hub for cheerful gatherings on any given day. However, today, the air was thick and stale with jealousy and mistrust over nothing more than protecting family baked bean recipes and denying elder stateswomen the joy of seeing newborns. Tomorrow's faith supper was sure to be eventful, and by week's end, the entire town would learn about its newest residents.

39

Frank moved off Blanche, pivoting on his elbow, being careful not to squish her breast before rolling on his back and feeling the sweat on his neck blend into the pillow beneath his head.

"The entire town knows about Mary and Roy by now," Blanche lamented, her head resting on Frank's shoulder post-coitus. "I would make a good mother, don't you think?"

The Hunt tavern had been quiet on Sunday night. Most of the patrons Frank served during the week had filled up on their free faith dinners at the Congregational and Unitarian churches. There wasn't much room left for alcohol after gorging on beans and bread.

"Of course," he assured her.

He never imagined himself as a father, much less a good and decent one, but maybe he'd attempt to challenge his deceased mother for telling him that he'd never amount to much in life.

"I could be a good father, too," he said.

"I guess we'd all be snappy dressers," she quipped.

He poked her in the ribs. "I knew my pinstripes tickled your fancy!"

Blanche stared at the ceiling and, without turning to face him, asked, "Why did you bring her here to Mrs. Gates?"

He realized her mind was racing and sensed her increased breathing, her chest rising and falling, and her muscles tensing. She had been more intelligent than him since the day they met when she had called him a snake oil salesman.

And he was.

"Why did you lie to me, Franklin?"

"Because I didn't want you to think we knew each other. I didn't want you to doubt that was somehow my baby which you *know* it's not!"

"So you met her off the boat, and then what?"

He sensed a draft in the room and the warmth leaving the bed.

"There's a monstrous voice careening out of control in my head, and I need to know."

He made his case by telling her the truth. "She was alone on the wharf. She needed help."

"So you *helped* her?" she asked, propping herself up on her elbow and leaning to face him.

"She came to give up the baby for adoption."

Blanche sat up, covering herself with the sheet. "Then why didn't you send her to Boston City Hospital?"

He sat up to meet her at eye level. "Because I remembered Mrs. Gates and Gertrude. I knew they could help."

"You knew they could help?" She scrunched her face so tightly that it resembled a dried apple. "Are you out of your mind? You knew the Gateses as a kid! What do you mean you *knew* she'd help?"

He realized she'd been right all along—he was a snake oil salesman. "My mother was right," he admitted, holding her stare. Accepting his fate of losing her, he turned away before she could see him mewl. She was the most beautiful woman he'd ever met and, undoubtedly, would never meet again. Her uniqueness, stature, and youthful maturity made her one in a million. Seeing her perfect face and figure reminded him of the mythological goddess statues he'd seen in Carrie's schoolbooks. Every time her eyes caught his attention, he softened inside. He had never known what love felt like, but this had to be it.

Without her, his life was nothing more than an empty room with bare walls, a cold bed, and a chamber pot. With her, it was radiant, and every day felt like a celebration.

His cheeks were streaked when he faced her again, and the sheets were dotted with his teardrops. "She never thought I'd amount to much, so I set out to prove her wrong and show I could be resourceful. Maybe if Gertrude, with her church connections, could find a home or orphanage for the baby, there'd be something in it for me. So yeah, I was nothing more than a snake oil salesman, working a grift."

She crossed her arms, fully covering her breasts. "You're an idiot, Franklin."

He didn't deny it. "The problem was that I spent my whole life angry with my parents. I realized I only needed to prove my worth to myself, not my mother, and I did."

Blanche sat up straighter, crossed her legs beneath her, and pulled the sheet to herself. "You might still be an idiot, but I'm listening. Keep talking."

He offered no resistance when he felt her tug at the sheet. It was time to bare his soul. "It was you. It was all you," he confessed. "You made me want to hold my head high, smile, straighten my shoulders, and work two or three jobs to show you I was resourceful. You helped me. You changed me."

He knew he was about to start tearing up again and hoped he wouldn't lose all of his newfound self-respect if he fell into weeping. "You're the most beautiful woman in the world. Whenever I see you, I feel like there's a flock of gulls inside me. I love you all to pieces, Blanche Chapin." He broke down into emasculating sobs. "I don't wanna ride out on a rail."

"You might *still* be an idiot, but you're *my* idiot, and you're not going anywhere, so knock it off."

His caterwauling shifted to sobbing, then to a simmer, until he looked at her with occasional sniffles.

"You're not fooling anyone. Deep down, you might have a good heart. After all, you *did* help her, so that means something." She dried his face with a wadded corner of the sheet. "Otherwise, who knows, the kid might have ended up as nothing more than a guttersnipe."

Frank's burst of energy left him exhausted, and he slumped, resting his head in his hands. He had expressed his feelings and expected the next sound to be her getting dressed and leaving the tavern room for the last time, never to witness his weakness again. He would miss her warmth and softness, the fresh scent of spring flowers on her skin and in her hair the most. He promised himself to hold no bitterness, knowing it would only taint his memories of her, and he wasn't sure how much time he would give himself before leaving to follow her, but he knew the train station would be his destination.

She cupped his face in her hands and tilted it to meet hers. "Didn't you say I was the reason you stood up straighter?"

He barely nodded, ultimately obeying her, and sat up straighter.

"You love me? All to pieces?" Their faces were so close her eyes darted between his. "That sounds pretty serious," she said, searching their darkness for confirmation.

"I *do* love you, Blanche."

"So we agree, then, that I'm the most beautiful woman in the world?" she asked.

Frank found that to be a funny way to reciprocate.

"You were right all along. Gertrude really did have connections."

"She did?"

"You and I."

He suddenly felt chilly and wrapped them both in the sheet, letting their combined body heat warm the air beneath the covers up to their necks.

"There might be a little problem," he confessed.

Blanche tightened the sheet around their throats, twisting it enough for them to feel it. "How little?"

"Mary said she's heading home soon and leaving the baby with Gertrude."

Blanche relaxed her hold on the sheet. "And the problem is?"

"She said she'll come back for him."

"When?"

"I dunno. Weeks?" he guessed, raising his hands.

"Then we better think of a plan before that time comes."

Blanche stretched her arms above her head, letting the sheet fall to her waist. "I can't think right now. I'm hungry."

"But, it's late. Everything's closed."

She slipped out of bed and strutted nude to the door. "This tavern isn't closed. Aren't you the barkeep?"

Frank's chest felt like gritty sand and still ached from his sobbing. His eyes were swollen, and he wiped his face with the sheet to wash away the wetness. His head felt like Little Joe had kicked it.

"Yes, but we can't go downstairs naked," he murmured, aware that he was embarrassed only for himself.

Blanche turned, hands on her trim waist, one slender leg crossed over the other with her toes pointed. "It's Sunday night, and we have the whole place to ourselves. Who's going to see us?" she asked coyly. She pirouetted and opened the door without waiting for his answer, stretching tall enough to fill the entire height with her hourglass figure.

She glanced over her shoulder, peering at him with one eye, her tousled blonde hair cascading down her back. "Franklin, I love you too. You're sweet… but if you *ever* lie to me again, you will wake up without your plums."

After delivering her directive, she silently vanished, tiptoeing into the darkness of the tavern hall.

40

The early April weather was downright balmy. Sunshine in the high sixties during the first week dried the roads and stopped the sap from flowing. Green buds on maple trees and the return of red robins added the first hints of color to the outgoing winter slate gray empty palette.

Homes across Lincoln were shutting down their coal fires as folks packed away their winter woolen clothes for lighter cotton and linens and ventured outside.

Frank no longer needed his rabbit earmuffs, leather coat lined with fur, or matching rabbit fur collar. He only took off his trademark felt derby hat while sleeping. Blanche had once asked him to wear it while she was riding St. George, and he remembered having to hold it in place with both hands.

It had been a much happier week since last Sunday's near-collapse of his relationship, and his daydream smile went unnoticed as he dozed to the rhythmic clopping sounds of Little Joe's hoof steps pulling the carriage down Lincoln Hill.

After mass had ended, he picked up Mrs. Gates, Mrs. Putnam, and Mary at the Congregational church and let Little Joe find his way back into town. His elbows rested on his knees, and the reins hung limp in his hands. As they passed the store, the town's sights and sounds went in one ear and out the other. He was supposed to be thinking of a way to convince Mary and

Mrs. Gates to give Roy to Blanche, but he couldn't focus on two things at once—use his brain logically or let the fog of love dull all the hard edges.

Other horse carriages, some open and some closed, funneled couples and families around the central circle into and out of town. He was the only daydreaming driver who didn't return the courteous waves of others. He had no need or reason to pull on his horse's reins, as Little Joe knew every road and stop in town. Still, he stared at the general store's front door as if corned with liquor, hoping to see Blanche come through, waving and smiling.

She did not.

The common buzzed with children playing baseball while their parents sat on the green grass, reading books or enjoying lunch from picnic baskets.

"It's good to see so many children outside and playing instead of being cooped up for another day," Gertrude said, looking out the carriage's open window. She ran her palm along the edge of the window, then over the cotton-filled seat cushion between her and Gladys. "I suppose we're all spending enough for J.L. to afford a new taxi carriage." To Mary, who was sitting across from them, she asked, "Do they have taxi carriages in Halifax?" She reached over and squeezed her distracted friend's knee, startling her. "Mary? I asked you if Halifax has taxi carriages?"

Mary blinked several times, gathering her thoughts.

"Sorry, I didn't hear the question. I was watching the children play and imagining when Roy would start crawling and walking. The thought of him eventually running around frightens me. Look at how quickly that school-age boy got away from his caretakers," she said, gesturing out the carriage window.

"I suppose," Gertrude said, exchanging puzzled shrugs with Gladys before repeating her question, "But what about taxi carriages in Halifax?"

Mary heard the question this time. "Yes, there are, but they stink. There are so many of them, and the streets are full of horse shit."

An audible gasp escaped from both elderly ladies.

"It's always damp from the harbor air blowing up the hill. When we lived on the north shore, it was much cleaner."

"Mary Jane, mind your language," Gertrude scolded her. "We just left the church." Gertrude pointed to Roy, who was draped across Mary's chest in his sling, sleeping to the rhythm of the carriage. "Wouldn't you feel embarrassed if the first words out of his mouth were stinky and salty?"

Gladys chuckled as Mary returned her attention to the window.

Frank turned onto Sandy Pond Road, and the town common faded from view.

Reaching into her dress pocket, Gladys extracted a small letter. "This came the other day while I was at the store. Carrie didn't know Mary, but Blanche did, of course. I offered to deliver it," she said, handing it to Mary. "I didn't want to do it in church, thinking it would be best to wait."

Mary accepted the letter and opened it carefully. "It's from my mother."

"So Carrie and Blanche saw this?" Gertrude asked.

"A'yup," Gladys answered in the affirmative.

"So the cat's out of the bag?"

"I don't think the cat was ever really in the bag," Gladys told her longtime friend. "The other ladies in the store, including Evelyn Donaldson, Rebecca Smith, and Maria Pierce, all know Mary's down from Canada, which means the whole Unitarian flock knows by now."

"I never told anyone I was your niece, either," Mary said. "I need to go back as soon as I can. My mother's in trouble."

Gertrude and Gladys leaned forward.

Mary's face darkened and tightened with distress.

"What's the matter?" Gertrude asked. "Can you read to us what she says?"

Mary read Rachel's letter:

Dearest Mary Jane,

It was so good to hear from you! Agnes and I are so happy you and baby Roy are safe and well! There is much to discuss! I care not to frighten you, but Sarah Ann has found us here! She wants to see you but knows you are in America. We think it best you and Roy stay! We will be fine. You will be a great mother and I am so proud to know I am a grandmother! Love Rachel

I love you too! And baby Roy! Love Agnes

Mary lowered the letter to her lap, grief-stricken sobs shaking her body as her head bobbed up and down. "Reading the last line of the letter from my baby sister makes me dizzy. What if these are their last words to me?"

Gertrude reached out to Mary, handed her a handkerchief from her sleeve, and then rubbed her knees. "Nonsense. You'll see them soon enough."

Mary took the handkerchief and wiped her nose. "Thanks."

When she tried to hand it back, Gertrude waved her off. "Keep it until we get home."

"Who is Sarah Ann?" Gladys asked.

Mary pulled Roy tightly to her bosom.

"You shouldn't know. This town can only handle one scandal at a time," Gertrude said.

Gladys placed a hand on Gertrude's knee and pledged her loyalty to her lifelong friend. "I think you've visibly aged in the past three months while caring for your two new charges. And Franklin's unexpected return after twenty years hasn't helped either."

Gertrude leaned between the coach seats and whispered to Mary, "I think we should talk about this more before making a hasty decision."

Mary pulled Roy closer to her chest, crumpling the letter in her hand. She shivered despite the warm cross breeze blowing through the open coach windows and the heat of Roy's body against her.

Pulling back on the reins, Frank brought Little Joe to a halt in front of Gertrude's Queen Anne. He set the handbrake before climbing down from the driver's seat, knowing that only a black bear emerging from hibernation in the nearby woods would frighten the aging, mature horse.

When he opened the carriage door and saw three faces, he realized he had forgotten to drop off Mrs. Putnam first, who lived closer to town next to the library. It didn't make any difference to him, but he hoped no one would cause a fuss.

"Mrs. Putnam, I apologize. I should have dropped you off first instead of making you…" he began his insincere apology.

Gladys waved him off. "It's nothing, Franklin. Time spent outdoors with friends is better than being cooped up in a lonely house."

"Alrighty, much appreciated," he said, extending his hand to Gertrude. He pointed to the side handles, which she grabbed before stepping one foot down onto the uneven gravel roadside.

When it was Mary's turn to exit the carriage, she hesitated, exchanging awkward hand gestures with Frank until she finally sat back down, lifted Roy in his sling above her head, and handed him to Frank.

He took the baby from her, and for a split second, he felt the urge to take off running down the road, hauling his catch home to Blanche while leaving the women and Little Joe behind. Hearing Blanche's words in his head, 'You're an idiot,' helped him ignore his moment of insanity.

"He's getting heavier," he said, patting Roy's bottom and swaying from side to side. When he spotted Mary emerging from the coach, he felt puzzled again about what to do until she demonstrated quickly enough that she could manage, stepping down without waiting for a helping hand.

"Thank you for holding him," she said, extending her arms to take him back.

Frank noticed the crumpled piece of paper in her hand and reminded himself to tell Blanche that Mary looked defeated. He carefully handed Roy back to her, not wanting to accidentally drop him on the hard ground while trying to read her troubled face.

He tipped his hat, and they thanked him for the ride home. Gertrude gave him a nickel for his services.

After watching the ladies safely return to the house, he turned his attention back to the carriage. "Okay, Mrs. Putnam, next stop is home," he said, reaching to close the door.

Gladys slid closer to the window where Gertrude had been sitting and raised her hand, palm out, to get his attention. "How about when we're back in town, you take an extra loop around the back of the common and drop me off at the tavern instead?" she asked.

"I can do that," he offered. "But Sundays are, you know, kinda slow, and I'll be manning the bar. I wasn't planning to open until after I'd put away and fed Little Joe."

She closed the door. "That'll be fine, Franklin. I'll wait, and people watch."

• • •

"I should leave tomorrow," Mary said, following Gertrude into the house.

Gertrude stopped and turned. "Can we at least change out of our church clothes and start supper before jumping into the pond?"

"Yes," Mary conceded, taking a deep breath and holding it. She would have to do better, reining in her emotions. Gertrude was not her mother, and she shouldn't allow herself to treat her that way. No matter how much, as a teenager, she and her mother had gotten emotional with each other, her mother would always be her mother, but Mrs. Gates had only become her dear friend out of the kindness in her heart. Gertrude could at any moment ask her to leave her home and her life.

Mary exhaled and walked over to Gertrude, bowing her forehead to touch the older woman's shoulder.

Roy squirmed and kicked his feet between them, letting them know it was his feeding time.

Gertrude hugged her, gently removing the sticks from Mary's hair and letting her locks fall free. "I know you're scared," she reassured Mary, running her fingers through her thick hair. "Let's make a change. I'll make us some supper, and afterward, you can read Walden while I braid your hair."

"I could fall asleep right here, standing up," Mary confessed. It felt so good to have someone else brush her hair.

Gertrude smiled. "Oh, don't do that," she said, pushing Mary upright. She hooked a finger into the edge of the cotton sling and peeked at the growing baby boy. "Looks like one of us is impatient for dinner."

Mary pulled him from his confines and slung him over her shoulder, patting his bottom. "He's getting heavier. When can he start eating porridge?" she wondered, completely unaware.

Gertrude swatted his bottom. "He's only two months old. We should have asked Gladys, but I thought we had a bit more time."

"What could it hurt to try?" Mary asked. "If we make it thin enough, he can't choke… right?"

Gertrude and her husband had never had children of their own. "Let's not take any chances tonight before bed. I don't want to lose sleep worrying that something terrible might happen in the pitch dark. We can try it for his breakfast."

"Okay," Mary replied. "Besides, your talk of jumping in the pond made me want to run a bath." She felt good about herself again now that she was shedding all the baby weight. The only exception was that her breasts were now more prominent, and she couldn't wait to see the look on William's face when he noticed her.

"I bet I can feed Roy and give him a bath at the same time!"

Gertrude chuckled. "Well, go have fun," she said. "But don't fall asleep with him in the tub!" she warned. "If you're serious, I'll check on you every minute."

Mary kissed her on the forehead. "You worry too much, Gertie," she said, then noticed the stunned look on Gertrude's face. "Sorry, I meant Mrs. Gates."

The elderly mentor smiled. "Gertrude," she corrected her young protégé as she and her growing infant son bounded up the stairs to change their clothes.

Gertrude waited until Mary disappeared into her room, then told herself, "Someday, you'll be my age. Then you'll know what worry really is and wish you were young again."

41

Annie Hatt cherished the view from her kitchen window, which overlooked Owls Head Bay. The all-white, four-square house with gable ends and a porch faced southeast, maximizing the view of the rising sun as it moved southwest throughout the day over Palmers Cove. Initially, the house had four bedrooms upstairs, but Richard and his boat-building brothers expanded it after their daughters, Ada and Omeda, were born. Reuben and Robert now had their own rooms upstairs along with their sisters, while the two youngest sons, Henry and Clifford, shared a room.

The fishermen's homes along the eastern shore were modest dwellings, as most of a family's income from cod and lobster was reinvested into maintaining and expanding their boats, traps, and horses. There were no tourists and few roads, but the Hatt family had grown throughout the area over the past century, establishing a large community where the lumber, farming, and fishing industries supported one another.

Annie poured a cup of coffee into a mug nearly as large as a lobster bisque bowl, cradling it in both hands as she watched the rising sun illuminate the boats scattered across the bay.

Coastal grasses were turning green, brightening the rocky granite coastline of the eastern shore. Waterfront piers bustled with local fishermen, launching dinghies and ferrying supplies to their anchored flotillas. Within the first hour of daylight, everyone navigated up and down the shoreline inlets, hauling and resetting their lobster and cod traps. By lunchtime, the day's catch was cleaned and racked to dry in the afternoon sun.

Spring was Annie's favorite season in the Northeast. The days in April and May seem to pass quickly for her, leaving her with too little time to appreciate the vibrant colors of mayflowers, lupines, and pink phlox in the flower beds surrounding her porch.

May was also when Richard and their sons would finish the schooner order placed last fall, having worked on it all winter. The remaining tasks included completing the sails and getting the vessel in the water for sea tests. The income from the sale to the wealthy Cox family in neighboring Clam Harbor could help expand the work shed, allowing the boys to build two boats over the winter. She and Richard also discussed giving all proceeds from the sale to Reuben and Robert so they could set out on their own and start their businesses. Reuben would undoubtedly follow in his father's foot-steps, while Robert preferred being on the water fishing instead of sailing.

It was a rare morning that Annie could enjoy being alone while the rest of the household lingered in sleep. She and Richard had savored a night of lovemaking that left her glowing warmer than the giant mug of coffee held firmly in her hands. The end of the winter boat project also meant that late-night work hours in the shop and Richard's fatigue disappeared, allowing him to see and appreciate his duties to her as his wife.

She inhaled another noseful of rich, earthy coffee, enjoying the view out the double window at Cable Island, when she felt Richard's strong arms wrap around her waist. She barely managed to keep from spilling the coffee, having not heard his approach. When he swept her silver-sprinkled chestnut hair away from her neck and planted a kiss that trailed down to her bare shoulder, she had to lower the mug to the counter, or she would have dropped it.

At fifty, his large hands were strong from years of manual labor, and he used them to turn her shoulders to face him. His face was weathered, his hair a mix of salt and pepper, and she felt every wiry stubble around his lips when he kissed her good morning, full on the mouth.

She sank into his embrace as all the good feelings from last night washed over her. When he let her catch her breath, she said, "Oh my, who are you, and what have you done with my husband?" She reached up to wrap her arms around his neck and kissed him again. "Don't answer that. I like the new guy," she teased, fluttering her lashes.

"I smell coffee," he said, glancing over her shoulder at her oversized mug on the counter. "I see you got a head start."

"I'll make another pot. The boys will be up any minute now," she said, loosening her grip on his neck.

"One more," he said, gently pushing his hands and fingers through her silky hair, kissing her forehead and nose. "How can you smell the aromas with such a tiny button nose?"

"It's big enough to smell coffee but small enough not to smell all the fish."

"Last night was fun, eh?" He pulled her close, letting his hands wander over her light housecoat, squeezing and tapping her bottom.

"Okay, it's official. You're not my husband," she said, pushing him away.

Reuben stepped around the corner wall into the kitchen. "C'mon, I don't want to see that stuff." He walked straight to the pot on the stove. "You're too old for that nonsense now."

He looked up at his mother's copper pots and pans, some hanging over the kitchen counter, most over the butcher block island, and none on the stove. "Has breakfast not even started yet?" he asked.

"You're twenty-seven, and the last time I checked, I wasn't running a bed and breakfast," his mother replied.

She slipped her arm through Richard's. "We should go with the backup plan and help them move out. I'll trade a bigger workshop for less money, more privacy, and a smaller larder." Looking for his approval, she asked Richard, "What do you think?"

Robert walked into the kitchen. "I'm starving. What's for breakfast?" he asked, rubbing his eyes and nudging his brother's shoulder.

"Your mother's right… you're leaving… and you can take your brother with you," Richard said, his face expressionless.

Robert appeared confused as he glanced around the kitchen. "I'm not sure if you're joking or serious. What's going on?" he asked.

"Nothing. They want to be alone, and you and I are standing in their way," Reuben replied to his brother.

"Reuben Norman Hatt!" Annie reprimanded her eldest son.

Richard waved his hand over the smooth, hardwood surface of the butcher block. A subtle, sarcastic smile crept across his lips.

The move didn't go unnoticed by Annie. "Don't even think about it!"

"So, what exactly is the backup plan?" Reuben asked.

Richard dropped his smirk. "Your mother says when we collect the money for the Cox schooner, you two can have all of it."

It was Reuben's turn to look confused. "But I thought we were going to use that money to double the size of the workshop so we could each work on new boats next winter?" he asked.

"That was the plan," Richard admitted. "But what do you think? I believe you're capable of building your own boats now. You've come a long way since your first skiff."

Reuben gazed out the kitchen window and pointed toward the bay. "Yeah, you sank the first one I built. What if the next boat I build by myself sinks?"

Robert shoved his brother and remarked, "Yeah, remind me to buy my first from someone else. I'd rather not drown."

Richard reassured his sons, "We'll continue working together, building and fishing, so don't worry."

"It's not like we're sending you away to Boston!" Annie chimed in.

Reuben and Robert exchanged glances and shrugged their shoulders. "Maybe we could buy a couple of places or build on some lots down in Southwest Cove," Robert proposed.

Ada and Omeda strolled into the kitchen. "What's for sale?" Ada asked. She had her father's height and her mother's pretty face. Her hair was flaxen blonde like all the Hatt children when they were young, reminiscent of her mother's hair from her younger days. Ada assumed it would darken to the same shade of chestnut brown as she grew older. Her hazel eyes were framed by the same long lashes she inherited from her mother, and her smile showcased straight teeth. At nineteen, there was no shortage of suitors—all the local teenage boys were smitten with her. If only she could someday find one who wasn't a cousin or who didn't smell like fish.

Annie waved them into the kitchen. "Never mind, girls, come help me start breakfast," she said, reaching for a pan over the island. "Pancakes, breaded cakes, or omelets?" she asked everyone. Richard and the girls voted for omelets with lobster chunks, while the boys only wanted pancakes. Breaded codfish cakes were last on their wish list.

Fifteen-year-old Omeda offered to help, but with Annie and Ada around the stove and island, there were too many cooks in the kitchen.

"Of course, sweetheart," Annie said, gently rubbing her still-sleepy youngest daughter's cheek. "You can bring the eggs and lobster meat from the larder. You remember which crock we filled with last night's leftovers?"

Omeda shot her mother a serious look and said, "I've been eating lobster since the day I was born. My first baby toy was a dried lobster crusher claw. I'll know which crock is filled."

Annie did not appreciate her daughter's sass. "Don't give me that look, young lady, or all you'll get are the salted codfish cakes."

After Annie had playfully swatted her daughter's bottom and sent her to the larder as punishment, she turned to the men of the house and asked, "So how much longer on the sails and cabin?"

"The interior is finished," Reuben said, hoisting a whole sack of wheat flour onto the stone counter so Ada wouldn't have to lift it. "With everyone helping, the sail work stitching can be done in a week, and then we can get it into the water. We'll attach the keel and ballast and then tour the bay to ensure she doesn't founder. That'll take another week or so. It'll be ready ahead of the end-of-May delivery schedule."

Robert said, "She's our largest build ever, and at thirty feet, we'll need help getting her down into the water."

"Charles plans to sail her along the coast from the Cape to Yarmouth, so we should at least take her out in as many conditions as possible before handing her over to him next month," Richard said.

Charles Cox made his fortune in the Halifax shipping import and export trade, having built a summer home on the shore above Clam Harbor, south of the Southwest Cove peninsula. The schooner would be moored there in the summer and docked in Halifax during the winter.

"Has he given you a name yet?" Annie asked. "You need to paint and varnish it with three or four coats before launch."

"Yes, he did."

"Well?" Ada asked, "What's her name? Can I paint it this time?"

"Whose name?" Omeda asked as she returned from the larder, carrying a basket of eggs and a crock of lobster. "Are we getting a new baby sister?"

"No, no more babies," Annie reassured her. "So?" she asked Richard.

Richard didn't know why he was making everyone wait. "She'll be named the Ivy Maud," he told them.

42

All the gravel roads in and around Lincoln were leveled, thanks to a week of warm weather and the effort that Frank and Little Joe put into pulling a road grader. Little Joe did most of the hard work while Frank enjoyed the ride.

Mary had put away the boots she had borrowed from Gertrude, which were as clean and shiny as when she first wore them in January. Light cotton shirts and skirts with no layers were all that were needed for the early April weather in Massachusetts.

She walked along Sandy Pond Road, heading into town to shop one last time before leaving. She wanted to order a new baby carriage shipped from Boston, or maybe Blanche knew of a family that was growing out of one she could advertise at the store.

Roy slept in his home away from home, the sling draped across Mary's chest, but he was getting too big for it, and Gertrude needed an infant carriage.

The roadside was adorned with yellow and white daisies, and the leaves of the maple and elm trees had fully unfurled, filtering the midday sun onto the dusty road.

Mary felt like Goldilocks, strolling along and enjoying the weather and temperature as if they were just right. She daydreamed that William walked beside her, holding her hand as they made their way into town from their own Queen Anne cottage. It didn't matter that neither she nor William had jobs or money, but maybe someday soon, this dream will all come true.

In the distance, she could see the town center and the library beyond. The walking exercise did her good. Her legs, back, and shoulders were getting stronger, and she always carried Roy around. He now weighed as much as the total baby weight she had lost from her midriff.

The day was warm enough for her to unbutton her shirt cuffs and roll her sleeves to her elbows. Roy's weight in the sling tugged at her collarbone, so she adjusted his position and unbuttoned her shirt collar, exposing her neck. The air felt cool and refreshing against her neck, evaporating the sweat that trickled down her décolletage.

Looking up at the sun, she remembered to ask Blanche if she could try on a wide-brimmed ladies' summer hat and if the store had any in stock today.

Despite the breeze stirring up some gravel dust, she could still sense a floral scent in the air, perhaps from apple or cherry blossoms, though she wasn't sure which one.

She paused at the corner of Sand Pond Road, facing the town common, and listened to the sounds of laughter from people enjoying their day. The sun was warm, and the air was fresh. She couldn't wait for William to arrive to see Lincoln, knowing their first picnic would be a visit to Thoreau's cabin at Walden Pond.

As she stepped into the store, her eyes still adjusting from the bright outdoors, she felt hands on her baby before she could recognize Blanche.

"Oh, can I hold him, please?" Blanche asked, bouncing on her toes like a schoolgirl.

"Sure," Mary said, lifting Roy's sling over her head, feeling as if she might float away with the burden of his weight lifted from her.

Blanche quickly removed him from the sling and handed it back to Mary before hoisting Roy onto her shoulder and patting his bottom. "Oh dear, he's getting so big," she said, cradling the back of his head and nuzzling the folds of skin on his neck.

Mary couldn't help but feel jealous as she watched Blanche kiss her baby's ears and twirl the tufts of his blonde hair. The thought of not seeing him for what she was sure would be weeks until her return with her mother, siblings, and William made her pause to wonder if she was making the right decision. Maybe she should stay and try to convince her mother through letters, but Rachel had already told her to stay, and now she had time to solidify her stance. Her gut feeling told her that she could only change her mother's mind if she confronted her in person.

Forge ahead with her plan and stay strong.

"Ms. Chapin?" she asked, interrupting the intimate moment that belonged to her, not Blanche, who was kissing his delicate outer ears with the tip of her tongue, clearly savoring the sweet oil of his soft skin.

Roy looked entirely content, sucking on his ring and middle fingers while a bit of drool dampened the white linen of Blanche's shirt. With his other hand, he clutched her ivory cameo brooch.

Mary reached up to pry Roy's fingers off the brooch, not wanting him to tug on Blanche's shirt collar, but she turned away slightly. "Oh, it's okay," she said, tilting her chin toward Roy, who was gripping her throat.

"I didn't want him to pull on your collar," Mary said, trying to free Roy's fingers. She glanced at Blanche's cameo brooch. "Whose portrait is that, if I may ask?"

Blanche gently covered Roy's fingers with her own, clutching his tiny hand along with her mother's cameo. "That's my mother. She passed away a few years ago."

"I'm sorry to hear that."

"I wear her every day and touch her when I need a sign or… if I'm feeling worried. It's self-soothing."

"A worry stone. I sometimes feel that way, too. I have a silver brooch that belonged to my mother, which I use as my worry stone." Mary held up her index finger and thumb, making a rubbing gesture. "I swear, during the trip down, I might have rubbed the color right off!"

Blanche slowly rubbed her thumb pad over Roy's fingers, still clutching her mother's cameo. "It might be a sign that my mother is reaching out to the innocent."

The two let a brief, uncomfortable lull pass between them. Blanche was in no hurry to steer the conversation forward until Mary asked, "Do you think we could order an infant carriage from Boston, or maybe I could place an advert on the entrance wall seeking a hand-me-down from a local family no longer in need?"

Blanche narrowed her gaze, seemingly studying Mary's bottomless dark brown eyes. "That depends on how soon you think you need it." Blanche grimaced, slowly twisting from side to side, and hugged Roy tighter to her breast. "You look good. I imagine carrying this little fellow around"—she gently bounced Roy higher onto her shoulder—"why, hefting him now, he's no longer little, is he? And it's pretty good exercise."

"For me, yes, for Mrs. Gates, not so much."

Blanche appeared to study the shorter young mother's face. "Well, Gertrude is much more frail than we are."

"I'm leaving Roy with her until I come back with my family and…" she paused, turning away from Blanche. She felt slightly judged as the taller, older woman looked down at her.

Blanche exhaled slowly, and a warm, glowing smile brightened her cheeks. "I'd be so honored to help Gertrude care for Roy while you're away for as long as you need. If we can't find her an infant carriage as soon as possible, I could have Carrie run the store, and I'd help Gertrude in whatever way she needs me. Unless…" she said, pausing and glancing up.

Mary could sense Blanche's strong desire to volunteer to care for Roy. She trusted Mrs. Gates but hadn't spent enough time with Blanche to establish a natural bond. Feeling conflicted, she glanced at Roy on Blanche's shoulder, smiling, bouncing, and carefree.

"I can talk more with Mrs. Gates," she conceded. "I think the time is close enough for me to leave, and he's probably ready to wean and start eating porridge, but Gertrude can't carry him outside or even up and down the stairs. We talked about turning her sewing room into a nursery."

"It seems she needs help."

Mary agreed.

"What if before you leave, I spend the day with Roy or only for a morning or an afternoon?" Blanche suggested, arching her finely groomed eyebrows.

Mary stood her ground, hesitant and unwilling to rush her answer as a group of customers flooded into the store in single file, and Blanche was the first to balk, offering, "I'll take care of the carriage. You don't need to worry about it, even if I have to go into the city to find a new one."

Mary wasn't ready to accept Blanche's offer to spend a day with her son as she watched each customer in the group file past her. She needed to touch her son's feet or pinch his cheek. When she reached out to take him from Blanche, she offered no resistance. "Thank you," Mary said, accepting Roy while Blanche tried to unhook his tiny fingers from her mother's cameo. Despite being small, he had a surprisingly firm grip.

"I'll let you know what I find out, probably by tomorrow evening," Blanche said, reluctantly releasing his fingers.

"That sounds great, and we'd really appreciate it," Mary said, tucking Roy back into the chest sling, eager to leave before he was fully settled. "I'll discuss it with Mrs. Gates, but okay, maybe we'll take you up on your offer. We'll see what happens when he tries a little solid food."

Blanche's face lit up. "Of course, there's nothing to worry about," she reassured, holding the front door open. "I'll stay in touch."

43

Mary's shoulders and back were relaxed as she hurried back to Gertrude's house, kicking up road dust. Before starting supper, she wanted time to feed Roy and discuss Blanche's proposal.

Gertrude was sipping afternoon tea on the porch when she spotted Mary. "The way you're high-stepping home tells me my days of walking faster than a box turtle are behind me."

Mary veered off the road, avoiding the Queen Anne's front stone walkway, and was about to mount the porch steps when Gertrude halted her with a hand.

"Hold on, missy. Wipe the dust off your shoes and fluff your skirt before coming inside."

Mary returned to the short grass of the front lawn and did her best to wipe her shoes clean, at least well enough to finish after supper with a rag. It wasn't easy to check her hemline since she couldn't bend over enough, holding Roy, to see if she'd shaken everything off.

"All right, that's good enough," Gertrude conceded. "At least as much as I can see through these." She tugged her wireframe spectacles off her ears and wiped the lenses on her apron. "What's the hurry?"

Mary stepped onto the porch and settled into a rocking chair. Now experienced, she deftly maneuvered Roy out of the sling with one hand while tugging her shirt free with the other, latching her baby to her breast.

Gertrude looked up and down Sandy Pond Road. "You might want to cover up. I know traffic is few out this way, but I still don't believe nursing is something done outside the home."

Mary glanced at her friend, wiggling her lips while keeping them pressed together. Sometimes, she felt like a sassy rebel, and this time, she quietly rebelled and pulled the cloth sling over Roy's head, covering him completely. If anyone happened to ride by, they would be none the wiser that anyone else was on the porch apart from the two ladies enjoying afternoon tea.

"I walked to the store and asked Blanche about getting an infant carriage," Mary admitted. "I know you can't do what I just did, and I don't want you to feel like you have to try either."

"Your reasoning is solid."

Mary scanned the road in front of the house, biding her time. "What would your thoughts be if Blanche were to help you while I'm away?"

Gertrude sipped her tea, gazing across the road where her lady slipper bed still lay dormant. "I'm upset with myself for not reaching out to the Donaldsons sooner. I had hoped you would reconsider your plan." She took another sip. "The Donaldsons are a good family with roots in Nova Scotia, and their farms are located outside town, away from gossip-mongering."

Mary kept listening as Roy continued nursing.

"I meant to speak privately with Evelyn to establish either a short-term or long-term arrangement for Roy's care, but the Chapins are a capable family," she relented, continuing to stare across the road.

She turned to face Mary and spoke softly, "If you had fallen out of the sky onto my doorstep without Franklin, maybe Blanche would have been a more logical choice."

Mary knew Frank had only been a gentleman since he shared his salted popcorn and peanuts with her on the dock. "I don't know if it's fair to judge someone by their past actions," she countered, unaware of their entire history. "You knew him years ago as a troubled teenager, but people can change, right? We change, that's what Thoreau wrote."

Gertrude focused her gaze on the lump beneath Mary's shirt. "Franklin came from a troubled home, and his parents couldn't keep him on the straight and narrow. His formative years forced him to be street-smart. I'm not sure if the Franklin you know now is the same street-smart Franklin I knew back then."

"But it's been twenty years," Mary insisted, holding her ground. "He was kind even before he met Blanche. They've been dating for almost three months. Maybe she's been good for him."

Gertrude didn't argue. "Okay, I'll let Blanche help, but… transplanting a lady slipper rarely succeeds. Mother Nature must have her reasons."

Mary watched her friend finish her tea, puzzled. "She mentioned that Carrie could help take over duties at the store."

"It's a family store, but Carrie is still the working school principal." Gertrude remained focused on the elm trees. "When Franklin was here, the school would close from March to May so the children could help with the spring plantings, then stay open until it was time for fall harvest."

Mary's eyes widened slightly, counting the weeks in her head. "So it works! That's why we saw all the children playing in town!" she exclaimed, surprising Roy. She repositioned him to the other breast without looking. "It'll give me a month. I'll hardly be gone, and you won't even have time to miss me."

Gertrude closed her eyes and smiled subtly, the afternoon sun on her face reflecting off her silver hair.

"We should think about how we're going to make his thin porridge tonight so we'll be ready in the morning," Mary said. "I'd like to leave as soon as possible, and I have no idea how many days he needs before we can be sure he'll be okay."

Gertrude opened her eyes. "I should think at least a week or fortnight," she suggested.

"I don't want to wait a fortnight," Mary argued. She detached Roy and slung him over her shoulder, proceeding to burp him while letting her shirt-tails hang out.

Gertrude turned away, huffing. "Even being partially undressed outside the house makes me anxious. I hope younger generations will uphold a sense of propriety."

Roy burped and spit up on Mary's shoulder, with some of it dripping down onto the porch floorboards.

Mary apologized, feeling the wetness soak through her shirt. "I guess I bounced him a little too much, being excited and all." She turned to look down at the drops and little puddles. "I'll clean that up."

Gertrude seized the opportunity to usher the disheveled young lady back inside. "Let's get you cleaned up. I'll take care of the porch."

"Okay," Mary agreed. "While we're getting supper ready, we can talk about when Blanche can take Roy for a day."

Gertrude hesitated, freezing in a slumped posture as she rose from her rocker. "A day?" she asked. "We agreed to help—not take."

Mary reached to hook her arm around Gertrude to help her fully stand, but the older woman shrugged her off and walked into the house. From the foyer, Mary heard, "We'll discuss this later."

44

Carrie Chapin placed a note in the mail slots of all her students' parents, asking if anyone had an infant carriage available to borrow, barter, or purchase. Dorcas Brown, one of Carrie's teachers at the Center School, had offered hers, but she no longer needed it as her youngest son was now her student.

Blanche pushed the empty carriage down Sandy Pond Road. She had set a one-week deadline for someone in town to volunteer; otherwise, she would have gone to Boston herself, spending top dollar on the best she could find.

She walked alongside Frank, not letting go of the maternal feelings that arose from gripping the crossbar and imagining little Roy's smiling face looking back at her. She intended to keep the handoff brief, wanting to spend as much time as possible with Roy today, keeping him all to herself.

She was in her own little world, lost in her thoughts and unaware she was walking next to Frank when he reached a hand towards the carriage and placed a two-finger grip on the edge of the crossbar to remind her of his presence.

She swatted his hand away.

The elm tree canopy had filled in over the road, creating a green tunnel to walk through as bright rays of sunlight speckled the roadway. The squeak of the carriage wheels and the synchronized footsteps were drowned out by the sounds of blue jays and crows as the birds flitted through the leaf canopy and circled above the treetops.

As Gertrude's cottage came into view, with its pink peonies, Frank broke the silence and asked, "Are you excited? Today's the day."

Blanche couldn't be bothered to turn and face him. "Of course I'm excited," she replied, a hint of annoyance in her voice.

"It's going to be a great day. You're going to shine brighter than the sun," he said in a higher octave than usual, attempting to sound convincing. "I love you, Blanche Chapin."

Blanche felt her shoulders relax. Frank was right. It would be a wonderful day. She knew she would be glowing until the moment she had to return Roy to Mary later that afternoon, and she would walk much slower bringing him back, that's for sure.

She turned and smiled genuinely at him. "I love you too, Frank Hosman," she said, knowing she owed him this moment that would never have happened without him.

Frank fell out of step, growing weak in the knees as he gazed into her eyes, which were the same color as the leaves backlit by the sun. He removed his derby and placed it on her head, stroking her hair.

She had French-braided it that morning, letting it cascade down her spine. She felt his fingers linger on her ear and trace her jawline. Her face tingled as she felt his fingertip glide from her earlobe to the cleft of her chin. Battling her emotions, she pantomimed—posing, smiling, and puckering her lips into kisses—while running a hand around the brim of his hat, pulling it down over her eyes, putting on a show for one.

Frank clutched his chest and pretended to collapse. "You're so beautiful it kills me," he gasped.

Blanche forced herself to relax as they approached Gertrude's front porch and found it empty. "Okay, no more fooling around. It's time to get serious." She handed him back his hat, which he held, expecting the ladies to emerge from the house.

Blanche walked up the front steps and knocked gently on the door frame.

"Should I leave the carriage here or take it onto the porch?" Frank asked.

Blanche turned to face him, shrugged her shoulders, and held her hands out, palms up, silencing him with a wave as the door opened from the inside.

"Good morning," Mary greeted them with a smile. "We didn't expect you this early, but I suppose you wanted to get a jump on the day."

Blanche couldn't hide her excited smile and enthusiastic nodding.

Mary stood on her tiptoes, peering over Blanche's shoulder. "Hello, Frank," she greeted him. "Are you coming in?"

He waved his hat. "I'd better stay out here and watch the carriage. It probably isn't something a passing horse thief would take a shine to, but… just in case it rolls away or the wind takes it."

Mary and Blanche exchanged glances, shrugged, and then stepped inside.

In the kitchen, Gertrude washed the breakfast dishes in the soapstone sink. When she heard their voices, she turned. "Good morning, Blanche," she said, drying her hands on her apron. "Big day."

"Good morning, Mrs. Gates. Yes, it is. I'm so grateful to help!" Blanche focused on the baby in the baker's rack drawer, feeling like she might jump out of her skin. It took all her internal strength not to rush over and grab him with both hands.

Hoping to appear subtle and in control, she took a slow, deep breath. She noticed everything arranged on the kitchen table: a mason jar filled with a brown liquid she assumed was thin porridge, a teaspoon for feeding, burp cloths, cloth diapers, two extra safety pins, extra linens, tinctures she recognized as lanolin ointment she sold in the store, knitted booties, a matching hat, and a canvas satchel bag.

"I think this is everything you'll need for today," Mary said, pointing to the items on the table. "And hopefully, it all fits in the bag. I call it my baby bag." She began packing and identifying each item. "His porridge—he'll probably want a couple more feedings today. Extra diapers, pins, clothes in case he has an accident, and this is an ointment for his bottom if he gets a rash, but you already know that since you sell it. And his hat and boots for when he's outside." She managed to fit everything into the bag. "I guess that's it," she said, pausing, tapping her temple with a finger. "Gertrude? Anything else I might have missed?"

The older woman had been watching instead of washing dishes. "Tissue paper? I don't think you want them carrying dirty diapers and clothes."

Mary walked toward the kitchen door. "Okay, I'll grab some from the bathroom."

Blanche was becoming impatient and still hadn't had a chance to hold the baby. "I have plenty at the store, so don't worry. Besides, it'll be Frank's job to rinse out any dirty diapers." She forced a laugh.

Gertrude redirected her focus to the dishes in the sink and muttered softly, "I wish I could be a fly on the wall to see Blanche Chapin change her first dirty diaper."

Neither Blanche nor Mary seemed to have heard Gertrude's snide remark.

"Oh, I almost forgot," Mary interjected, pointing to Roy in the drawer, still napping after breakfast. "The best advice I can give you from experience is when you change his diaper, either lean to the side or keep your hand in front of him as a shield. Otherwise, he'll get you."

Blanche didn't think anything could ruin her day. "Or else?" she questioned, pushing herself to laugh again.

"Or else he'll spray you right in the face," Mary said. "Believe me, you only let that happen once. The first time he got me—both eyes and mouth! It wouldn't stop! I had no idea a baby that small could shoot out so much pee! It's funny now, but it wasn't funny then!"

Blanche willed herself not to react, only to smile. She was sure that Mary was being overly dramatic. "Advice taken," she said, stepping closer to the drawer where she hoped to finally get her hands on her little boy.

Mary picked him up before Blanche could ask. "Let's check his diaper one last time," she said, moving him to the table. "I don't smell anything, but let's make sure."

Blanche felt like a newborn colt on wobbly legs as she watched Mary deftly undo the safety pins in each hand at the same time, pull his diaper back quickly and then forward to shield his tiny button penis in case he peed, and then refasten each pin.

Blanche hoped Mary did not see her blank stare.

"Don't worry, it's all practice," she reassured Blanche, picking up Roy and placing him over her shoulder. "I guess that's it. Walk you out?" she asked, handing Blanche the baby bag.

Mary led the way through the foyer, pausing inside the front door. She turned to Blanche and said, "I'm trying to convince myself not to have second thoughts as I wrestle with instincts beyond my control. I miss my mother and sister. They're missing out on Roy's growth, and he's changing every day. They won't have any memories of him as a baby."

Blanche remained unempathetic as she watched Mary's face contort, struggling to hold back tears. She hoped Mary wouldn't cry, as feigning consolation was not her strong suit. She didn't care who Mary's family was; they were not the foremost plight between her and the baby she coveted.

Once Mary regained her composure, she pushed open the front door and stepped onto the porch. "Hey Frank, sorry we kept you waiting," she said apologetically. "I had to do one last diaper check." She poked Roy's bottom. "He's all set to visit with his Uncle Frank and Auntie Blanche," she said, smiling and winking at them.

She lifted Roy off her shoulder, holding him at arm's length, admiring his father's eyes staring back at her. She covered his face and cheeks with kisses before settling him into the carriage and wrapping him in a blanket cocoon.

Blanche smoldered at the Auntie reference and stepped behind Mary, handing the baby bag to Frank. She glared at him, her eyes boring into his, making it clear that she was not amused.

Frank's shoulders trembled slightly.

"So, do you have any plans for the day?" Mary asked.

Blanche pushed her demons aside, crafting a smile that peeked through her dimples. She tilted her button nose toward the clear sky and wiggled her pouty lips as if considering her options or waiting for a sign. "I don't know," she replied coyly. "Maybe we'll visit the girls at the library, swing by the store, stroll around the common, and have lunch on the grass."

"Sounds like quite a parade," Mary said.

"It'll be a Roy town tour parade," Blanche countered.

Gertrude stepped out of the house onto her porch, wringing her hands in her apron, and gave a curt wave. "I'll have supper ready when you bring him back before sunset. There'll be plenty if you want to stay and tell us all about how things went," she said. Her words sounded more like a request than an offer.

Frank perked up at the mention of a free meal and waved back at Gertrude in acknowledgment. "I'm sure it'll beat anything we could scrounge up at the tavern."

Mary reached into the carriage and gave her son another gentle rub on his cheek. "Have a fun day, and don't miss me too much. Okay, Boodle?" She turned to Blanche and Frank. "I call him Boodle. I have no idea why that name popped into my head," she admitted with a shrug. "I just think he looks like a little Boodle."

Blanche would give him a nickname of her own. "Cute," she said, gripping the carriage's crossbar tightly and looking at Frank. "Shall we go? Ready for an adventure?" she asked him, catching herself before she nearly said *our* adventure.

Frank nodded. "I was told I'd be the sole passenger on this outing."

Blanche winked at him. "Oh, we'll see."

They trundled down the road towards town.

Mary waved goodbye, tears streaming down her cheeks as Frank, with Blanche, pushing the carriage holding Roy, rolled past the property line. She leaned forward, poised to run after them, when an arm wrapped around her waist, holding her back. "How long am I going to stand here?" she asked.

"Just breathe. They'll be back in no time," Gertrude said. "I'm betting they bring him back after lunch. The first time little Roy lets loose his stinky porridge breakfast, neither one of them will be able to cope. I bet they'll hightail it to Carrie for help, and then it'll be all over town by the morning paper," she said, giving Mary a small hug.

Mary wiped the tears from her face with her hands. "You think so?" she asked her friend.

Gertrude took a handkerchief from her apron and handed it to Mary. "One has street smarts, while the other was raised with a silver spoon."

Mary watched them move along the road as Blanche's white linen shirt swayed against the gray gravel. She stepped off the porch and faced down the road, taking a step and cupping her hands around her ears.

•••

Blanche couldn't take her eyes off Roy as she pushed the carriage along, never once looking to stay on course. She didn't even realize Frank was focused on the road, watching for oncoming horse carriages and adjusting to stay centered. She was too absorbed in her obsession to bond her face and the sound of her voice with her baby.

She visualized what she wanted, desired, and coveted, willing everything to come true.

Roy smiled and giggled at her cooing.

Her breasts felt tender, softly swaying beneath her shirt. She swore they felt more engorged with each deep breath.

She told Mary the truth when she said she and Frank would visit the girls at the library. She wanted to browse for books on motherhood and had no intention of sharing her baby with Rebecca and Maria.

There was so much to plan.

"We need to find suitable housing," she told Frank. "As much as I've enjoyed living with you above the tavern and away from my family's generational house, I can't endure either of those while raising my child." Noticing Frank's sharp intake of breath, she stopped pushing the carriage and turned to face him. She needed to rein in her emotions and take a slower approach to motherhood. She was focusing only on the outcome, not the journey. A journey that must include Frank, or else she'd be nothing more than Mary. *Our* child," she corrected herself, pulling him into a kiss by tugging on the lapel of his vest.

He met her gaze.

"We both made good money last month. Isn't that enough for a down-payment?" he asked her.

"I don't want to work at my family's store anymore. I want to be a stay-at-home mother." She did not want to sound cruel. "And I don't want you working two or three jobs either. You can't sustain that pace."

He turned away, looking straight down the road.

She already knew the answer but challenged him. "If I… *we…* want to keep my family's monthly allowance, then you know what needs to be done."

"With your eyes and perhaps one day a face framed in silver instead of blonde, you are indeed one of a kind and possibly the prettiest woman I've ever seen in New England… or Canada. Your beauty will undoubtedly outlast me."

Well said, she thought, flattering.

With a blossom-scented breeze on their faces and the morning sunlight shining in her hair, glinting in her eyes, he made his offer, "I'm sorry that I won't age as gracefully as you, Ms. Blanche Chapin, but if you can look past that and forgive me, it would be my pleasure to make you an honest woman and mother, making me the happiest, proudest husband in this whole town."

It wasn't the proposal she expected, nor was it close to anything she had dreamed of as a little girl, but he certainly had his own sense of style and directness. Fortunately for him, she didn't need his money.

"Why, Franklin Hosman, for a former snake oil salesman, you sure do say the sweetest things." She extended her hand, which he took gently, and kissed. "So you're the husband, and I'm the honest woman?"

Frank blushed. "I know I'm an idiot and never intended to fall in love and lose my pants, but will you marry me and be my wife, Blanche Chapin of Lincoln, whose face could launch a thousand ships?" he asked, kissing her hand again and hoping to hide his embarrassment.

"I believe that will work out just fine," she admitted.

"Is that a yes?"

"Yes, it's a yes."

Roy raised his legs and thumped them down in unison inside the carriage, flailing his arms and chortling.

"I believe the little fella agrees with your decision," Frank said.

Blanche smiled, visualizing what she wanted, desired, and coveted. She was willing everything to come true as she pushed the carriage closer to town, distancing herself from *her* son's biological mother—a mere nuisance for the moment.

45

Blanche felt grateful to see the library's front steps as they made their way through the town center along Trapelo Road. The dull ache in her arms and legs didn't bother her as much as the pinched toes in her boots. She hadn't walked this far since her schoolgirl days, going to and from school up and down Lincoln Hill. The boots she wore today had the lowest heels of all her shoes, but she still reminded herself to find something wider and more comfortable at the store or in Boston when Roy was old enough to travel by train.

It was a tight fit, but the carriage managed to squeeze between the wrought iron hitching posts at the entrance to the library's walkway. The nine stone front steps were too steep, marking the end of the line for the carriage.

"I'll be quick," Blanche told Frank. "I'll take him inside, and you can sit and nap in the shade." She pointed to the chestnut trees east of the library, near the cemetery, and Frank gave a curt nod. "Besides, you don't want to hear Rebecca and Maria gushing about baby talk anyway."

She kissed him, then scooped up Roy, placing him over her left shoulder. He was alert but quiet, his eyes on the trees swaying in the warm spring breezes. She pulled a cloth from the bag and draped it over her opposite shoulder, then settled Roy snugly into place and gave his bottom a quick pat.

"When I come back, we can check his diaper by the trees, then head to the tavern to open it and freshen up." She kissed him again before he could object.

He watched her climb the library's front steps, hitching his breath with each step until she reached the top landing, where she pirouetted, extended her arm, and wiggled her left ring finger.

He tipped his hat and admired the mason's craftsmanship on the library's southern-facing exterior. If he had mastered the skills needed for that job, he could afford to buy her the big diamond she deserved.

Blanche understood that they needed a down payment for a house, and perhaps they could arrange a deal with Mac Donaldson to help build their home. As she watched him pushing the empty carriage across the grass, she figured he wouldn't be able to nap while worrying about money.

"Oh! Look who's here!" shouted Rebecca Smith, standing behind the librarian's front desk. She turned and vanished behind the oak bookcases, reappearing from around the side of the desk, making a beeline for Roy. "Is that who I think it is?" She peeked around Blanche, looking behind her. "Just yourselves today?"

Blanche answered her nosy question, "Just us, thanks."

"His eyes are open! What a beautiful blue! He's going to be a heartbreaker when the girls start swooning over him someday."

Blanche smiled and gave Rebecca a brief glimpse of the baby while her above-average height restricted the librarian to a fingertip handshake.

"Thanks for stopping by. Maria and I have been anxious to see how fast he's growing—and how he has! Is Mary with us today?"

Annoyed at having to repeat herself, Blanche shook her head and looked around, expecting Maria Pierce, the co-librarian, to appear from between the bookshelves at any moment. "I'm taking care of him today while she's preparing for her trip. I stopped by to browse some books."

"Oh, well, that's very kind of you. Would you like to sit down and read some children's books?" Rebecca asked with a hint of envy in her voice.

Blanche hesitated, choosing her words thoughtfully. "Could you perhaps direct me to the parenting or infant section? I mentioned to Mary that I would bring her and Mrs. Gates something informative to read about infants at this age."

"I see, yes, of course." Appearing slightly snubbed, Rebecca donned her librarian face again and pointed down the open hall. "We have a shelf of all the published issues of Godey's Lady's Magazine. Right this way," she said, taking the lead.

Rebecca paused near the bookcase beside the library's gothic fireplace, an iconic feature visible east of the main entrance. The mid-April weather was warm enough that a fire was no longer needed. She knelt and pointed to the two lowest shelves of the oak case. "These are all the old issues from 1830 to 1878. Be gentle with them. You'll find them quite interesting. Everything a Victorian woman needs to know is within those pages, from fashion to motherhood."

Blanche didn't bother to ask Rebecca if she knew which issues might cover infant feeding or wet nursing. She would look herself if it meant pulling every issue. Hopefully, Frank was enjoying a good nap. She had told him she would be quick, but that seemed less likely now.

"Would you like me to hold the baby while you take a look?" Rebecca offered.

'How dare you?' Blanche thought. "We'll be fine, but thank you for offering." Blanche looked at her boots, where her toes pinched, and her arches ached. "I'll sit and hold him in my lap while I read through the magazines."

"Are you sure you wouldn't like a chair?"

Blanche grew impatient. "I'm good, thanks."

"Okay, then. I'll get back to work. The books aren't going to put themselves back on the shelves now, are they?" she quipped. "If you need anything or have questions, just holler. I'll hear you."

When Rebecca rounded the cases and finally left her alone, Blanche lowered herself to the floor and sat cross-legged, propping Roy in the crook of her knee. The sting of her pinched toes overshadowed Victorian etiquette and the hardwood floor. She unlaced her boots and pulled them off, letting Roy grab her braided ponytail as it hung off her shoulder and dangled over his face. The pinch on her pinkie toes disappeared as soon as her narrow-toed leather boots were off. She glanced again toward the end of the row before removing her wool stockings as well. The extra comfort padding of the socks had bunched up all the space at the front. She rubbed her toes, the balls of her feet, and her heels, relishing the cool air against her skin. She wanted to sit there and wiggle her toes, but she'd be offended if Rebecca or someone else came around the corner, catching her. She pulled her feet under her dress, hiding them from view. If Rebecca tried to evict her from the library, she'd bribe her silence with a few moments to hold her baby.

The sight of her bare feet exposed in the library was a risk she was willing to take, but letting Roy try and nurse from her, while she read in public, was too taboo, no matter how much she craved to bond. Her maternal drive chimed the noon hour, ringing in her ears like church bells.

46

Mary collapsed onto the bed in Gertrude's upstairs guest room, a place she had called home for the past three months and where she had given birth to her son. The clothes she planned to pack into her canvas bag for her trip home were neatly folded and stacked at the foot of the bed. The bedroom window was open, lifted halfway up its sash, allowing the afternoon spring breeze to waft through the room. The dipping sun's rays illuminated the floating dust in angled columns of light down to the floorboards. The sight of the dust made her nose itch, and she pulled a handkerchief from her dress pocket, along with her mother's letter.

Rereading it made her eager to rush to the train station:

'Sarah Ann has found us here! She wants to see you but knows you are in America. We think it best you and Roy stay! We will be fine.'

Mary couldn't stop wondering what her mother meant by telling her to stay in America. Three months ago, Rachel didn't want to be a grandmother, but now she is both proud and fearful. What exactly had William's mother said? Does Sarah Ann want to make amends?

Reaching for her bag on the floor next to the bedside chest, Mary was convinced she was doing the right thing by leaving Roy here, far away from Sarah Ann, but she flinched as panic rose in her throat. Her mother's silver brooch wasn't pinned to the outside, and she needed it for the trip. She sprang off the bedside, pulled open the top drawer, and rifled through the garments she hadn't already laid out. She worked her way from top to bottom, feeling over the bottom of each drawer with her bare hands, but came up empty.

She grabbed the canvas bag and looked inside, finding it empty. Holding it close to her face, she carefully examined where the brooch had been attached and confirmed that the two tiny holes in the material were still there, so she wasn't crazy to think it was missing.

She dashed out of the bedroom and halfway down the stairs, leaning over the railing, and shouted toward the kitchen, "Gertrude! Mrs. Gates!"

Gertrude rushed out of the kitchen and called, "Mary?" Her voice trembling, she asked, "What's the matter, sweetheart?"

"I can't find my mother's silver brooch! It's not pinned on my bag!"

Gertrude stopped, inhaled deeply, and closed her eyes.

Panic remained on Mary's face. "Gertrude?"

"I heard you, Mary. I thought you'd fallen, and I was moments away from joining my Roy, too." Gertrude took another breath and released it with a whoosh. "I nearly dropped the place setting I was arranging for supper!"

Mary felt sorry for her but still experienced an invalidated panic. "I'm sorry," she said, hearing Gertrude whispering, reciting a quick prayer.

When Gertrude finished rubbing her hands on her apron, she seemed calm. "Given the circumstances, I understand why you think it's missing, but I assure you it's safe. We gave it to you when you were in labor."

"Yes!" exclaimed Mary, recognition washing over her face. "That's right, I did, didn't I?"

"Yes, you did. While Gladys and I were cleaning up—oh, no need to relive that part—I put it in the nightstand drawer to the right of the bed."

Mary slapped her forehead with her palm. Naturally, she still hadn't checked the one drawer in the room. "I'm really sorry. Did I actually frighten you?"

Gertrude smiled and offered a quick wave as she turned and walked back to the kitchen.

Mary bounded back up the steps, knelt in front of the small oak nightstand where a nighttime water pitcher stood, and found the silver brooch alone in the drawer as Gertrude had promised.

She turned her knees to face the bed, rested her elbows on the mattress, and prayed to Saint Anthony, rubbing the smooth surface. When she was done, she kissed the metal, feeling its coolness, and then pinned it back where it belonged on her bag.

She rushed back down the stairs, holding onto the railing for safety, and entered the kitchen. "Do you need my help?" she asked Gertrude, catching the aroma of chicken broth wafting from the stove.

"Not at all, dear. The soup is simmering, and we still have bread. I didn't need to make fresh."

Mary filled her lungs. "Chicken?"

"Your nose doesn't lie."

"Yum. I'll go outside and wait on the porch for them."

"I'll make us tea and join you shortly."

Mary skipped down the foyer and onto the porch, feeling nervous and excited.

47

Blanche left the library still barefoot, taking small steps to keep her feet hidden beneath her floor-length skirt and her tightly rolled boots tucked under her arm. Once she noticed the front desk was empty, she quickly exited through the front door and down the stone steps, holding Roy securely with both hands over her shoulder while trying not to drop her boots. She could hear him cooing in rhythm with his staccato voice as he bounced his chin on her shoulder.

The soft, cool grass felt wonderful beneath her bare feet as she walked across the shaded lawn toward Frank, who was resting against the base of a chestnut tree on the east side of the library as instructed.

She sat cross-legged, facing him, and roused him from a light catnap. After straightening her legs, she rested her feet on his thigh as he lifted his hat off his face with a finger and sat up straighter.

He smiled and rubbed the balls of her feet. "You're absolutely stunning, and you know it."

A devious smile took shape on her face. "You have no idea how good that feels. My pinkie toes did *not* survive the walk into town in these boots. How do they look? Bad?" she asked him.

Lifting one foot for a closer inspection, he lowered it and then raised the other. "Methinks the lady doth protest too much," he replied. "I think you look as fine as wine."

"Oh, really? Do you quote Shakespeare to all the girls?" she asked, teasing him.

She leaned backward, lying flat on the grass, and turned Roy facedown onto her chest, one hand on his back and the other patting his bottom rhythmically. "I could lie here all day and night," she said, bending a knee and feeling the breeze waft up her legs.

Roy sucked on his fingers, his eyes closed and breathing shallowly, and she wished he would drift off to sleep, feeling her heart beating against his own.

"It beats a day of hard labor, that's for sure, but we can't stay here all day, as much as I'd love to," he said, sliding his hand up her calf and lingering with a featherlight touch.

"I don't think I can push that carriage back to Gertrude's," she said, rotating her foot at the ankle. "I'd need to borrow some different shoes from the store."

Frank looked west past the library and the town common.

A chestnut fell nearby, followed by a squirrel barking in the tree above. Blanche instinctively covered the baby's head with both hands before sitting up and leaning in to shield him better.

"Speaking of the store, how are you going to handle this little side hustle with your family?" he asked.

She noted Frank's poor choice of words. "It's not a hustle," she scolded him. "I'll tell them I'm helping Mrs. Gates, and it's a family situation that's not my concern."

Roy began to squirm, either uncomfortable being pressed against her chest or unsettled by the sharpness in her tone. Whatever the reason, she stood and bounced him, shielding the top of his head from any further potential nut droppings.

"You'll ask my father and tell him we're looking for a house. Maybe he'll be generous, but"—she raised her left hand with the palm facing inward, again, showing him her bare ring finger—"the sooner, the better."

He nodded.

"Forget the shoes. Let's take Little Joe." She gestured toward Roy's infant carriage. "It should fit on the back, right?" she asked him.

Frank nodded again. "Good. I was getting hungry. And it's never too early to eat supper."

Roy started to fuss and sucked on his two middle fingers as if he were trying to bite them off if he had teeth.

"Should we feed him first?" he asked her, rummaging for the bag and searching for the jar of porridge.

Blanche tucked Roy into the carriage. "I'm not giving him that cold stuff. It probably belongs in a pig trough," she said, sitting back down and pulling on her stockings and boots. "Let's go, I'll feed him on the way."

48

Mary didn't wait for them to reach the house when she spotted Little Joe plodding along. She jumped off her rocker and skipped to the roadside, waving at Frank, who waved his hat in response. She was excited to hear about their day. Hopefully, Roy hadn't caused any trouble.

Just as she had initially panicked about her missing brooch, her first sinking thought upon seeing Little Joe was that something was wrong with Roy's carriage; perhaps it had broken. Finding another would delay her plans by at least another week.

She ran up to Frank as he reached Gertrude's property line. "Where's…"

"It's tied on the back, don't worry," he told her. "Blanche will find her sea legs and more comfortable shoes on the next trip."

He brought Little Joe to a stop, tied the horse's reins to the handbrake, jumped down, and tipped his hat to Mary again. He tapped his knuckle on the side door, then walked to the back of the coach to free Roy's carriage.

Blanche opened the door when she was ready and extended her arms, handing Roy to Mary, who reached out to grab her son and showered his face with kisses, telling him how much she missed him today.

"How was he?" Mary asked her.

"He was a prince, nothing less."

Frank hoisted the infant carriage up the steps and onto the porch. "Did I remember something about staying for supper?" he asked, setting it by the front door. "We can chat and eat at the same time." He sniffed and followed his nose into the kitchen.

Blanche gestured for Mary to enter next and then followed behind, struggling with the baby bag. The jar of porridge inside weighed a few ounces less after some had been poured out the coach window onto the gravel road.

Mary gently placed a calm and satisfied Roy into the sewing room's makeshift nursery—another empty chest of drawers, slightly larger and deeper than the one in the kitchen.

Gertrude shot Frank a stern look, pointing at his head.

He removed his hat and set it on the baker's rack, looking a bit sheepish. Then, he pulled out a chair at the head of the table for Blanche and motioned for her to sit first, which she did with a smile and a nod of thanks.

Gertrude's kitchen smelled of chicken stock and fresh garden vegetables. She filled the bowls, ladling in chunks of carrots, russet potatoes, yellow sweet onion, and tender pieces of dark thigh meat, all seasoned with salt, black pepper, and finely chopped chives.

Frank was the first to grab a hunk of day-old bread and dunk it, greedily chomping on the salty, fatty juices before tucking a bib napkin into his shirt collar. Drops of golden stock and white-soaked bread crumbs clung to his black mustache, and he blushed at the disapproving looks from all three women, wiping his mouth with one of Gertrude's fine linen napkins. He apologized, lowering his eyes.

Gertrude touched his wrist and told the guests at the table, "A hearty appetite is nothing to be ashamed of—it's a sign of good health."

Mary turned to Blanche and asked again, "So everything went okay? No trouble? Roy behaved himself?" She wanted to sound excited but realized she sounded far more nervous instead.

"Everything went fine. We walked to the library, and I read him some children's books—Roy, not Frank," Blanche quipped, eliciting a short chuckle from Gertrude and Mary. "Then we sat under the trees and lounged on the lawn. He loved watching the squirrels play. We napped in the shade for a while, then woke up and checked in on Carrie at the store, where we freshened all our diapers."

Mary giggled, but no one else reacted.

"Then Little Joe chauffeured us around town in our very own parade."

Mary was impressed but wondered if Gertrude was correct, assuming Carrie had changed Roy's soiled diaper instead of Blanche or Frank. "Wow, it sounds like everyone had some fun times." She glanced down at the open baby bag on the floor, peeking at its contents. "Looks like he even had time for a bit of porridge?"

The corners of Blanche's lips lifted slightly into the faintest of smiles. "Yes."

Mary was distracted and disarmed by the older woman's deep eyes and alto voice. She was the first of the two to break eye contact, lowering her gaze and noticing Blanche's steady pulse reflected at the base of her throat through her open shirt collar. She wished she had Blanche's calm fortitude, and she hoped she could summon her own when she faced Sarah Ann.

"And you sure you have the time to help Gertrude?" she asked Blanche directly, not even glancing at Frank. "I might be gone a couple of weeks."

"He'll be my top priority! I'll be at Gertrude's beck and call."

Frank slurped the last drops of broth from his tilted bowl and stood, pausing before glancing at Gertrude.

"Go ahead. Help yourself to seconds, Franklin," she told him.

"So, I'm okay if you're okay," Mary told Gertrude.

Gertrude took a spoonful of broth after pausing for a moment. "I'm sure we'll set up a schedule and settle into a nice routine," she said, looking directly at Blanche.

"That sounds wonderful. I suppose that settles it." Blanche replied, finally taking her first spoonful of soup. "So good, Gertrude." After wiping her lips, she said, "I guess this means I need to invest in a comfortable pair of walking shoes. My legs are going to get some exercise, for sure."

Frank perked up his ears and arched his eyebrows.

Mary turned her attention to Gertrude across the table. "I believe I'm all packed, and we've set up the downstairs sewing room as a nursery, so you don't have to risk going up and down the stairs anymore."

Gertrude looked puzzled, and a silence lingered until Mary decided to break the quiet, which she did.

"I don't see any reason to wait any longer. Honestly, if I did, I think I'd only get more anxious than I already am. I need to get home and see my family. I'm not sure how long it will take to convince them to come back with me," she said, her cadence picking up speed.

Blanche startled, almost inhaling a spoonful of soup down her windpipe, coughing and choking a bit. "So, you'll be returning *with* your family?" she asked Mary, her green irises swimming in a sea of white.

Mary felt the swell of emotions rising in her chest and the weight of tears pooling in her eyes. Only a deep breath kept her first sob in check. "Yes," she admitted. "I miss my mother, younger brother, and sister, and… I miss William… Roy's father." Hearing herself say William's name was too much to bear. She grabbed the nearest napkin, covering her face to muffle her sobs.

Blanche remained slack-jawed but gently placed a soft hand on Mary's shoulder.

Frank looked as uneasy as a long-tailed cat in a room full of rocking chairs. "I think I'd better go check on Little Joe," he said, grabbing a piece of bread and excusing himself from the table. "Little Joe thanks you for the bread, Mrs. Gates."

Gertrude tensed and leaned over the table, grasping one of Mary's wrists.

Mary lowered her napkin, locking her watery eyes on Gertrude, the woman who had treated her like the daughter she never had for the past three months. Behind the Ben Franklins, her slate gray eyes were steady, and her short, cropped, matching silver hair resembled Mrs. Claus. All she was missing was a red coat and a white sash collar.

She tried to anticipate how the upcoming weeks would unfold. Her biggest concern was whether Gertrude could physically care for Roy, but she also worried about whether Blanche and Frank would behave. The last thing she needed Blanche and the rest of the town to hear, aside from Gertrude and Reverend Richardson, was that her mother had committed an unforgivable transgression.

"I think I want to catch the train first thing in the morning," she said, glancing at the same wooden spoon pocketed with her bite marks on the table, wishing she could sink her teeth into it again.

Blanche and Gertrude rubbed Mary's shoulders while the three women exchanged sidelong glances.

"I think it's best…" Blanche began, turning to Gertrude. "For *safety*… Frank should accompany Mary back to Boston."

"Oh, I could—"

Gertrude interrupted Mary. "You arrived practically in the dark, if I recall. Do you remember how you and Franklin got to North Station from Lewis Wharf?"

"It was pretty crowded," Mary admitted. "There's no need for me to get into a kerfuffle, I guess, trying to find my way back."

"It's settled then. We'll return at first light. Instead of this being a goodbye supper, we'll have another parting breakfast?" Blanche asked Gertrude, who hesitated before nodding. "I'll drop you both off at the station, and then Gertrude and I will start our new schedule. I'd better have Frank let me take Little Joe's reins on the ride back into town for practice," she said, enthusiasm lighting up her face and voice.

Mary walked Blanche out after she thanked Gertrude for the delicious supper, telling her they would see her again sooner rather than later at first light.

"Everything will work out the way it's meant to," Blanche told Mary as she linked her arm through Frank's elbow and gazed up at him. She turned to Mary and said, "Once everything sugars out… it'll all be fancy." She poked Frank in the ribs, then dug her fingers deeper, making him flinch. "Frank told me that a few times last month." She winked at him after he shifted away, and she tugged on his arm, grabbing his attention. "We'd better get going, and I'll fill you in on all the plans." To Mary, she said, "We'll save all our hugs and goodbye kisses for the morning."

"I'll hold you to it. Have a good night," Mary said with a quick wave.

"Help me up, cowboy," Blanche told Frank, extending her hand. "I'm driving us home."

Frank obliged, holding her hand as she stepped up and then supporting her rump as she settled into the box seat, which made Mary giggle.

Blanche swatted his hand away.

After they arrived at the town common, she finally broke the silence between her and Frank. "We have a couple of weeks to get our ducks in a row. Did you enjoy living in the city?" she asked him.

Not taking his eyes off the road ahead, he replied, "Opportunities, yes… but I like living here with you."

"We are packing for Boston."

49

"I appreciate you bringing me back to the city," Mary said, sitting across from Frank as they rode the Fitchburg Line east toward Boston's North Station at the end of the line. "I didn't mean to keep you away from Blanche all day."

The eastern Massachusetts countryside stretched along both sides of the train, painting a broad swath of green brushstrokes. The scent of burning coal wafted through a few open windows along the line of coaches.

Mary sat facing forward, eager to focus on her destination while trying to forget what she was leaving behind. Her nervous energy needed an outlet for small talk. "I'm glad you and Blanche found each other," she said, rubbing her brooch and feeling the warm friction on her fingertips. "You two make a lovely couple."

Frank smiled at the compliment but didn't take his eyes off the window. "I've often thought about working the rails and traveling across the country from coast to coast. Being a brakeman in a caboose would have suited me just fine." He turned to focus on Mary. "But I'd probably end up a crumb boss in some rail gang camp instead."

"It's comforting to know that you two found each other so late…" She paused, lost in thought. "Maybe there's still hope for my mother," she said.

He shifted his eyes to the passing outdoors. "Are you saying we're ancient?"

She gasped, mortified. "No, I only meant…"

He chuckled softly. "That we're old."

She did her best to step back. "Older?" She cringed awkwardly, a hint of rouge flushing her cheeks.

"Yes, we're older, middle-aged. It means we've seen more, that's all."

"I feel like I've seen plenty," she admitted, looking out the window, remembering that awful night when she stood in the copse between their farms and watched her mother stab William's father in the back with a kitchen knife.

"You've faced some tough choices, and I get it." He paused until she made eye contact again. "Three months ago, while sitting on that bench… the situation you found yourself in that made you run away… I never judged you."

Mary sat slack-jawed and speechless, hoping to let go of her simmering unease when Frank broke the tension by changing the subject.

"I asked Blanche to marry me."

Mary's jaw dropped, and her mouth fell open.

"And by the way, you're the first to know, aside from her, of course." He waved his hands wildly, laughing.

Mary waited, biting her tongue until she couldn't hold it any longer. "And?"

"Oh, she said yes. Why wouldn't she? I'm a catch and a snappy dresser," he replied, chuckling at his own joke. "I'm going to try and find a ring in the city this afternoon."

Although Mary knew her fairy tale wedding would never come true, she was happy for him—no big church wedding for her and William with Roy as a toddler.

"She'll love it, no matter what," she told him, her dark brown eyes hiding the green of envy. "Do you think it's possible to wait until I return?" she asked. "I'd like to witness at least one wedding in my lifetime."

Frank shrugged, showing her a confused look, then shook his head from side to side. "Of course you will. Don't be silly."

"I wouldn't even know to ask you whether you thought the ceremony would be held in the Congregational or Unitarian church," she admitted.

Mary had left her baby, who would be spending weeks in the care of a woman she had known for only a couple of months. Her eyes flickered with curiosity, and she had questions. She held her hands out, palms up, moving her lips with no words.

"I see you have questions," he assuaged her. "Neither of us is religious. Call us humble and private. Probably more fitting for us to go to Town Hall," he said, reciprocating with his hands out, palms out. "We've somehow managed to wait this long to find each other, so it certainly doesn't seem crazy to me to wait a few more weeks until you can be a witness."

Mary's eyes continued to flicker as more last-minute questions clamored for attention behind them. "She's so beautiful in such a charming little town. How is she not married?" she asked him.

Frank's shoulders slumped, and the color drained from his face. "We haven't talked about our pasts, only the passion in the here and now."

"Has she been engaged before?"

"I don't want to know how many men in town have previously courted her."

Mary saw him shiver as if the hands of the Devil crept up his back and settled on his shoulders, and the Devil's breathy taunts whispered in his ear.

"I don't need or want to know," he replied. "My mother always told me I wouldn't amount to much, so thinking too much about those things makes me doubt myself."

Mary leaned forward, wanting to extend a hand or even step across the aisle to embrace him, but she refrained. "I'm sorry to hear that. I understand doubting oneself."

Frank waved his hands wildly as if he were swatting away flies.

"The Chapins are well connected with deep roots in Lincoln and quite well off." He was revealing nothing new that wasn't untrue. "If I were J.L.— that's James Lorin—her father, and I had a daughter as beautiful as her growing up, I'd probably do some serious vetting. And knowing Blanche now, I bet she fended off all those unworthy suitors with a heavy stick." He beamed, appearing lost in thought. "She simply found me too charming and irresistible. The timing was right. We were both in the right place at the right time. Good things come to those who wait, right?"

Mary breathed deeply and exhaled, "And that was us, too, at the right place and the right time."

"Touché."

"Frank?" she asked, her voice soft. "I'm nervous… all over again."

The click-clack of the train on the rails was the only sound in the coach as their eyes met, and they searched each other for the right words.

"I'm sorry," he said, breaking the silence. "You were anxious back then and must be even more worried now with what's at stake."

She gave a barely noticeable nod.

"Three months have passed, and I imagine you still don't have the answers."

She shook her head. "No, not really."

"But you have a plan?"

"I have a plan."

Mary shared her plan with him: to persuade her mother and siblings to leave Canada and convince William's mother to let him come along. (Things could go wrong at any point, but good things come to those who wait, right?)

When Frank asked her why it was up to William's mother, she side-stepped the question. "If the boat were to sink on either crossing or anything else goes wrong while I'm away, would you and Blanche take care of Roy?"

Frank appeared to be conflicted, and she held a blank face, waiting for his response.

"Of course, but don't think that way. You can't think that way. Everything will work out."

"A month."

"What?"

"If I don't return in a month, will you keep him?"

Frank dry swallowed a few times before confirming. "Yes, but we all need to show patience."

"Then it's settled. I need to leave knowing I have at least one firm answer… and you'll sort it out with Gertrude?"

He looked stunned. "Yes, of course."

Mary finally stopped rubbing the brooch, as her thumbprint felt like it was on fire.

•••

"Good luck finding a ring!" Mary said, unwilling to say goodbye on the dock. "It should complement her green eyes, you know."

Frank rolled his eyes. "I'm fully aware of her eye color… her best feature."

"Can't you just say yes?" Mary rolled her eyes. "And it doesn't hurt that she's as tall as a Viking."

"I hadn't noticed, but thanks for the reminder," he deadpanned.

It had been three months since they had encountered each other on Lewis Wharf, and it was as crowded and bustling now as it had been then, except everyone was dressed in fewer and lighter clothes for the warmer weather. Opportunistic seagulls floated above on the trade winds, searching for dropped food. The smell of kelp and seaweed, heated by the sun, in the salty air was more pungent than Mary remembered.

The S.S. Halifax's steam whistle echoed against the merchant facade. "Do you have your ticket?" Frank asked. "I want to double-check. Show it to me."

Mary complied, taking the ticket out of her shirt pocket.

"And your bag, I see—check." He tugged on the satchel's strap over her shoulder. "Whew, good thing we remembered not to leave it on the train!"

The ship's whistle sounded again, and they looked to see the boarding passengers on the gangway dwindling.

"Alrighty then," Frank declared, seemingly unable to say goodbye.

Mary stood on her toes, reaching up with her fingers to tug at his vest lapels, and pulled him down to kiss his cheek. Tickled by his mustache, she let go and rubbed the itch from her lips.

"Don't forget!" she said, pointing at him and shaking her finger.

He ignored her gesture. "Have a safe trip, Mary Jane Nutting. We'll see you again soon." When she didn't turn to leave, he said, "Now skedaddle! You'll miss your boat, and I can't stay here another night."

She relented and walked away, turning once more. "If not green, then blue's a good choice!" she shouted over her shoulder.

•••

Frank wandered through Boston's North End, searching for an engagement ring for his tall-as-a-Viking fiancée. He couldn't afford an emerald, sapphire, or diamond, and it wouldn't be the perfect ring. Still, he was determined to find something special, and before closing time, he did, at E.B. Horn Jewelers in the downtown crossing district—a nearly one-carat pale faceted blue zircon mounted on a thin gold band.

The salesman assured him that, although less expensive than other gemstones, it was a charming, popular Victorian choice and a rare color.

He wanted to please Blanche by gifting her the baby boy, but not at the expense of Mary's free will to willingly give him up for the best.

PART THREE

50

The S.S. Halifax did not sink while returning to Nova Scotia from Boston, docking safely at Noble Wharf within Halifax harbor. Mary exited the dock, crossed Lower Water, cut up Salter Street, walking past Saint Paul's Cemetery. She took her first deep breath and shifted the canvas satchel to her other shoulder, noticing it felt heavier this trip with more new clothes rolled tightly inside. She promised herself that after hugging and showering her mother and siblings with kisses, the first order of business would be to write Gertrude, informing her that she'd arrived home safely and thanking her again for the new clothes.

Her memory of navigating the southern hillside swiftly returned, along with the musty smell of horse-drawn carriages and the odor of sewage flowing downhill toward the harbor.

She pressed on, moving diagonally through the cemetery headstones and across Morris Street at Rottenburg and Church into the vast cemetery at Holy Cross. The midday sun felt warm on her skin, and the grass was lush and soft underfoot. She was almost at Kirby's Lane and making good time when she gave her feet and shoulders a rest, sitting against the base of a maple tree to catch her breath. She didn't want to doze off, so she glanced down the hill at George's Island, wondering what Roy was up to that morning and whether he had a good night. Did he miss her and realize she was gone, and who was he with now?

Mary rubbed her shoulders, flexed her toes, and wanted to remove her boots but knew the small rental on Kirby's Lane was nearby, just beyond the other side of the church. The eastern sunlight reflected off the chapel's three stained glass lancets, giving the medallions rich hues reminiscent of gemstones: ruby, sapphire, and emerald. The emerald stained glass surrounding the portrait of Saint Patrick reminded her of Blanche's eyes, and she smiled at herself, thinking and hoping Frank would find an equally brilliant colored stone for his bride-to-be.

• • •

Inside Our Lady of Sorrows Chapel, Rachel and Agnes sat in the pews, praying. They had prayed every day since receiving Mary's letter, unsure of when or if she would return this month despite Rachel urging her to stay safe in America.

"I'm feeling a bit famished," Agnes declared. "If we don't start supper soon, I might have to nibble on some of Mary's beads." She held up the strand of rosary beads that Bishop O'Brien had given to Rachel, and when she bit down on a glass bead, her tooth clicked.

"It's not a real piece of soft gold," Rachel told her youngest daughter.

It was always difficult for her to leave the chapel, especially on sunny afternoons when sunlight flooded the interior, streaming through the colored stained glass windows. This stood in sharp contrast to their dim little rental, which had only one front window that allowed in just enough sunlight to illuminate the depressing dust particles.

"We can leave now," she said, giving in to her daughter.

Together, they kissed their beads and carefully pulled the strands over their thick red braids, flipping the ends over so they hung around their necks. If they didn't replace the cotton strings soon, they'd find themselves picking up beads from the floor on their hands and knees.

• • •

Mary flexed her shoulders and pulled the canvas satchel closer, preparing to stand and make her way across the cemetery, past the chapel to Kirby's Lane, when she saw two female figures emerge from the far side of the building. They wore muted gray outfits—she guessed shirts and skirts—but the red hair, braided between their shoulders, ignited a spark in her heart and fortitude. Clambering to her feet, she threw the satchel strap over her head and stood indecisive and paralyzed, her boots seemingly glued to the grass.

Her mouth was dry, and the insides of her cheeks were stuck to her teeth. "Mom?" she cracked a barely audible whisper, unable to catch her breath. Watching the two women walk away, she licked her lips and swallowed, remembering to inhale deeply this time, and shouted, "Mom!"

The taller woman hesitated, gripping the arm of the other, her ears cocked to the open air as she swiveled her hips.

"Rachel! Agnes!" Mary called out to them from across the other side of the cemetery.

The taller woman turned to the other, pulling her closer as she surveyed the chapel grounds. Her head swiveled left and right, and her eyes scanned the rows of headstones.

The shorter, younger woman was the first to see Mary across the cemetery, and she waved frantically. "Mother! It's MJ!" she shouted, breaking free from the other woman's grasp and waving both hands above her head.

Mary raced up the hill, weaving through the listing stone markers as her boots snagged on clumps of grass. The heavy thud of the satchel against her hip caused her to stumble several times before she reached the chapel entrance. The three women grabbed and embraced each other before finally tumbling onto the grass.

"Oh my God, it's you!" Rachel cried, pressing her forehead against Mary's and rubbing noses. "Oh"—she smothered Mary's face with more kisses—"I can't believe I told you to stay away!"

"Mom!" Mary exclaimed, catching her breath between kisses.

"I was so scared for both of you!"

"Mom! It's okay."

"Where's the baby? Is he all right?" Agnes interrupted, pulling Mary's face toward her own.

"Yes, he's fine, Agnes."

Mary held their chins and declared slowly, "Roy is fine. He's adorable, perfect, safe, and sound with Mrs. Gates. She's the elderly lady who took me in." To her mother, she said, "Mom, you're going to love her."

Mary winced and rolled away from her bag as the sharp points of the brooch jabbed into her lower back.

They all tried to sit up gracefully but failed miserably, brushing off the loose blades of grass from their clothes and hair. Giving up, they embraced once more, locking arms tightly, before getting to their feet and walking toward their temporary home away from home.

Mary settled in the middle, wrapping her arms around her mother and sister's hips. "I don't want to waste much time, but I have a plan. I've fallen in love with Lincoln, and I think we can make it work. You'll both love it! I'm sure of it."

Agnes jumped with excitement, but Rachel did not. "Mary—"

"Mom, listen to me," Mary interrupted. "The moment Roy was born, I saw how beautiful he was, and everything started to change. I didn't name him William because I felt so lost. I didn't think I'd ever see him again." She closed her eyes, holding back tears, remembering the days before she got pregnant when everyone was happy. When she finally opened them again, she said, "Mrs. Gates helped me after Frank—"

"Frank?" Rachel interrupted.

"Yes. I'll explain later. He's a friend who introduced us."

Rachel looked at her daughter impatiently, which brought everyone to a halt. "Mary!" she called out rather loudly.

Mary steadied herself, taking a few deep breaths. "Okay… I met Frank after I arrived in Boston. Let's say my emotions revealed my plight, and he helped guide me out of the city, believing his former mentor, Mrs. Gates, could help me." She glanced up at the heavens. "It turns out she was an angel—my guardian angel."

Rachel wrapped her daughter in a one-armed hug, pulling her tight to her bosom.

"She's a widow, and her husband was named Roy. He was a sharp Harvard man who loved his rose gardens but left her too soon. She lives alone in a beautiful, quaint Victorian house outside of town, surrounded by all of his flower gardens, and… it has a soaking tub with hot running water!"

"Well, it sounds like someone did have a guardian angel. Everything seems too good to be true," Rachel said.

Mary looked up at the sky again, feeling the pang of impending reunion tears. Even though she had been away for one day, she missed her son and her Walden.

"I want us to start a new life there as a family, and I'm going to ask Sarah Ann if William can come with us."

Rachel and Agnes looked away, leaving Mary feeling that she had said something wrong—so much so that neither of them could face her. "What? What did I say?" she pleaded.

Rachel halted them in the middle of Tower Road. The front door of the rental unit, their home away from home, stood feet from Kirby's Lane. She cupped her daughter's face in her hands. "He's gone, Mary."

Gravity dragged the first wave of tears down Mary's cheeks. "He's not gone, Mother. I'll talk to him. I won't have to convince him to come with us. I know he still loves me!" Flashes of sadness and anger flickered across her face.

Rachel began to cry, and Agnes moved closer to her sister. She wrapped her arms around Mary's waist as she looked over her shoulder at their mother, sadness and recognition evident on her face. Agnes held her sister tightly, steadying her.

"William is gone, Mary," Rachel whispered, leaning closer. "Sarah Ann sent him off to the army. He's gone to Victoria… I'm sorry."

Mary shook her head in denial, feeling buoyed by Agnes's grip. "No," she said, wiping the tears from her eyes and leaky nose. "I'll write to him. It's not too late. He still loves me, and he'll come back."

They stood together in the middle of the road, crying beneath the canopy of chestnut trees.

• • •

Abigail Fletcher sat leaning against the base of a maple tree, watching the three women—a mother and her daughters—roll about gleefully, hugging and kissing on the cemetery lawn outside Our Lady of Sorrows Chapel.

It was her day to sit and watch, taking turns with her older sister, Lydia. If they saw Mary return, with or without her baby, they would deliver the news to their mother.

Unlike the three women who laughed, hugged, and cried tears of joy at their reunion, she, her sisters, and their mother had only wept tears of grief and loss over the past.

• • •

The small kitchenette table at Kirby's Lane had two chairs, and Mary and Agnes were sitting closely together as one, hip to hip, when George opened the front door and stepped inside.

"I know, boots off," he said, bending down to untie the knots.

He kicked off his boots next to the door and didn't notice the two girls sitting in the same chair at the table in the shadows until he spotted their different hair colors. Fancying himself a Shakespearean theater actor, he played the scene stoically, aided by the ale shared with the Monteleone brothers. However, he recognized the wavy, dark brown hair that belonged to his sister, whom he had missed these past three months, as she faced the kitchenette wall behind the sink. He could see her concentrating intently on Rachel's face, smirking, biting her tongue, and trying to stifle her laughter.

Mary jumped up, twirled around, and threw her hands over her head, all ten fingers splayed like a geisha fan. "Ta-da!"

George didn't blink or react; the ale had dulled his startle reflex. With a straight face, he asked, "Who's this?"

His older sister took the bait. "It's me!"

He leaned in closer, bringing his fingers to his chin, and scratched his cheek, appearing baffled, then suddenly clear. "Oh! It's you!" he exclaimed. "I didn't recognize you, not looking all fat as a house!"

"George Wilson Nutting!" Rachel scolded him.

"Oh, nice!" Agnes jumped into the fray, disapproval washing over her freckled face.

Mary and George met in the middle, embracing and spinning each other around.

"You look great," he admitted. "Where's my nephew?" he asked, looking around. He lowered his voice to a whisper, "Is he sleeping?"

"He's not here," Mary told him.

George looked stunned. Had she abandoned him and come home as planned?

His sister could see his anguish and reassured him, "It's okay, don't worry. You'll get to see him. I have a plan to share with you all."

She addressed everyone in the room. "I don't see any point in waiting, and it's not like we have to decide and pack up tonight…"

"Pack tonight?" asked George.

"We have some time," Mary reassured him. "I need to write a couple of letters, giving ourselves a few weeks as a buffer for anything unexpected, but I don't see any reason we have to stay." She scanned the room, looking at each face. "I fell in love with this small town in Massachusetts, made some friends, and there's plenty of work and a good life." She surveyed their faces again. "I need you to trust me."

George glanced at his mother, sensing that she knew what he was thinking even before he spoke, and it wouldn't be about missing his beer cronies. "But what about?" He glanced around the room. "Does she know? Did you tell her?" he asked timidly, lowering his voice to a whisper.

"We told her," Rachel said.

"I'm not worried," Mary said. "I'm writing William a letter tonight, and I'll send it first thing in the morning. The army will know where to send it." She took a deep breath. "I'm just going to think positively for now."

The excitement and three pints of ale were giving George a headache, so he walked to the sink and poured himself a glass of water. He and the Monteleone brothers had each bought a round at the pub, and he hadn't expected to do this much thinking afterward.

"What if she was lying?" he questioned his mother. "What if she didn't push William into the army? What if she only said that out of spite, and he's here in Halifax with them?"

The women in the room assessed each other's reactions to what George had proposed.

Mary's face lit up with hope.

Agnes's eyes flickered, judging.

Rachel was the voice of experience. "She's not. I believe her. The irony of sending William clear across the country, as far away as possible from here, away from Mary, that's true spite." She lowered her head and spoke into her hands, muffled, "I took Robert from her, and she took William, cutting off her nose to spite her face."

Mary comforted her mother and rubbed her back. Finally, she told them, "He'll come home… he'll come home."

51

A horse-drawn funeral carriage moved slowly along Mumford Road before entering Mount Olivet Cemetery through the main gate on Olivet Street. The driver stopped the horse alongside a freshly dug grave missing its headstone. High clouds and drizzle blanketed the Halifax west-end hillside in a palette of grays, fitting for a funeral that matched the bleakness of the undertaking.

When two more coaches stopped behind the lead hearse, no mourners stood graveside. The second driver stepped off, opening the door for sisters Euphemia, Hannah, Lydia, and Abigail. A third driver released the handle for sisters Alice, Clessia, and Frances, followed by their mother, Sarah Ann Fletcher. All of them wore black dresses and hats, with black veils keeping the light swirling drizzle out of their eyes.

What remained of the Fletcher family stood rigid next to the carriages, waiting for the three pairs of drivers to remove the casket and bear it to the open gravesite. The older sisters were most upset with the irony that it was April Fools' Day, facing the fraught reality of burying their only brother today, a stressed teenage boy struck down too soon by influenza and pneumonia in the damp coastal air of the Pacific Northwest.

"Why are we here?" asked six-year-old Frances, the youngest, tugging at her mother's dress.

"Why aren't we burying him next to Dad in Eastville?" asked Euphemia, the eldest at twenty-seven. She had left the family farm with her sister Hannah to move to Halifax for jobs and husbands.

Sarah Ann reached for her youngest's hand as Clessia and Alice sidled closer to their older sisters, Lydia and Abigail. "Because it's an army grave plot. It's out of my control," Sarah Ann lied to them all, keeping her anger low in her gut. If that whore wanted to choose to be with her William so badly, then let her reunite with him here.

As the drivers returned to their carriages, Sarah Ann led her daughters to William's graveside, trudging through the soggy brown grass and spring green shoots; she couldn't care less about soiling her boots and dress, as she had no intention of ever wearing them again.

She couldn't bring herself to move her son into a more formal casket; instead, she chose to leave him in the pine six-sided casket that the army had shipped back to Halifax, adorned with brass handles and lined with white linens. She had signed off, taking possession at the train station two days ago, and had formally identified his body. He was dressed in his simple Private's CEF uniform and looked handsome even in death, his once shaggy cornsilk hair shorn bristly short. The anguish that gnawed at her heart was knowing she would never again see his eyes, now forever hidden behind sewn lids.

She wanted to leave her gold wheat chain necklace with him, adorned with a single-carat fancy, vivid blue diamond. It had belonged to her mother, Euphemia, who passed it to her after his christening, seeing how perfectly it matched the luminous color of his eyes. But today, having always worn it, she decided not to place it in his clasped hands, which were hidden beneath his uniform hat. She refused to disturb him, ultimately choosing not to bury this final memory with her son.

There was no service, priest, or spoken words—only final goodbyes. She watched each of her daughters, one by one, touch their brother's raindrop-covered casket when Frances, the last to approach, pulled a wilted pair of crocus stems from her dress sleeve and placed the purple and white flowers on the lid.

Sarah Ann hoped her son might be looking down from Heaven and seeing some color this April Fools' Day.

52

Mary gave herself two weeks to reconnect with her family and stop worrying about waiting for a reply from William. She had written out all the details of her trip to Boston, their son's birth, and how they would thrive in Lincoln, including the possibility of someday building a home near Flint's or Walden Pond. She signed the letter with her love always and quoted Thoreau: "Things do not change; we change." She even doodled a rough map, with an arrow from the peninsula of Nova Scotia pointing to a dot west of Boston labeled "Our New Home!"

"It's only been a week. How many days is the train?" Agnes asked her sister.

Mary didn't need a week to recount her time in Lincoln and encouraged her mother to continue cleaning the houses around the university. There was no reason for them all to catch cabin fever. She planned to stay with Agnes and home-school her in the ways of life, including the realities of childbirth, but she softened the harshness of pain to avoid scaring her younger sister. They enjoyed more fun, giggles, and outright laughter while tracing the lines of her stretch marks—an experience Rachel had never shared with either of them, yet Agnes seemed morbidly enthralled.

"I don't know. A week each way? Seems like a reasonable guess," Mary replied.

"You didn't ask the Postmaster?"

"No, sorry."

"What happens if…" Agnes started.

Mary shook her head, looking away. "I can't think about that right now." She dismissed the thought, changing the subject. "Gertrude's kitchen table is much bigger than this. Her kitchen alone is bigger than this entire place!"

"You're preaching to the choir."

Mary covered her sister's hands with her own and leaned over the small kitchenette table barely larger than a nightstand, their knees bumping. "Shall I say it again?" she asked, eyes widening and mouth agape.

"Do it!" Agnes insisted.

"Her house has an indoor bathroom *and* a soaking tub with running hot water! I never even saw an outhouse the whole time I was down there!"

Agnes squealed. "Let's go! Just leave a note for Mom and George saying we've gone ahead. They can take the boat tomorrow!" She shook Mary's hands like a rag doll.

A light knock on the front door interrupted the sisters' reverie. They tightened their grips on each other's hands, staring into one another's eyes, paralyzed.

"Maybe it's the mail," Mary whispered, attempting to free her hands.

Agnes shook her head, but Mary pulled her toward the front door, her stockings sliding across the varnished wooden floor.

"Who is it?" Mary asked through the closed door.

"Mary?" a woman's voice called from outside. "If that's you in there, I'd like to talk to you. This is Mrs. Fletcher…William's mother."

Agnes shook her head vigorously, gripping her sister's wrists tightly, attempting to drag Mary back away from the door.

Mary forced herself to break free, twisting the knob with her right hand, and nudged Agnes behind the door. The brass knob felt warm against her fingers from the sunlight, and the door opened smoothly without a hint of a squeak from the hinges.

She opened the door halfway, glancing beyond Sarah Ann and over her shoulder, and spotted a horse-drawn carriage waiting along Tower Road. She firmly pushed Agnes further behind the door to keep her out of view from William's mother.

Sarah Ann Fletcher took a step backward onto the walkway, distancing herself from the threshold. She wore a light-collared white shirt adorned with pleats and delicate ruffles on the cuffs. Her hands were clasped and relaxed in front of her while her lightweight skirt danced in the spring breezes flowing up from the harbor. Her hair was loosely pinned and frizzy as if she hadn't brushed it in days or weeks, with a noticeable gray wave that hadn't been present the last time Mary saw her. Despite the sun shining high in the sky, she wore no hat to shade her eyes.

"I was hoping we could go for a ride," Sarah Ann said, turning slightly and gesturing behind her while keeping her eyes on Mary.

Mary was unsure how to respond, yet she felt Agnes tugging at her sleeve like a dog pulling on a rope held by its owner.

The motion didn't escape Sarah Ann's notice. "Are you not alone?"

Agnes stepped out from behind the door and puffed out her chest. Her high mound of thick red hair, a trait shared with her mother, made her appear inches taller than her five-foot-two-inch frame. "Mary isn't going anywhere with you, Mrs. Fletcher."

"Hello, Agnes. It's nice to see you again. Your hair looks stunning, and you're blossoming into an exceptional young woman."

The three turned toward the road, hearing a horse neigh as another coach passed by. Sarah Ann's driver attempted to calm his horse, which eventually settled after clomping a few times against the carriage's hand brake.

"You're welcome to join us, Agnes." She turned to Mary and pointed north along Tower Road. "I feel I must show you something. It's only a short ride further up the hill, and I do promise to have you all back by supper time."

Agnes tugged harder on Mary's arm.

"I give you my word… I'm not here to hurt you… either of you."

Mary realized it would only upset Mrs. Fletcher if she didn't go with her, and if she wanted to earn any goodwill that could help persuade William to join her, she should go now and get it over with, trepidations be damned.

"We're not dressed to be seen in public," Agnes said, revealing her stockings.

"It's quite all right. I'll wait in the carriage until you're proper."

Sarah Ann returned to her carriage, where her driver held the door open until Mary and Agnes joined her and climbed inside. They sat across from Sarah Ann, holding hands, unsure of where they were headed or what fate awaited them for the rest of the day. Although Sarah Ann had promised they would be back by supper, Agnes had persuaded Mary to leave a written note on the table for their mother to find before they got dressed.

They rode up Tower Road, with Sarah Ann gazing out a side window, silent and lost in thought until the coach crossed Spring Garden Road. The Halifax Public Gardens were in full bloom, showcasing yellow daisies, red tulips, boulder-sized deep ruby-red azalea bushes, and pale blue wisteria vines that draped over every pergola along the winding maze of walkways.

"I've spent many days here, sitting in the gardens. It's not only the colors"—she fanned the air near her nose—"it's the ocean of fragrances. You can almost taste the smells. It keeps the mind clear."

Mary understood but knew Agnes did not, noticing her puzzled expression, but someday, she would.

Sarah Ann turned away from the window, focusing on Mary. "Tell me about my grandchild?"

Mary could feel the pleading behind the widow's dammed-up tears on the verge of overflowing, and when she told her it was a boy, Sarah Ann let out a great sob that contorted and flooded her face.

"He's three months old with William's blue eyes, blonde hair, and my nose and disposition."

They rode for another block or two before Sarah Ann thoroughly composed herself. "Will I ever be able to see him?"

Mary and Agnes exchanged a silent glance, their eyes flickering with unspoken questions, before Mary nodded to her sister and turned to Sarah Ann. "I suppose that depends on you. I know you told my mother that you sent William into the army. Is it true? He's away?"

"Yes."

"Did you do that for me? For my mother? Out of spite?"

"Yes… lying on the admission papers by a year was never questioned."

Mary squared her shoulders. "Two wrongs don't make a right."

Sarah Ann sighed and looked away after struggling to maintain eye contact. "I see that now."

"When the army finds out he's only sixteen, will he be kicked out?"

Sarah Anne squinted, appearing bewildered. "Discharged?"

"Yes, and then… will you let William come with me to Lincoln so we can be a family?"

Sarah Ann faced the two young women, looking anguished and stung. "No," she barely whispered.

Mary felt her face flush as warm blood rushed to her cheeks. "You won't give us your blessing so William can be with me and… *our son?*" she crescendoed.

Her face down, Sarah Ann whispered louder, "I can't do that. I'm sorry."

"Why?" Mary shouted. "Tell me *why* you can't let him go?"

"He's gone."

"He's *not* gone! He's just away!"

Agnes pressed her face against the carriage window, watching the rows of white marble and gray granite headstones scattered across the open green grass slip past. She fumbled to find her sister's hand, finally squeezing it, and then slapped her thigh to get her attention.

Mary followed her sister's gaze out the window, covering her mouth with a hand to stifle her dread. "This can't be happening," she whispered through her fingers.

She bit her tongue to wake from this cruel nightmare, hoping she'd be rewarded by finding herself back in their dusty, dim kitchenette, regaling Agnes with more vivid descriptions of Gertrude's lovely home. Her disappointment peaked as the taste of copper and rust filled her mouth, having bitten her cheek.

"What have you done?" she asked, tears catching at the corners of her lips, the taste of salt mingling with her blood. "Is this truth or yet more spite?"

When the coach came to a complete stop, Sarah Ann said, "It's closure. For all of us"—she pinned her chin to her chest—"I hated your mother and you"—she dabbed at the corners of her eyes—"and this is how God has punished me."

"Punished *you?*" Mary spat, swiping at Sarah Ann's downturned face, striking her with the speed and quickness of a catamount.

Reaching past Agnes, stunned into silence, Mary fumbled for the door latch, not waiting for the driver. She pushed the door open, nearly stumbling headfirst before grabbing a handle, awkwardly swinging into the side of the carriage, and bumping her knee. She dropped to the grass, frantically scanning up and down the row of stones, finding nothing to ease her panic. Ducking behind the coach to the other side, she spotted a grave site with greener, finer grass and forced herself to look at the marker.

Pvt. W.H. Fletcher, 1876-1892

Sarah Ann approached from behind. "We laid him to rest at the turn of the month, before his birthday. The army said he fell to influenza and pneumonia."

Agnes stood at the rear of the carriage, partially hidden from view, too scared to witness, but ran to Mary's side, clutching her as she fell to her knees.

The ground was soft atop the freshly dug grave, and Mary collapsed her full weight, sinking her knees into the soft earth and grasping fistfuls of new grass shoots and dirt, unable to resist the urge to dig. Agnes wrapped her arms around her sister and squeezed, halting the painful futility.

Sarah Ann wiped her face with trembling hands. "I come here every day without my daughters and kneel alone, apologizing to my son." She struggled to capture Mary's attention. "I'll stay this last time and wait as long as you need."

After enough time to feel the sun on her lower back, Mary finally broke her silence. "You were going to build us a home near Walden Pond," she whispered to William, facing where his upturned face would be listening beneath the soil. "I'll never be able to forget your handsomeness because our son is you... reborn."

Agnes shielded her hurting sister as Sarah Ann approached, revealing the red scourge marks on her cheek, now faded to pink.

"I want you to have this," Sarah Ann said, reaching into her collar. She slipped her mother's necklace over her head, careful not to snag it in her untamed hair, and stared at the gold necklace with its vibrant pendant. "I can no longer bear the weight of it on my heart." Cupping it tightly, she blew softly into her hands before offering it to Mary. "I don't want to burden you with any family heirloom history, but I thought maybe you'd like to keep it… for William… and your son. Perhaps he might cherish it someday as a reminder of his father long after I'm forgotten."

Mary viewed the extended olive branch with suspicion and turned away, not wanting to look at or accept it.

"Even if you never want to keep it, I understand, but it's of significant value. It could help ensure your family thrives in America."

Agnes, eyeing the gold chain, grabbed it from Sarah Ann's hand and shoved it to the bottom of her dress pocket.

"My heart is broken… as I know, yours is as well. Look at what two wrongs hath left us," Mary said, brushing her hand over the fine-bladed grass. "Two graves to visit when we're melancholy over who we miss and what will haunt us and our children." She stood, lifting Agnes with her. "Our debts are paid. Your family dies here, and mine… someplace in America." She bent a knee before raising two fingers to her lips, kissing them, then placed her hand on William's headstone for the first and last time. Remembering the day he burst through the treeline with Duke, she whispered, "I'll always love you."

She rose to her feet and growled at Sarah Ann, "Take us back now, and *you* ride with the driver. We don't wish to speak with or see you *ever* again."

53

By the time Rachel rushed to the doorway to clutch her daughters, Sarah Ann's coach had already vanished down South Street, passing by Holy Cross Cemetery. It left a painful closure that would take years to heal, yet never to forget.

"Where in the heavens have you two been? And what kind of a note is *this* to leave me?"

"Mom!" Agnes shouted, attempting to divert her mother's fright. "We had no choice. We didn't know where Mrs. Fletcher wanted to take us. It's not Mary's fault."

"Mrs. Fletcher?" Rachel plunged her fingers deep into the folds of her Scottish mane and massaged her temples. "Sarah Ann was here and confronted you?" Tears streamed down her face as she sobbed. "I knew it! She wants me arrested! Or take the baby! She wants restitution, doesn't she?"

As they retreated into each other's arms, they sank to the wooden floor at Kirby's Lane, their hips and kicking feet holding the front door open. If Agnes hadn't been the one to close it, their cries and screams would have alerted any patrolling constables in the south end to come running.

Rachel's anger faded when she noticed Mary crying and Agnes comforting her. "What's the matter? What's wrong?" she asked Agnes, joining her in soothing Mary's shoulders.

"William's dead, Mother. Mrs. Fletcher took us up the hill to Mount Olivet to see his gravesite for ourselves."

Rachel held her heartbroken daughter. "Oh, sweetheart," she rocked Mary.

They collapsed onto the floor, drained from talking and crying, until someone attempted to open the front door, slamming it against Agnes's feet, who screamed within the dim shadows.

"It's just me home from the pub!" shouted George. "Stop yelling. You'll wake the dead across the street." He poked his head inside. "What are you all doing on the floor in the dark?"

Mary stumbled into the kitchen, rubbing her pins and needles. In the darkness, her wandering hands searched for the oil lamp and matches. With the lamp lit and her face glowing, she declared, "We're leaving! I need my son!"

"Oh, Mary," Rachel said, moving toward the light. "I can't afford for all of us to pick up and move somewhere else. Please use your return ticket instead of us." She glanced at George and Agnes in turn. "We'll find our way someday"—turning her attention to her son, who appeared guilty—"and you stop thinking it's your fault for drinking what might have been saved."

Agnes plunged her hands into her dress pockets, withdrawing one empty hand that she slipped into her hair.

The abrupt move caught Rachel's attention. "Do you have something to say?" she asked Agnes.

Agnes shook her head once.

Mary took her mother's hand. "I have another plan," she assured her. "I know someone who might have a boat. They may not be pleased to meet you, but I can smooth things over." She set the lamp in the center of the small table and pulled out a chair. "It's time to write another letter, and we won't wait for a reply that could take weeks. We're going to pack our clothes and go," she declared to her family, who were huddled around the kitchenette table, their faces illuminated by the oil lamp.

"Hold on a second," Rachel said, attempting to soothe her daughter and serve as the voice of reason. "Where exactly does this someone live?"

"Owls Head."

"And where is this Owls Head?"

"I dunno, but it's on the coast because Annie said they were boat builders and fishermen. It shouldn't be that difficult to find on a map."

George grumbled.

"You've drunk your last fill with the Monteleone brothers," Agnes scolded him.

Rachel shushed her. "Where'd you learn to sass like a sailor?"

Agnes grumbled.

"Whose Annie?" Rachel asked Mary.

"Annie and Richard Hatt. I met them on the boat the day I left." Mary slowly shook her head and shrugged. "Well… maybe they met me instead." She collected her thoughts. "I'll cash in my return trip ticket, see where we stand, and then find someone to take us along the eastern shore."

George stood with his back against the lone hanging cabinet that held a few sparse dishes belonging to the landlord. "What will we do when we get there, if we even find it, and these people don't want anything to do with us? Then what?"

"This woman cared about my well-being." Mary sighed and lowered her voice. "Yes, it's true. I panicked and left her and her husband in Boston, but she'll remember me. I *know* she will. They went there to buy stuff for their boat business." Her face lit up, and she turned to George. "It's not going to happen, but whatever, we'll clean fish for a living for the rest of our lives if we have to."

"Eww," Agnes exclaimed. "Are you trying to make me throw up?"

"I don't want to stay here either," Rachel admitted.

"Neither do I," Agnes said.

They all turned to George.

"What? Like I'm going to let the three of you up and float away somewhere into the North Atlantic?"

"So it's settled then," Rachel proclaimed for everyone. "Are you sure these people will help us?"

Mary glanced at each of them in succession. "I convinced you, didn't I? And I knew that would be the hard part."

54

So you spoke to J.L.?" Frank asked his fiancée.

"I believe it would be wise to postpone any financial discussions until after he's convinced that you're the right long-term investment for his daughter," Blanche said, directing one of her piercing eyes at him and raising a finely trimmed blonde eyebrow, urging him to respond.

The calendar showed Mary's self-imposed deadline was only a week away. He had promised her that he would acquire a ring in the city, which he did, and he was holding onto it, waiting for Mary to return and claim her son, who was now suckling at Blanche's breast.

He adored her and was deeply in love with her, wishing only for her father to gift them a new home, yet he didn't want to share her with anyone else.

"Is it safe to sleep with him between us at night? What if we accidentally crushed him in our sleep?" he asked her.

Pressed against her chest, she told the infant, "I would never let anything like that happen to you."

She stimulated his feeding, gently caressing a pudgy cheek near his lips with the knuckle of her finger. "Why do we have to bring him back now? This is a mother's most intimate moment."

Frank walked a fine line, resting his hand on Blanche's knee. "Because that's the arrangement with Gertrude… we alternate nights."

"But we only started this week, and I love it," she whined. "I pray she doesn't return."

"We have to get dressed. We need to open the store, so we're bringing him back now."

"One more week, right?"

"She said a month, so let's give her a month to return. If she doesn't… then we can have him."

"Does Gertrude know about this arrangement? Why would she trust our word—your word?"

"I don't know, but it's a valid question, I'll give you that."

Blanche shifted Roy to her shoulder, gently patting and rubbing circles on his back to burp him.

When her gentle patting became firmer, and Roy didn't burp, he reached for the boy and took him from her. "What are you thinking?"

Blanche stared beyond him over his shoulder, her jaded eyes fixed on the void.

55

After cashing in her round-trip S.S. Halifax ticket, Mary said goodbye to her family at Noble Wharf and walked a block to the corner of Bedford Row and George Street, where she mailed her last two letters at the post office built the previous year on the former site of the Cheapside Market, established in 1753.

She addressed one letter to Mrs. Gertrude Gates in Lincoln, Massachusetts, wanting Gertrude to know that she was bringing her family and the heartbreaking news of William back to Lincoln. The other was to Mrs. Annie Hatt in Owls Head, Nova Scotia, telling her that she was sorry, desperate for her help, and might arrive by boat before this letter reached her.

"Do you have a map of Nova Scotia?" she asked the postmaster. "I didn't see one in the lobby."

The postmaster was a weathered man in his late fifties with a thick gray mustache longer than the hair on his head. It hung over his upper lip and was paired with equally bushy eyebrows. His face was covered with enough hair to keep warm in the winter, but not his chin. He wore a white shirt and black trousers held up by suspenders and a gold pocket watch chain that shined against the black wool, and Mary swallowed the lump in her throat when it reminded her of her father's.

"Something I can help you with?" he asked, glancing at both letters.

"Do you know of this town Owls Head? I'm sure it's somewhere along the eastern shore."

He held up Gertrude's letter. "That'll be five cents for the international letter, and yes, it's not big enough to be called a town, but it's up the coast along the Ship Harbor mail route."

Mary handed over a nickel from her ticket refund. "Do I need to travel by boat, or is it close enough for a taxi carriage?"

The postmaster eyed her, wiggling his mustache as he pondered. Mary thought it resembled a giant moth ready to take flight from his face.

"How soon are you looking to get there?"

"Very."

"Then you'll need to take a boat, but that's expensive."

Mary glanced behind her at the empty lobby. "How much does it cost?"

"A lot."

"Then a carriage?"

"Quinn's stagecoach will get you there. It's the mail run from here up to Sheet Harbor. Stops at Porter's Lake, Musquodoboit Harbor, Lakeville, then Ship Harbor will be your closest stop."

"How far?"

"I'd say about fifty miles or a long day. It leaves promptly at 6 am."

"Room for four? I need to get there."

He rubbed his mustache. "All I can tell you is that it leaves every Monday, Wednesday, and Friday at 6 am sharp, so get there early." He glanced again at the letter addressed to Owls Head. "Do you still want to mail this letter?" he asked, holding it up.

"Sure. Always good to have a backup plan, right?"

Mary first spotted her mother on the dock, recognizing her and her sister's signature auburn manes amidst the undulating crowds. Agnes and George were sitting with bags at their feet. Mary searched for her canvas satchel and sat beside her siblings, pulling it snugly between her feet. "So, I have good news and bad news," she said, rubbing the silver brooch under her thumb.

"No more bad news," complained Agnes.

"A boat ride is beyond our means, but the mail stagecoach can take us nearly all the way."

"So, no boat is the bad news?" Rachel asked.

"Not really." Mary wasn't looking forward to staying up all night or sleeping on the street, but she had no other options. They had already left Kirby's Lane behind, and even if they hadn't, there was no way she would have wanted to climb the hill again, and she certainly wasn't going to make her mother do it either. "It leaves here at 6 am, and we need to be at the front of the line if we want all four of us to get on board. Otherwise, we're stuck here another two days."

With heads bowed, they sat determined, aware they had come too far to change their course again.

• • •

Lydia and Abigail Fletcher stood in the shadows under the eaves of Lower Water Street, across from Noble Wharf, as they watched the Nuttings huddle by the dock entrance, assuming they were waiting to board the next ship bound for Boston.

Lydia leaned against the building wall with her raven-black hair, heated from the morning sun, pulled up and off her neck into a ponytail, letting the shaded granite stone cool her skin. Her onyx eyes scanned the street and dock, watching to see if anyone approached the family ultimately responsible for her father's and brother's deaths.

Convincing her sister to follow them down the hill from Kirby's Lane was an easy ruse, promising Abigail a day of shopping downtown for new clothes.

Lydia took her sister's hand and gently squeezed it in rhythm with her pulsing heart. "So, what would you think?"

Abigail followed her sister's leer across the street, focusing on the two women with rich hair who were unmistakable after weeks of surveillance. "What would we think?"

Lydia turned to her younger sister and asked again, "What would you think... about us seeing America?"

"We do have all these bags of new clothes and Grandma's allowance burning a hole in our pockets."

The sisters knew their infant nephew was there, and if they could bring him back to heal their family, they would do it for their brother.

"For William," Abigail declared.
"For William," Lydia agreed.

56

Annie Hatt loved the feel of the soft dirt under her knees as she weeded and scratched in her flowerbeds. She inhaled the scents of her daisies and lilies, careful not to stick her nose into any flower a pollen-collecting honey bee occupied.

Charles Cox's schooner, the Ivy Maud, was finished, and she turned to see if she could spot Richard and Reuben out on the water in the bay, putting her through her sea trials.

It was an exceptionally prosperous year, and the payment for the schooner, their largest ever, would support them through the following spring. Although Reuben and Robert had moved out, they remained close as neighbors in Southwest Cove, which ensured the family's building and fishing businesses operated smoothly.

Squinting into the sun, attempting to block the reflection off the water, the first throb of a headache made her feel the bubble guts, and she vomited her breakfast into the dirt of the flowerbed.

"Oh, dear," she murmured to herself. "That certainly came on fast."

Scratching the vomit into the soil, she spit out the remnants left in her mouth and wiped her nose on her already soiled long sleeve, adding laundry to her already busy list of chores.

She was forty-seven years old and had six children. Half were adults, while Clifford was nearly six and no longer entirely dependent on her. She was three weeks late for her period, so the morning sickness didn't come as a shock, but this seventh child certainly wasn't planned.

"At least, please be another girl," she whispered, rubbing her stomach as she spoke to the unborn child.

The white sails masted to the thirty-foot schooner were highly visible against the dark waters of the bay as her boys returned to dock in Palmers Cove.

"I hope your father's heart can handle the news," she whispered again.

"What news?" Omeda asked, sneaking up on her mother.

Omeda knelt on the grass beside her mother, deliberately timing her arrival a bit too late to help pull weeds. Her hair faded from blonde to chestnut, its golden highlights shimmering in the morning sun. Approaching sixteen, she stood eye to eye with her mother, unlike her older sister, who had inherited their father's height. Always eager to please, they were best friends, supporting each other in the kitchen and caring for their two younger brothers.

She sniffed the air. "What's that smell?" she asked, leaning closer to her mother and taking more exaggerated lungfuls of air.

Annie knew there was no reason to keep secrets within the family. "I was sick a minute ago. You're smelling it in the dirt, right there," she told her daughter, pointing to the freshly scratched topsoil. "It'll fertilize the crocus bulbs for next spring."

"Eww."

"No, not eww, it was morning sickness." Annie realized Omeda was too young to remember this natural part of pregnancy. "I'm pregnant again," she said, bracing herself.

Omeda reacted swiftly, crossing her arms over her chest and huffing. "I don't want another brother! Ada and I are already surrounded by too many as it is!"

Annie opened her arms, inviting Omeda into an embrace. "I'll do my best."

Omeda relaxed and hugged her best friend. "And we just got our rooms too." She squeezed her mother for emphasis, then pushed away, hearing sounds coming from the front of the house. "Neighbors are here," she said, turning towards the noise.

"You hear someone?"

"Yes, I hear voices out front... women's voices."

"Help me up," Annie asked her daughter, pushing down on Omeda's shoulders for support.

The house stood vacant. Richard and Reuben were on the schooner with Ada, who went along for the trip to catch a spring tan, and Clifford and Henry were with Robert out lobstering.

Knocking sounds.

"Hello? Is anyone home? Annie?" a woman's voice echoed.

Annie thought they weren't strangers, though she didn't recognize the voice as belonging to any of her neighbors. Something about it felt familiar. Taking her first step after standing up too quickly made her stomach gurgle with more bubble guts, but she hurried around the side of the house toward the front porch and door.

Three women and one man stood in the shade on Annie's covered front porch. Their travel bags rested on the side of Cove Road at the head of the walkway. She didn't recognize them until one of the younger women spotted her rounding the corner of the house.

The young woman recognized Annie before Annie remembered her. "Annie Hatt?" the woman inquired, quickly leaving the porch and walking down the steps.

Annie met her halfway, recognizing the young woman's face as the lone traveler they'd accompanied to Boston. She saw she was no longer pregnant, and no one was holding a baby. Her emotions were roiling, and she couldn't stop herself from welling up. "MJ! Mary!" she shouted. "You're alive! And safe!"

Mary closed the distance between them, embracing the wonderful woman who had worked so diligently to comfort and help her. "Annie! I'm so sorry!" she exclaimed, burying her face in Annie's neck and crying.

Tears soaked their shoulders.

Annie clutched Mary as if she were her daughter, caterwauling, "We couldn't find you! You needed boots! We never got you new boots!"

Omeda moved to her mother's side, not recognizing these strangers. "Mom?" she interrupted, tugging at her mother's shirt.

Annie released Mary, wiping her eyes and nose on her soiled sleeve, and tried to rein in her emotions. "Mary, this is—"

"You must be Omeda," Mary finished for her. "The good-natured one," she said, gently touching Omeda's elbow.

"Mom?"

Annie turned to her youngest daughter. "It's a long story. I'll explain more later," she said, pointing to Mary. "This is Mary Jane. Your father and I met her on our last trip to Boston."

Omeda looked unconvinced as she glanced toward the bay, searching.

Rachel approached, knowing everything about the woman who had offered to help her daughter when she had faltered. The coach ride had been long, bumpy, and arduous, and there was nothing to do but fill the hours with conversation.

"This is my mother, Rachel, and that's my younger sister, Agnes, and my brother, George," Mary said, pointing to each in turn.

Omeda instantly appeared envious of Agnes's luscious hair, ogling it briefly before giving George an untrustworthy flinch.

"Rachel," Annie said, extending her hand. She sensed the thickness and weight of the air between them, knowing this woman was the reason Mary's baby was not present. "Mary Jane spoke of you—"

"It's all bad, I'm sure," Rachel interrupted. "I feel so..." She trailed off, dropping her chin to her chest.

Annie could see the guilt washing over Mary's mother. "Why don't we all go inside and have something to eat and drink? You must all be tired from your trip up here."

"You have no idea," Agnes interjected.

"My husband, Richard, should be home soon. He's out on the bay with a schooner we built over winter."

"We?" Omeda scoffed.

"My husband and older sons," Annie corrected herself to satisfy her good-natured but sassy daughter.

"I can't believe you remembered and made it here!" Annie said as she led the way into the house, followed by Mary, Rachel, George, Agnes, and Omeda, who brought up the rear.

"I like your hair," Omeda said, tapping Agnes on the shoulder.

"I like yours too," Agnes confessed. "Mine is too much work, brushing and braiding, day and night. I like winter. It keeps me warm, but it's too hot in the summer."

Omeda smiled, appearing eager to socialize with another girl. "I'm almost sixteen."

"I'm nearly eighteen," Agnes said, gesturing towards her brother. "And George is almost twenty-one."

"He seems quiet."

Agnes shrugged. "He's all right. He means well."

Everyone gathered around the butcher block island in the kitchen to enjoy water and tea.

Annie's kitchen was much larger than Gertrude's. It even had a water view from the window above the elbow-deep soapstone sink. Copper pans hung over the counter above the stove, while copper pots were arranged by size over the kitchen island.

"Your kitchen is incredible," Mary said. "I think it's bigger than our entire farmhouse back in Stewiacke."

"Wait… you came down from Stewiacke?" Annie asked, sipping from a glass of water. All she could think about was drinking and not feeling hungry. "I assumed you rode all day with Quinn."

Mary glanced at her mother and nodded before turning to Annie. "No, not there… and yes, we did. That's why we're here."

Annie let her silence linger, aware that Mary would fill the void with more answers.

"We came to ask for help."

"May I ask if the help might have something to do with who's missing?" Annie prayed, scanning everyone's faces in the kitchen.

Mary swallowed and licked her lips. After taking a long drink of water, she said, "My son, yes."

"You had a boy! How wonderful! And?" Annie urged.

"He's in Massachusetts. I left him *temporarily* in good hands to come home and convince my family to return."

Annie still did not leap to respond.

"I wrote you a letter the day before we rode the mail coach. I wasn't sure how or when we could get here. We're out of money and food, and we don't have any friends," she paused, stopping short of mentioning their former friends.

"I don't fully understand why you need our help. Why did you leave us in Boston?"

Mary turned to Rachel, sniffling, her emotions on the verge of erupting. "I felt guilty and such a burden. It was my fault that I got pregnant."

"No, it was my fault," Rachel cried. "I'm the guilty one."

"You weren't a burden to us," Annie said, starting to cry as well. "We were meant to find each other on that trip… on *that* day… so we could help. We had the means." She composed herself. "Richard and I were terrified when we lost you that morning. I felt so guilty for leaving you alone on the dock while I signed some foolish papers."

Rachel clasped her hands over her heart. "You showed such kindness toward my daughter."

Annie remained focused on Mary, needing more answers.

"I'm sorry, I felt like I was being such a burden, and Frank helped—"

Annie threw up her hand, stopping her. "Who is Frank?"

"He was a guy who worked in the warehouse where you and Richard were signing whatever papers you needed to sign."

Annie covered her mouth, her skin starting to itch with anxiety.

Rachel flinched at her abrupt movement.

Unfazed, Mary said, "He told me his supervisor had taken you and Richard to the train station office. I remember it was something about setting up the delivery schedule. I made him take your bag back into the warehouse so it would be there when you were done."

Annie and Rachel exchanged glances, and in that moment, they understood each other.

Mary couldn't stop herself. "Frank said he knew a midwife who could help deliver my baby, and I was so sure then that I wanted to give him up, but I was all jumble-headed and confused. But thank God, it all worked out!

"We took the train to Lincoln, and Mrs. Gates was so kind. Her best friend is the town midwife, Gladys. They're so sweet, Gladys and Gertie. Well, Gertrude is. Gladys, not so much. But, I fell in love with the place and the people, and I want us all to go back, but we can't all afford the trip, at least not all together."

Mary finally stopped talking and reached for her empty glass.

Annie closed her eyes, allowing most of what Mary said to go in one ear and out the other, and breathed deeply, scolding herself for being so careless that day at the wharf. She should never have left Mary alone. Fleeting memories of the dapper man in pinstriped pants who had locked eyes with her flickered in her mind.

"MJ... Mary," Annie said, filling a new glass with water. She carried it from the sink around the end of the kitchen island to where Rachel and Mary sat, placing the glass in front of Mary. She leaned on the island, closing the space between their faces. "No one helped us. We never had to go to North Station. We never saw our bag again after leaving it with you on the dock. Do you understand?"

"No," Mary whispered. "You didn't?"

Annie slowly shook her head from side to side.

"He lied?"

"Who did you leave your son with?" Annie asked.

Rachel looked at her daughter, waiting for an answer.

George flexed his fists under the counter.

Agnes and Omeda found each other's hands and squeezed tightly.

"With Mrs. Gates, but we agreed that Frank and his fiancée, Blanche, would help watch him."

"Mary Jane Nutting," Rachel scolded her daughter, turning away and biting her fist.

Mary's lips quivered, and tears drizzled down her cheeks, dripping and splattering onto the butcher block. "Frank rode the train with me back to Boston. Before I boarded the ship, I made him promise that he and Blanche could keep Roy if something went wrong and I didn't come back in a month."

"Mary? And this was when?" Annie probed, her stomach churning from stress and morning sickness.

"Three weeks ago."

Annie turned and dry-heaved over the hardwood island, grappling with her deepest maternal fear of losing a child.

Richard was the first to notice his wife's distress as he entered the kitchen, followed closely by Reuben and Ada. He immediately locked eyes with Omeda and searched her face for any signs that she was hurt.

"Annie!" he shouted, rushing across the room to his wife's side. He wrapped an arm around her waist and lifted her face to his. "What's wrong?" He scanned the kitchen, eyeing the strangers in his house, pressing his wife's face to his shoulder. "Who are you people?"

When his eyes reached the last dark-haired woman, he said, "It's you." He hugged his wife tighter. "What's this about?"

Annie pushed herself away from her husband's chest and out of his grip. An hour earlier, she had been alone, smelling her perennials and enjoying a tranquility she seldom had the chance to enjoy by herself. Now, everything felt like a full moon tidal surge. "Richard," she said, gaining his attention as she placed her hands palms flat on his chest and focused her eyes on his.

"Mom's having a baby!" shouted Omeda, her voice soaring into a squeak.

Annie huffed and turned to her daughter, disappointed that she had not been allowed to ease into the news, which was, at that moment, the least of all their worries. "Thank you, Omeda."

Ada rushed to her mother and wrapped her in a bear hug, ignoring the strangers in the kitchen.

"We need to focus," Annie pleaded. "Yes, I'm expecting again. I know it's a shock and a surprise. This baby is still nine months away, but we have more pressing issues at hand." She steadied herself, accepting Richard's kiss and squeezes. "Richard"—she waited until she was sure she had his full attention—"this is Mary Jane's family: her mother, Rachel, her brother, George, and her sister, Agnes. This is my husband, Richard, our oldest son, Reuben, and our oldest daughter, Ada." She squinted at Omeda. "And you've already met our daughter Omeda, the tattletale."

Richard glanced at them and nodded in acknowledgment but remained silent.

"We need to sail to Boston as quickly as we can." She tugged at his shirt lapels to keep his attention. "We need to get Mary's baby and bring him home."

Reuben stepped forward, unable to remain silent any longer. "What? Who are these people? What exactly is going on here?"

Rachel stood. "I'm not sure why I let my daughter convince me—maybe we should step outside. We had no idea." She looked at her children. "Let's leave this family in peace. C'mon now," she urged them to follow.

Omeda and Agnes exchanged a fleeting hug before Agnes left the kitchen, dragging her feet.

George followed her. "It's a pleasure to meet you, sir," he told Richard.

Reuben stood his ground, unsmiling and on guard.

As she left, Annie grasped Mary's arm, delivering a smile at her. "Don't… you… leave," she emphasized slowly. "I'm not going through *that* again. Do you understand?"

"Yes, ma'am," Mary assured her. "I hear you." She told Richard, "I'm so sorry. Please forgive me."

Mary walked out of the kitchen, lingering over her shoulder, her eyes uncertain with fear and embarrassment.

Ada moved to join Reuben and took a stance. "How do you know those people?" she asked again, repeating her brother's question to their parents.

"They met her on the boat to Boston. She was pregnant then," Omeda blurted out.

"Omeda!" Annie scolded. "Do you mind?" She glared at her daughter. "As a matter of fact, why don't you go outside with them? It looks like you've already managed to make a new friend."

Omeda bolted out of the kitchen like a wild colt. No one had to ask her twice.

Annie turned to her children. "Yes, your father and I met Mary Jane on the ship to Boston while buying supplies to finish the Ivy Maud. She was an expectant mother out of wedlock—"

Reuben and Ada huffed, leaving Annie bewildered by their lack of empathy. How could they make her question how she had raised them?

"Do not judge, lest ye be judged. Matthew 7," she reminded them. "She needed help, and we are a helping family"—pointing at Reuben—"We helped you and your brother. Aunts, uncles, and cousins help each other. The people up and down the eastern shore help each other… that's what we do."

"You should have seen your mother," Richard said. "When we lost that girl in Boston, she broke your mother's heart by walking away from us."

"Richard, listen," Annie said before sharing everything Mary had confessed about Frank's grift and falsehoods.

Richard took a deep breath to steady himself. "So this isn't finished… is it?" he asked his wife.

"I'm afraid it's not. And we know what we have to do."

Richard stared at the bay through the window above the sink. "Well… there's nothing like an actual sea trial to determine if she's seaworthy."

Annie didn't see a problem with it. "We'll tell Charles it's how we conduct business. A full sea trial is essential. He's waited all winter"—waving a dismissive hand—"so he can wait another week or two."

Richard scanned the room, looking at everything they had built. "It might be dangerous. Do we really want to do this?"

Annie placed her hands on her midsection. "We do."

"Well, you're not going, that's for sure."

"It has to be you," she said, looking at her oldest son. "And, of course, Reuben and Mary."

"I'm not sure two of us can handle a thirty-footer alone in the open water." Richard closed his eyes. "Imagining a worst-case storm, we'll probably need Robert."

"No," Ada said. "We can't afford to have all three of you gone. Robert stays. I'll go. I can sail, and besides, I'm not letting Mary sail off into the North Atlantic alone."

Annie knew she was right and, feeling dehydrated, poured herself another glass of water. "It's decided then. I'll go, let them know, and then we'll start supper. We have extra mouths to feed, and I hope we have enough to eat."

"Mom, we always have extra fish. We're up to our ears in dried cod," Ada said sarcastically. "If I eat any more codfish, I'll grow scales and fins and swim into the bay. Maybe I'll swim to Europe and find a nice husband."

"But you'd be a codfish," Reuben reminded her. "Who would want to marry a codfish?"

"Shut up," she said, punching her brother's shoulder.

57

B lanche sorted the day's mail during a lull in sales. Giddy with excitement and anxiety, she wished the clock would spin faster. It was her day to keep Roy overnight, and the workday hours weren't passing quickly enough to satisfy her needs.

The Donaldson brothers were on their lunch break, gathered around the cold, unlit wood stove that had been shut down for the season, discussing how nice it was to be ahead of schedule on the Center School's renovations, thanks to the stretch of pleasant weather.

Spring clothing sales had peaked, and by late morning, the morning rush of fruit and vegetable sales had depleted the store's stock.

It wasn't the address on the letter to Mrs. Gertrude Gates, Sandy Pond Road, that caught Blanche's eye, but rather the Halifax postmark. She hesitated, pinching the letter by a corner, holding it steady, while her free hand moved to her cameo. She wore her mother's portrait as a talisman on her collar and rubbed it as she contemplated her next move—whether to slip the letter into Gertrude's pigeonhole unread or to read it.

She looked around the store. The Donaldson men weren't paying her any mind, and the rest of the store was vacant, so she traced her fingers along the back flap of the envelope, hoping it would already be loose, making her decision easier. The letter was clearly from Mary, and she was eager to know its contents. Was Mary coming back, and when? Was she delayed? Or had she chosen to stay in Canada? Perhaps the latter. (She could only hope.)

Placing the letter on the counter, she noticed the back flap was neither loose nor tight—something a sharp opener could slip under and lift free. How could she reseal the envelope, she wondered while scanning the post office space, hoping an answer would come to her. Glancing behind the register, she noticed the rows of tinctures and paused at a resin and tree sap product that would only need a finger smudge to reseal it.

Blanche slid a letter opener under the flap and gently pried it away from the back, feeling the seal separate. If it ripped, then what? Read it and destroy it? She didn't want Gertrude to know that a letter had been opened. So why not just tear it open, read it, and dispose of it? She had a plan and a backup plan, so she opened the envelope, avoiding tears, and withdrew the letter, unfolding it flat on the countertop. After reading the note, she crumpled it along with the envelope in one hand, pounding on the countertop with the other, while the Donaldsons all turned to stare.

58

I'll go with my sister," George told the Hatts. "You could use my help on the ship, and Mary could use my help once we get there."

Ada stood straight, matching her older brother's height, and planted her fists on her hips. "It's not a ship, it's a schooner." She glared at the Nutting siblings. "Have either of you ever been on the water before?"

Mary raised her hand sheepishly.

"That doesn't count," Ada said, lowering her fists.

George looked down at his feet. The coastal air was crisp and fresh, a stark contrast to the Halifax hillside. He closed his eyes, remembering the smell of dried hay on their inland farm. It was a place he knew he would never return to, but he could adapt. "Never, but I'm a quick learner."

He noticed Ada's button nose and long lashes, trying his best to smile warmly, but he feared he had failed miserably.

"I say we spend as much time on the bay before we tackle the full crossing," Ada said, raising her hand, appearing to start a vote. "They're no use to us or themselves if they're puking as bad as Mom."

The color drained from George's face. "Puking?"

"Ada!" Annie said. "Don't be mean."

Omeda provided the official term. "That means seasick."

George realized he had to do whatever it took to safeguard the women in his family. "I can handle it," he asserted.

"Handle what?" Robert asked, poking his head into the family kitchen and letting loose his baby brothers, Henry and Clifford, who clamored to their mother's side, wrapping themselves around her legs like octopuses. "And who are these people?"

Agnes gaped as she slowly untied the cloth from her braid, lifted her hair high above her head, and arched her shoulders.

Robert scanned the faces of the outsiders and stopped to focus on the young lady with the lion's mane of red hair cascading through her fingers.

59

W e're leaving." Blanche's final demand to her fiancé urged Frank onward as they walked across the town common toward the tavern. "We need to pack a couple of bags before we pick up Roy. It's our night to have him, and we'll be gone before Gertrude knows what to do in the morning."

"So we're just pulling up stakes and taking him to Boston?"

"I don't see any choice. We need to leave before Mary gets back."

She quickened her pace, eager to gather their belongings from above the tavern. They would take the little money stashed under the bar and add it to the small amount of cash she dared take from the store, where she would leave a note on the register for Carrie to find in the morning, letting her know that she and Frank were going to the city for a few days of rest.

Blanche was no longer winded as she arrived at Gertrude's front door after the walk from town. The weeks of exercise had strengthened her lungs, and with a growing infant, Roy had added definition to her arms, shoulders, and legs. Frank couldn't seem to keep his hands off her bottom, which now felt as firm as it did when she was twenty. (So she claimed.) He was stuck to her like hide glue, a marionette on strings.

Gertrude opened the front door before Blanche could knock. "Afternoon," she greeted them. "We were in the front room and heard you coming up the steps."

Gertrude had forgone getting her hair cut for the past few weeks, mainly because she had been housebound with Roy, and it now nearly brushed her shoulders. She tucked it behind her ears, removed her spectacles, and wiped them on her apron. Her shirt, always ironed, was wrinkled and unbuttoned at the collar. The skin on her face appeared thinner with more noticeable lines, perhaps indicating she hadn't been drinking enough water lately.

"I'm sorry I'm not presentable," she said apologetically. "But Roy's been wearing me out lately." She waved them inside and pointed to him lying on his belly on the rug, head lifted, smiling and drooling, flailing his arms and legs like a swimmer paddling across Flint's Pond. "He must be getting close to crawling. I can't leave him alone anymore."

Blanche slid past Gertrude into the front room, lifting Roy into her arms and over her shoulder. "Are you trying to run away?" she whispered into his ear, bouncing him gently on her shoulder.

She slid Roy off her shoulder, holding him aloft with one hand under his chest and the other gripping an ankle. Then, she spun in a circle so he could fly like a bird. He squealed, drooling as her skirt billowed like a merry-go-round canopy.

"Oh, be careful!" Gertrude pleaded, clearly anxious that Blanche might lose her grip.

"Don't worry, he loves it! I won't let him fly through the front window."

Frank stepped into the room, arms slightly extended, looking ready to dive to one side or the other in case he needed to catch a soaring infant who waved his arms and kicked his feet, showing everyone that he was having a great time.

Gertrude's heart stopped pounding against her rib cage when Blanche stopped spinning, but her face remained flushed as she fanned herself with her hand. "I made something new for him. Give me a moment, and I'll go fetch it from the sewing room to show you." She walked down the foyer, pausing to grasp the newel post at the base of the stairs before continuing to the back sewing room, her shoe heels clicking on the wood-paneled floor.

As she vanished around the staircase, Blanche jerked her head and widened her eyes to signal Frank. "Let's get moving… we're going to miss the train."

He nodded like a marionette.

When Gertrude returned, holding what appeared to be a cotton sack, she told them, "I sewed him a sleep sack. He can grow into it. I made the sleeves a bit longer. You can roll them up, and the length is a little long, so his legs will still fit as he grows. And"—she held up the drawstring—"I sewed in this drawstring instead of leggings, so you can pull it tight at night to keep his feet warm."

"Just like Santa's toy sack," Frank said, oblivious to Blanche's scowling look directed at him.

Blanche had never sewn anything in her life, yet she smiled. "What a wonderful idea, Gertrude. We'll use it tonight."

Mary's return, a knock on the door, and missing the last train to Boston were driving Blanche paranoid. She imagined herself pulling the sleep sack over Gertrude's head and tightening the drawstring until there was one less connection to her and Roy's disappearance—someone who could talk.

"Slow night at the tavern?" Gertrude asked Franklin.

"There's a water leak under the bar. I had to close and can't look into fixing it until tomorrow morning."

Blanche smiled; once a snake oil salesman, always a snake oil salesman.

Gertrude shook her head. "Oh dear. I think that place needs a fresh start. Tear it down and have the Donaldsons build something new. Being so close to the new library, it's such an eyesore now."

"That it is," Frank agreed, once more oblivious to Blanche's pursed lips and scowl.

"We should probably get going," Blanche suggested, unable to hold back any longer. "Is his bag all packed, by any chance?"

Gertrude looked at Franklin. "Don't you want to try convincing me to stay for supper?" she asked, knowing that if either of them agreed, Franklin would be the one to do it.

"We can't, really," Blanche apologized, not offering Frank an escape. "I want to keep walking to see the pond. We'll turn back before it gets dark"—she poked Frank in the ribs—"this one needs all the exercise he can get because Little Joe does all the work making deliveries." She forced a chuckle at her joke.

Gertrude looked a little dejected. "Alrighty, then. I'll pack his bag and dish out some fresh porridge I made this morning."

"How about you pack his bag?" Frank asked. "Don't forget this cute new sleep sack. Is that what you call it? And I'll dish the porridge in the kitchen. Maybe I'll have a spoonful or two to tide me over on the walk up to the pond." He looked at Blanche, gently touching the tip of Roy's nose. "And you're in charge of him."

In the kitchen, Frank quickly scanned the table, counters, and baker's rack for a pencil and paper. He took a hefty spoonful of porridge and shifted his eyes around the room, returning to the baker's rack to open the two drawers. They contained nothing but place mats, cloth napkins, and cookbooks. He took another spoonful, winced, and opened the cabinets on either side of the sink, which only held spectacles, mugs, and tea cups. On the middle shelf of the pantry closet, he found a piece of paper and a pencil with Gertrude's shopping list. He wrote a note on the back and turned to place it on the table but hesitated, instead putting the note with its shopping list back on the shelf where he'd found it in the pantry. He left the dirty porridge spoon in the sink, washed his mouth with a glass of water from the tap, and picked up a small, empty-lidded crock from the counter by the stove.

He met Gertrude at the bottom of the staircase, where she handed him the baby bag, and he tucked the empty container into a corner at the bottom.

Blanche handed Roy to Frank. "Could you please put him in the carriage for me? I'd like a glass of water before we leave," she said, walking down the foyer into the kitchen, where she walked to the sink and picked up the same water glass from the counter that she had heard Frank pour for himself. As she sipped from the glass, she scanned the countertops and the empty table, noticing only the dirty spoon in the sink.

After a brief pause at the baker's rack, looking into the drawers and even checking the top shelf because she could, she left Gertrude's Queen Anne cottage for the last time, feeling satisfied.

60

Lydia and Abigail Fletcher stood on Lewis Wharf, looking down at their shoes. "America feels the same under my shoes. How about you?" Abigail asked.

Lydia sniffed the air. "It definitely smells better," she admitted, noticing the cleaner, saltier air without the stench of horse manure and musty sewage. "It's cleaner, too. I like what I see so far."

The two sisters stood in the shade, considering their next move. Their mother told them that Mary had wanted her blessing to allow William to go to a town called Lincoln. It had to be somewhere outside Boston along a commuter rail line.

"Should we find the nearest train station or eat first? I'm hungry. I dunno about you," Lydia said.

"I need to pee first, then eat, but not lobster. There has to be more to eat around here besides seafood."

Lydia watched the people entering and exiting the granite doorways. Those going in were empty-handed, while those coming out carried shopping bags. Before leaving Halifax, their shoulder bags were well stocked. "Let's head inside," she said.

They found and used the same washroom Mary had used, unaware it was where Frank had thrown the Hatts' bag into the trash.

In the courtyard, Lydia stopped the first couple carrying shopping bags. They appeared to be moving confidently, unlike her, who felt lost. The gentleman wore a tweed herringbone newsboy hat and an off-white loose-fitting shirt beneath a matching tweed vest. His trousers were wool, despite the warm early May weather. The woman wore a wide-brim sun hat, the edges adorned with lace, a white pleated shirt buttoned at the collar, and a thin belted linen skirt.

The only difference between her attire and theirs was the sun hat that Lydia coveted, which she used to draw their attention. "Excuse me, but I love your hat. Did you purchase it nearby?" she asked the woman, touching her elbow before letting her pass by.

The couple halted, and the woman spun around. Her complexion was olive, her thick eyebrows shaded her dark brown eyes, and her high cheekbones complemented her full, kissable lips.

Lydia's pulse quickened, and her pupils dilated.

The woman adjusted her bags and pointed to where they had come from. "Yes, Murray's Toggery Shop."

Lydia's eyes swept over the woman's figure. "Thank you."

"Pleasure."

"We're just visiting." Lydia saw no reason to share details. "Is there a nice place nearby for lunch?"

The man and woman exchanged snickers, glancing at each other to determine who would respond first. The man gestured first, giving her the honors. "This is the north end of Boston. I hope you enjoy Italian cuisine." Her accent sounded almost royal, and her broad, radiant smile exhibited good hygiene.

Lydia returned the smile. "I do like Italian."

Abigail tugged at the man's elbow. "And where is the nearest train station?"

He pointed across the courtyard to the distant corner, where a sign guided travelers to North Station.

"Much obliged," Abigail said, turning her attention away from her coquettish sister, who continued exchanging grins with the Italian woman.

61

Frank pushed the carriage down Station Road, feeling the strain in his legs and ankles, and he couldn't wait to drop into a cushioned seat, fearing he only had enough strength to lift the carriage with Roy up the stairs from street level to the railway platform.

He watched Blanche walk to the ticket window, knowing she was buying two tickets to North Station, but he had a more straightforward plan, which he hoped to convince her to adopt soon.

The shrill steam whistle announced the train's arrival from Silver Hill, which meant their departing train on the parallel tracks would arrive shortly from Concord.

Blanche sidled up next to Frank, hooking her arm around his elbow while bending and wiggling her free fingers at a dozing Roy lying in the carriage. They made a dapper couple and proud parents.

• • •

The Fitchburg rail cars slowed to a crawl, coming to a final stop, and lurched Lydia and Abigail forward in their seats. The conductor had announced this as the Lincoln stop at South Station, so they disembarked onto the platform, which was no Lewis Wharf. The later hour likely accounted for the decrease in commuters, as there were no randomly zig-zagging crowds arriving and departing, seeking places to shop and eat, or headed home from working an overtime shift.

Lydia no longer needed her new decorative hat, as the sun had set, leaving the station in a dusky afterglow. After the bumpy ride, she and Abigail arched their backs, stretching their muscles, and hoped their full bellies of pasta and meatballs would finally have a chance to settle.

No one seemed to be boarding to continue up the line, but Lydia spotted a well-dressed couple with an infant carriage standing proudly on the station platform, waiting and looking up the vacant rails. The man wore a black derby hat, vest, and mottled pinstriped black pants, which was something she had never seen before. The woman was tall and lithe, as tall as the man, with long braided bright blonde hair, delicate eyebrows, pale skin, and a button nose. The Italian woman had fuller lips that were more attractive, but this woman had fuller breasts.

She gently nudged Abigail's hip with her own. "Let's go see the baby."

• • •

Frank couldn't help but notice the two young women who stepped off the arriving train. They were well-dressed, with the raven-haired one appearing slightly overdressed with her decorative lace hat, while the chestnut-haired woman seemed younger and more tomboyish.

They must have noticed the infant carriage and approached with smiles because babies attract all women, like fish, to fresh bait. That's how he caught Blanche without a net.

"Good afternoon," said the woman with shiny raven hair. "I couldn't help but notice a new baby." She leaned closer to the carriage, lifting the brim of her hat with her hand so it wouldn't obstruct her view. "Is it a boy or a girl?"

"He's a boy, our son. His name is Roy," Blanche said, reaching into the carriage to pull the edge of the blanket off his chin.

"How lovely! You must be very proud parents."

"We are, thanks."

The raven-haired woman leaned in further, closer to Roy's face. "He has such beautiful eyes."

• • •

The blonde woman stood inches taller than Lydia and appeared older, similar to the man. Age lines were etched around the corners of her lips, and her green eyes were shiny, even in the fading light of dusk.

Lydia couldn't help but notice the baby boy's eyes—the vivid moonstone color reminded her so much of William's.

She wished the new parents well and, along with Abigail, walked up Station Road, the only road, toward what she hoped was the town center.

The sign over the building's facade read *"J.L. Chapin's General Store,"* but it was dark and closed for the day, so Lydia looked north up Bedford Road while Abigail looked east, scanning the town common.

"I think I see lights over there," Abigail said, pointing. "This isn't Water Street or the north end of Boston. There better be a place to stay. I'm not sleeping on the grass under a tree."

"Are you worried that everyone will see your green gown tomorrow?" Lydia teased her, knocking her off balance with her hip.

"Very funny, as if I don't know what that means." Abigail stuck out her tongue.

Lydia smirked. "You learned from the best."

The sisters walked across the town square, where fallen chestnuts crunched under their shoes until they reached the Hunt Tavern. The interior was illuminated by a couple of oil lamps perched on the bar, and there were no patrons other than a man wiping down liquor bottles behind the counter.

Lydia knocked on the glass door to get his attention. He was bald, with matted dark gray hair wrapped around his head from ear to ear. His white collared shirt was open at the collar, revealing gray chest hairs longer than those on the sides of his head. Noticing her, he wiped his hands on a dirty apron tied around his waist, which hadn't seen a day's rest in decades.

He crossed the room and opened the door slightly. "We're closed. Come back Friday night," he said, his voice grinding as if he had rocks in his throat.

Lydia lifted her hand, placing her pale palm flush on the door glass. "Do you rent rooms?"

The bartender swung the door open a bit wider, peering more closely at the two young women outside. He seemed wary, scanning them from head to toe, and let out a grunt, exhaling heavily.

Abigail waved his dry breath away from her face while Lydia reached for a handful of silver coins within her dress with her free hand. "We have money. We can pay," she stated, exposing her palmful of coins to him.

He beckoned them to enter. "Welcome to the Hunt Tavern, ladies, the hub of Lincoln. Will you all be needin' two rooms and a drink? Or one room and two drinks?"

Setting aside their fear, the sisters moved to a table closest to the bar and sat, crossing their legs and fluffing their skirts, careful not to reveal what they'd purchased at Murray's Toggery Shop in North Station for protection. Confident that their garter belt daggers were within quick reach, Lydia replied for both of them, "One room, two drinks. Canadian whiskey, if you have it."

• • •

"I don't know how far we should stray from North Station tonight," Blanche told Frank. She hadn't thought through any details beyond their plan to escape Lincoln for the anonymity of the city. Trying to contain her growing fear of uncertainty, she believed it was better to confront a problem than to succumb to panic.

Frank delivered the news to her. "We're not going all the way to North Station."

Blanche stared at him, confused, instinctively hugging Roy to her chest. "What are you talking about? What are you trying to say?"

He grasped her hand, coaxing it away from the baby. "I have a plan, Blanche."

She squeezed his hand, unsure whether to trust him. "I have friends in Salem. They'll help us," she told him.

He seemed caught off guard. "Salem?" He hesitated, tilting his head, appearing to weigh her offer. "No, we shouldn't go all the way into the city." He turned slightly to face her directly. "My father still lives in Waltham. We'll get off at Roberts station."

"Your father is still alive? I thought…"
"My mother passed away a long time ago, not my father."

62

Richard Hatt held his wife's head against his chest, gently stroking her chestnut hair and massaging her scalp as they failed to fall asleep. "How could another day start so normal, only to become a traveling circus? I can't believe you're pregnant," he said, gliding his hand up and down her bare arm draped across his chest.

Annie chuckled. "I think youthful naivety is precisely how it all started," she said sarcastically, stopping his hand. "But it's too late now. I can't get any more pregnant."

Holding his wife was the only thing keeping Richard from a full-blown panic attack. "We're really going to do this in the morning?" he asked her, knowing the decision and plan had already been discussed over dinner. "How did we get ourselves into this?"

Annie tilted her head, resting her chin on his chest, and looked into his face, softly illuminated by the waxing moonbeams streaming through their bedroom window. "You should have asked yourself that same question before you chose our seats and sat next to a pregnant woman who was all alone."

After dinner, finding places for everyone to sleep had turned into a juggling act. George went to stay with Reuben, where they were likely getting the least sleep, probably talking about all the deckhand jobs needed to keep a thirty-foot schooner sailing smoothly. Ada and Omeda, who were staying with Robert, had given up their rooms for Mary and Rachel.

"I like Agnes. She sure is a spitfire, that one," Annie proclaimed, tapping her fingers on Richard's chest. "I guess what they say about redheads is true." She heaved a sigh. "We'll be fine, plenty of hands to hold down the fort."

Fretting and reluctant to leave, he draped a leg over her, clinging and trying to will himself to sleep.

63

Gertrude found herself unable to sleep soundly in her empty house. Years ago, she had lost the phantom sensation of her late husband lying next to her in bed. She had become accustomed to hearing Mary's footsteps in the kitchen or moving up and down the stairs at all hours of the day.

She missed their morning tea and scone conversations, and the kitchen table now felt twice as long this month as it had during the past winter and spring.

Her slippers slid across the wooden floor with a whispered rasp as she took her place at the head of the table before running a pot of water for tea.

Depression was sapping her sense of taste and smell.

She always went to the sink first to fill a pot of water and admire Roy's flower beds through the kitchen window. Seeing the vibrant colors in the morning sun was refreshing, but today, she felt weary. Maybe she'd push herself to be productive and bake a loaf of bread.

The tablecloth was no longer bright white. It was muddied in places, with stains from spills over the years, and had not been thoroughly washed. Perhaps it was time to replace it.

She brushed loose crumbs over the edge of the table into her palm and took them to the sink. Spotting the dirty spoon coated with dried porridge, she hitched a breath, remembering that she'd forgotten to store the leftover porridge. Turning to the stove, she noticed the uncovered pot of leftovers, and it didn't matter whether it had spoiled overnight or not; she couldn't risk feeding it to Roy.

She scolded herself as she shuffled toward the pantry. "I'll need to add oats to the delivery list and better check on the flour, too." She opened the door and looked for her paper list. "Gertrude, what are we going to do with you?" she asked herself, bringing the paper and pencil back to the table.

She jotted down the oats and then checked her only bag of flour and yeast to make sure she had enough to bake a loaf or two of bread, which she did.

Satisfied that her list was short, she resumed filling a pot with water from the tap, noticing Roy's roses were beginning to bloom, which made her smile. "Oh," she quipped. "Bonemeal. I should get some for the roses."

She picked up her list from the table and returned to admire the roses, her husband's pride and joy, a daily reminder of his work and dedication.

Holding the list closer to her face, she slid her spectacles up and down the bridge of her nose and noticed that the writing looked strange with the morning sun shining from behind. She turned the paper over and read Franklin's note on the back. "Oh dear!" she gasped, clutching the note tightly to her heart with arthritic hands. "Franklin, what have you done?"

64

Lydia and Abigail dressed and left the tavern at the first morning light. There was no sign of last night's bartender, so they helped themselves to some bread and dry-aged cheese from the kitchen larder. The bread looked fresh, soft, and yeasty, with the start of white mold spots, and the cheese was overly dry and bitter, so they spat it out like men into the trash, eating more of the bread until the cheese taste was gone. They washed down the last pieces of bread with a pitcher of tepid water that tasted metallic but still wet and satisfying.

"Let's walk around the town square. I don't want to get my shoes wet with dew," Lydia said. "That general store over there"—she pointed through the stand of chestnut trees that towered over the common—"should open soon. Someone there will know Mary Jane and where we can find her."

"Let's hope so," Abigail said.

"I don't think there'll be a problem. This whole town seems smaller than our old farm property,"

The town center was quiet at sunrise, except for the chattering of gray squirrels racing up and down the trees, frantic to start the nut-gathering spring season.

Abigail studied the gothic brick building to her left, unaware it was the town library. "If the store doesn't pan out, we passed an official-looking building last night. Either that one or the place over there must be the town hall or library. They definitely don't look like houses where people would live."

A horse neighed in the distance, somewhere between the store and the neighboring house.

Lydia linked her sister's arm. "Let's walk slowly. We have time. Maybe by the time we get closer, someone will come out to open the store."

They had not yet taken their first steps when a woman appeared from the house holding a pot and a bag. She turned right and unlocked the store's front door.

Abigail pulled her older sister's arm. "We're still not going to get our shoes wet. Let's walk around."

The bell above the front door jingled as they entered the general store and watched the woman set a pot of boiling water on the unlit potbelly stove, then place the bag behind the counter to fetch a broom.

"Good morning, ladies. You won this morning's hot beverage of choice contest," she said, pointing to the kettle on the stove. "It's first come, first served—coffee or tea while the water's hot."

Lydia and Abigail scanned the store, starting with the kettle on the wood stove in the sitting area, panning past the woman, who was older, her hair a mix of gray and browned butter, no longer blonde. There was an abundance of vegetable baskets, canvas sacks, and piles of new clothes, far too numerous to possibly outfit what so far seemed like a rural ghost town this early in the morning.

"Tea would be lovely," Abigail said, accepting the shopkeeper's welcome.

The woman lifted a couple of mugs off a shelf at the end of the counter. "Sitting over there or here?" she asked, gesturing with the mugs.

Lydia took a step forward. "We'll have some with you at the counter. That'll be fine, thanks." She was pleased that the woman had noticed her and her sister looking around, pretending to be interested in the inventory.

"I don't recognize you ladies, but it's nice to meet you. I'm Carrie Chapin, and I've lived here my entire life. My family owns this store. We're just visiting, aren't we?" she asked, reaching for the kettle.

"That's right," Lydia replied. "We came in from Boston last night."

"Last night?" Since she wasn't the one shopping, Carrie seemed to have the time to gossip. "You must know someone, then. Where did you stay?"

"The tavern across the way."

Shock registered on Carrie's face. "The tavern? Oh my. It's seen better days, but I hope Frank treated you well."

"He was a dirty old man, but even a couple of whiskeys couldn't bring our guard down, although he tried," Abigail said.

The shock remained etched on Carrie's face, and her mouth gaped. "A dirty old man? That doesn't sound like Frank. He's engaged to my sister!"

Abigail scrunched her face in disgust.

Lydia looked out the window, bored and wishing this introduction would wrap up quickly. "We came to visit a friend and see her new baby. Maybe you know her, Mary Jane Nutting?"

The Fletcher sisters witnessed the recognition on Carrie's face before she answered.

"Oh, yes, I know Mary. She's been staying with Mrs. Gates."

"Is she still there?" Lydia asked. "We haven't heard from her since she told us about her baby… and we just came to see him and check on how they're doing."

Carrie squinted at them. "As far as I know, yes. Mary and Roy should be there at Gertrude's."

Lydia and Abigail exchanged looks.

"Her son is named Roy?" Lydia asked, forcing a fake smile. "I can't believe she never actually told us his name yet. We'll have to tease her about that."

Abigail finished her tea.

Lydia did the same before pushing their mugs toward Carrie and dropping a coin on the counter. "Thanks so much for the tea. It's not too far of a walk?"

Carried seemed to hesitate. "No, not at all. Out the door, take a right on Sandy Pond, and then it's the first house on the left. A big Queen Ann with a white picket fence out front. You can't miss it since it's the only one within sight of the next."

The sisters were headed for the front door when Lydia gently halted Abigail with a light touch. It took all of her strength to stay composed as she posed her question, "Give our congratulations to Frank and your sister... she's?"

"Blanche... thanks."

Lydia smirked, nodded slightly to her sister, placed a hand on her arm, and said to Carrie, "You might want to tell your future brother-in-law to keep his old gray-haired hands off his fiancée and away from women young enough to be his daughters."

Carrie's mouth fell open. "Franklin isn't gray! He has black hair and a black mustache. And he's certainly not old!"

"Oh! I'm sorry! A misunderstanding, perhaps the wrong barkeep?" Lydia lingered a moment, feigning shock, then recognition. "Frank would have been the one with the black derby hat, then?"

Carrie Chapin's stuttering confirmed that Frank and Blanche Chapin, along with their nephew, were the couple at the train station last night.

Leaving the store, Lydia assured Abigail, "This Mrs. Gertrude Gates will most certainly tell us where to find them."

65

"Ada! What are you wearing?" Annie Hatt nearly dropped the large bowl of pancake batter, but Rachel saved the day by catching her arm, preventing the mess from hitting the floor.

"What? You expect me to climb all over the deck, handle the rigging, and keep George's yack off any skirt of mine while he's leering at me climbing and sliding around?"

Annie shook her head. "Ada, you look absurd."

Omeda was unperturbed, but Agnes appeared verklempt. "Nice pants," Omeda chimed in. To Agnes, she said, "She does this all the time. Mom's embarrassed because you're all here."

Annie cast a sour look toward her youngest daughter. "Omeda? Must you?" To Ada, she asked, "Are those your brother's pants? You might be the same height, but that belt's too long and looks ridiculous on you, wrapped like that."

"Reuben added a hole, so what?" Ada retorted.

Rachel and Mary remained discreet.

"No one is going to see us out in the open ocean. I'll pack some real clothes to change into before we get to Boston."

Mary broke her silence, teaming up with Ada. "I believe women should have the freedom to wear trousers. It's all about comfort, right?"

"I occasionally spotted bloomers around town," Rachel admitted.

"Mother, that's awful," Mary said. "You never wore those while working, did you?"

Rachel shifted the conversation. "Who wants more pancakes?"

"She doesn't want your brother looking up her skirt," Omeda told Agnes.

George glanced sheepishly at Ada and shook his head. "Reuben said to meet down at the dock? I guess I'll go. I probably shouldn't eat anything now that you all have me feeling paranoid." As he left the kitchen, he whispered, "I can't believe I lived with three women, and now here I am with three more."

Rachel heard her son and playfully smacked the back of his head.

Annie glared at Ada, feeling sorry for the young man. "Maybe you should take it easy on the first trip around the bay... okay?"

Ada looked out the kitchen window. "It looks like there's a stiff breeze out there. I see whitecaps. I bet I can make him scream so loud you'll hear him up here."

Annie turned to Rachel. "She doesn't mean that. She's just teasing." To Ada, she called her daughter's bluff. "Your father won't let you roll the keel over that far."

Ada nudged Mary. "Are you ready?"

"I'll take the next ride. I don't want to have nightmares about my brother screaming."

"Can I go, Mom?" Agnes pleaded.

"Absolutely not."

• • •

On the bay, Richard, Reuben, and George held firm to the rigging ropes, leaning against the tilt, as Ada piloted the Ivy Maud to full speed, rolling the keel further and further and picking up speed over the whitecaps.

George screamed, but at least he didn't throw up.

• • •

"It'll take us at least two full days, maybe three, so we're sure we have at least a week's worth of provisions stocked?" Richard asked. His eyes sought a final answer from Annie, hoping she'd change her mind. He didn't dare to ask one last time if embarking on this journey was the majority's final decision because he didn't trust his voice not to falter. He was responsible for the safety of four souls, including his two children.

"I built plenty of storage in the cabin and a full water tank. I think we're ready," Reuben reassured them all. He gave his brother, Robert, a final handshake and hug. "Try not to miss me too much while I'm gone." He leaned toward his brother as if to kiss him on the cheek.

"Knock it off," Robert said, swatting Reuben away. "Next time, it's my turn to have all the fun."

Richard hugged his wife.

Mary embraced her mother and sister, while Omeda embraced her sister and brother, and Henry and Clifford held tightly to their father's legs.

"Okay, enough. Let's go. It's time to shove off. We're burning daylight here, folks," Annie said, breaking up their lingering pity party.

The crew of the Ivy Maud cast off, waving their goodbyes as they set out on a 300-nautical-mile, round-the-clock beeline to the port of Boston.

Henry and Clifford clung to their mother's leg like thistles, waving goodbye, while Annie wrapped an arm around Rachel's waist, who, unable to bear waving, instead covered her face.

Agnes tentatively touched Robert's elbow as a subtle gesture. He glanced sideways and lifted his arm around her shoulder while she released his elbow and clasped her hands, fidgeting.

On the water, Ada raised the sails in her brother's oversized trousers as Reuben steered southeast out of Owls Head Bay.

Everyone stood on the shores of Palmers Cove until the Ivy Maud vanished around Yankee Rock, eventually changing course and heading southwest.

66

I should have bought a sun hat in Boston," Abigail complained.
"You can borrow mine," Lydia said, lifting hers off her hair.

"It doesn't go with my eyes," Abigail teased her. "Why aren't we heading back to the train station?"

Lydia rubbed her sister's back, feeling the dampness of sweat on her shirt. She could see a house on the left up ahead. The afternoon sun filtered through the canopy of elm trees that hung over the roadway, yet the humidity in the May air remained oppressive. "Patience," she said, tugging at the back of her sister's shirt like a bellows. "They could be anywhere between here and Boston now. We didn't see them board an outbound train last night. Believe me, if Mother had gotten… *Roy's* name, I can hardly even say it," Lydia spat. "His name should be William! If we had an address here or had known his name last night, we'd already be back on the boat heading home."

•••

Gertrude sat hunched forward on her loveseat in the front room, casually dressed in yesterday's white shirt and charcoal skirt, her hair unbrushed. She had forgotten her plan to walk into town for a haircut with Gladys after reading Franklin's note, which she clutched in her lap. The note was wrinkled, and the pencil writing had smudged.

She opened the front and back doors to let a morning cross breeze waft through the house. The shade of the interior room was chilly enough for a shawl, but she couldn't muster the effort to climb the stairs.

She still couldn't believe Franklin had allowed such a thing to happen. 'Where was Mary Jane? Why hadn't she written?' she thought, squeezing the note between her fingers while a dull ache throbbed in her swollen knuckles.

She opened the note, reading it for the dozenth time that morning:

> Mary asked me to care for Roy if she did not return within a
> month, so Blanche and I have taken him <u>home!</u>

She and Franklin knew that Mary's home was in Canada. Were they so presumptuous as to take a child and flee to Halifax? The questions kept swirling in her mind, and if they had caught the train last night, then yes.

She crumpled the note before unfolding it once more. Why did he stress home?

A knock at the front porch door startled her, prompting her to shove the note into her dress pocket before getting up to see who it was. She pushed herself off the loveseat with her fists. Her knees cracked, and she paused midway to regain her balance, feeling more like an eighty-year-old woman who shouldn't be living alone anymore.

Another knock. "Mrs. Gates?"

Gertrude did not recognize the young woman's voice. "I'm coming. Who is it?" She entered the front foyer and saw two young women standing on the porch through the screen door. "Yes, I'm Gertrude Gates. What can I help you young ladies with?"

"My name is Lydia, and this is my sister Abigail. We're Mary's friends. We came to see her and her new baby. Is she here? May we come in?"

Gertrude gave the overly cheerful-sounding young woman a thorough once-over. "Are you really friends of Mary Jane from Canada?" she asked them.

"Yes, we are. Is Mary Jane here?" Lydia asked, aware she wasn't after watching the Nuttings walk away from Noble Wharf and not board the S.S. Halifax with them three days earlier.

Gertrude suspected these women weren't Mary's true friends, as she had never mentioned having any since she and her family had lost all their friends when they were forced to flee their farm and hide. She noticed the tension in Lydia's neck as she flexed her fists and relaxed her hands. "She's not here. I'm sorry," she said, reaching for the edge of the front door to close it.

Lydia yanked open the screen door and shoved the old woman further into the foyer hallway. Gertrude stumbled over her heels and fell awkwardly onto the bottom steps of the staircase, injuring her backside.

Abigail twisted her head, scanning the road for anyone who might have seen them. She felt for her dagger under her skirt before stepping over the threshold and shutting the door.

Lydia lifted her skirt and drew her dagger. Pointing it near Gertrude's eye, she covered her mouth with her other hand. "Is there anyone else in this house?" she whispered directly into the old woman's ear.

Gertrude shook her head once.

Abigail moved to the kitchen, passing through the back rooms, the bathroom, and up the stairs. When she returned to the bottom, she told her sister, "Looks like she's alone." To Gertrude, who was still sitting half on and half off the bottom step, she whispered, "Nice bathroom. I'm jealous."

Lydia took Gertrude by the arm. "Help me," she told Abigail, who helped by lifting the old woman's other arm. "Let's go somewhere more comfortable, shall we?" Lydia led Gertrude into the front sitting room, where they settled onto the loveseat. Abigail sat in the chair beside the fireplace and tossed Lydia's sun hat onto the sofa table.

Lydia tapped the flat side of her blade against Gertrude's cheek. "Scream, and you'll be a long way from a doctor."

Gertrude nodded, flexing what little tissue muscle she had.

Lydia slowly removed her hand.

"You must be William's sisters," Gertrude acknowledged, maintaining her glare at her closest abuser. "If you're seeking revenge, it wasn't Mary's fault." She turned her face away from the cold touch of the dagger blade.

"Who are you to say!" Lydia screamed.

Gertrude flinched at the girl's tone but maintained her composure. "I don't know what kind of manners they teach young women in Canada, but you two gals seem a bit rough around the edges."

Abigail stood up. "We're wasting time, Lydia."

Lydia seized Gertrude by the jaw, her fingers and thumb pressing into the older woman's jowls. She raised the pointed blade to Gertrude's eye, locking her wrist and elbow behind it, her shoulder poised to thrust. "I'm only going to ask this once. Where did this Frank and Blanche duo take our nephew last night?" she asked through clenched teeth. "They kidnapped him. They're the bad guys. Not us."

● ● ●

Gladys walked into the general store, striding up to the counter like a constable searching for answers from witnesses at a crime scene.

"Good morning, Gladys. Come for early tea?" Carrie asked, wiping down the counter.

"No, thank you. I shouldn't be here."

"Beg pardon?"

"Gertrude was supposed to come over earlier for a haircut. However, she was late, so I gave up and told myself to walk to the store instead, and here I am, checking to see if she was lingering in here, gossiping or something, but I can see she isn't, so I'll be on my way."

Carrie felt a tingling at the back of her neck as if being watched. "She's not here, but—"

"But what? I haven't got all day. It's not like her."

Carrie understood children, having been a teacher and principal at the Center School for years. She recognized how they could be manipulative, and the two young ladies' tone had appeared overly intrigued, almost stale.

"Two young gals came in this morning. They were strangers to me but claimed to be Mary's friends. They stayed at the tavern last night, but I had a feeling—"

"She doesn't have any friends other than us."

"They said they were here to see Mary and her baby."

"Bullshit!" Gladys shouted, spinning on her heel. "I'm off!"

"Wait!" Carrie shouted after her, then ducked down behind the counter. Standing up, she said, "Let's take Little Joe!"

• • •

Abigail saw the horse-drawn carriage through the front window as it passed by the house. It stopped near the front walkway. "Someone's here," she said.

Lydia loosened her grip on Gertrude and whispered, "Shhh," placing a finger on her lips. To Abigail, she said, "Go see who it is. If it's not Frank and Blanche, don't answer." To Gertrude, she whispered again, "If it's our good old Frank and Blanche with our nephew, you might be off the hook."

Abigail approached the front window, shielding herself behind the drapes. The coachman's seat was empty, and from this angle, she couldn't see anyone on the walkway or porch steps. She pulled the drapes back, craning her neck to press her cheek against the glass, trying to get a closer look at the front door. "I don't see anyone," she whispered to Lydia, who signaled her sister toward the door, pointing the way with the tip of her dagger.

• • •

Carrie's idea was to stop Little Joe before they reached Gertrude's house and get off the carriage. She released the handbrake and patted him on the rump, urging him onward, which he did slowly.

"What are we doing?" Gladys asked.

"Let's go around back and come in through the kitchen. If everything looks okay, we can say we wanted to see the flower garden and join them for tea."

"And what if everything isn't on the up and up?" Gladys asked. "Then what?"

Carrie drew the compact Iver Johnson .32 caliber revolver, Fitchburg's finest, from her dress pocket. "Then we think on our feet and come up with a new plan."

Gladys was a tough old bird, having seen more blood and women's insides than a career cattle butcher, yet she was still abhorred. "Where did you get that? You're a teacher, for God's sake!" she shouted through her teeth.

"Not anymore. The store has a till that's always full."

"Put that away, nobody's armed here."

Carrie pushed the revolver back into her pocket, and together, they sneaked toward the back of Gertrude's house.

• • •

Abigail pressed her ear to the front door and heard nothing. She opened it slowly and quietly, enough to feel the breeze brushing against her face. Satisfied no one was there, she stepped outside, keeping her blade concealed against her waist. The horse carriage remained parked, its seat empty and doors closed. "Somebody might still be inside the carriage," she told Lydia.

"Go check," Lydia said. Then she asked Gertrude, "Who are you expecting? Anyone?"

"No… no one."

Abigail slid her dagger into her waistline at the small of her back, opened the door, and stepped onto the porch before descending the steps. At the foot of the walkway, she called out, "Hello? Is anyone in there?"

There was no answer.

She walked to the carriage, stepping aside, one hand on the hilt of her dagger as she reached for the door handle.

She opened the door and peeked inside.

Empty.

She hurried back toward the house, up the front steps, and into the foyer, dagger extended.

• • •

Carrie entered the empty kitchen through the back screen door, guiding Gladys down the back hallway past the bathroom and sewing room. They paused to watch a young woman with chestnut-brown hair walk out the front door.

She tightened her grip on the revolver when she saw the woman slip a knife into the back of her skirt.

Her heart pounded in her chest, her knees gave way, and she slid down the wall into a sitting position on her haunches. She pressed her finger to her lips, pleading with Gladys to stay silent.

Another young woman's voice from the front room asked, "Who are you expecting? Anyone?"

• • •

Abigail hadn't been outside in the bright sunshine long enough for her eyes to adjust, so she spotted the two women crouching in the hallway as soon as she re-entered the front foyer.

She stepped toward them, her blade raised high, recognizing the woman from the store who struggled with the folds of her dress.

"Lydia!" she called out to her sister.

The sitting woman drew a deep breath as she pulled a gun free and squeezed the trigger before taking aim, notching a hole in the floorboards between her feet. The woman lifted the handgun higher, clamped her eyes shut, and squeezed off another round.

"Abby!" Lydia shouted, shoving Gertrude off the loveseat and onto the floor, where the frail old woman struck her head on the corner of the sofa table.

Abigail turned her head toward her sister's voice. She felt so cold, and her legs were numb. Hadn't she just been walking and sweating outside moments ago? "Frances," she whispered, blood trickling from the corner of her mouth. She couldn't bear the thought of her baby sister growing up without manners. She was determined not to let Frances become as angry or jaded as her older sisters and mother. Look at where it had led them—from an idyllic, quiet country farm to an international chase and kidnapping. It felt almost as if they had all fallen under a curse. "I'm sorry," were her last words, seeing nothing but the deep black of a starless night sky as her glassy open eyes lost their shine and focus.

Lydia stood frozen in abject horror, staring at her younger sister's white shirt, which was soaked with an expanding scarlet bloom.

Gladys rushed past Carrie to aid the fallen woman, paying no attention to Lydia or her blade.

Carrie stepped over Abigail's prone akimbo legs and into the front room, where she saw Gertrude on the floor, blood rivulets cascading down the side of her face.

Lydia flexed and raged. "You! Where are they?" she screamed and huffed so forcefully that her cheeks bellowed. She raised her dagger, pointed, and stepped towards Carrie, who let her advance three steps closer before Gertrude coughed out, "Shoot!"

Lydia pointed her blade straight at Carrie's heart and tightened her grip as she leaped with her linen skirt billowing around her wake.

Raising the revolver, Carrie screamed, her eyes wide, and shot Lydia at point-blank range. She didn't miss. The bullet disappeared into her pale forehead, punching through a strand of her black hair. She dropped the gun, yelling, "I couldn't take my eyes off the knife! I only meant to scare them!"

Gertrude struggled to stand, leaning against the sofa table and couch as she paused to catch her breath. Her gaze was fixed on the lifeless girl who, minutes earlier, had wanted to take her eye or slit her throat. "That's what you get for having such bad manners." She dabbed at the blood on her temple and cheek, swooning until Gladys came to help her up.

67

Land ho!" yelled George, leaning against the foremast and watching the jib sail to avoid being knocked overboard.

Mary climbed out of the cabin with Ada, where they had both napped. "What are you, a pirate?" Mary asked her brother.

"I could get used to this," he said, pulling his sister closer by the shoulders. "Do you smell that air?"

"It's the same air we've been breathing for two days."

George was proud of himself for helping Reuben and learning the ropes. "This here is the jib sail," he said, tapping the sail attached to the foremast and bow. "Up there is the fisherman's sail, underneath it is the staysail, and behind us towards the stern is the mainmast and mainsail. Pretty good, eh?"

"So sailing is more fun than bricklaying?"

George missed tipping back pints with the Monteleone brothers. "Can't drink and sail, so I must reserve my final answer."

"Do you know how many doggeries there must be in the city of Boston?" she asked, not caring to see the truth or if her brother cared to answer. "Zero, as far as you're concerned. You're not leaving my side while we're here."

Richard and Reuben guided the Ivy Maud into Boston harbor, passing Deer Island and heading deeper into the inner harbor channel toward the North End seaport. Richard knew the S.S. Halifax docked at Lewis Wharf, and North Station was their final destination, where he hoped to barter a deal or trade with the harbor master to moor as close to the dock as possible.

"Time for me to change and get all dressed up," Ada said, ducking inside the cabin. "Keep your brother out while I'm changing."

George sighed, giving his sister a doltish look. "You know, she's cute, but when do I break her heart and tell her tall girls are not for me?"

Mary cringed. "Really?"

"She's a bit too manly for my tastes."

"You mean bossy."

"Same thing."

Mary punched his shoulder. "I'm going to make sure our bag is packed. When our feet touch land, we should head straight to North Station. I gotta see my boy!"

•••

Franklin Hosman and Blanche Chapin found themselves walking Sandy Pond Road once more. "We're doing the right thing, Blanche, and you know it," he said, watching her push the carriage along as she kicked up road dust with each step like a petulant child.

"I don't understand what this has to do with you talking to your dead mother."

Franklin had dreamed—or perhaps he had been awake and hallucinating—seeing his mother and hearing her say, "It's good to see, for once, you finally amounted to a hill of beans, Franklin." He didn't believe in ghosts, but he accepted the dead would find a way to speak when advice was needed, whether it was asked for or not.

"She said she was proud of me," he admitted, linking his arm through hers to slow her down. "If we had disappeared into the city or gone on to Salem, whatever that might have involved, with a kidnapped child, could we ever look at him and tell each other we were proud of what we had done?"

Blanche ignored the hypothetical question, instead asking, "Is that Little Joe's carriage in front of Gertrude's house?"

•••

Gertrude allowed Gladys to tend to her wound, stopping the bleeding that had slowed from the superficial cut above her brow.

Carrie Chapin slumped on the bottom step, her head down, and the revolver dangled from her fingers between her knees as she slipped into a state of shock. She dropped it, not hearing it clatter to the floor.

"I can stand. I'm all right," Gertrude said, looking down at Lydia Fletcher's lifeless body, blood seeping into her wool paisley rug. "That's never going to clean, is it?"

The three women exchanged weary glances, aware that none of them had answers or anything to say that could help justify the self-defense killings.

A knock at the front door made their heads snap in unison. "Gertrude? We're back. May we come in?" asked Franklin.

Gertrude stepped over Abigail, almost landing on her backside again, and turned to hush her friends before cracking open the front door. "Franklin, Blanche," she greeted them, each with a cold, stone-like tone, lingering on him with a squinted glare.

"I'm sorry we're late, Mrs. Gates," he said, looking at Blanche. "We took a trip into the city to pick out some new outfits for Roy and lost track of time."

"Not time! Days! And I know where you were, Franklin," she said, setting him straight. She looked at Blanche. "And I know what you were planning to do. You should be ashamed of yourselves."

Blanche studied Frank, who finally broke the tense silence. "Why is Little Joe here?"

"I brought him," Carrie said, stepping into view behind the screen door and standing next to Gertrude.

Gertrude touched her finger to the screen, pointing at Blanche and then jabbing at Franklin. "I got your little note this morning, and I know what you two were planning. Why did you come back?" She snorted, jabbing the screen door again. "I don't want to hear about it now, but I'll make sure everyone here and in between Concord and Boston knows unless we all agree to keep our mouths—shut."

She pushed open the front screen door so they could see inside.

• • •

Mary was the first to step off the Fitchburg Line and onto the Lincoln train platform, followed by Ada, George, Reuben, and Richard.

"It looks charming," Ada said. "When will we get a railroad built between Halifax and Ship Harbor?" she asked her father.

Richard winked at his son. "Why would we want to ride the rails when we can ride the sails?"

Ada burst out laughing.

George extended his hand from the platform, pointing toward the roadway. "Lead the way," he told Mary. "We're burning daylight."

They met Little Joe's carriage at the intersection of Station and Sandy Pond Roads, and Mary recognized Gladys and Carrie. "Afternoon," she greeted, waving to the women. "It's great to see you, Mrs. Putnam!"

"She's the midwife who delivered my baby," she told the group.

Carrie brought Little Joe to a halt. She returned Mary's wave, managing a pained smile.

Gladys neither waved nor managed a smile. "Good to see you too, Mary. And who are your friends?"

Mary introduced her brother, followed by Richard, Reuben, and Ada. "My mother and sister stayed behind."

"So, this is goodbye then?" Gladys asked, smiling now.

"Yes, I'm afraid so." Mary didn't want to explain further and didn't trust herself not to panic. She simply wanted to find Roy and take him home. "Is Blanche at the store?" she asked Carrie.

"Not today, I'm afraid."

Mary forced herself to keep swallowing the lump rising in her throat.

"But you're in luck with perfect timing," Carrie said. "We just left Gertrude's after dropping her and Frank off, and there's someone else there anxious to see you."

Mary's eyes widened, and her heart fluttered. "So…" she started, unable to catch her breath. It had been weeks since she'd seen her son.

"He looked pretty dapper in his new little suit. Oh my, wait until you see it. He's grown!" Carrie said, glancing at Gladys, who was subtly shrugging her shoulders. "Why don't you all hop in, and I'll turn Little Joe around? He needs the exercise."

Mary bounded up the front steps and knocked on Gertrude's door, letting herself and her posse inside without waiting for anyone to answer. "Mrs. Gates!" she shouted, noticing the front room was empty.

"In the kitchen!" came the reply.

Mary hurried through the foyer and down the back hall toward the kitchen, too excited to tell everyone to follow her.

Richard was the caboose and noticed a small hole in the floorboard. He used his boot toe to smooth the splinters over and kept walking.

Roy was perched on Blanche's lap, bouncing from his knees. He wore a little man's suit and resembled Frank perfectly, complete with pinstriped pants, a vest featuring a tiny watch pocket, and a newsboy hat.

"Apparently, either no one makes a baby-sized derby, or they're hard to find," Franklin said, tipping the brim of the tiny wool hat atop Roy's head.

Mary wasn't sure she liked what she saw, but she was grateful her son was right there within her reach. She took him from Blanche's hands, showering his cheeks and lips with kisses. "Mommy missed you so much!" she told him, rubbing their noses together.

Blanche pinched and rubbed her cameo talisman. No one would ever see her cry.

"Perfect timing!" shouted Gertrude over everyone's introductions and handshakes. "We're having tea and coffee, so I'll put more to boil."

After everyone's emotions calmed and Mary felt ready to let him go, she handed Roy to his uncle, George. Everyone listened as the Hatts regaled Franklin and Blanche with tales of their ocean journey.

Mary noticed Ada looking out the back door and beckoned her to follow her outside into the flower gardens.

"Everything is so beautiful," Ada said, gazing at the roses, daisies, azaleas, and lavender lilac bushes. "This is so many more flowers than my mom's garden. The salt air and cooler breezes probably don't help them much."

Mary surveyed all the rose bushes and noted how much work Gertrude had put into them, keeping them weeded and the soil freshly turned. "Roy is named after Mrs. Gates's late husband. These were his pride and joy, Lincoln red roses. She keeps these gardens beautiful because it's her only way to keep his memory alive. She told me his epitaph reads, 'He is just away.' She's not letting him go."

"Why didn't you name your son after William?"

"I felt I needed to let William go, but the more I fell in love with this town, the more I wanted him here with us."

"And now?" Ada asked.

"And now he, too, is just away but never forgotten." Mary leaned into the roses, inhaling the petals. "Roy William Nutting, but we can't stay now. We have to go home."

Gertrude had quietly crept up behind the young ladies and bristled at the news she overheard.

Mary turned and saw her old friend. "Oh, we didn't notice you sneaking up on us. I was telling Ada all about Roy's beautiful roses. How do you keep them so lush and fragrant?"

Gertrude smiled. "Bonemeal… lots and lots of bonemeal. It's the best fertilizer for rose gardens."

"We have plenty of fish bones in Owls Head," Ada said. "I'll give my mother your advice." She turned and nodded toward the back door. "I should rouse the guys so we don't miss the last train."

Gertrude watched Ada walk back to the kitchen. "Pretty girl, so tall with such beautiful eyelashes."

"I know. Just like her mother. I'm so jealous."

Mary took a deep breath. She didn't want to deliver bad news but had to be honest with her mentor. "I can't stay, not without William and… I know Frank lied to me."

Gertrude placed her hands on Mary's shoulders. "Don't worry about Franklin. Everything will work out fine here." She pulled Mary in for a hug. "It's best that you go home and be with William," she whispered.

Mary recoiled, shoving her aside. "Why would you say that?"

Gertrude nearly fell, her hand instinctively going to the bruise above her brow. "I… I thought that's what you always wanted. To be with William?"

"I did." Mary clenched her teeth. "But I wrote you that he's dead!"

Gertrude recoiled, covering her face with both hands. "I never received any letter!" she coughed through her knitted fingers.

"You didn't?"

Mary enveloped her mentor in a bear hug after seeing her stricken and speechless.

Gertrude thrashed her head against Mary's shoulder as she listened and cried over what Mary had written but had not yet received.

• • •

After Mary, Roy, and her new family members left to catch the last train of the day back to North Station, Gertrude, Franklin, and Blanche sat around the kitchen table like they had months ago, staring at each other with mutual distrust. The difference now was that they all knew they were guilty liars, bound by an agreement and an understanding.

Gertrude spoke first. "Those two girls were intruders, looking to do me harm if I didn't hand over Mary's baby!" She pointed a crooked finger at Blanche. "Your sister had the good wherewithal to come and save us." She was mad enough to spit but controlled herself. "But were you two here to help? No! You were off kidnapping, of all things! You should be ashamed of yourselves!" Removing her spectacles, she leaned closer and whispered, "Those girls came all the way down from Canada, and nobody here knows them. Only Carrie, Gladys, you, and I saw them in town. But, if perchance constable Jimmy Farrar comes sniffing around asking questions, you'd do right to keep your mouths shut, and this will all blow over."

Franklin looked to Blanche for confirmation.

Her face showed no tells.

Things would never be the same between them.

"Yes, ma'am," he replied for both of them, sliding a hand under the table to protect his plums.

• • •

"All right, Mister," Mary told her son, standing him on one of Ivy Maud's cabin beds. "Time to go home." She didn't want to think about Frank or Blanche while tugging his little suit off. "Well, you do look adorable in that little hat. Maybe we'll keep it as our little secret," she whispered in his ear as she unbuttoned his vest. "Someday, you'll inherit your grandfather's pocket watch, but it's certainly not going to fit in this…" She paused as she dug her finger into the tiny vest's front pocket and pulled out a delicate gold ring with a pale blue stone.

68

"It's a girl!" Ada shouted as she ran down the stairs to make the announcement.

Richard Hatt expressed relief, saying he was too old to teach another son how to catch fish and build his first skiff.

Ada and Omeda hugged, slapped hands, and danced an Irish jig badly when they heard the news that they had a new baby sister to groom in their likeness.

One-year-old Roy joined them, his jig-dancing mimicry wobbly at best before he fell onto his buttocks.

Upstairs, Rachel and Mary hugged Annie for a job well done while Rachel dabbed a damp cloth on Annie's forehead, and Mary squeezed her hand.

"Well?" Mary asked Annie. "What do you think? Have you and Richard chosen a girl's name yet?"

Annie fluttered her long lashes and allowed Rachel to wipe the sweat from her face, even as cool air flowed in from the bay into the upstairs bedroom.

Mary shook her head at her mother and then smiled at Annie. "Yes, we know, even after giving birth, you're still beautiful," she teased. "So… what's the name?"

Annie Hatt beamed. "I think it's obvious… isn't it? We wouldn't all be here if it weren't for the Ivy Maud."

Mary nodded in agreement. "Sounds perfect."

69

Sarah Ann and Frances sat in the front pew of Our Lady of Sorrows Chapel, their fingers intertwined around rosary beads—Sarah's top hand covering her seven-year-old daughter's hand. Together, they sat alone in the empty chapel on a weekday that neither could likely remember the name of.

Despite staying in touch with her older daughters, Euphemia and Hannah, both of whom live in Halifax with daughters of their own, Lydia and Abigail disappeared a year ago and have yet to be heard from since. Encouraged by Euphemia and Hannah, Sarah Ann filed a missing persons report with the Halifax Regional Police. Although the case remains open, she couldn't shake the feeling in her heart that they were gone. Abigail wouldn't have left Frances.

"Mommy, why do we keep having to come here? It's so boring."

"You know why we need to be here." She squeezed her daughter's hand. "Saint Anthony needs to see our strong faith for him to find your sisters."

Frances yanked her hand away. "He's not doing a very good job."

Sarah Ann closed her eyes, willing her strength to flow into her daughter. "It's not his job, and what do we say?"

"Patience." Frances kicked out a foot, striking the kneeler. "I'm bored," she said, raising her voice. "I wanna go home and play with Alice and Clessia. Why don't you make them come here?"

Sarah Ann would have snapped a year ago, but time had dulled her, not mellowed her. She softly replied, "You know why." She shuffled and rotated the beads in her hand, aware she needed to keep Frances focused on hope despite her boredom.

Frances rubbed her thighs, leaned over the kneeler, and grasped the front of the pew. Then she sat back, crossed her arms over her chest, and gave her mother a pouty lip. "I don't know why."

Sarah Ann knew her youngest didn't understand any of this. For her, it was about innocence. In her mind, if Frances prayed, perhaps Saint Anthony or God Himself would reward that innocence. If Abigail wanted to be found or could be found, she wouldn't let her baby sister down.

Sarah Ann gently cupped her daughter's face. "When we pray here, I believe Abigail can hear us calling," Sarah Ann reassured her.

"Why can't we pray at home at bedtime and during grace?"

"Every little bit helps. What's wrong with that?"

Frances restored her pout. It was too much to expect from her.

"They aren't coming back, are they, Mother?"

Sarah Ann welled up to the brink of breaking but quelled her emotions without a hint of anguish in front of her youngest. "It's all about our faith, dear." She rubbed her daughter's head. "I'll tell you what, when they come back, I'll scold Lydia, and you can scold Abigail. How's that?"

Frances giggled, then suddenly froze in thought. A wave of sadness washed over her furrowed brow. "No," she finally replied. "We'd be too happy to see them."

"You're probably right," Sarah Ann said, standing up. "Are you ready to go?"

"I already told you I was bored, didn't I?"

"Yes, you did. You did at that." Sarah Ann took her daughter's hand. "Come along, and no slouching."

Frances waited for her mother to turn toward the aisle before sticking out her tongue.

Together, they walked hand in hand out of the chapel, with a mother smiling down at her innocent daughter, knowing they would only ever have sorrow—with or without Saint Anthony's help.

70

Franklin Hosman had decided to return to Halifax the moment he slipped what would have been Blanche's engagement ring into Roy's little suit pocket.

He wished he had never gone home.

His mother had told him from her deathbed that he'd never amount to a hill of beans. Her ghost acknowledged that he was doing the right thing by bringing Roy back to Mary and not falling for Blanche's immoral ways, but then he found himself burying two beautiful young women he didn't even know in Gertrude's rose garden. Now he was back in Halifax, propped up at the bar in a local doggery—fallen to the bottom of his bean hill.

He looked at his hands and swore he could still see dirt from Gertrude's garden under his fingernails, no matter how many times he tried to scrub them clean. He turned his palms up and covered his face, taking a deep breath and exhaling through his fingers before clutching his beer.

Another man's voice at the bar near Franklin asked, "Let me guess… girl troubles? Any guy sittin' at a bar with his fingers firmly wrapped around a pint and lookin' as dejected as you has gotta have girl troubles, am I right?"

Franklin pulled his shoulders back as he turned to look at the two men holding court on the corner of the bar—laborers wearing overalls, dirty-billed hats, and mustaches tainted with beer foam. "The thing about it of it is… you are most correct, my friend," he admitted. "God's honest truth? I followed a girl to Boston from here, then ended up parlaying her"—he cut himself off and held up his hands, palms out—"wrong choice of words. So I ended up finding who I thought was the love of my life, a different woman, but she turned out to have a dark"—he paused and looked up—"soul? I guess that's how you'd describe her."

One man elbowed the other and snickered, "So at least she had a soul, alive and breathing, am I right?" He guffawed and took a hefty swig of his beer, restocking his mustache with foam.

Franklin matched gulps and dug himself deeper when he said, "And she was a goddess. I've never met anyone as beautiful as her… and won't again"—he drained his suds—"She was like a big lobster you haul outta the trap with both hands"—he spread his hands shoulder-width apart—"but when you turn her over and see she's nothin' but all black on the underside, you know the right thing to do is toss her back in the drink and move on."

The men exchanged bewildered looks. "You mean you let her go because she was pregnant? That's cold."

Franklin shook his head. His days of thinking quickly on his feet were over. "No, that's not what I meant." He glanced around, hoping another glass of beer would make its way down the bar, but when none appeared, he said, "I mean, she was beautiful and intoxicating, smelled like roses, but once you looked deeper, she had a dark side. I'm not ashamed to admit she ended up scaring the hell out of me."

"Well, in that case, my friend, let's get you another round," he suggested as he waved to the bartender. "I'm Tommy, by the way," he said, extending his hand.

"Thanks, name's Franklin."

"No shit!" Tommy exclaimed, hooking a thumb at his brother. "So's his!"

Frankie Monteleone raised and tipped his pint glass.

When a fresh pint of Keiths sat before Franklin, Tommy asked, "You gotta job around here? What line of work are you into?"

Franklin began to lift his glass, sighed, and set it back down on the bar before revealing the truth. "I don't have a job right now, but I used to be a mason's apprentice around here. The timing wasn't right, and then that girl came along, and whaddya know."

Tommy sputtered a bit on his beer. "No shit! Whaddya know is right. We're brickmen." He winked at his brother. "We had a buddy once. He couldn't stack bricks for shit, either." He gave his brother a nod, waiting for the return nod, giving the go-ahead. "So hey, you believe in second chances? Wanna give the work another try?"

Franklin raised his beer and gave the Monteleone brothers a salute. "When do we start?"

71

The Chapin's General Store doorbell jingled as Gladys Putnam strode in-side with the same unwavering confidence she had always shown every day in Lincoln for decades, walking purposefully to the interior counter, where she abruptly stopped, holding her worn leather clutch bag by its frail straps with both hands in front of her like an oversized Scotsman's sporran. It had carried many of her midwife necessities over the years, but today, on this visit, it was almost empty.

She stood at attention, looking up and over the counter at the taller Blanche Chapin, and after a moment of silence, she reached into her bag and withdrew a tiny folded note. She slid the note across the counter, letting it rest directly beneath Blanche's sullen downward stare.

Blanche didn't know precisely what might be written inside the note, but she had an intimation of what words the old midwife would utter in the preface. Her energy was gone, and the fight had left her. Her once radiant, creamy complexion had faded, replaced by a pallor reminiscent of vintage lace. Once like faceted emeralds, the shine in her eyes had turned dull and dry—her hair was the same.

She reached for the note, covering it with her hand, unconcerned that Gladys might see her unkempt nails, ragged from biting.

"It's time for you to leave Lincoln," Gladys stated, arching her arthritic shoulders. She waited for Blanche to make eye contact. "I'm only the midwife. Where the path leads us *after* is not within my control." She paused as Blanche curled her fingers around the note, then opened it to read what was written. "That is where you'll find my sister in Danvers."

Blanche appeared defeated. "I lost them both," she muttered. "I'm—"

Gladys interrupted her. "You're *never* too old. That's up to you."

"Your sister is in Danvers?"

"The village coven has endured for two hundred years... she will welcome you in."

"I had no idea where or how to find them."

"Now you do... and this is your final courtesy."

Gladys paused briefly, locking eyes with Blanche before turning on her heel.

A wet shine blossomed in Blanche's eyes as she smiled, watching the old woman turn and stride out the door.

72

Agnes Nutting, will you have Robert Hatt as your husband? Will you love, comfort, and keep him, forsaking all others and remaining true to him as long as you both shall live?"

"I will."

"Robert Hatt, will you have Agnes Nutting as your wife? Will you love, comfort, and keep her, forsaking all others and remaining true to her as long as you both shall live?"

"I will."

• • •

During the wedding ceremony overlooking Owls Head Bay, where both families now called home, Annie Hatt whispered to Mary, "MJ, who are those adorable little flower children?"

"I don't know, Annie, but they sure would make a cute couple, wouldn't they? Someday?"

"Someday," Annie agreed. "And by the way, where did your sister get that gorgeous gold necklace?"

Mary didn't lie. She answered the woman she now called mom, "Something borrowed, something blue."

73

I vy Maud Hatt, will you have Roy William Nutting as your husband? Will you love, comfort, and keep him, forsaking all others and remaining true to him as long as you both shall live?"

"I will."

"Roy William Nutting, will you have Ivy Maud Hatt as your wife? Will you love, comfort, and keep her, forsaking all others and remaining true to her as long as you both shall live?"

"I will."

• • •

"Don't they make a pretty darn good couple?" Mary asked Annie. "Do you remember what we said? That *someday* is today."

"I do." Annie turned to her friend. "That someday never came again for you. Why Mary?"

Mary listened to their children's wedding vows, letting her eyes drift across Lake Sunapee and high into the spectacular fall foliage treetops of the White Mountains. After she heard her son complete his vows, she turned to Annie and shrugged her shoulders ever so slightly. "Trust... It died a long time ago." She smiled at her surroundings. "I'm still content. That hasn't changed." She reached over and squeezed Annie's hand. "Everything will work out… not to worry."

Annie patted Mary's hand, closed her eyes, and smiled. A tear emerged as she nodded, letting the moment pass between them.

"I'm so sorry your mother isn't here to enjoy the day, but did she enjoy her time here on the lake?" Annie asked.

"She did, thank you." Mary thought about Rachel's passing, knowing she was laid to rest here with her while William was just away. She would see him again. "We'll drive up and visit soon. How are Agnes, Robert, and George Roy? I can't believe he's a teenager already. Where did the years go?"

"I know. And your brother had a daughter here in New Hampshire, too?"

"Yes, she's nine… and thank you for bringing Agnes's necklace down for Ivy to wear today. Please give her our thanks."

Annie Hatt looked at her daughter from another mother. "It's Ivy's now—something borrowed, something blue."

Epilogue

Marie sifted through her soon-to-be grandmother Evelyn Nutting's jewelry boxes, searching for a necklace to complement her wedding dress and earrings.

She lifted a ball of gold chains, some delicate and thicker than others, most tarnished, when Celeste, her matron of honor, urged, "We gotta get going. It'll take us an hour to get to Copley Square if there's traffic on Storrow Drive, and I've already got the Nile River running down the crack of my ass."

Marie couldn't help but catch her fiancé's grandmother's disbelief. "Ignore her, Nanna. She's from Jersey," she said, chastising her best friend.

"You can wear my blue garter," Celeste offered, attempting to coax things along.

Marie's dusky voice deepened with stress as she searched for the elusive, perfect trinket. "I don't want to wear something concealed just because it's blue." She helped Celeste untangle the chains. "Now I understand what it must feel like for an Emperor penguin to find *that* pebble. This is important."

Marie's fingers parted a clump of chains, catching a glimpse of deep blue. "I think I see something tangled in here."

"Patience is golden, right?" Celeste said.

Marie huffed, her focus unwavering on the task before her. "I believe you mean that patience is a virtue and silence is golden, which would be a big help right now."

"You got it?" Celeste asked, watching Marie's fingers expertly untangle the chains.

Marie held up the gold wheat chain necklace with a vivid blue gemstone. "I got it, and it's perfect! It matches my vintage blue engagement ring! Thank you. You were so kind to pass it along!" Marie thanked Evelyn again and gave her a robust, warm hug.

Evelyn studied the necklace through her readers. "I believe that was Ivy's necklace, but I don't ever remember seeing her wear it."

"Is that a sapphire?" squeaked Celeste, reaching to touch it before it was grabbed away.

"I love it! It's precious," Marie said, hooking the clasp behind her neck and then rubbing the faceted carat stone between her thumb and finger before laying it high across her chest.

Evelyn admired her soon-to-be granddaughter's warm beauty, knowing she would be her grandson's perfect bride. "Why don't you keep it. It's yours now." She softly stroked Marie's cheek with the pad of her thumb. "Someday, pass them both along to your daughter."

Something old, something borrowed, something blue.

Acknowledgments

First and foremost, I wish to thank my wife, Laura, and our wonderful children, Taylor, Connor, and Samuel (yes, he's named after our family's accused and hanged Salem witch, Samuel Wardwell, September 22, 1692).

To the actual Mary Jane, Roy, and Ivy, their daughter Evelyn, and her daughter, my mother, Lyn.

To my grandfather, Gordon Leslie Wardwell, who passed away at the too-young age of 23. His epitaph reads, "He Is Just Away."

Thanks to Vanessa Brown, Becki Dabbs, Tania Engel, Tim Faust, Joanna Fonseca, Mary Koeppel, Czarina Muro, Kathy O'Neil, and Angie Turgeon-Ladeau for reading the early drafts of the manuscript.

Max Fonseca, for his tongue-twisting and catchy colloquialism, "The thing about it of it is."

Thomas and Elizabeth Monteleone of Borderlands Press, thank you for the encouragement and for calling me a writer, even though that's not the occupation I listed at the bottom of my tax return.

I'd also like to sincerely apologize to any New England anthophiles who may have taken umbrage to the April and May floral growing seasons across the Northeast. Lady slippers bloom in late May or early June; including them in the story was essential to me.

A special historical thank you to:

Donald Hafner, President, Lincoln Massachusetts Historical Society.

MacLean, John C. (1987), A Rich Harvest: The History, Buildings, and People of Lincoln, Massachusetts; Published by The Lincoln Historical Society.

Ragan, Ruth Moulton (1991), Voiceprints of Lincoln: Memories of an Old Massachusetts Town and Its Unique Response to Industrial America; Published by The Lincoln Historical Society.

Amber L. Laurie, Curator of Marine History, Nova Scotia Museum Collections Unit, Maritime Museum of the Atlantic.